THE RHINO CONSPIRACY

THE RHINO CONSPIRACY

Peter Hain

MUSWELL
PRESS

First published by Muswell Press in 2020
Typeset by M Rules
Copyright © Peter Hain 2020

Peter Hain has asserted his right
to be identified as the author of this work in accordance
with the Copyright, Designs and Patents Act, 1988

*This book is a work of fiction and,
except in the case of historical fact, any resemblance
to actual persons, living or dead, is purely coincidental.*

A CIP catalogue record for this book
is available from the British Library

ISBN: 978-1-91620-771-4
eISBN: 978-1-91620-772-1
Muswell Press
London N6 5HQ
www.muswell-press.co.uk

Printed and bound by CPI Group (UK) Ltd, Croydon CR0 4YY

For Elizabeth

PROLOGUE

The butt of the high-powered rifle had the old familiar feel, nestling against his shoulder as he crouched in the safari park.

In recent years his shooting had been mainly rabbits. Also guinea fowl – they were terribly difficult to get a clear shot at. But he was by far the best of all his friends. When they all went out for a weekend's shooting, if anyone was going to get a guinea fowl it would be him.

His eye was still in.

Amongst his circle these days, he was something of a legend. Over a cold Castle or Windhoek beer after a shoot, his friends would pull his leg about his 'mysterious' past. But he would never let on, never say what he used to do.

But, now into his forties, he was fretting about his accuracy – whether he could stay rock steady during those vital seconds when the target came into view, exactly as was required.

It was one thing downing a bird, quite another a person.

He hadn't done anything like this for nearly a quarter of a century.

That seemed a lifetime ago. And then of course, at the very pinnacle of his military career, he hadn't needed to squeeze the trigger. Mercifully his had been a quite different duty on the momentous day when Madiba took the first steps of his long walk to freedom.

Then the Sniper had been holed up from dawn in the Cape winelands overlooking the secure Victor Verster compound in which Madiba had been incarcerated for the last few of his twenty-seven years in prison.

The Sniper, tall, muscled, especially around his shoulders and arms, had been a young man in the South African Army, renowned as one of its most proficient, when his commandant had suddenly summoned him

1

one day in early February 1990 on direct instructions from the office of President de Klerk.

The mission was a special one, not the usual offensive attack, but one of defensive protection for the old gentleman who held the future of the nation in his hands. The newly revered one, transformed from the terrorist ogre his parents had always spoken darkly about. 'If they ever let him out, his people will push all us whites into the sea,' he remembered his dad repeating in his thick Afrikaans accent.

But that was then. On this special day, nothing must go wrong, could go wrong. The walk to freedom had to occur. His orders were very specific and very humbling: spot any potential assassin or assassins and shoot them, or otherwise the nation, which had been so perilously poised on the brink of civil war and financial meltdown, might be dragged back to the cliff edge – then to tumble over into murder and mayhem.

The Sniper had found a good spot amidst all the fynbos and aloe in a large clump of boulders. From there he had both a clear view of Madiba's prison compound, the gates through which he would walk and, more importantly, any vantage points from which a shot could be fired at the great man.

From early light when he had scrambled into position – having scouted the spot late the previous evening, returned to base, eaten and grabbed some sleep – he had his binoculars trained on the surrounding landscape.

In the hills by the roadside he looked continuously for anywhere an assassin could be. There were certainly enough of them out there. Extremists, neo-Nazis, white fundamentalists, nutty ideologues: all sorts amongst whom there could be danger on the big day.

The Sniper knew exactly where to look – because he knew exactly the sort of place someone trained like him would choose, camouflaged in the stony scrub, dried out by the searing heat of the summer now just at its peak.

But the problem was the nutter might not have been trained like him. Might not be a professional. Might be a wild card, an opportunist, in some ways much more difficult to anticipate. Perhaps even a martyr, not too bothered about escaping, just doing the horrendous deed, come what may.

That was the real nightmare.

Which was why he had an African spotter, down below, much closer to the prison gate, binoculars searching intently, scrutinising everyone, everywhere, without revealing his true purpose, a permanent smile diverting attention from laser eyes and the concealed microphone under his shirt front through which he could mutter to the Sniper above.

The Sniper scoured the terrain, watching, waiting. First a few arrived, then more, then a swelling crowd, boisterous, starting to *toi toi*, to sing, expectantly, ecstatically.

It was joyously chaotic. And that was the problem. It was almost anarchic. TV outside-broadcast vans had rolled up by the dozen for live coverage. Reporters were talking to camera or interviewing anybody remotely authoritative, or even mildly interesting, just to fill programme space. More and more people were arriving. Cars and vans were parked up anywhere, everywhere they could find space.

And then the allotted time came and went. Through his earpiece the dreaded news that there was a delay – a long one. Madiba was ready, but his wife Winnie had self-indulgently been delayed at the hairdresser's. Keeping her man, keeping the nation, keeping the whole world waiting for hours.

Typical, the Sniper thought. The woman was trouble, had been a real menace with her incitement of the young comrades into 'necklacing' and thuggery.

The Sniper knew nothing of the decades-long ordeal she had been through: the banning, beating, banishing by the old Special Branch. He had no comprehension of how she had had to bring up their two girls from toddlers to women amidst all the brutal attempts at humiliation. No understanding of the burden she carried as the wife of the globally heroic freedom fighter. He had no sympathy for her. She was just spoiling things for the man he was charged with protecting – protecting at all costs.

He sipped at his water bottle, the liquid now as hot as the sweat running all over him, as he lay prone among the rocks, seeing everything.

Then a cavalcade swept down towards and through the gate. 'She's arrived – about bloody time,' a guttural clipped message came through his earpiece. 'Copy that,' he acknowledged.

Stretching a little to ease the aches not even his ultra-fitness could stem, he focused hard, scanning constantly.

The chanting was reaching a crescendo. This was impossible: how could he possibly do his job in the swirl of figures down below?

And as if that wasn't bad enough, his spotter croaked excitedly in the earpiece, 'I can see Madiba now, boss. He's walking to freedom, boss. But I can't see through my binocs any more, boss. They've misted up. Sorry, boss, can't stop crying, boss. Never, ever thought I would see this day.'

The Sniper recalled that amazing moment. His mission then was to target the assassin. Now it was to be the assassin. How ironic.

Yet, just as his duty then was to protect Madiba, now he passionately believed he was protecting the legacy of Madiba.

The first text stated *shortly*, the second *imminent*. Minutes later his phone flashed and buzzed again.

Although he knew it was coming, the meeting had been too important to drag himself away, the information to which he had been confidentially exposed too alarming, the task that followed too serious.

Now he had just eight minutes as he jumped up, said his goodbyes and hastily headed for the exit across the bare wooden floorboards, passing the real-ale handles on the bar top to the Clarence pub, to begin hurtling down Whitehall, not sure he would make it.

He had to get there on time. It was crucial. If he failed there would be all manner of repercussions. And he didn't want that. Although noted for his independence of spirit, he prided himself for being conscientious, and didn't take liberties with his obligations to vote when required.

Bob Richards kept himself reasonably fit in his late fifties. A regular gym goer, he didn't do fitness heroics but ate carefully and was in much better shape than most of his colleagues, male or female. He had observed them – almost all of them – fill flabbily out, not just from age but from fast food and caffeine grabbed between incessant meetings or media interviews or events. And from stress: stress and pressure, all the time on a treadmill of commitments.

But he wasn't used to running a distance and was soon out of puff. He kept glancing at his watch, worrying. The minutes ticked by, beads of sweat surfacing on his brow in the cool evening as he darted between startled pedestrians on their way home from surrounding government offices.

Past Gwydyr House – the Wales Office, and around two hundred years before, the venue for dispensing compensation to slave owners after the abolition of slavery. That always tickled him. Compensation for the owners? What about the slaves?

And all the time his mind was pulsating at the haunting briefing he'd been given – and the responsibility he must discharge to honour the values, the traditions for which he had once campaigned.

Even if he could keep up this pace, he wasn't sure he would make the deadline. He was slowing visibly as he lurched past the grey, gaunt Ministry of Defence building, with its tunnel under Whitehall. Four minutes to go.

He ducked left into 1 Parliament Street to avoid traffic-light delays across the road to the Palace of Westminster, and dodged left past the security officers, who immediately recognised a familiar face, pressing a button and waving him through the normal visitor barrier.

Now he could hear the rasping bell ringing, summoning him insistently. Down the stairs. Around the corner. Doors opening automatically. Across the courtyard. Panting up more stairs. Pushing through another set of doors.

Past the Despatch Box coffee shop and across the Portcullis House atrium. Nobody paying a blind bit of interest – sprinting adults, mostly well out of shape, normal for these voting moments. Sweating like mad, down the escalator. Spotting a few others desperately running as well.

Quickly. Don't even think you are knackered. Just keep going.

Through a corridor joining the modern building and the old palace. Left under an arch into the open courtyard where the smokers congregated. Then right, pressing open the door, his pass not needed because a vote was on, clambering up winding stairs, pushing past gossiping colleagues coming the other way, having completed their duty.

Muttering to himself: 'Out of my bloody way!'

On his left, the Leader of the Opposition's office. On his right, first the Foreign Secretary's, then the Prime Minister's office.

Seconds to go, back of the Speaker's Chair just ahead, figures pouring out of the Noes Lobby to his left. On the right a doorkeeper poised, ready for the summons.

'Lock the doors!' The doorkeeper, catching sight of him but determined nevertheless to carry out her duty on time, began to wrench the doors closed.

He burst through the narrowing opening, catching his shoe and tumbling to the carpet of the Ayes Lobby.

He had made it. Only just. Utter relief. His vote might be vital, for his party whips weren't sure how many defectors might be in the other lobby.

But what a way to run a bloody country.

5

CHAPTER 1

Winter had passed, spring was fading, the nights not so bitter, the vegetation grey-brown and sparse, and the sun rising higher in the day over Zama Zama.

The Owner of the wildlife park, over two hours' drive north-west from Durban, had named it to capture – using the indigenous Zulu language – the essence of his project: 'keep trying' or 'try again'.

Because that's what it meant, recreating from scratch a game reserve in primeval African forest where, over a hundred years before, elephants, rhinos, giraffes, zebra, kudus and a variety of other antelope had once roamed until hunted, shot and exterminated by the most viciously damaging species on Earth: man.

Whatever you did, however hard you worked, the bloody animals would do their best to foil you. Breaking out of the surrounding fence to search for water during droughts that came so often these days, causing havoc, threatening the licence preciously gained but subject to periodic renewal.

You could never relax from the constant threat of poachers, not just locals wanting an impala for the family, but a more recent menace: organised, criminal poaching of elephants and especially rhinos for their precious tusks or horns.

'Keep trying': Zama Zama. The Owner had never given up, and gradually daily crises diminished, then stopped, and it soon morphed into a flourishing wildlife park, both a haven for conservationists, who worshipped their African heritage, and a beacon for caring tourists whose dollars and pounds and euros underpinned the whole project.

It was early morning, a reddening sky on the horizon, the majestic

African light creeping over the camp, on which were clustered a score of tents. Well, that's what they were called, but the thick canvas contained en suite facilities – a bath, toilet, external shower, where you stood gloriously naked facing the thick surrounding bush – as well as a comfortable four-poster double bed in which staff placed a hot water bottle in winter as they turned down the sheets while residents were out enjoying a *braaivleis* washed down by a glass of Pinotage, glinting ruby around the campfire.

Later, safely tucked up in their beds, they would hear the grunts, barks, screams and bird calls of the marauding wildlife. Or the leopard padding about nearby, its sound that of deep rhythmic snoring or sawing wood.

Now dawn was just breaking as a few hardy souls made their way sleepily from the tents towards the main building for a welcome cup of hot coffee or a rooibos tea. It was dark, the sky beginning slowly to morph first from black to red and purple, then, as gradually the light crept up, to light yellow with trees and bushes darkly silhouetted on the surrounding hills, slowly merging into hazy and finally bright blue. Two female nyala grazed languidly across a gorge at the edge of the camp, taking little notice of the couples strolling along. Elegant, with gentle white stripes on the sides of their fawn coats, the bucks were used to these intruders and so didn't scamper away, as impala were prone to do, but watchfully kept their distance.

Soon the two park rangers would gather the few sleepy souls and make off on foot out of the camp for a bushwalk, the air dewy, as the bush and its life slowly awoke with movement and sound on another crisp, fresh day.

Isaac Mkhize, a Zulu, was ahead with a rifle, strong, wide-shouldered, fit but with a small paunch. Steve Brown, from an old white English family in Natal's Midlands, was to the rear, bearded and slim, instructing the visitors firmly to walk in line and never to overtake the lead ranger.

There had to be discipline on a bushwalk because in the wild the unexpected could always happen. They might stumble upon a predator stalking a prey – in which case they might become the prey. Or step inadvertently upon a puff adder with its lazy but lethal bite. Or emerge into a clearing to confront the matriarch of the elephant herd protecting a three-week-old baby and seeing an intruder as a danger.

Almost always, however, the bushwalks were threat-free. Only once, when guiding walkers in a game park in the Okavango Delta in

Botswana, Isaac Mkhize told them amusingly, had they suddenly encountered elephants as if out of nowhere.

A young bull had begun stamping its feet as if to charge, and Mkhize had quickly instructed the guests to slip quietly out of sight, upwind, behind thick bush and stay absolutely still and silent as he distracted the bull away. But as he carefully withdrew – didn't run because that would show weakness and encourage a charge – the bull continued to advance, trumpeting menacingly.

Mkhize, worried not least because one prime duty of a ranger was not to leave guests in the wild, kept his eyes on it all the time, walking backwards, continuously glancing over his shoulder, increasingly worried as he could see no cover in the scrub. Then, out of the corner of his eye, he spotted an old termite mound turned into an aardvark hole, dark grey and weathered. He slid behind it, heart pounding, spotting an opening and crawled in, down towards a dark cavern, hoping not to tread on a snake stirring from its winter hibernation.

If the young bull had seen him or – more likely because elephant eyes are poor – smelled or sensed his presence, it could easily have stamped upon the mound, crushing Mkhize underneath. He had witnessed them pull giant trees to the ground, leaving a trail of destruction in their wake as they ate their way through thick vegetation, devouring leaves and grass, almost anything green.

He wasn't in a panic, because rangers were trained never to panic – but he was tense with strain, the sweat pouring down his face, worrying him as much as anything else because the scent of perspiration could attract the bull. He could hear it stamping about, near and above.

Finally, after what seemed an eternity, but was just a few minutes, the bull mercifully wandered away. Mkhize remained crouching for a further five minutes before inching back out into the open, searching for any sound or sign of elephants.

Above, the raucous dulcet whooping of a hadeda, the dark-grey ibis of sub-Saharan Africa, its wings green with iridescence; a large bird, its beak black with a thin red streak. Otherwise a fresh tranquillity all around. Mkhize cautiously made his way back to find the relieved and tense guests, crouching exactly where he had instructed, thankfully, because it was a career-terminating crime for a ranger to lose a guest.

He was a fount of knowledge on these walks, as well as on game drives, which he and Brown also led. Game drives were offered to guests in open vehicles, normally elongated Land Rovers or Toyota Land Cruisers, and were very different experiences from the walks. Usually wildlife displayed a total disinterest towards humans in the vehicles. It was almost as if they weren't there. A lioness with her cubs might stroll past a parked vehicle less than a metre away, so close a guest could reach out and pat her on the back. Not that such behaviour would be wise.

But if any guest stepped out of the vehicle, they became a threat, perhaps the target for a kill, especially if, as often happened, the lioness hadn't eaten for a week and her cubs were starving. The difference between being inside and outside the vehicle was surreal.

On a game drive the day before in Zama Zama, Brown had been driving the Toyota while Mkhize regaled the guests with stories from the bush when there was a sudden loud barking.

'What's that?' asked one of the guests, Piet van der Merwe, a white business consultant from Johannesburg. 'Wild dogs?'

'No – baboon,' Mkhize replied. 'Probably warning there's a predator around, maybe lions or leopards. Let's go and see.'

Experienced rangers had an uncanny sixth sense about wildlife. They could sniff out danger, anticipate a sighting, spot a brown snake eagle searching for prey with its razor-sharp eyes from high on a distant tree.

Brown drove off-road, following the now incessant baboon barks, Mkhize giving directions.

'Up there.' He pointed towards a gaunt tree stump, all its foliage and bark stripped by elephants.

A large male baboon was perched up on top, silhouetted about four metres high, staring out in front. Brown drove carefully past and stopped as Mkhize searched about with his binoculars. Not that these were always necessary, with rangers' eerie ability to spot everything – any bird, any animal, anywhere, however camouflaged.

Mkhize explained that baboons were not territorial because they would roam far and wide in search of food or water, sometimes as much as fifteen kilometres. They had to drink daily and could dig for water.

Van der Merwe kept asking questions. Normally rangers liked nothing more than to pass on their immense knowledge to naturally inquisitive visitors. But there was something about the Joburger that Mkhize didn't like, though he couldn't pin down what it was.

Yes, van der Merwe was gregarious – one of the lads with a cold Castle beer relaxing around the campfire before the evening dinner, always

10

offering to buy the two rangers another, which they appreciated. Never more than one, or at most two, beers, however – and only at night. Game rangers were always on duty unless they went on leave, as they did for two weeks after every eight.

But van der Merwe was unusually persistent. Was the fence around Zama Zama always electrified? Did any humans ever penetrate? What about poachers? How good was security?

On the one hand Mkhize and Brown didn't mind because they were used to curious guests, with whom they frequently became friends; it was always nicer when you could get on with the guests, have a laugh and a leg-pull, for that helped them to do their jobs. They enjoyed the continuous, fascinated enquiries. On the other hand, this guy was different, and they couldn't quite place him.

Scouring the open *veld* beyond the trees and bush as their vehicle slowly moved forward through thick grass around a metre high, Mkhize carefully responded to van der Merwe's questions.

Now the baboon's barks were like a guttural chorus.

Mkhize pointed. 'Over there, ahead and to the right. Zebra.' A small herd were walking unhurriedly, perhaps three hundred metres away.

'Look in the grass just before us. Maybe a predator is on a stalk.'

The guests, excited, craned their necks, eyes swivelling, van der Merwe asking advice.

'There it is,' said Mkhize quietly. 'A lioness, over to our right.'

She was treading carefully through the grass, almost impossible to see as she blended into her surrounds, taking not the slightest notice of the vehicle, let alone its humans intruding into her terrain. She had one thing and one thing only in mind: a kill.

'Probably there will be another lioness, maybe her mother or sister. They often hunt together,' Mkhize added.

And – yes – there to the fore, but on the left this time, was the second lioness, this one crouched still as her partner circled around towards the unsuspecting zebra.

'The lions are too far away. Zebra would outrun them. They have to crawl much, much closer to sprint and pounce,' Mkhize explained patiently.

'They must be really pissed off with the baboons,' van der Merwe remarked.

'Yah, totally. An occupational hazard for all the big cats,' Mkhize replied. 'They normally hunt at night, but are opportunistic and will stalk and kill during the day if they spot something. They can go days without food, but when they have a kill they will gorge themselves then sleep and gorge again. They stalk brilliantly, keeping their eyes fixated on the prey and crouching as they walk, ready to freeze instantly if their prey lifts a head.'

'They are not built for long chases, though if they have to, they can run around a hundred metres very quickly before pouncing. If they caught one of those zebra they would jump on top and pull it down, then bite the throat. Lionesses normally do all the hunting; males are lazy buggers. But all lions, male and female, rest for around twenty hours daily so that they are readied for the intensity of hunting, stalking and chasing. They are the super-predators, the most dominant of all.'

Brown interjected: 'My guess is the zebra will shoot off at some point.' He switched off the engine, asking everyone to be still and silent.

The zebra continued to graze, the lioness to move invisibly nearer, her partner crouching, the baboons barking. The circle of nature: killers, victims, vigilantes.

Van der Merwe shifted, irritated at the baboons. He was thirsting for a kill, other guests also eager but more ambivalent. Mkhize's mind went back to a gory experience in Botswana's Chobe National Park, where four lionesses had taken down a three-month-old elephant that had fatally strayed away from its mother after the herd had finished drinking from a river.

They first gouged out the baby's eyes, leaving bloodied red holes as it stumbled, bewildered and distraught. Then they tore at its stomach, its insides trailing out as it desperately tried to run. Next they climbed on its back, pulling it down, savagely tearing into it as it tried to struggle, then twitched and lay prone, its flesh disappearing into greedy, munching mouths, blood dripping, until the cubs were beckoned in to take their fill.

On the top of a nearby torchwood tree vultures had begun arriving by the dozen, ready to swoop down and scavenge the remains.

Some of the guests couldn't watch. Others, like van der Merwe, were transfixed by the trauma, drawn by the dramatic spectacle few game visitors ever saw, knowing they were very fortunate to be just a stone's throw away, yet somehow also feeling dirtied simply by being there.

But in Zama Zama that morning, time seemed frozen, each animal before the vehicle, and the baboon in the trees behind, playing out their roles.

Then the dominant male zebra, its penis long and dangling, almost like a fifth leg, looked up, turned and began galloping away, the rest of the herd following.

Disappointingly for the guests, it was over. The two lionesses converged and walked off, outwardly unconcerned, to lie on a mound and rest, as Brown drove up close to allow prime photos and videos.

'Shit, man!' van der Merwe exclaimed in frustration. 'That would have been a lekker kill.'

Then he asked casually, 'What about the rhinos? When can we try to see them? I've only another full day left.'

'Hopefully late this afternoon or early evening,' Mkhize replied. 'No guarantees, but we plan to head where we think they might be.'

Down on the southern tip of Africa at the base of the spectacular Cape Peninsula, the compact settlement of Kalk Bay nestles, its front along the shore of False Bay, which spreads deep in all shades of blue around in an arc before disappearing over the horizon towards the Antarctic thousands of kilometres to the south.

It is more Mediterranean than African, with changes of season sometimes in one day, often within a week. It could be damp and misty, bakingly dry or pulsatingly rainy, warm or cool, hot or cold, with a gentle breeze or a ferocious wind driving in from the Antarctic known as 'the South-Easter'.

The name False Bay originated from the first sailors to circumnavigate Africa, who, returning from the east, mistook it for Table Bay and thought they had reached Cape Town, only to be disappointed that their hopes were 'false'. About forty kilometres wide, the Indian Ocean mingles in the bay with the Atlantic, its seas warmer than the cold Atlantic-only west coast of the Cape Peninsula just around the corner.

To the rear of Kalk Bay, houses climb higgledy-piggledy up the mountain, which spreads down close to the shoreline. These dwellings, both small and large, are mostly British colonial in style, with corrugated iron roofs and wooden verandahs, ideal for a sundowner, savouring the stunning sea view. They run along the busy but narrow street, mountain side of the railway.

Kalk Bay is engagingly attractive rather than beautiful, and now the Veteran moved easily among its residents, mostly whites like him.

If they were of a certain age, they all knew of his background. Armed

13

and dangerous he had once been, in the African National Congress's underground organisation, uMkhonto we Sizwe (Zulu and Khoza for 'Spear of the Nation', shortened to its more familiar acronym MK), launched by Mandela in 1961 with a mission to perform sabotage but with strict instructions to avoid killing civilian bystanders.

The Kalk Bay people recognised him as a prominent, even venerable local citizen, genial, smiling and chatting in the summer sun under his wide-brimmed hat, rather tubby these days, as he made his way through a crowd of locals, joined by tourists scanning craft shops or heading for one of the eateries.

He would often walk down for lunch at the Harbour House Restaurant and sample the local fish brought in that morning at the small local port and auctioned off by the Coloured women who ran the market by the dockside. There they filleted snoek – the speciality of the area, an oily, barracuda-like fish much sought after locally – for queuing customers amidst the bustle of work, chatter and exchange of money.

In a corner of the restaurant overlooking the sea, the Veteran would sip his favourite but not expensive Sauvignon Blanc over lazy long lunches with friends and point out the seals frolicking and showing off by tossing fish in the turquoise waves below.

Heading rather more quickly towards eighty than he would have preferred, he had been enjoying his retirement from active politics in Parliament and twelve years as an ANC minister. He would tell friends, 'Now is the time for the new generation. I can advise and support – but I have made my main contribution.'

And nobody could question that contribution or question his credibility as a struggle veteran of the ANC, making him such a threat to the governing elite if he openly criticised them for betraying Mandela's legacy.

But now he had to admit to a different problem. Although his infectious political enthusiasm remained undimmed, he simply didn't have the physical energy of old. The spirit was still willing but the body less so. He tired quickly.

Yet he didn't think of himself as 'old'. Some men considered themselves old even when they turned thirty. Or forty. Or fifty. He thought he was still young two decades earlier on his sixtieth birthday, not denied but celebrated in a raucous gathering with his comrades, the Pinotage and the Sauvignon Blanc wine flowing freely with the Windhoek beer.

Nevertheless, he was forced to concede, he couldn't undertake this new challenge on his own. He needed help from a younger protégé. Someone to do the legwork, to be out there, reporting back to him.

But who might that be? Some of the younger activists were into what he scornfully regarded as 'ultra-left adventurism' – followers of the populist and opportunistic but extremely astute and eloquent former ANC Youth leader Julius Malema, now commander of the Economic Freedom Fighters (EFF).

Too many other youngsters were in the ANC for entirely the wrong reasons – to clamber on board the gravy train into position, power and money. And for that same reason, too many other young people were totally alienated from the ANC, wouldn't join, and wouldn't get involved in politics, even though they were highly political.

How to find a suitable younger activist, the Veteran pondered?

CHAPTER 2

The safari group had enjoyed a nice lunch washed down by a glass or two – or in some cases rather more – of wine or beer.

Some had slept, others merely rested or taken a swim in the camp's pool.

Gradually they dribbled into the lodge and gathered, ready to climb aboard for the afternoon drive.

It was often difficult to keep a group to schedule, Isaac Mkhize mused to himself. Some were sticklers for time. Others showed little respect and always found an excuse to turn up late, irritating the hell out of him. But Brown always countenanced: 'Set the rules and go with the flow. Unless there are blatantly disruptive offenders, let the group assert its own codes of conformity.'

To be fair, he acknowledged to himself, most were dead keen. Especially, he noted, a striking young African woman, like van der Merwe visiting on her own: Thandi Matjeke, in whom, Brown noticed, Mkhize seemed especially interested. She was unusual: young whites, not young blacks normally did safaris. But she had won a prize to be a guest at the reserve – and jumped at the opportunity because she loved wildlife.

Other guests had paid well, and wanted to experience all that was on offer. But it was usually the ones who were late who complained first when the vehicle had to return in the gathering gloom before the night came down like a curtain – unless, of course, there was a full moon.

The weather was on the cusp from winter to early summer. Hot now in the mid-afternoon, but within a few hours as dusk fell, the temperature would plummet, and so the guests were advised to bring extra clothing, particularly to cope with the cooling wind as the Land Cruiser swept along the dusty, rutted tracks which, in the rainy season, became muddy and treacherous.

It was hard to conceive of the parched dry land being deluged with rain. Of the way the *veld* was transformed almost overnight, its bare dusty soil suddenly sprouting lushly with greenery. Bushes, shrubs and trees swiftly stood proud, thick and green, instead of thin, dishevelled and grey. Plants pushed through dung, tiny frogs and tortoises appeared from nowhere. Sicklebush, or Kalahari Christmas trees flowered, resembling Chinese lanterns, the upper part lilac, the base yellowy-brown, favourites for herbivores from giraffe to duiker. Flying ants were everywhere. Little black beetles called toktokkies ran around. The incessant high-pitched din of cicadas was ubiquitous. Life was reborn – quite literally as Christmas approached, newborn antelope with gawky, spindly legs stumbling about.

Guests never wanted rain. Rangers always craved it, and Mkhize was desperate. There hadn't been any rain for months and months. The bush was parched, hardly any green in sight. The drought across the southern African *veld* was crippling. Trees shorn of leaves, bare bushes everywhere and grass confined to streaks of grey was bad news for all the herbivores, reducing them to near scrawny skeletons, making them easy targets for predators, who were thriving.

Zama Zama had had to turn on the taps fed from reservoirs higher up for the watering holes. The elephant herd – so intelligent – sometimes searched out the pipes, dug down and lifted them clean out of the ground, drinking straight from the broken bits gushing out, cutting off supply to the camp.

The guests had clambered safely aboard. Young newlyweds were hugging, seemingly sleepy still. Van der Merwe, middle-aged and moustached, with a lean, tall frame, though stooped, was chattering as usual. 'What chance of rhinos?' he asked.

'Same as I said before lunch. No guarantees,' Mkhize replied, ever patient, concealing his irritation.

Brown next to him, swinging the steering wheel and pulling away, added diplomatically, 'We'll do our best.'

'The rhinos here are "white rhino". But not really white, as we hope you will see for yourself. More like grey. The difference from black rhino is not colour but lip shape – black ones have pointed upper lips, white ones squared lips,' explained Mkhize.

17

'Their different lip shape is diet-related. Black rhinos are browsers, getting most of their food from eating trees and bushes, using their lips to pluck leaves and fruit from the branches. White rhinos graze on grasses, using their big heads and squared lips lower to the ground.

'Their horns are composed of keratin, the same material as fingernails. In the black markets of China, Hong Kong, Taiwan, Singapore, Vietnam, Laos and Thailand, rhino horn can be more valuable even than gold and platinum, or heroin and cocaine. Some use it as a party drug, others for medicinal purposes, despite the absence of any scientific evidence that it can improve health.'

He went on: 'They are in danger of extinction because of poaching to feed this voracious demand. We have a number in the reserve, mostly orphans. Their mothers were all killed for their horns. We took them in and reared them, otherwise they would have died too. The babies we have to bottle-feed until they are able first to feed themselves, then be released safely from our orphanage into the wild.'

The rhino orphanage was high up on a hill in the middle of the reserve, with security so tight that guests could not visit, causing both disappointment and understanding: the project was in a vital, precious race against time.

'How many in the reserve?' van der Merwe wanted to know.

'We never say,' Mkhize replied carefully. 'It's Zama Zama policy. Poachers are everywhere. We've even had rangers and security guards bought off by the criminal gangs. It's dangerous. Big business. Huge amounts are paid, with plenty for bribes.'

Brown interjected again: 'That's why we have a shoot-to-kill policy for poachers.'

'But surely that's not legal in South Africa?' van der Merwe asked pointedly.

'In Botswana shoot to kill is the law for poaching, brought in by President Khama. In South Africa it is a matter of self-defence,' Mkhize replied carefully. 'Kill or be killed.'

He paused, turning around to face the guests sitting on the three bench seats on the Land Cruiser: 'It's war out there. These bastards have AK-47 assault rifles. They don't mess about. To get those rhino horns they will murder anybody, destroy anything. We've lost some good people shot by rhino poachers. It's a war zone. Once they kill all the rhinos, that's it. It's a race to save the species from extinction.'

The guests were startled by the sudden vehemence from a ranger who had seemed an easy-going soul.

As if sensing that, Mkhize continued: 'For me this is personal.'

He pointed out towards the rolling hills of the reserve. 'This is my land. My ancestors have lived off this soil for centuries. I grew up in the region. I learned about the bush from my dad: about the tracks that different animals leave and how to trail them. He took me out with him, taught me how fragile nature is.'

'He also taught me what was safe and what was dangerous.' Mkhize pointed to clumps of skinny upright trees with greenery on top; they seemed to be everywhere. 'Tamboti. Poisonous to humans; contains a toxic latex, blistering you, damaging your eyes and can even cause death if eaten; you burn its wood and you can get diarrhoea and headaches. It is destructive of other plants and foliage. But tamboti leaves are used by elephants as a laxative and browsing antelope like impala eat them.

'My dad wasn't educated, but he kept explaining how, if we humans don't protect the wildlife and nurture nature, we endanger our own future. So I decided as a boy that was to be my mission.'

Van der Merwe said nothing, but in answer to a question from Thandi Matjeke, Mkhize elaborated.

'After school I studied to be a ranger and took the necessary trail guide qualifications. But it was not until I came here to Zama Zama that I fully understood the threat of today's poaching. I am not talking about a villager who makes a small hole in our fence, scouts about and traps an impala. It's like fighting paramilitary militia. These people have back-up and huge resources behind them. The local police help us, of course. But even they are powerless. The rhino poachers seem to be above the law.'

'But that is unforgivable!' Thandi exploded, Mkhize and the guests were taken aback at the loud, passionate outburst from someone who had seemed quiet up until then.

'This is our heritage!' she exclaimed. 'Our heritage. It's part of what makes Africa so special, so unique. Where else in the world can you find such an amazing variety of wildlife? Rhinos have been around for fifty million years. They are prehistoric. To kill them is not just criminal. It's Armageddon!'

The whole Land Cruiser fell silent. Who could follow that?

*

Several years ago, the Veteran had watched the television footage with mounting horror.

How was this possible in the rainbow nation he had fought so hard and so long to secure?

The lethal conflagration around Lonmin's Marikana platinum mine near Rustenburg brought back memories of the Sharpeville Massacre in 1960, when apartheid police gunned down sixty-nine innocent people; many women with bullets in their backs had been running away.

But this was over fifty years later, apartheid now long gone, his own ANC having been in power for a couple of decades.

Marikana should never have happened.

Yet for the thirty-four black miners killed that Thursday in August 2012 it certainly had.

Admittedly many had gathered armed with 'traditional weapons' – spears, machetes and clubs – as they demonstrated for higher wages. In the weeks before, ten had already died at Marikana, the attacks blamed on union infighting. Tensions were running high.

But how could even that begin to justify police opening fire on these striking workers? And not the white supremacist police of old, but predominantly black police officers directed by a black police chief appointed by the majority-black government of his own ANC – the heirs to his old comrade Nelson Mandela. The icon he had cherished, had battled alongside in the ANC they both worshipped.

What was even worse, the great majority of dead miners – twenty-two – had been shot in cold blood away from the main confrontation. As the official inquiry into the massacre heard, the machine guns used were 'weapons of war', not those appropriate for riot control.

Lawyers representing the families of the dead miners insisted that the massacre was pre-planned, invoking chilling testimony. Guns were planted on some of the corpses, and witnesses claimed to have been intimidated – even tortured – by the predominantly black police. As disturbing was the rest of the firepower deployed that day – helicopters, army units – seemingly the entire firepower of the state. His state. The ANC state.

The more the Veteran discovered about Marikana, the more the implications were seismic – testing the ANC like nothing else since they first took power in 1994, when he was a minister. The 1994 miracle of Mandela's rainbow nation – and even the joyous, bubbling football World

Cup showcase two years before Marikana — had been expunged by the ferocious clash over higher wages.

Expunged not just for the millions who had looked to the ANC for redemption and release from apartheid and the suffocating legacy of poverty and unemployment, but expunged for him too, he sadly reflected as he pondered the implications.

The Veteran weighed it all up. Under the ANC South Africa had made huge advances, especially in civil rights and democracy, a joy to behold compared with the evil of apartheid.

In just two decades, the ANC government had built more than three million new homes. It had created four million jobs. Millions more South Africans had running water and electricity. Some economists said that income per capita, in real terms, had risen by almost a third. Massive state bursaries had opened up the country's universities to 400,000 new students, mostly black. He was proud to have helped deliver all that during his twelve years as a minister.

These achievements were even more remarkable given the horrendous legacy of apartheid: the shanty towns; the lack of healthcare; the forced displacements; the dehumanising education system, designed to keep the black majority as servants for white masters.

But he knew that in other respects living conditions of poor blacks, including migrant workers like the Marikana miners from the deprived rural regions such as the Eastern Cape, had hardly improved.

What infuriated him was the evidence of corruption in all levels of government. How could that have happened? The ethics and principles of the struggle leaders had been vanquished. He had even heard a former struggle comrade making excuses: 'When you haven't had enough food and you now have a chance, you sometimes eat too much.'

For him, Marikana was a symbol of all that had gone wrong.

The police that day were confronting a cauldron, the ugly massacre developing out of the mostly simmering but sometimes explosive resentment at the chasm between expectations and delivery. Two million people annually were taking to the streets protesting about their predicament, about poor service delivery and the creaming-off of government contracts by a favoured few. Unemployment among black youth remained shockingly high at sixty-five per cent in some communities.

A symbol of the new order became the Life Esidimeni scandal, where the ANC-run Gauteng provincial government in 2015 outsourced care of mental patients from professionally run institutions to unregistered, fly-by-night facilities, its party leaders pocketing the savings along the way, and causing the deaths of over 140 mentally ill people, victims of greed and corruption.

The Veteran had a responsibility – no, a duty – to act.

But he knew that when he did so there would be a cost. Old comrades would be angry at him, accuse him of damaging the ANC, to which he had dedicated his life. Friends would cut him off. Old political opponents might quote him approvingly, opportunistically. And of course he would be a target for 'fake news' smears, especially on social media: that came with the territory of being a critic of the President.

All that he felt he could cope with. He was used to the tough side of politics. After all, in the freedom struggle he had been an ANC hardman himself, not someone to cross, especially when he was underground, identifying and distinguishing the honest and dedicated from the spies and self-seekers.

In politics – especially the life-and-death politics of the anti-apartheid struggle – hard decisions were always necessary and they sometimes came at the expense of lost friendships, or jealousies and bitter rivalries. You simply had to develop a thick skin, especially if your fellow party members undermined you, as also happened. He had learned to endure all those downsides because the cause was noble and the cause was his life.

Occasionally it even endangered his life because he had been one of the main assassination targets of the apartheid security forces.

But pondering what exactly he should do now – as he saw it to re-energise that same noble cause – the last thing on his mind was that his life would again be in danger – this time from his own side.

CHAPTER 3

Young and vivacious, if sometimes headstrong, Thandi Matjeke was a 'Born Free'.

One of twenty million, or forty per cent of the population born in South Africa since the end of apartheid in 1994, she had never experienced its horror or oppression, which had intruded into every nook and cranny of the lives of her parents and their fellow Africans.

Never been shot at by the ruthless old security forces, like the schoolgirls and boys had at Soweto in 1976. Never known an activist relative to disappear into the clutches of the Special Branch, without discovering what had happened to them.

She had grown up in the 'rainbow nation', her childhood spent in the small family home in Atteridgeville, one of the old satellite black townships ringing her country's capital city, Pretoria.

But, unlike most of her fellow Born Frees, she had read voraciously about the worst racial tyranny the world had ever known. She knew about Mandela's history and that of his close ANC comrades: Oliver Tambo, Walter Sisulu, Govan Mbeki, and Ahmed Kathrada. Knew about Chris Hani, the inspirational next-generation ANC leader gunned down by a white racist so cruelly, just before the transition.

She was inspired by their courage, determination and passionate commitment to democracy, to human rights, to social justice. They were her heroes. So were the tiny handful of whites who joined their freedom struggle, sacrificing all the privileges apartheid conferred on them, like Joe Slovo, Ronnie Kasrils, Denis Goldberg, Bram Fischer, Rusty Bernstein, Harold Wolpe, John Harris, Hugh Lewin, Peter Brown, André Odendaal.

Among these whites were women like Ruth First, Helen Joseph, Hilda Bernstein, Eleanor Kasrils, Sarah Carneson, Myrtle Berman, Barbara Hogan, Adelaine Hain, Val Rose-Christie. As a strong-willed young feminist, Thandi was especially inspired by them.

Even more so by African women like Albertina Sisulu, Adelaide Tambo and, before she went AWOL, Winnie Mandela. They carried forward the struggle and brought up their children over the long decades while their men were on Robben Island; amazing mothers of Africa, each and every one of them, followed by a younger generation like Cheryl Carolus and Zohra Ebrahim.

As her grandmother was dying, she had been summoned to her bedside to hear stories from the past. Stories the frail old woman felt were important. Like when the Special Branch had raided the home of her white mistress and master, and she had secreted the suitcase full of their activist documents away in a slot between a kitchen cupboard and the cooker, standing there doing a 'dumb *kaffir*' routine expected of her by the arrogant white intruders.

Or playing the same dumb role when the family moved and the Special Branch weren't sure to where, answering the door to the officer with the big hands, nicknamed 'Bananas' van Zyl, pretending to know nothing.

Or attending the funeral of John Harris, the only white man to be hanged in the struggle, her retching sobs resounding in Pretoria's small Rebecca Street crematorium, packed with supporters, who were each photographed and their names recorded by the Special Branch.

Or suddenly facing eviction from her tiny home in Lady Selborne township after the authorities had ordered workers to take off the roof, forcing her and all other black Africans to move out to make space for whites, even though she and her three children had nowhere else to live. As the workers moved in to kick her out, she was officiously informed she had to go on a list and wait for a house somewhere else, many kilometres away.

Thandi Matjeke felt herself to be different from the school friends who seemed to know nothing of the struggle, nothing of the bitterness and terrible hardship. Nothing about where they had come from.

She was probably more beautiful than the lot of them, with her shiny, smooth skin, mischievous eyes and sense of fun. Keeping herself trim by jogging, exercise and careful diet, she turned men's eyes and drew them towards her.

But no man dared to take advantage like they did far too often with other young women. Some of her peers even saw her as rather stuck-up – the young men because she usually said 'No', the women because she wasn't like them, obsessed with their phones, lipstick, fashion or the prevailing celebrity culture.

At times she even felt aloof. But surely she wasn't abnormal, she asked herself? She enjoyed the company of men – if they were respectful, intelligent and interested in her, not just her body. She even enjoyed the odd flirt with them.

But she carried herself proudly. She was Thandi Matjeke. A Born Free but not a Born Forget. She knew where she had come from, what her people had been through.

Above all, she knew from her history that to betray the values of the freedom struggle was the ultimate betrayal.

Thandi – translated as 'the beloved one' – stood tall despite being small in height.

They had been out on the game drive, bumping along for about an hour before the Land Cruiser came up over a high ridge and the landscape opened up before them, rolling away as far as the eye could see. It was hazy in the lowering heat of the late afternoon, shadows creeping along the valleys and on the hillsides, both light and dark shades of green blending into brown and grey.

The sky, laced with a dry, now cooling wind, was orange and fringed pink. The view reminded Mkhize of a line from one of his favourite authors when at school, Alan Paton: the landscape of KwaZulu-Natal was 'lovely beyond any singing of it'.

Brown pulled up and switched off the engine for them to savour all they could see, pointing out where the reserve's fence a couple of kilometres away delineated the border of their land.

They chatted for several minutes. Then Mkhize pointed towards a water pool a kilometre or so down to the right.

'I think there might be rhinos down there. Let's go now, in case they move.'

There was an air of excited expectation as the Land Cruiser swept down the hill, the pool at first out of sight and then swinging into view; the water was perhaps a hundred metres long and fifty metres wide, two rhinos lapping innocuously together.

They seemed prehistorical, bravura live relics of an ancient past dating from the Cretaceous age, with elephants and hippopotamuses the largest in the animal kingdom. Weighing up to 2,300 kg and up to two metres high, they lumbered about snorting and whinnying, almost incongruously breathtaking.

The scene was so peaceful, the giant specimens so innocent, it was almost incomprehensible that their huge horns could ever be ripped out of their heads, leaving them bloody and reduced to a shadow of their former regal selves.

As if reading the awestruck guests' minds, Mkhize broke the silence. 'You cannot imagine why human beings would destroy them. But they do. Ruthlessly, leaving their victims mostly dying from extreme trauma.'

'How exactly do they remove the tusks?' Thandi Matjeke interjected.

'Some poachers first drill the rhinos with their AK-47s, often crippling them by shooting at their legs. Then they hack off the horns with axes or *pangas* – machetes – as the animals lie prone on the ground, the top of their heads reduced to a bloody stump of open flesh, bone and cartilage.'

'Other poachers skilled at skinning zebra use their knives, having shot the rhinos with a hunting rifle. They prise the horn loose from the dome-like base in the animal's skull. If it is a female with a baby calf, it's even more heartbreaking to see the little one trying to suckle for days in burning heat from its dead mother,' Mkhize explained. 'I've witnessed that myself and it fills me with wild rage about the perpetrators.'

The guests lapsed into a stunned, still silence, finally broken by van der Merwe. 'Do any survive?' he asked quietly.

'Sometimes, but it is painful to see. Their horns are their main defence. Without them they are nothing, just big lumbering giants, lost and bewildered. If you heard their piercing screams after having had their horns chopped off alive you would never, ever forget,' Mkhize replied, noting that for the first time van der Merwe seemed less cocky. 'That's why a shoot-to-kill policy for poachers is so tempting for all rangers.'

'What about security for the rhinos?' Thandi asked.

'They have armed security guards with them all the time, twenty-four hours every day of every year. They will be watching us now, not too far away, one of them probably up a tree, scanning the bush for poachers. They radio in every half hour, day and night; if they don't, an alert goes out to every ranger, who immediately grabs a gun, clambers into the nearest vehicle and rushes to where the last call came from. These guards are tough men; they have to survive in the bush on their own with some of the most dangerous animals around, and they know they are targets to be killed all the time. There's plenty of other security I cannot discuss.'

Mkhize suddenly morphed from expert guide to evangelist. 'South Africa has around eighty per cent of all the white rhinos in the world. But rhinos killed by poaching is at an all-time high. There is massive demand. In Vietnam, for instance, rhino horns are used in traditional medicine or as a middle-class delicacy. They fetch up sixty-five thousand dollars a kilo – maybe a hundred thousand.

'If it was humans we would call it genocide. And the death toll is rising.'

As he paused, turning to the guests in despair, they noted his eyes were glinting moist in the disappearing light.

Just a hundred metres away, two armed guards watched the vehicle from their vantage point in the shade of a yellowwood tree.

They worked twelve-hour shifts, swapping over with a second team, and then a third for back-up, illness or leave.

They were both local men from a nearby village, had been carefully selected, vetted and then trained. The arrangement so far had worked well. The villagers recognised the guards were doing important, and by local standards, well-paid jobs. The local chief had long declared his allegiance and full cooperation. In an area where unemployment ran as high as sixty per cent, the game park was a vital source of jobs – all sorts of jobs, from cleaners and gardeners to chefs and bar staff, with a route into management as well.

But Zama Zama's head management had no illusions about the sheer scale of the security threat. Well before the rhinos had been introduced to the park, security had been a nightmare. Initially they had been rec-ommended a group of Ovambo from Namibia, said to be experienced at security work. But they proved unreliable and security breaches happened almost daily.

The old verity – everyone has their price – certainly seemed to apply. Guards who regularly patrolled the reserve's fenced perimeter to look for illicit entry openings were bribed. Or members of their family were offered inducements if a guard turned a blind eye; and although the guard was often the only breadwinner among a dozen family members including both sides of in-laws, that was hard to stop.

Guiding guests on bushwalks, Mkhize would habitually discover wire traps to catch antelope, set by local poachers, stuck between clumps of bush. Bending down, he would carefully untangle these for depositing back at the camp. With his eagle eyes for footmarks on the dusty trails, he would also spot alien human footmarks, explaining to guests that rangers and guards all had standard boots with standard special markings. Gradually the reserve management working with the local chief were able to regularise security procedures without entirely eliminating breaches.

Then the orphaned rhinos were introduced. And the threat level became very different.

The Veteran's wife had died of cancer several years before; the only consolation was that it had taken her venomously and swiftly, devouring her in weeks without the suffering of drawn-out pain.

She'd been very practical about it, putting her affairs in order and instructing him to seek out another partner, though amidst his anguish at the time that was the last thing he could ever imagine himself contemplating.

He missed her desperately. Her love, emotionally and physically – they'd been so close that he still ached after her. Also, her companionship – politically and not only personally. Because she had been a struggle figure in her own right.

Indeed their two boys, small at the time, often regaled friends with the story about opening the front door to two burly Special Branch, and anxiously calling their mother, who was brusquely handed an envelope containing a banning order that ran for five years and was expressly designed not only to terminate her role as an activist, but to make her a non-person.

It was a six-page document running to three thousand words. She was prohibited from taking part in any political gathering and was publicly silenced, as she couldn't be quoted in any media. She was also barred from 'any social gathering, defined as any gathering at which the persons present also had social intercourse with one another'. In practice – her own family excluded – she was limited to being in the company of not more than one person at a time.

However, the courts were not at all certain of the law in all circumstances. A judge once upheld an appeal of one banned person against a conviction for playing snooker with a friend, and a magistrate was unable to inform another banned individual whether or not it was legal to go to the local cinema. Confusingly, she was permitted to take her sons to see their favourite Johannesburg football team, Highlands Park, because apparently that did not involve her in a prohibited social gathering.

Entry to any educational premises was also blocked – so banned university students couldn't complete their degrees, and his wife could no longer walk into her boys' schools and discuss their progress with teachers – despite having done this assiduously over the years. One or two daring teachers walked over to the school fence where she stood on the other side, on the pavement. She had tried to substitute for their father's absence underground by being present for their rugby or cricket matches, but those too were on school fields and therefore out of bounds to her.

Restricted to the Johannesburg magisterial district, she couldn't enter factories, or any 'native [African] location, native hostel or native village' or 'Coloured or Asiatic area'. Had she wished to, she couldn't even go to church or attend the birthday parties of her own children, held in her own home. She was not allowed to attend a funeral, even of a close relative, or a family reunion or to visit a relative in hospital.

Her banning order also prevented any communication with another banned person. Which meant that comrades of theirs in Pretoria – who were the first married couple to be banned – even had to be granted a special exemption, enabling them exceptionally to continue to talk to each other.

The Veteran often regaled audiences with this Orwellian twist, a useful anecdote to illustrate both the absurdity and the icy persecution of apartheid. But these days, each time he mentioned it, he winced inwardly. The pain of her absence never left him. They'd been inseparable in love and in struggle, in family and in sacrifice.

In Zama Zama that night around the campfire they enjoyed a *braaivleis*, and Mkhize became even more animated.

'Over the past five years in Kruger, around five hundred poachers from Mozambique next door have been shot dead by rangers. But these are local people who are destitute. It's the big crime mafia who make all the money.

'It's become such a complicated problem. Not just about rhino protection but poverty. Young men in these villages who cannot get jobs see rhino poachers almost like role models. The poachers build themselves

29

nice houses. They drive expensive cars. They wear posh clothes. So there's no shortage of recruits. In some luxury reserves near Kruger, well-heeled tourists enjoy plush bush lodges with spa treatments, campfire dinners and dawn and dusk game drives. But the rhinos they see do not have horns – they've been removed as a safety measure. And on night-time game drives, guests are not allowed torches in case they are confused with poachers.'

Encouraged by his spellbound guests, Mkhize warmed to his theme.

'The poachers are usually poor and black, risking their lives for high rewards. The guests enjoying these luxury air-conditioned lodges are usually well-off and white. As they relax over a drink or delicious food, like you are doing, they haven't a clue about the frantic battles in the dark surrounding bush between poachers, rangers and rhinos.'

'Where will all this end?' someone asked.

'I really don't know. Very poor communities surround these exclusive lodges in parks like Zama Zama. For some local poachers there are no other jobs. It's life and death – for them, not just the rhinos.'

Mkhize elaborated further: 'Wildlife is seen as something for rich whites, so poachers can be seen as sort of Robin Hoods. Kill a poacher and you can turn these communities against wildlife protection.'

'So what on earth can you do?' Thandi asked.

Mkhize shrugged, giving her a smile, then continued. 'I have no time for local poachers, but their life is dangerous. If they survive, they risk capture and prison. If there's a gunfight, the death rate is high, because they're shot on sight. They are desperate for money: husbands, uncles, brothers and sons – often the family provider. Kill a poacher and there will always be someone waiting to take his place. Unless we deal with poverty in these communities and stop selfish people in other countries paying so much money for rhino horn, we are fighting a losing battle.

'Although most poachers doing the dirty work are black, above them are whites, usually in a chain of command that includes syndicate bosses making most of the riches supplying markets in the Far East. Some white poacher bosses even have helicopters. Illegal wildlife trafficking is big bucks, like drugs, arms, human trafficking.'

He paused, looking sheepish. 'Sorry. You are meant to be relaxing – not having a sermon.'

But his guests, enthralled, urged him on.

'The problem is completely out of hand. And not just rhinos. Around thirty thousand elephants are being killed every year in Africa, along with dozens of wildlife rangers trying to protect them in "ivory wars".'

Thandi interjected animatedly. 'It's not just big crime but big business, with tusks transported from Africa then converted into ivory memorabilia for Asian consumers. It's militarised slaughter.'

Thandi was in full flow, Mkhize in a glow of admiration, the other guests entranced.

'Ivory for arms is also fuelling other terrorist groups like Boko Haram and Islamic State. There's lots of high-level state corruption underpinning it everywhere in Africa.'

Mkhize nodded and grinned, turning the other guests. 'How do I follow that?'

Laugher broke the tension and drinks were sipped before Mkhize continued.

'Poaching wiped out almost a third of Africa's elephants over the ten years to 2014. In 1970 there were around sixty-five thousand black rhinos in Africa; today only around five thousand remain.'

Mkhize paused, and Thandi quickly intervened: 'The only way to stop this is by totally cleaning up the governance of Africa, by shaming Asia, and by establishing a United Nations Treaty to ban the trade in what I think should be branded "blood ivory", like the treaty in 2003 to ban trade in "blood diamonds" from African conflict zones. The global ban on trading rhino horn obviously isn't working.'

Instead of the normal laughter, chatter and the clinking of wine and beer glasses around the *braai*, a stillness descended over the group's last night in Zama Zama. Just one person smiled inwardly. Mkhize was captivated by this vivacious young woman.

CHAPTER 4

As a teenager in the 1970s, Bob Richards had been with his parents to anti-apartheid events in London. He was the only one among his school-mates to go, enjoying the hustle of marches through London's streets, the banners, the chanting and the camaraderie – except the picketing outside South Africa House in Trafalgar Square, which he found quite boring.

Although he had been too young to join the 1969–70 campaign of direct action against the visiting all-white Springbok rugby team, he loved listening to his dad entertaining him with tales of clambering over the pitch-side fence at Twickenham and running among the players to stop the match. Of how one friend had chained himself to a goalpost, disrupting play until police found bolt cutters to prise him loose. Of how a young woman had been booked into the team's Piccadilly hotel, dis-covered where the players were staying and gone round in the middle of the night injecting solidifying agent into the door locks so they couldn't get out of their rooms on match-day morning without breaking open the doors.

And then later the same morning of how a man dressed impeccably in a suit – and therefore looking the very opposite of a caricature protester with long hair and casual clothes – approached the driver of the team bus, engine idling as it waited for the team to board, told him the manager wanted a word inside the hotel, jumped behind the wheel and chained himself to it, driving the bus off and slewing it off the road. The mighty Springboks were so chastened, they voted to go home for Christmas halfway through the tour.

As he grew older, went to university and got caught up in the swing to the left led by Labour MP and cabinet minister Tony Benn in the mid-to-late '70s, he joined the party, becoming very actively involved, first elected a local councillor and eventually an MP. All the time, however, he remained involved in the British Anti-Apartheid Movement and, after South Africa's transition to democracy, continued to maintain close links with South Africa through the movement's successor, Action for Southern Africa.

As an MP, encouraged by the campaigning group Global Witness, he secured a House of Commons adjournment debate – a timed half-hour debate occurring after government business has ended for the day – on the subject of Zimbabwe and blood diamonds. He had followed the issue closely, appalled at how illicitly mined diamonds in conflict zones like Sierra Leone and Angola were used to purchase arms by terrorist groups to prosecute their murderous wars. Richards reminded fellow MPs that in 2003 an international treaty banning blood diamonds had helped stem the flow of diamonds for arms, contributing to the defeat of the terrorists.

But, Richards pointed out, there was now a different kind of 'blood diamond' from Marange in Zimbabwe. The history of Zimbabwe, he added, had been punctuated with violence. Cecil Rhodes' exercise of colonial power in southern Africa was built on a monopoly of violence. Ian Smith's racist Rhodesian regime used violence against opponents demanding democracy until late in 1979, when it was swept away by the liberation war and popular resistance. And then Robert Mugabe's ZANU, first elected in a landslide victory in 1980, betrayed the freedom struggle they once led by systematically using violence as a political strategy to maintain both power and the privileges of an increasingly corrupt ruthless mafia surrounding him.

Richards paused, looking around the chamber to emphasise his point: 'In the Marange fields in eastern Zimbabwe is one of the world's richest deposits of alluvial diamonds. Nearly every soldier in Marange is involved in one way or the other in illegal mining, forming syndicates of diamond panners whom they then protect and escort, smuggling the diamonds into Mozambique.'

Having been an anti-apartheid protester himself, Richards always went out of his way to praise campaigners, as he now did: 'Global Witness deserves our thanks for unearthing devastating evidence on Zimbabwe's blood diamond trade run by Zimbabwe's military-industrial complex with its links to Chinese companies.'

Richards paused again, well aware that he had covered a complex chunk of detail and was at risk of losing his audience. But not the attention of the Veteran, who had come specially to listen to him, and was sitting watching from the public gallery.

Richards described how diamond revenues were being siphoned off when the Zimbabwean Treasury needed teachers and nurses, not attack helicopters and secret police thugs.

'Let us be clear: Zimbabwean military-controlled blood diamonds are now sold within Europe including the UK, appearing on wedding rings. The World Diamond Council and governments with a substantial diamond trade must act to block blood diamonds from Marange, or the whole diamond trade could well find itself tarnished and targeted by boycotts and protesters, just as was threatened until it acted in 2000.'

Richards sat down, just within the time set by Commons protocol to enable the relevant government minister to reply. Which she did in the usual boring manner, reading out in an 'it-says-here' script written by civil servants to rationalise the government's stance of doing as little as possible to disturb commerce.

After Richards' meticulously researched and passionate speech, hers was about as exciting as watching paint dry.

Sitting in the special section of the public gallery immediately behind the reinforced glass security screen in a seat arranged by Bob Richards, the Veteran was one of the few members of the public present for the debate, the chamber virtually empty. He had been impressed. Richards was definitely a chip off the old block. The Veteran knew his parents from their activism during his time spent intermittently in London from the late 1960s to the early 1980s.

The Commons adjourned until the next morning, Speaker John Bercow – detested by many of his fellow Conservatives for his irreverence and modernising reforms, but admired by others as probably the most radical Speaker of modern times – rose from his seat and was escorted in a procession out of the chamber, the doorkeepers and ushers soon afterwards collecting any papers left on the benches.

Before they locked up for the night, a few MPs wandered in with excited guests, pointing out where the two contestants clashed at Prime Minister's Questions, the weekly Wednesday midday bear garden with enthralled TV viewers worldwide. It was less a traditional means of holding the government to account and more one of mutual point-scoring to feed an insatiable media.

The Veteran got up from his seat and thanked the gallery ushers – one of whom he had established was a Chelsea football fan like him – and exchanged a bit of banter on who would win the Premier League. Then he made his way round and down the stairs. His knees were not in the best shape and it was a bit of a climb down before he emerged into the Members' Lobby, the traditionally exclusive area for MPs and political journalists.

Richards was waiting and escorted him down the stairs to the Strangers' Bar. They pushed through the door into a heaving noise of animated chatter, and Richards headed for the bar, where he ordered two pints of one of the week's real ales. This time it was Reverend James, a silky real ale from South Wales.

Richards handed across a glass with a nice head of froth on top and beckoned the Veteran through another door onto the terrace outside. 'Liked the speech,' the Veteran said, slurping down the beer. 'And good stuff, this,' he added, pointing at the glass. 'I miss a decent pint. We only have lager in SA; a cold one is great in our hot weather, but it's not like British real ale.'

'Thanks on the speech. Much appreciated coming from you,' Richards replied, slightly awestruck as he always was when the two met, even though the Veteran never pulled rank and treated him as an equal.

They chatted away for an hour, Richards getting another pint for each as the Veteran admired the view across and down the Thames. There was Vauxhall Cross, headquarters of MI6, away to the right. Lambeth Palace – where the flag flew if the Archbishop of Canterbury was present – stood across and a little to the right. The Eye – the moving wheel with pods from which to view London – was on the left.

It was one of the nicest spots in London, the Veteran decided. Although he had a healthy contempt for the brutality and venality of Britain's imperial history (not least over South Africa), he had a soft spot for the grandeur of Parliament and the UK's penchant for regal pomp and ceremony.

As they sipped their second pints, the Veteran remembering how the first always slipped down but the second took longer, they continued talking about the state of both British and South African politics, agreeing that democratic governments across the world, who all followed the neoliberal economic agenda, were fast losing touch with their voters, spawning a sometimes dangerously reactionary populism.

'Neoliberalism hasn't delivered for ninety per cent of the population since it started dominating policy, with Reaganism in the US and Thatcherism in the UK,' the Veteran argued. 'The middle classes have lost out, not just lower-income groups. That's why there's so much discontent – also the parliamentary left, too, which throughout the democratic world has adopted a "neolioberal-lite" agenda. A little less austerity than the conservatives. Big mistake.'

Richards nodded. 'The way to reduce borrowing and debt after the global banking crash of 2007 to 2008 was for government to invest more to grow the economy more quickly, as had happened after the Second World War, not to cut and cut.'

Agreeing, the Veteran moved to change the subject. 'I was impressed with the way you exposed the Marange blood diamonds situation. If I ever need help on something else that needs exposing, might you be up for that?'

'For you, of course,' Richards immediately replied. 'But if I use parliamentary privilege to name and shame, as I just did, I need to be absolutely certain the case is rock solid.'

'That goes without saying,' the Veteran smiled.

A struggle hero, the President's head of security, Moses Khoza, had been detained with him on Robben Island, alongside Mandela, Kathrada, Sisulu, Mbeki and the other leaders arrested in the early 1960s. But they weren't of the same generation of detainees. Khoza had arrived as a militant young activist from Soweto, a sprawling complex of twenty-eight townships outside Johannesburg, including Orlando, where Nelson and Winnie Mandela, along with Walter and Albertina Sisulu, had their original small homes.

When Khoza was a boy Soweto had no electricity, no proper shops, no modern amenities, just vast numbers of box-like concrete houses with water standpipes and drainage. He had lived with his parents in one of these, sharing their single bedroom with his brother and two sisters.

By then the official population of 600,000 had risen to well over a million – in fact nobody knew what it really was – and it had become the murder capital of the world as Africans killed Africans in a downward spiral of despair and mutual destruction epitomised by apartheid.

Then on the morning of 16 June 1976 everything changed – both for Soweto and for South Africa.

Before that moment any resistance had been crushed, the leaders imprisoned or banished. Many were murdered by the state – in exile by letter bombs or shootings, at home by 'slipping in showers', or 'falling out of windows' while in police detention.

On that fateful June morning white policemen opened fire on a group of schoolchildren protesting peacefully against an edict the previous year forcing them to be taught in Afrikaans – alongside English, the official language of the country. But for Moses Khoza and his fellow Soweto youngsters, Afrikaans was the official language of apartheid, of the ruling Afrikaner whites. He had joined scores of children carrying placards with slogans such as 'Down with Afrikaans', 'Blacks are not Dustbins', 'Afrikaans Stinks', 'Afrikaans is Tribal Language', 'Bantu Education – To Hell with it'.

The first child to be killed was twelve-year-old Hector Pieterson, whose photograph flashed around the world, was of him dying while being carried by his crying brother. Moses Khoza had been at school with him, crammed together to be taught in the same classroom, even though he was two years older. Khoza fled in panic and shock, his classmates dying around him amidst the terror of police bullets and beatings indiscriminately unleashed on the children wearing their school uniforms.

In the hours afterwards, none of them could fully comprehend the enormity of what had happened. Then the fear in him turned to anger. He rounded up his fellow students, their older brothers and sisters, in some cases their furious fathers and uncles too. They started stoning and setting on fire any police vehicles they came across. They knifed police dogs unleashed upon them; they burned and looted official buildings and vehicles. 'Uncle Tom' black policemen stationed in Soweto were killed, as were two white officials. The township exploded.

Local media denounced them as a bloodthirsty mob. But to Khoza the people power was exhilarating, even intoxicating. For as long as he could remember in his young life, both his elders and his youthful peers had been submissive, accepting their plight as the inferior, the oppressed, forced to bow down to arrogant, ruthless white rule under which black lives were dispensable.

Now suddenly – as if a slumbering volcano of bitterness had erupted out of nowhere – the youth had hit back. The youth were in charge. They weren't going to say 'Yes *baas*' like their elders. They were saying

'No' – determined to fight back, regardless of the danger. If by their resistance they provoked further police and army violence, then so what? Their lives were worthless anyway. They were prevented from acquiring the skills to progress beyond rudimentary, low-standard schooling. They were despised, beaten, spat upon, treated like shit. They had nothing, so they had nothing to lose.

Khoza's mother tried to restrain him, pleading, 'They will kill you. You cannot win.' She was terrified of losing her eldest boy. Yet even she could see in her two younger children the gleam of admiration and new respect for their brother Moses. That was what it came to, she had to admit, wailing in frustration: self-respect.

A storm of resistance was unleashed, with Soweto at the centre and virtually under martial law as an occupied territory. On four days in August 1976, with Moses Khoza among their leaders, the students organised work boycotts – called 'stay-at-homes' – by Soweto workers, which seriously crippled business in Johannesburg.

Shock waves tore through the country as black communities took to the streets in a display of defiance at the hated white oppression, greater even than that following the Sharpeville massacre sixteen years before. It met with a predictable response: protesters shot down mercilessly, in the back, head, chest. By the end of the year more than six hundred were dead and over six thousand were arrested.

Although the hated Afrikaans decree was withdrawn, many student leaders fled to escape the police. A new movement of Black Consciousness organisations developed, with a fresh generation of activists and militants, their young leader the inspirational Steve Biko from the Eastern Cape, long a stronghold of ANC radicalism from where Mandela, Sisulu, Mbeki and others hailed. Biko wasn't remotely anti-white but instead asserted a sense of black pride, of black self-empowerment.

Khoza, now a prominent figure, left home to escape detention, living in different houses, sometimes slipping out of Soweto on clandestine missions, one of them travelling 1,300 kilometres to meet Biko outside King Williamstown, where he was based. The pair discussed the uprising, where it might be going, how they could sustain the momentum. Biko, although insistent that the Black Consciousness Movement must stand apart from the ANC, was better read than Khoza and explained to his more impatient younger colleague the valuable role the ANC had played on the past.

'But now we are the vanguard,' Khoza insisted, 'and they are the past. They are history. We are the future.'

Late one evening in September 1976, Khoza made his way through Soweto's back lanes, the familiar polluting smoke from primitive paraffin stoves belching from the tiny houses in a failing attempt to keep the bitter cold and wind at bay. He sought out the address he was aiming at – not an easy task, since Soweto's labyrinth of streets were a nightmare to outsiders. Often he didn't know the people we was to stay with, and would just turn up, mutter thanks, and gratefully eat before collapsing exhausted until he rose and left the next morning, sometimes never to see his hosts again.

He tapped gently on the kitchen door. It was made of flimsy corrugated iron, wind howling underneath and through yawning gaps around it. The door creaked and then was suddenly flung wide open, catching Khoza by surprise, for normally someone would first peer carefully out. A blaze of light burst forth, blinding him. A harsh shout – then suddenly he was grabbed by three bulky men clad in dark sweaters and jeans shouting, '*Kom, kaffir, kom!*' The hated Afrikaans again.

Before Khoza could resist, he was bundled out of the front door as a police van roared and burst around the corner, catching only a glimpse of a terrified old couple huddled on the corner of their bed, their hands and mouths bound, eyes pleading forgiveness. He was thrown unceremoniously into the back of the van, his head skidding on the metal floor and thudding against the wheel arch, the three men jumping in afterwards as the van pulled quickly away. He was too dazed and shocked to think straight and decided to lie limp as he got his orientation, the van bumping over the rutted roads, racing through Soweto.

Someone must have betrayed him. You never knew who could be bought, Steve Biko had advised him. A leader underground – because that was what he had become – needed to be open and generous, yet trust nobody. Nobody at all.

A kick was aimed at his solar plexus, the pain stabbing through him. 'We got you now. Not so big any more, are you, boy?' one of his dark-clad captors sneered. He steeled himself not to react, not to give them any satisfaction from the kicks, the searing pain and the abuse.

On Robben Island the first insider news of the nationwide revolts that had followed Soweto reached Nelson Mandela and his fellow prisoners when young Black Consciousness rebels, defiant and aggressive, started to flood onto the island, many having been savagely tortured in detention.

Moses Khoza was one of them. He had been sentenced in Pretoria to ten years after a perfunctory trial with no defence lawyer. Chained together with three fellow Sowetans, he was forced to stand in the bowels of an old ship, which rocked in the heavy Cape rollers as white warders urinated down on them through their only channel for air and daylight, a single porthole to the deck.

The island, its reputation cold, inhospitable and oppressive in the apartheid times, had, after Sharpeville in 1960, been established as a prison to hold not just common criminals but also waves of black political prisoners, under a brutal regime of white warders. Humiliation was constant.

For Khoza, life became pounding stones in the heat during the day under constant harassment and intimidation by white warders determined to break the spirit of the 'politicals'. The bleak wind blew through his freshly issued khaki prison garments, grim guards armed with automatic guns constantly watching.

As an African he was permitted 5 oz of meat daily, where Coloureds were allowed 6 oz; he was permitted ½ oz of fat, Coloureds 1 oz: the precision of apartheid penetrated the island, just as it did every part of life outside the prison, where interracial sex, park benches, sport, jobs, schools and hospitals were banned.

He was now seventeen, facing the next ten years in a cell so tiny – under three metres by just over two – that as he grew taller both his head and feet bumped up against the walls as he lay in his bed. There was a small, barred window through which the wind would blow, freezing in winter, with just three thin blankets and a straw floor mat on which he huddled trying to keep warm as he slept.

Encountering the ANC leaders who had arrived over ten years earlier, he found their spirit admirably steadfast. But they seemed to him out of touch, didn't seem to understand the new radical appeal of Biko and the Black Consciousness Movement, with its call of 'Africa for the Africans'. However, one of the old guard, from the moment Khoza met him, seemed different. Nelson Mandela, thin yet somehow regal, exuded authority in a way that struck Khoza profoundly.

The militantly assertive young activist was intrigued. Mandela had a certain aura about him and was quick to promise court action if attacked or threatened by warders. The Robben Island regime had never come across any prisoner like Madiba before, confident as a lawyer of his rights, oblivious to their petty humiliations, and almost imperious in his disdain, though always courteous and respectful if treated accordingly.

Impressed rather than threatened, like some comrades, by the cocky belligerence of the young rebels, Mandela sought Khoza out, shaken to find that he was almost as sceptical of the ANC as of the apartheid government, having been told that Mandela was 'a sell-out'.

In his clipped, precise grammar Mandela asked Khoza and his young militants to give lectures on the new wave of militancy to the older prisoners. These were organised, Khoza having to admit to himself that some of his comrades seemed sectarian and immature in their preoccupation with blackness and exclusion of whites, but noting that Mandela was careful not to respond aggressively.

Gradually, Khoza and most of the rebels came to admire the resilience of the veterans, surprised that after so many years on the island they were still so courageous, mentally alert and determined to fight on.

After four to six months, the excitement of having been at Soweto had died down in Khoza's mind. He smuggled Mandela a note asking some political questions, and Mandela wrote back in his own careful hand with three pages of the ANC's history.

Khoza read it over and over. Then he made up his mind. He would join the ANC. But he was accused of betrayal by his young comrades, one hitting him on the head and nearly killing him with a garden fork. The prison authorities charged the culprit with assault, but Mandela and Sisulu interceded, wanting to avoid an open rift between old and young, and asked Khoza not to make a complaint. He refused to testify, which undermined the charge and brought him closer both to Mandela and to the younger activists. Many other young comrades soon followed Khoza into the ANC – including, finally, his attacker.

But all that seemed a lifetime ago. South Africa had changed, and Moses Khoza had changed.

He liked to think of himself as the same man who had fought for his people's freedom. Others saw someone rather different. He was part of the new governing establishment, getting things done, he would explain to friends and former comrades sceptical of the President's regime. He would highlight to them the ANC's many undoubted achievements in office, including while he was working in the presidency.

41

And when they complained of corruption, of the President's new private palace with its swimming pool and lavish facilities paid for by the taxpayer ostensibly as 'necessary for security', he dismissed it all as 'media smears'.

Yes of course, he had become used to his more than comfortable house in one of Pretoria's prestigious suburbs, and the government driver who sometimes took him to and from work. Before university in England, his son went to perhaps the best school in the country, Pretoria Boys' High, still state-funded but now also dependent upon substantial fees. His daughters similarly attended the less well known but also esteemed Girls' High. He enjoyed his wine stock – not expensive vintages, because good quality South African wine was very affordable.

And why should he not enjoy such privileges, he asked himself?

'It is our time to eat now,' he said to old friends. 'Why shouldn't we enjoy the fine things of life? Surely the struggle was about spreading opportunity denied under apartheid to all, and not any longer just to a small white elite?'

The problem was, his friends retorted – sometimes to his face, though often between themselves, as they thought he no longer listened, maybe even no longer cared – opportunity wasn't being spread to all. Under the president Khoza served so faithfully, a new black governing elite had replaced the old white one. Just as self-serving, with tentacles of illicit business links, and sadly even more corrupt, if that indeed was possible.

His sceptical friends simply didn't understand the pressures and realities of government, Khoza told himself. They had no idea at all. His key security role in the presidency meant the hours were very long and often his work took over his weekends, at the expense of family life. He missed seeing his son play cricket at the school's sumptuous arena – proud he was developing into a fine young cricketer.

The friends also didn't comprehend how hard it was delivering better community services, the absence of which protesters now took regularly to the streets to decry. Getting the system to work properly was really difficult. That needed dedicated people like him.

What he didn't tell them – and hardly liked to admit to himself – was the incessant demands from his extended family of children, in-laws, cousins and second cousins. They all seemed to want some largesse from him: it was the way of his circle of relatives. A job here or there – yes, he could secure that, whether the relative was qualified or not, for presidential cronyism was rife. Help with the odd child's school fees – maybe.

But to satisfy all these great expectations required him to supplement his income. It was not his fault, he insisted to himself. Although he had a good salary, it simply wasn't enough. He wasn't betraying his principles: they remained what they had always been. He was fundamentally the same person who had served on Robben Island for a better South Africa. But, really, he had no alternative. Anyway, all the extra cash he was able to generate was not for him personally: it was for the greater good of his circle.

Isaac Mkhize was in full flow, with another safari group mesmerised as they watched a herd of elephants close by. Elephants, Mkhize explained, had recently passed an intelligence test that demonstrated mental capabilities not previously understood by scientists.

'We knew before that they can recognise themselves in a mirror, something rare for animals. But the new test meant they had to pick up a stick and hand it to a researcher. And sometimes the stick might be tied to a mat, and the elephants had to understand they had to get off the mat in order to pass the stick – a level of understanding and self-awareness that is very rare in the animal kingdom. It probably means elephants are much better than we ever thought at understanding someone else's point of view or interest. Pretty significant where there are conflicts between people and elephants, for example over land and resources.'

'Do any other animals show this sort of self-awareness?' a middle-aged woman from Scotland asked.

'Yah, great apes, dolphins and, funnily enough, magpies. But elephants are almost certainly the most intelligent animal on the planet. They console each other by touching and "talking" to each other – rather like we humans do. An elephant might go to a member of their circle who is upset and gently touch its face with its trunk – or even put its trunk in the other elephant's mouth. Putting trunks in each other's mouths is a sort of elephant handshake or hug – it's tender and intimate. They are strongly social animals with concern for others. If there is a distressed group or individual in the herd, nearby elephants tend to huddle together and rub or stroke each other. You see babies nuzzling their mothers continuously.'

'So, we're so different, yet quite similar?' the woman asked.

'Yes and no,' Mkhize replied. 'Most adult females usually have a single calf and won't give birth again until these are self-sufficient, at around four years old. This means males are constantly frustrated, because females are only rarely sexually receptive and must be sought out and often fought over. Such competition means that, though capable of fatherhood from around fourteen, males will be lucky to achieve it before their twenties, partly because they will be seen off by stronger rivals.'

'Males preying on females,' the woman quipped. 'Rather like the plight of women today!'

Mkhize winced, embarrassed, 'I've been talking a lot. Have you had enough?'

'No!' chorused the guests.

'Also, elephants can use infrasonic frequencies to communicate over long distances. We sometimes hear these as a sort of "rumbling", but now scientists believe elephants use their sounds like humans speaking or singing. They greet, communicate, shout, chat and console each other in rumbles, sometimes loud and sometimes quiet; sometimes throaty and sometimes buzzing.

The following day it was Mkhize's turn to take leave. As always, he faced it with mixed feelings. On the one hand he liked the fortnight's break. The demands were unrelenting as a ranger: seven days a week, 24/7 sometimes. At home he could sleep in late. He could hug his mother, a large matronly figure who ran the whole wider extended family like the matriarch she was. Sadly, his dad was no longer alive, and he often missed him agonisingly, especially the chance to talk about a particular wildlife experience or issue.

He could also catch up with the very few friends he had time for these days. His girlfriends had come and gone, lost interest when he went away for such long periods. He knew rangers who had children through several such relationships with different women. But that wasn't for him. He was no saint – liked to bed an attractive girl if she wanted that, and provided he had a condom – but on one thing he would not budge. If he was ever to father a child, it would be with a woman he cherished and remained with. So he could be a proper husband and parent, like his own dad had been.

On the other hand, he loved the life of a ranger. It was what made him who he was. It wasn't just a job. It was a mission. Being out in the bush, close to nature. Protecting, nurturing the animals. The moment of sheer exhilaration when he could lead the guests to witness something unique for them, even if was routine for him. (Not really routine – he always

44

got a thrill from the experience.) Teaching guests, learning all the time from new questions they asked, for some of which he had to look up the answers. Whenever he left Zama Zama for a break it was with a sense of loss; whenever he returned it was with the same old excitement; if that ever left him he would get another job, or so he told himself.

Then he jerked back to focus on this spell of leave, because it contained a different promise. Among the emails left by the friendliest guests – most never followed up – was Thandi Matjeke's. He planned to travel all of eight hundred kilometres to Pretoria to visit her.

Mind you, when he had invited himself via the erratic camp email a week after she had left, Thandi responded coolly. She wasn't unfriendly: how nice it would be to catch up with him and to follow up their discussion about the toxic wildlife trade, she replied. And suggested they meet early one evening in a bar where there was live music and where you could grab some food. Well, at least that was a start, he thought – maybe.

He had never come across a girl quite like her. Not one to take liberties with, he imagined. How right he was.

As he was leaving his office at the end of a long day, Moses Khoza's phone buzzed – his personal one, for he always carried two. Only his official one was declared and under his name.

He pulled it out of the inside jacket pocket of his suit and found a text from a friend who was a self-described 'business consultant'. It asked for a meeting, and soon. No name, no venue, no time. Just the usual: at his home that night after his wife and kids had gone to bed, not in the house but in his garage, accessed via the double-locked secure side door off the street for which Piet van der Merwe had been given his own keys.

CHAPTER 5

After a few sleepless nights wrestling with his conscience and having emotional and difficult conversations with his closest comrades, the Veteran finally decided he simply had to speak out.

His disillusionment had started when he was ejected from his job as a minister, having previously served under Nelson Mandela and then Thabo Mbeki.

Admittedly he had been critical of Mbeki over his eccentric denial of the HIV-AIDS epidemic, his pusillanimity towards Robert Mugabe's tyranny next door, his high-handed style and his reliance upon an ever-smaller elite of confidantes and securocrats, all distancing him from both his ANC rank and file and public opinion. That had triggered his downfall and troubled the Veteran.

But it wasn't losing his ministerial job that had disillusioned him. 'The only thing inevitable about a ministerial career is that it will end,' was his motto. The reason was very different. He was appalled by the stance of the new president and his tightly organised followers. If Mbeki had been toppled for ideological reasons – the Veteran might have strongly disagreed but nevertheless understood – that was just politics. Mandela and his young comrades in the ANC Youth League had toppled the party's old guard in the late 1940s and early 1950s because they believed the leadership was not militant enough to resist the relentless advance of apartheid.

No, this president's faction had quite different motives. To capture power for themselves, to elevate and enrich themselves and their cronies. Back in the years of exile, the Veteran had worked closely with the President and seen how he never missed a chance to line his own pockets.

46

And now in his years of office that was happening again – except on a gigantic scale. 'They are looting the country,' he bitterly complained to fellow ANC activists.

But Marikana was the final straw. Betraying everything Mandela and people like him had fought so hard for. The state gunning down defenceless strikers. Not the apartheid state. But the ANC state. A black police chief giving orders to mostly black policemen to turn their weapons of war upon poor black miners in an operation blessed by an overwhelmingly black government. The Veteran's government – or so it once had been.

He publicly resigned from his party, issuing a long, emotional but powerfully reasoned media statement, which was covered prominently on front pages and in broadcast bulletins: 'The ANC is destroying the legacy of Mandela and his fellow leaders. I cannot be complicit in this,' the Veteran thundered. 'For the last few years I have tried to persuade my fellow ANC members to change direction. But the corruption and cronyism are endemic. People are joining the ANC and standing for representative office, not to serve the people, but to enrich themselves by corrupt means.'

His resignation statement created a storm. He was denounced by the ANC leadership but privately praised by former Robben Islanders, including Mandela's closest surviving Rivonia Trial comrades, Ahmed Kathrada, Andrew Mlangeni, Denis Goldberg and Eddie Daniels. If Mandela and other Rivonia stalwarts like Walter Sisulu and Govan Mbeki had still been alive, he was sure they would have responded similarly. But other former ANC friends turned on him as someone scorned by losing the privileges of ministerial office. Politics could indeed be cruel: honest reasons deliberately misrepresented and twisted for ulterior motives.

But at home in Pretoria, Thandi Matjeke was enthused. At last someone prominent was saying what she felt. And doing so not as one of the white 'I told-you-so' brigade, eager to seize upon any ANC government fault or failure to express their lingering resentment at the transition to democracy and African-dominated government, ending perhaps the most privileged lifestyle in the world. Doing so instead as someone of impeccable freedom-struggle integrity and credibility.

She vowed immediately to contact the Veteran to offer her help. She reached for her iPhone, hovering over the Twitter app and then Facebook. But she paused. Maybe making contact openly was too impulsive – and a tendency to act on impulse, she knew deep down, was a persistent personal flaw. Sometimes it was right, because she could seize the initiative and provide creative leadership. But sometimes it was rash and counterproductive.

'Think, Thandi, think,' she told herself out loud.

She got up to collect a glass of sparkling water from the fridge in her parents' small but comfortable family home. And then, not at all impulsive, but considered and calculated, she worked out what she must do.

The senior judge in the Constitutional Court was dapper, always impeccably dressed in pressed suit, ironed shirt, cufflinks and tie. He carried himself well – regarded as a model for the job he did, helping to guard the country's Constitution, which had emerged out of the transition from apartheid to be the envy of both civil libertarians and judicial experts across the world.

Justice Samuel Makojaene was also known to be untouchable, appointed by Nelson Mandela and irritating to presidential successors. Perhaps this was the reason that, when the Chief Justice retired, Makojaene was passed over despite many believing he was by some way the best qualified for the top job. Internally he seethed at the snub, for he didn't have a low opinion of his own professional standing. Externally he smiled knowingly to those who told him he should have been appointed on merit, flattered but determined not to concede or reveal his true feelings, which might compromise the judicial integrity upon which his reputation and that of the highest court in the young democracy rested.

Instead, he quietly got on with the job, ensuring with his justice colleagues that the new Chief Justice – not renowned, unlike Makojaene, for any forensic knowledge of the law – was soon hemmed in and provided with draft judgements that kept to the highest standards expected from the Constitutional Court, much to the frustration of the President, who had appointed him. Especially when the court issued a landmark judgement that the President had acted unconstitutionally in defying a ruling from the Public Protector to pay back millions of rands wrongly purloined for his own private purposes.

Makojaene, although apparently austere and measured in a manner befitting such a senior member of the judiciary, had passionate convictions and values going back to his youth. Those unaware of his background might have been astonished that this man who now went about his work

48

with almost regal dignity was once a young militant in the 1960s. Then he had stood in the Pretoria dock facing white justice, aged fifteen in the obligatory khaki shorts for black prisoners. The judge was white and so were the prosecutors and police. There seemed little future for him.

To crush his spirit he had been charged in 1963 with subversion for joining a demonstration in his township in protest against the Pass Laws. Organised by the banned Pan-Africanist Congress (PAC), an Africanist rival to Mandela's ANC, many of his school friends had joined Poqo, the PAC's underground youth wing, which had a fearsome reputation for anti-white pogroms. Although not actually a Poqo member, Makojaene got caught up in the spirit of rebellion against the white state. The young comrades rejected Mandela's ANC as too moderate, too accommodating. They weren't racists — indeed they were victims of racism. But they believed that Africans had to assert their own power by organising as Africans alone.

The courtroom epitomised for Makojaene the slogan all his young comrades had preached — 'ourselves alone' — and he felt beleaguered, bullied and besieged. His mother, tearful and helpless in the gallery reserved for non-whites, watched as the police officers queued to give evidence against him. The charge of 'subversion' was so all-encompassing there was no chance at all for him, even though he hadn't actually committed any specific crime.

He felt he was on trial for who he was, not what he had done. On trial because he was born black.

Only one person in the court came to his aid — and in a manner that truly astonished him. A youngish white woman, petite with dark hair, attended his hearings and each day brought him a bowl of hot soup. And most important of all, a bar of chocolate. Chocolate! His favourite. Such a luxury. Drenched with nervous sweat on the day he was sentenced, he could feel the chocolate melting in his pocket as he yearned to munch it.

He could tell the police and the court officials were furious with this woman, burning with resentment that one of their own, a member of their *volk*, could consort with this 'black terrorist'. He had no idea who on earth she was. Nobody told him her name. Yet there she was, seemingly fearlessly indifferent to the hostility displayed by officialdom toward her, smiling quietly, supportively and anxiously at him as he was marched away to serve ten years imprisonment on Robben Island. He noticed the police and judge gave her looks that could have killed.

49

Samuel Makojaene never forgot her. Indeed decades later, after studying for and taking his junior law degree on the island, he would confide to friends, sipping tea in his large book-lined office in the Constitutional Court: 'That tiny white woman changed my whole attitude to life. I realised for the very first time there was some goodness in whites. I just wish I knew who she was.'

Mkhize had Thandi's absolute attention as he described the planet's last three northern white rhinos, none capable of breeding and therefore virtually extinct.

'They are constantly protected by heavily armed guards as they graze on the grassland of the Ol Pejeta Conservancy in Kenya, the last of their kind on earth. The northern white once roamed Africa in its thousands. Around two thousand survived in the wild in 1960, but after that they were hunted and wiped out.'

'What's the difference in a northern rhino?' asked Thandi.

'It is smaller and hairier than its southern cousin,' he replied, going on to describe how in 2016, international scientists attempted to do the impossible: to rescue the species from extinction, by planning to remove the last eggs from the two female northern whites. Using advanced reproductive techniques, including stem-cell technology and IVF, they aimed to create embryos for surrogate rhino mothers – something never done before.

'It's really exciting,' Mkhize was animated now.

Thandi looked sceptical. 'But that must be hugely costly? Surely the resources used to create northern white embryos would be better spent protecting other rhino species? I don't like the idea of people being let off the hook by science instead of being forced to behave responsibly.'

'Good point,' Mkhize said, 'But the scientists insist that unless they act now, the northern white rhino will be extinct, all killed for traditional medicine in China, and as a luxury cure for hangovers and other ailments in Vietnam.'

'Hangovers!' Thandi exclaimed, her normally serene face twisted in disgust. 'Aren't some people just so revoltingly obscene?'

Thandi placed her hand gently on his knee, giving him a comforting squeeze. The two had rendezvoused, as she had first suggested, in a lively Pretoria bar, tables tumbling untidily out from a verandah under adjoining trees, waiters of all colours serving, some customers eating, others just drinking, African music playing.

She had been rather warily reserved at first, as if she was simply being polite. She had agreed to come because she had enjoyed meeting him in Zama Zama. And learning from his expertise and love for the wild. She didn't want him to jump to any conclusions. Still, he had travelled all the way to see her: that demanded courtesy.

But now she had touched him. Only lightly, of course. Nothing serious. Nothing, necessarily, to read into that. But, she could tell, he rather appreciated it. Did she really mind? No, she supposed not.

'Let me get you another drink,' she said.

'You got the last one. It's my turn,' he exclaimed.

'No. You are my guest in my home city. Do you fancy a bite?'

So that was that, he thought, watching as she swivelled to catch a waitress's attention.

After they had ordered, Thandi almost abruptly changed subjects. 'I am working tomorrow, but in the evening plan to attend a meeting addressed by an ANC veteran critical of the current regime. Do you fancy coming with me?'

He had never been to a political meeting before, wasn't too sure he liked the idea much, but he certainly did like spending more time with her. 'Yah – of course,' he said.

Thandi looked pleased. That at least was good, he thought.

51

CHAPTER 6

The meeting was packed, with standing room only, people straining in through the main doorway to listen, the atmosphere bubbling.

Thandi and Mkhize had got there early, she striding purposefully down to the front, him awkwardly in tow and taking his seat somewhat gingerly, relieved only to be sitting close up next to her.

From the moment the Veteran was introduced, he was wildly cheered, seemingly with an umbilical link to those listening, a cross section of old and young, black and white, women and men. Thandi was enchanted.

'In the struggle days I used to be a target for assassination,' he began, then paused. 'After my recent pronouncements maybe I will be again!'

He looked up smiling as giggles turned into roars of merriment.

'Comrades, over twenty years ago, the radiance of Nelson Mandela's "rainbow nation" shone down upon the world, consigning apartheid to history. But, tragically, since then South Africa has gone from hero to zero. People have lost faith in our party's ability to govern. Our president loots the country and financially benefits his inner circle.

'International investors turn their backs on a nation they once favoured, and – generations ago – colonially plundered. The President suddenly sacks our respected finance minister when he refused to approve monstrously costly nuclear and airways deals, which were also a passport to more looting. Shock waves race through the financial markets. The rand crashes. The stock exchange goes into meltdown. Our country's credit rating is downgraded to one level above junk status. But the President doesn't care.'

'Veteran activist Eddie Daniels – a former Robben Island inmate – told me his heart was torn at the time of the last general election. Eddie

52

could no longer bring himself to vote ANC, but he felt he would betray Mandela if he voted for anybody else, so in the end he didn't vote at all. My old friend, struggle stalwart Denis Goldberg – who was convicted with Mandela at the 1964 Rivonia trial and served twenty-two years in jail – called for a clear-out and renewal of the ANC leadership "from top to bottom". He added that corruption and patronage was now "so deep-rooted that it is endangering our democracy".

'None of these voices must be ignored! Our rulers must go! Our people must be free again! We demand honesty and principle, not corruption and cronyism!'

Thandi rose to her feet, Mkhize hesitantly joining her, a crescendo of clapping bursting out as the Veteran helped himself to a glass of water, looking at everyone until silence again descended and people sat down.

'Thanks to Mandela's extraordinary leadership and insistence on reconciliation, South Africa was transformed from a police state to a constitutional democracy. So when did the dream of our rainbow nation turn sour?'

The Veteran's question hung in the air. Mkhize caught Thandi's eye. The meeting was still. Waiting, expectant, for his answer they all knew anyway.

'The President – our president, elected by our great party – has encouraged corruption to flourish on a scale that poses a huge and cancerous threat.'

There was resounding applause.

'But not just that,' he added.

'Cronyism has replaced merit – not only in the public services, but also in the parastatals, which play such a vital role in the economy – bankrupting electricity, airlines and water supply.'

The Veteran looked up, saying nothing, eyes on an imaginary horizon.

'So, why am I, someone schooled in Marxism, worried about these failings of capitalism?'

His rhetorical question hung invitingly.

'Because – my friends and my comrades – I tell you if we cannot competently run the system we inherited, we shouldn't be in government in the first place!'

Thunderous applause broke out.

Then he lowered his tone, looking beseechingly upward.

'But what pains me – maybe most of all – is that – protected by ANC leaders in return for political support – our National Teachers Union seems to have abandoned its proud history in the struggle for freedom and justice. Jobs-for-cash rackets and patronage systems in provincial education departments run by union officials. Defending teachers who don't bother to show up in their classrooms but expect to get paid. Good schools with good teaching is our children's future. Without that they have no future. Our – mainly our African children – are being betrayed!'

The Veteran was now in his element, clapping breaking out continuously.

'And – as bad – betrayed by our own party and our own trade union.'

He lowered his voice, silence following him.

'Do you know this?' he asked.

'At one time, our ANC government spent more on education than any other developing nation. School attendance had doubled since the dark days of apartheid. Fantastic. And yet. And yet. Out of 140 countries in the recent World Economic Forum's Global Competitiveness Index, South Africa was ranked at 138 for the quality of its education, below desperately poor, undeveloped states like Burundi, Benin and Mauritania.'

'That,' the Veteran thundered, 'is absolutely, totally bloody criminal!'

There were shouts from the hall of – 'Yes, criminal! Yes, criminal!' – amidst another burst of clapping.

Now there was no stopping him.

'Unemployment among black youth remains shockingly high, and South Africa is now one of the most unequal societies in the world. The gap between rich and poor has actually widened since apartheid. Widened – absolutely, totally, completely shameful!'

Another round of loud applause.

'Of course people say that the widening inequality gap is happening right across the world because of neoliberalism. But that is no excuse at all.'

He paused again, taking a sip of water, the meeting spellbound.

'The symbol of all that has gone wrong happened on the sixteenth of August 2012. Marikana.'

He lowered his voice and the atmosphere could have been cut with a knife.

'The police were ruthless, in a killing mode, arrogant like too many in the ANC: if you're not one of us, you are free game.'

Once more the Veteran had struck a chord with his audience as thunderous clapping erupted. He paused for effect, the meeting growing silent and expectant.

'A wealthy white-owned corporation pitted against its poor, black migrant workers.'

Another pause, then his key point.

'For me the Marikana massacre is about the unresolved legacy of our struggle. Under apartheid, government and big business were run exclusively by the white minority. When white rule finally came to an end, the fear was that white businesses and investors would flee. Instead a deal was struck, and compromises were made for the sake of a peaceful and economically stable transition. A black majority could run the government, but the white minority still ran the economy. It is hard to see how any other course could have been adopted by our leaders. For that reason I went along with it. But now I see this as "the devil's pact": a terrible betrayal of the poorest of the poor.

'Around the ANC has grown a kind of predator state, where a powerful, corrupt and demagogic elite of political hyenas is increasingly using the system to enrich themselves at the expense of the poor they are supposed to represent!'

This time, Mkhize was among the first to his feet.

'You know something?' the Veteran asked, pausing then lowering his voice, his face sombre. 'I wouldn't be surprised if we don't face a popular uprising – spearheaded by unemployed youths. In fact, I might even join it – if they allowed old codgers like me along!'

Mkhize bellowed with mirth, almost startling Thandi.

'Just look at the FeesMustFall movement, when protesting students forced the President to reverse planned fee increases, and to pledge billions of rand for student grants and debt relief. What they showed, our students, is that resistance to government injustice can force change. And that contains a clear message to the ANC: if you don't change, the people will force you to change – or kick you out!'

As he said these words, the Veteran was conscious that – just like the bad old days – there would be informers in the meeting who might well report back.

'My friends, do not lose hope. There is still much in South Africa to inspire confidence. Thank goodness, we have a vigorously independent media: outspoken talk radio stations and online investigators like the *Daily Maverick*. Yet where Madiba always championed freedom of

55

expression, this president has forced through secrecy legislation with draconian powers to prevent journalists from exposing corruption, nepotism and state abuse. We must fight this!'

Thandi – with the rest of the meeting – again erupted with applause. Mkhize, however, was silent; he hadn't followed the secrecy legislation, didn't really know what it was about.

Although the Veteran had now been speaking for over twenty-five minutes, the audience was hungry for more, and he had by no means finished. Thandi looked sombre, Mkhize thoughtful – he was still not accustomed to political meetings. The language and the format were strange to him, though he had to admit he was rather enjoying it. Although he had come simply to accompany her, now he felt part of the occasion.

'My friends, the choice is that stark. Change or die. And do please remember what Madiba said to senior activists in 1993, and I quote: "If the ANC does to you what the apartheid government did to you, then you must do to the ANC what you did to the apartheid government."

'I repeat to you that quote, because I want you to remember it if you remember nothing else of what I have said tonight: "If the ANC does to you what the apartheid government did to you, then you must do to the ANC what you did to the apartheid government."'

The Veteran's pause this time was dramatic as the audience absorbed the almost insurrectionary meaning of what he said. Near the front row an African man who blended invisibly into the crowd checked his iPhone recorder was still running: it was.

'Now I want to conclude, because you have probably had enough of me tonight!'

'No! No!' came shouts from the audience.

He smiled and then continued, 'Perhaps we all expected too much. Perhaps it was naïve to think that the ANC – my ANC, my ANC! – for all its moral integrity, its heroic historic role and its constitutionalist traditions, could be immune to human frailty, especially in the face of such immense social inequalities. Could any political party anywhere in the world have done any better?

'I get irritated with outside observers who have never been able to view post-apartheid South Africa in a nuanced way. Our country has either been romanticised as "Mandela's miracle", or cynically dismissed as "going down the pan". But neither of these perceptions is accurate – and they never were. After transition from apartheid under Madiba, it was always going to be a bumpy road because of the enormous problems dumped on our laps by generations of apartheid and colonialism.

'Don't lose heart. We never did in those long bitter years of struggle. And don't lose faith. Because our beautiful country remains an inspiration: joyously transformed from evil and horror in spite of the many challenges that remain. The "rainbow nation" is an ideal for which a generation of South Africans sacrificed their lives. Tens of thousands suffered imprisonment, torture and exile in the process, some my close comrades.

'Tonight I urge you not to give up. For to do so would be an equal betrayal. Joint the fight! Campaign! Organise! Justice and liberty is on our side! We will fight and we will win!'

The standing ovation was spontaneous and prolonged. Both Thandi and Mkhize leapt to their feet, clapping enthusiastically, everyone wreathed in smiles of joy – even the man with the iPhone recorder, to ensure he blended into the crowd.

The Veteran, too, was delighted. But sweat poured off his face. And as the adrenaline ebbed, he suddenly realised how deeply drained and terribly tired he was.

There was a bubble of enthusiastic chatter as the crowd drifted away. iPhone Man headed out quickly – though not too quickly, ensuring he merged with the rest. His task was to brief the President's security chief.

As Mkhize held back, Thandi pushed forward to join an excitable small group around the Veteran. When she spotted an opening she introduced herself.

'I want to help you,' she beseeched him.

He smiled, encouragingly yet also searchingly, at the bright, enthusiastic young woman standing imploringly in front of him.

'Of course. But I'm a bit knackered now, you know.'

'Then please can I come to see you while you are still in Pretoria? Tomorrow would be fine for me.'

He stared at her, then grinned. 'Okay. Can you give me your name, cell number and email? If I get a chance I will call you to see what we can fix.'

Thandi quickly scribbled down her details. 'Please do call,' she pleaded. 'I am not a hanger-on or some weirdo. I want to do something. That's why I came tonight.'

Although the Veteran, from long, sometimes bitter experience, was wary of strangers, he was also by temperament an open, convivial person.

'I promise to call – if not tomorrow, then later tonight.'

'Thank you so much,' Thandi replied. 'See you tomorrow, then!'

'And your friend?' the Veteran enquired quizzically of a nervous, shy Mkhize hovering behind her.

'Ah – my friend Isaac! His first political meeting ever. He is a game ranger.'

'Welcome!' the Veteran extended his hand. 'Game ranger, hey? Hope you are sorting out those bloody poachers. I think they're connected to the state capture and corruption I was talking about tonight.'

CHAPTER 7

It was early morning and the Jacaranda City was in full bloom.

Pretoria's broad streets, parks and gardens were speckled with beautiful jacaranda trees and the city seemed carpeted in their distinctive blue/purple colour, especially when seen from the hills surrounding the central zone – one hill containing the centre of government, the Union Buildings, the other its tranquil Freedom Park, a monument to those who fought in the freedom struggle.

Jacaranda petals lay across the pavements and streets as iPhone Man drove up from the city and over the hill along from the Union Buildings to the Bryntirion Estate, containing the presidential compound set apart from about twenty double-storey ministerial residences. His credentials were inspected and checks made through phone calls at the kiosk alongside the gates guarded by armed police.

He swept around a score of ministerial homes and buildings set in a graceful park with trees, wide lawns and well-kept flower beds surrounded by intimidating security fencing, and pulled up near the President's Herbert Baker-designed official home, with its adjoining offices where presidency staff like Moses Khoza worked. Khoza awaited him in his office, 'President Security Chief' emblazoned upon the door, and was briefed fully on the Veteran's meeting before being handed the downloaded speech on a memory stick.

'Are you saying he actually urged the overthrow of our government?' Khoza asked.

'Absolutely – you just listen to the speech. It was crystal clear. Twice he repeated that Mandela quote. Twice. And he incited the meeting to fight, to organise – it was revolutionary stuff.'

After iPhone Man had departed, Khoza pondered long and hard. He felt genuinely torn. On the one hand the Veteran had been a much-admired comrade. They had worked together in exile after Khoza had been released from Robben Island. On the other hand, this was an outright threat to the regime – a democratically elected regime, quite unlike the apartheid governments.

Such incitement simply could not be tolerated. It was bad enough having to set the police on millions taking to the streets in public service-delivery protests right across the country each year. But the protesters were ordinary citizens, not popular leaders of the Veteran's stature.

The packed meeting on which iPhone Man had reported was indeed proof of mutinous intent. And that had to be dealt with.

At the same time, but on the other side of Pretoria, Thandi and Mkhize were enjoying an early morning coffee, sitting outside a small café where they had agreed to meet after going their separate ways the night before. Although Mkhize had been disappointed at her crisp goodbye and peck on his cheek, at least she had suggested they meet up again at breakfast time.

The sun was up but the early summer heat had not yet blanched the city and the birds were in full song. Pretoria, Mkhize noted, had a much cosier, less metropolitan feel than bustling Johannesburg. It was more human, he decided. The city centre was full of Africans, the leafy, sprawling suburbs with their manicured gardens much less so, black servants and an elite of black residents excepted.

He was listening intently to Thandi. She had hardly stopped talking, enthusing over the meeting.

'He was brilliant – totally brilliant.'

'But what exactly did he mean by poaching, state capture and corruption?' Mkhize asked. 'I've been thinking about that ever since.'

'I'm not sure – we will have to ask him,' she replied.

As if by telepathy, her phone rang.

'Can you come and see me in an hour?' the Veteran asked. Airily assuming the young woman would be available at such short notice, he gave her details of the address of the friend's home at which he had stayed overnight before he had to fly back to Cape Town International Airport and then home to Kalk Bay.

*

60

Moses Khoza had summoned one of his most trusted security officers and briefed him closely as they wandered on the grass outside his office.

They chatted intently, looking at the fine view of the suburbs spreading out down below and the rolling hills on the horizon. He didn't want to talk inside his office and their phones were both switched off in their pockets to reduce any chance of being overheard.

For missions like this, the President simply did not wish to know and certainly did not want to be consulted.

It had to be totally deniable.

Getting on for fifty years before, the Veteran had recruited and organised a group of young activists known as the London Recruits, as part of a small and secret operation organised by ANC and South African Communist Party activists in exile in London.

They had undertaken daring missions – some solo, some in pairs – right into the heart of apartheid South Africa. Some had flown into Johannesburg on scheduled flights posing as carefree young white tourists with 'suitcase bombs' in their luggage. These had thousands of leaflets concealed in false bottoms with a timing mechanism to activate a small bomb, which exploded, showering the leaflets round city centres. Detection would have been simple with modern airport security measures, but the activists were operating in quite another era and their cases were stowed with other passenger baggage in aeroplane holds, to be collected on landing.

The Recruits were assisted by the South African government's policy to promote tourism in breach of the boycott organised by international anti-apartheid campaigns. All of them were white and arrived at airports to be warmly welcomed. Most dressed smartly, one in a specially purchased new white linen suit and a fedora hat. Each had been instructed how to assemble the small bombs, tasks to be accomplished in their hotel rooms. One pair had meticulously followed their instructions and training. They had purchased half a dozen cheap plastic buckets and a sheet of thin plywood, which they inserted inside the buckets to carry the leaflets. Then they inserted the pipe bombs. With the buckets in the back of their rental car, they were dressed in bright scarves and fancy coloured hats to distract attention from any witnesses noticing them leaving the devices.

Driving to their destination in Durban, they were stopped by several burly armed police officers in plain clothes. The bombs were timed to detonate in twenty minutes. Horrified, they were trapped, already imagining the imprisonment and torture the Veteran had warned about.

Then, in a stroke of genius, and in his haughtiest English upper-class accent, one of the Recruits exclaimed: 'We are British tourists!'

The plainclothes policeman looked startled. 'Sorry sir,' he stammered in a thick Afrikaans accent. 'There's a lot of thieving around here, stolen goods and so on, and you are driving a Johannesburg car, where a lot of the thieves come from. Please show us your passports and we won't trouble you any more.'

'What a beautiful country you have,' the Recruit beamed as the passports were cursorily inspected.

'Yah, we are proud of it,' the officer replied, smiling and waving them on.

These escapades took place during the late 1960s and early 1970s, when the resistance had been all but closed down inside the country, with Nelson Mandela and many ANC leaders imprisoned and others suppressed by a ruthless police state. So when the blasts sent leaflets up into the air to scatter, they created a huge impact in local newspapers and were an immense source of succour to depressed, isolated anti-apartheid activists. The authorities were bemused and disturbed, for they had no idea whatsoever as to either the source or the delivery mechanism; they thought they had closed the resistance right down.

Reporting the story, one evening newspaper said: 'The significance of the "bombing" lies in the precision with which the operation was executed and the relatively sophisticated equipment.' The operation was repeated the following year – again causing consternation. Africans present rushed to pick up the leaflets and were elated as a tape-recorded broadcast blared out from a loudspeaker on a rented car or hotel-room balcony. Leaflets smuggled in were showered from rooftops, and banners were unfurled from buildings with the slogan 'ANC FIGHTS!' Others had a message from Nelson Mandela on one side and instructions for making Molotov cocktails on the other side.

In the 1980s, when the resistance was in full swing again, one of the London Recruits drove a large safari vehicle across the Zimbabwe border, the dozen safari lovers on board blissfully unaware their bench seats were constructed over a false floor containing scores of machine guns and arms for the ANC's underground wing uMkhonto we Sizwe.

The London Recruits were a project so secret that leading anti-apartheid campaigners abroad knew nothing at all about its existence, let

62

alone its provenance. It was the Veteran's baby. The Recruits worked in small self-contained cells unknown to other cells, only to the Veteran. Other members of the central unit helped to locate safe houses in London where planning and work could be undertaken.

Pubs, parks and university campuses were used as rendezvous points for contacts and recruits. Briefings on missions typically occurred on the Stamford Bridge terraces of the Veteran's favourite football team, Chelsea. At what used to be known as 'the Shed End', amidst the hubbub, noise and jostling of the Chelsea fans during home matches, confidential conversations could not be monitored by directional microphones. Instructions could be given, queries answered in the thick of the raucous crowd.

Hampstead Heath on early mornings or late afternoons saw clandestine experiments with the leaflet-bomb devices and sessions teaching the Recruits techniques of counter-surveillance and methods of passing on secret documents or messages.

The operation's headquarters were located in a three-storey apartment in the London suburb of Golders Green. It had a discreet back entrance, and one of the Veteran's colleagues had constructed a hidden room, its door concealed in a large wardrobe with a back panel that slid open to provide access. Inside, the unit had detailed maps of South Africa and work tables. There was a small darkroom for photographs to be developed, and for the storage of cine films of locations in South Africa, including the coastline of the east coast, where guerrillas might be landed by sea.

Because of the project's extreme sensitivity, the Veteran had been scrupulously cautious about recruitment. Most were young activists on the left, members of the Young Communist League or the International Socialists. Some he had met during his own clandestine work in London at the time, as he flitted in and out from ANC bases in Tanzania, Angola or Zambia. He would warn each Recruit: 'If you get caught, you will be severely and repeatedly tortured.'

He was paranoid about penetration and informers. Much of that was routine during the Cold War, where proxy battles infected the Southern Africa theatre. The ANC, shunned by the West – Mandela himself denounced as a 'terrorist' by Margaret Thatcher and Ronald Reagan just a few years before being freed as a global hero – was a target, not simply for the apartheid security forces but for Britain's MI5 and America's CIA. The Anti-Apartheid Movement had informers from all these intelligence services in its ranks. Prosecution evidence against one leading figure in an Old Bailey trial for organising militant protests against racist South African sports tours contained a verbatim transcript of the entire proceedings of its 1969 Annual General Meeting.

The Veteran had established his own technique for gently interrogating those he had identified or been recommended as London Recruits. He would give no prior indication at all of the purpose of chats he had set up with each individual on their own. Nor would he tell them anything specific until he had satisfied himself they could be trusted. He would talk around their political views, probe their involvement and experiences, and double-check the credibility of the replies against his deep knowledge of left-wing politics and ideologies.

When Thandi rang the doorbell she was blissfully unaware she was about to be vetted like those young London Recruits once were.

She had come alone. Mkhize waited in her parents' battered small Toyota parked outside, not a little sore.

'I asked to see him. I have something sensitive and important to discuss. Very private,' she had explained.

'Private?' He seethed inwardly.

'Yes. Private.' She touched him on the knee and looked him in the eye. 'Just give me a bit of space.'

'Of course,' he smiled awkwardly, enjoying the touch.

He was confused about her. Drawn – intensely drawn, he had to admit to himself – but also a bit in awe. And he hadn't felt that before about the girls he had been with. Nice girls, yes, but not to be in awe of. This one was awesome. Truly awesome.

He watched out of the car window as the door opened and the Veteran beamed broadly, noticing Mkhize looking out of the car window. Good, he thought, she's being extra-careful.

'Come in. Come in. How are you?'

'Fine, thanks very much.' Thandi was nervous.

'Fancy a cup of coffee? Or a rooibos?'

'Rooibos, please,' she stammered. What was wrong with her? She fidgeted.

The Veteran switched on the kettle. The homeowners had gone to work, leaving him in alone.

'So,' he said. 'Why you? Why me?'

'I just think someone has to do something. I feel a responsibility.'

64

'Responsibility? To what exactly?'

'To our ideals. What has happened to them? I don't know. They seem to have disappeared. Everyone just seems to be out for themselves. The corruption and cronyism you talked about. It is like a cancer, it is getting everywhere. What would Nelson Mandela think? We should be ashamed.'

The Veteran looked at her. A vibrant young woman, charismatic with youthful energy, her dark skin glowing with health, speaking with passionate idealism. Silence now hung between them. He had learned to use silence. It was so powerful. People were enticed by it. They had an urge to fill it – to fill the vacuum. It seduced them to say something. Silence also made them feel respected, not badgered.

As did Thandi. She relaxed, and began her story. Not hesitantly. Fluently.

'I was brought up to support the ANC as our salvation.'

'Why?' he asked.

'My grandmother told me about it. She was a housemaid. Not a political campaigner. But she was sort of an activist in her own way. She told me when she went to work for a young white couple and their four children here in Pretoria, she had no idea they would become notorious. At first she thought they were just like all the other whites. Born to rule. But then she realised they were very different. She told me how Africans came to their house – the house she kept clean and tidy – as equals. She had never before witnessed this. She knew her place as a housemaid. Seen but not heard. Obedient – always.

'But my granny discussed politics with the white woman, became her friend, understood what was going on, tried to help as best she could, especially when the Special Branch raided. She told me how the officers tried to humiliate her. But she kept her dignity, stayed quiet, always watching.

'She told me what apartheid was like for us blacks. Because my generation – us Born Frees – haven't a clue. That really makes me cross. My granny told me about the destruction of her home and the forced removal to make space for new white suburbs in old black township areas like she had lived in. She told me about the police brutality towards our people, how our lives were worthless. She told me about our leaders imprisoned on Robben Island – about their sacrifices for a better future.

'My Granny told me about her fifteen-year-old nephew, allowed by the white activist couple to stay with her for a few days in her servants'

65

quarters. He had walked back there, whistling to himself, stepping into the road to make way for a bunch of white youths filling up the pavement. But they pulled him back and just beat him up on the spot, kicking and punching. "Don't you dare walk on our pavements, *kaffir*," they shouted at him. "Let this be a lesson to you." He came back to Granny terrified, crying, bleeding and bruised all over.

'She told me about the struggle. And I went to the library and read more. About how Mandela and our leaders had been peaceful and respectful for generations. Until in the 1950s they realised that wasn't getting them anywhere. With apartheid spreading its tentacles, things were getting worse all the time. So they opted for militant but still non-violent action, like strikes or the stay-at-home days by black workers, who refused to travel in to work in the white cities. And then how the leaders were arrested and charged and banned.

'So reluctantly, very reluctantly, they were left with no alternative but armed struggle. Even then, their targets were not allowed to be people, just government property and infrastructure.'

The Veteran nodded sympathetically. 'And what did you think when you heard all about that?' he asked.

'I was inspired. I even read Nelson Mandela's *Long Walk to Freedom*. It was amazing. What a man! Eight hundred pages – the longest book I have ever read, but I could hardly put it down.'

'No,' interrupted the Veteran, 'I meant what did you think about the armed struggle?'

'Oh,' Thandi paused, her forehead wrinkling. 'Well, I don't like violence, because there's always a danger of people getting hurt. But what else were they supposed to do? Just give up?'

'Some said the armed struggle alienated liberal whites – the ones who said they didn't like apartheid,' the Veteran replied.

'You're playing devil's advocate with me!' Thandi exclaimed.

They both burst out laughing.

She had spunk, this girl, the Veteran thought to himself.

Thandi, flushed now, ploughed on to make her point. 'Mandela and the other leaders were banned or in jail. The ANC was made illegal, so were other anti-apartheid groups. Also so-called "liberal opinion" often wasn't that liberal. Yes, their consciences were pricked. They found apartheid embarrassing, even distasteful. But when it came to the crunch, they just went along with it, and enjoyed its benefits like other whites.'

He suddenly switched subjects. 'Tell me about your parents. Your friends. Any relationships you have had, and so on.'

'Relationships?' Thandi exclaimed, suspicious and prickly now. 'Excuse me, but what's that got to do with you?'

He smiled reassuringly. 'I am sorry, but everything has to do with me. If you are going to help me in the way I absolutely need, I must know all there is to know about you.'

'But all I want to do is help,' she replied tartly.

'Yah, I realise that. And I am very grateful. But let me explain.'

He had probed enough to have made up his mind about her. She was the genuine article. That had been his instinct from when they first met the evening before. And he had developed a sixth sense for people, born out of long and bitter experience in ANC intelligence during the liberation war when informers were everywhere. Some he had trusted turned out to be apartheid agents.

Their conversation had only reinforced his initial instinct, indeed reassured him.

'Thandi, don't take offence. This is routine. In the struggle, in order really to trust someone – sometimes with your life – you had to know pretty well everything about them. Any vulnerabilities, any hidden allegiances, any obligations. Sometimes people were turned by the security police because something in their life made them vulnerable – debt, illicit sexual relationships, for instance – not because they were traitors to the cause. Also, you had to know that they really were who they claimed to be. That is why I asked you those personal questions.'

'Okay,' she said hesitantly, her bristling demeanour abruptly subsiding as it suddenly dawned on her that she was being seriously assessed. But for exactly what, she wondered?

'Anyway, let's talk frankly. I think, no I know, you are genuine.'

'Well, that's very generous of you!' She laughed impertinently.

'I am not as energetic as I once was. I am not a kid any more, you know.' The Veteran smiled ruefully.

'You aren't too bad for an old codger!' she retorted, repeating his self-deprecating description the evening before.

'Well, that is very generous of you!'

They were even now, and it hadn't escaped his notice how she could be both impudent and respectful.

'If I am to have any impact in bringing about change, I need someone

67

much younger to give me the legs I no longer have. Do you want to be that person?'

Thandi was completely taken aback. When she volunteered she had hoped to be a mere foot soldier, not his lieutenant. Her mind was in a whirl. What did this mean?

'Do you really think I can do that?' she asked, 'I'd love to support your work, of course. It would be a real honour. But I don't know if I'm capable of taking on all the heavy responsibilities. I certainly don't want to let you down.'

'No chance. Of that I am confident. But let me ask you another question. I have a feeling I could be a target. The people at the top will hang on to power at all costs. I am not saying they will definitely endanger us. But if we represent a real threat, they might. I want you to be clear about that. Things might get nasty. If you walk away now I will be disappointed, but I will fully understand and respect your decision. What I wouldn't want is for you not to have been warned.'

'I am not worried about that,' she replied.

Thandi was of an age and of a temperament where taking a risk wasn't a consideration. Her values, her idealism, her sense of duty propelled her, like many young people involved in radical politics. They didn't have family responsibilities. They weren't bothered about money beyond the necessity to survive. They didn't think anything would ever happen to them. Their security wasn't a consideration.

'What about your job?' he asked, wondering if she actually had one.

She explained she worked a few days as an early morning production assistant on a weekday breakfast time online radio station. It gave her plenty of time – even if not much income. But then she didn't need much. She stayed with her parents, the apple of their eyes. She was pretty frugal. Yet somehow she seemed to have enough cash to enjoy herself when those of her peers also in work, but unlike her full-time, were always strapped for cash.

The more he got to know her, the more impressed the Veteran was.

'You have the advantage of being what they call in the trade a 'clean skin'. You aren't known. You haven't been involved in the ANC. You haven't made friends or enemies in politics. So we can do things together without getting noticed. That's a major reason why you could be effective – provided we are very careful, and you are especially careful. For believe me, what I have in mind, the governing elite and their cronies won't like at all. They are bound to retaliate in some way. How exactly I can't tell now.'

'I want to help anyway, whatever is involved,' she responded confidently, still somewhat heady at the turn of events. Unsure what exactly she was letting herself in for, she was nevertheless excited.

'That's good, let's shake on it, then.' He extended his hand and she hers. It felt warm to her, though a little rough on her smooth skin.

'Now, here are all my contact details.' He handed over a sheet of paper. 'This cell number is not my usual one. It is not under my name. I will get you one like it. We will only contact each other on that pay-as-you-go phone. All right?' He paused quizzically.

'Yes, of course,' she mumbled.

They had been talking for well over an hour, she suddenly realised, and felt guilty about Mkhize.

'Oh my God! Isaac is still sitting in the car outside. How rude of me.'

'Never mind, we will get him in, because I also want to talk to him – about poaching.'

'Really?' her mind raced. 'But I don't know him that well.'

Then she became a little indignant. 'We only met recently. He's not my boyfriend, you know!'

'Now, now.' The Veteran chided, amused – which made her even more indignant. 'I will explain that leaving him outside wasn't your fault. It was mine. But before I do so I just want to cover some more things about what I might want you to do with me, and check you agree.'

They talked for another ten minutes in detail.

'That's great,' he said, beaming. 'Now I will have to grovel to your non-boyfriend. Can you bring him in?'

When Thandi rushed outside, flustered, embarrassed and ready to apologise profusely, she found Mkhize fast asleep in the passenger seat.

He looked so peaceful, almost innocent, and she found herself considering him intensely for the first time. She knew he was interested in her, but was she really interested in him? Maybe? He seemed different from the others who had tried to inveigle their way into her life. Mmm . . . but she was too busy to think about that now. And anyway, she was likely to be very busy from now onward.

What to do? The Veteran wanted to speak to him, yet she felt guilty enough without disturbing him. She tapped gently on the window. He didn't stir. She tapped again. Still no response. She turned and started to walk back.

As she got to the front door, preparing to explain, doubly embarrassed now, there was a commotion behind her. Mkhize had finally woken, had yanked open the car door and was calling to her.

Come, she beckoned.

He sloped up to her, unsteadily wiping the sleep from his eyes. 'Sorry,' he said sheepishly.

'Don't worry! It was me who was embarrassed, leaving you stuck in the car for so long.'

'You needn't have bothered. I get so little sleep when I'm working, I just catch up when I'm off – even when I don't want to. Not very considerate, is it?'

Thandi laughed, her eyes sparkling. He was quite fun really, she thought, an easy-going guy. This one might, just might, be worth getting to know better. But no time for that: she had so much to do.

The Veteran showed them in, oblivious to the interaction, though noticing they were both flushed. *Aha*, he thought, *these non-boyfriends.*

'Thank you for leaving us to talk,' he said to Mkhize. 'I'm sorry you were stuck outside for so long. It was really good of you, but I had no alternative. Now the reason I would like to talk is poaching. Not just ordinary poaching. I'm really interested in poaching that agencies of the state turn a blind eye to.'

Mkhize said nothing, shrugging his shoulders. This was new to him – not something that he had ever considered before. He knew from experience that there was local poaching, and then there was poaching directed by big crime syndicates, sometimes of course exploiting poor local men. He had caught poachers, he had shot at them, but he hadn't imagined government collaboration might lie behind them.

The Veteran spent half an hour quietly interrogating Mkhize without the ranger having the faintest notion that was what was being done to him. All he thought he was doing was explaining who he was and what he had done in his life.

Piet van der Merwe was in a nostalgic mood as he carefully worked out a plan.

He had first been involved in the Rhodesian African Rifles in their war against black guerrilla fighters. When that failed and Ian Smith's racist rule in Rhodesia gave way to majority rule in the new Zimbabwe, van der Merwe, like his contemporaries, went to South Africa and joined its Defence Force, SADF.

From there they launched attack-and-destroy missions into the newly independent Zimbabwe, with the objective of destabilising and reversing majority rule. Some were caught or killed. But, because they had deliberately dressed in old Rhodesian Army camouflage uniforms, South Africa's military chiefs were able to deny all knowledge.

He was also a member of the SADF's 32 Battalion, known as the Buffalo Battalion. Nicknamed 'the Terrible Ones', it had been formed in 1975 with black and white soldiers, many of whom were mercenary recruits from the Angolan Civil War who fought alongside Jonas Savimbi's murderous UNITA rebels. Operating hand in hand with South African forces, UNITA at one time controlled large parts of Angola's southern and eastern regions, creating mayhem and havoc, with hinterland towns like once-modern Huambo becoming uninhabitable, blown-out shells. Fertile farming lands were abandoned and infested with landmines. The Buffalo Battalion was to the fore of this battle, its brutal but effective prowess important to the apartheid state in its objective of destabilising and undermining new majority-rule governments around South Africa's borders.

Piet van der Merwe performed a shadowy role, focusing upon logistics and procuring resources for the Terrible Ones, who were also mercilessly efficient in their attacks on South West Africa's liberation movement SWAPO. His links to government and the security forces, combined with his business acumen, made him a key figure, although he was meticulous about staying out of the limelight, his name never appearing in reports on the battalion's more infamous incursions into neighbouring states.

Investigators later discovered that ivory and rhino horn smuggling was integral to the covert South African war in the neighbouring states, with high-ranking South African army officers and officials directly involved in the 1970s and 1980s. SADF helicopters were used to ferry horns from slaughtered rhinos and elephants. A CIA front company was also implicated in flying cargoes of illicit rhino horn out of conflict areas.

UNITA chief Jonas Savimbi was quoted in 1986: 'We export ivory, rhino horn and leopard and antelope skins to help pay for our war.' And all of these could be found at times in SADF crates labelled 'military hardware'.

71

The 32 Battalion was ignominiously disbanded on 26 March 1993 after a bloody attack on unarmed African civilians in the South African black squatter settlement of Phola Park, east of Johannesburg. That notorious event, just a year before the final transition from apartheid to majority rule, with the ancien régime still clinging on while simultaneously negotiating with Mandela, stigmatised and stained the reputation of the Buffalos.

But van der Merwe was never named, and his only real worry came during a commission of inquiry established by President Nelson Mandela. To van der Merwe's relief, however, he wasn't called as a witness or even mentioned in the long list of characters identified. He had covered his tracks well, but you never knew what might be unearthed, he had worried, as key witnesses were summoned.

When Judge Kumleben published his 226-page report in 1996, van der Merwe rushed to get a copy and found a devastating indictment of SADF, its lies and cover-ups. Anxiously, he read Kumleben's key conclusion: 'The SADF officially, though covertly, participated in the illicit possession and transportation of ivory and rhino horn from Angola and Namibia to South Africa between 1978 and 1986.' The inquiry also heard how SADF had 'aided and abetted the slaughter and destruction of elephant herds and rhino in Angola and Mozambique'. South Africa had been a 'clearing house' for the handling and delivery of these horns from other African states, principally to the Far East. Not only was this SADF involvement illegal, but it was also 'sanctioned by highly placed personnel in SADF, state officials and ministers of state.'

Meanwhile, van der Merwe slid unobtrusively away to build a new role in his world of business deals and mercenaries, ready to serve new masters – like Moses Khoza, even though the former liberation fighter could well have been a target of the Terrible Ones during the 1980s.

In his new life van der Merwe moved seamlessly between government buildings and his shadowy world, on good terms with anyone wanting a deal. Always on the lookout for new opportunities, he quickly came to realise that procuring and smuggling rhino and elephant horns could be very lucrative indeed. But he was determined to stick to planning and fixing, at all times to be nowhere near the action. That would be far too compromising. He had got away with much over the decades and was determined to stay in the clear now.

*

After probing Mkhize, the Veteran had satisfied himself that the ranger was authentic, an engaging combination of tough canny bush operator and political innocence. Thandi had been agitated about the relentless questions, though she had learned so much more about her 'non-boyfriend' as a result.

When they had adjourned to get themselves snacks from the house owner's fridge – what the Veteran referred to as 'fixings': avocado, cheese, tomato, salad, hummus and bread – they sat around the kitchen table again to resume their conversation.

'I suspect the rhino trade may go high up into the state, like it used to be under the old apartheid regime,' the Veteran said. 'During the liberation struggle, we knew this was going on. There were reports of all sorts of scams. But we could never get enough hard evidence for the media to publish. Today wildlife crime is also linked to the drugs trade, money laundering, gunrunning, prostitution and human trafficking – all the worst sort of serious international crime.'

Mkhize interjected. 'Yah, we've always suspected and sort of known that at the end of the chain from poor local poachers are the big men. But what about the government, where's the proof?'

'The key thing is to look at the patterns,' the Veteran replied, 'and to try to work out what's behind them. That's what I used to do a lot of when I was heading up the ANC's underground intelligence. You've always got to be very careful of making one plus one equal three by simply juxtaposing different slabs of information. But my nose tells me there's a bigger picture somewhere if we can put all the fragments together.'

The Veteran paused, staring directly at Mkhize. 'Are you up for helping me to put this bigger picture together?' he asked.

The ranger was hesitant. 'I don't know if I can really add much,' he replied. 'Your world is a mystery to me.'

Thandi had been sitting back listening, fascinated as the two men engaged, but now she leaned forward, touching Mkhize gently on the arm.

'Of course you can help,' she said, encouraging him. 'You may know very little about each other's professions, but together you will know much more about what is really happening on the ground.'

Mkhize shrugged his broad shoulders, muscles bulging. 'Okay,' he said, but still seemed diffident.

Munching his sandwich, the Veteran went on. 'Good. So what do we

73

know, then? I will begin, you interrupt when you want to. Let's start with South Africa's Endangered Species Protection Unit, the ESPU. In 2002 the ESPU was disbanded by the police commissioner, along with a lot of other specialist police units covering corruption, child protection, sex offences. This was despite the ESPU being very successful in infiltrating smuggling networks. Levels of crime in each area, including wildlife, substantially increased afterwards. I know its staff were redeployed to police stations, but the ESPU's expertise and effectiveness was completely lost. So why was that done?'

'Yah, I read about that during my training,' Mkhize said. 'Also I've always worried that, although everything on the surface seems geared to tackling smuggling and stopping rhino slaughter, there's been a pattern of bad apples in the system, which makes me wonder how serious the authorities are.'

Mkhize was in full flow now. 'Something else. Yes, the South African Revenue Service has a division called the Customs Border Control Unit, which targets smuggling. But billions of dollars of rhino horn somehow get through undetected. There's also the National Research Group, which targets smuggling and trafficking illegal substances alongside money laundering and tax evasion. But, again, smuggling continues regardless. Why and how?'

The Veteran interjected, 'Yah, and what about when the South African National Parks was exposed in 2012 for manipulating figures to conceal the extent of rhino-horn smuggling? And that in 2009 there emerged links between smuggling and senior ANC politicians?'

'That's interesting,' Mkhize added, 'because our game-reserve owner complained in our team meeting a few weeks ago that when anyone in our world points a finger at government shortcomings over rhino, anonymous sources attack us on social media and sometimes in the press.'

'That sounds like the so-called "information peddlers" who operate on the fringes of the secret state and are used to smear people hostile to the presidency,' chortled the Veteran. 'I'm expecting lots of that myself after last night's speech.'

Then he switched their conversation, Thandi was glued to every bit of it. 'People always talk about China as the magnet for rhino horns. Actually, the USA is a massive market for the whole illegal wildlife trade – second only to China. But Vietnam has become just as important.'

Mkhize, animated, interjected again. 'Yah, look at what they got up to in Swaziland, where rhino hunting is legal. Although most of the safari rhino hunters are rich Americans and Europeans, ranger friends have told me that the Vietnamese are very different. They tend to be much, much poorer people from Vietnamese cities and villages funded by so-called benefactors, always unnamed. They come for the horns, not the hunting. Some of them actually need teaching how to shoot when they arrive at the game reserve! It's outrageous. We have a name for it: "pseudo-hunting". Actually, it's not hunting at all – it's straight shooting. They aren't trophy hunters at all, they are criminals.'

'What's the bloody difference?' Thandi cried loudly looking furious. 'The rhino are dead anyway. Surely that's the crime?'

'I completely agree, but the law doesn't, unfortunately,' Mkhize replied. 'Even worse, the price of rhino horn jumped after those people went hunting, creating even more incentive for this criminality.'

The Veteran asked, 'What about the "Boere mafia" of professional hunters and their syndicates? I seem to remember reports of a "rhino slaughter farm" with decaying remains in mass graves.'

'Yah, you're right,' said Mkhize. 'After a leading Boere mafia figure, Dawie Groenewald, was arrested by the FBI, he pleaded guilty and was convicted by a US court.' By the way, there are two great books by the conservationist Lawrence Anthony, *The Elephant Whisperer* and *The Last Rhinos*. He explains that Africans have never hunted for trophies, only for survival, for food. He calls Africans "the original conservationists".'

Mkhize continued where he had left off earlier. 'Demand for rhino horn has grown massively in Vietnam. It's a bigger market than China now. Vietnamese advertisements claim rhino horn can treat everything from cancer to hangovers, and it's used as an aphrodisiac: doctors in state hospitals regularly prescribe it for patients. It's become the "in thing" for the Vietnamese rich – ground rhino horn taken with wine is a serious fashion drink.

'Another delicacy in Vietnam is from poached lions and tigers, both also endangered species. Their bones are boiled down into dark brown gluey bars and sold like chocolate bars in Vietnam's hotels and restaurants. Vietnam also has posh "wild-meat restaurants", where wealthy people show off by eating illegally traded wildlife.'

The Veteran interjected. 'Yah, but now look at the political picture. The Vietnamese Embassy in Pretoria has been known to use a diplomatic bag for getting rhino horn out of South Africa. The Geneva Convention for diplomats grants border-free passage for all consignments from embassies to their home countries worldwide. And Vietnamese diplomats have been exposed for their complicity in the trade. The Taiwanese Embassy in Swaziland was once also exposed for using its diplomatic bags to smuggle horn and ivory.'

'That's interesting,' said Mkhize, 'because our reserve owner was tipped off that, very soon after one of our rhinos was killed, a Taiwanese ship that had been anchored quite near to us in Richards Bay suddenly left in the middle of the same night.'

The Veteran interjected: 'The growth of the middle classes in East Asia is the real culprit, driving a massive new demand for ivory. In the black market the wholesale price shot up from over a hundred dollars per kilo to over two thousand dollars now.'

There was pause in the animated discussion as they digested all this information.

Then the Veteran came back to his theme. 'Remember the South African police investigation into links between the security minister and a Chinese rhino-horn smuggler who had hosted him regularly at his massage parlour in Nelspruit?'

'I think corrupt politicians at the very top of our government are up to their necks in all this, turning a blind eye, raking off a slice of the immense profits, using the state's apparatus to facilitate the slaughter and the smuggling to the East. If we can expose that together, we kill two birds with one stone. Protecting the rhinos and protecting our young democracy to preserve Madiba's legacy.'

Thandi understood immediately. Mkhize began to do so as well: now the connections were clear, he could see he too might well have a role alongside the Veteran – and therefore, more importantly, alongside Thandi too.

CHAPTER 8

The heat had risen to a mind-numbing 47°C as the rhino bull heaved, belched and snorted, desperately trying to manoeuvre under the shade of a marula tree. Its ears twitched, its breathing pulsated, a colossus in its prime and in charge of its own territory.

Or so it thought, completely oblivious to the silenced rifle pointing directly at it, with a live round in the chamber and ten more in a magazine. The rounds were soft-nosed – the purpose to explode on impact, creating maximum damage, tearing apart the hide. Often poachers used sharp-pointed ammunition, but with the option of cutting the tips off in order to fragment upon impact.

The royal giant hardly heard the sharp whoosh emanating from the gunman crouching behind a nearby bush, only felt the searing agony in its hide as the first bullet exploded. Its distressed screeching tore through the midday haze and boiling silence of the bush, as it staggered and fell, legs splaying as it struggled to remain upright. Circling around as if drunk, bewildered by being unable to smell the source, dust billowing, it took a second bullet and collapsed, still trying to climb up. A third bullet, blood spouting, eyes glazing over vacantly, it finally, wrenchingly subsided and died slowly as hunter and tracker gazed down at their stricken handiwork. A good night and half-day's work, they nodded, satisfied, and got out the *pangas* to hack viciously at the base of the horns, stuck them in a bag and slunk off, eyes roving constantly in fear of pursuers.

Fifty metres away one of the two guards assigned to constant protection of the beasts lay prone over a large rock, blood congealing around a gaping knife wound. Of his partner there was no sight nor sound.

In no time at all swarms of white-backed vultures began scavenging greedily, hissing and clambering over each other to gorge a share of the meat. Soon they were feeding right inside the carcass, tearing the flesh away. They bobbed from one leg to another, their wings spread so that they controlled the carcass area.

But then the lappet-faced vultures started arriving. Known as the 'king of the vultures', the largest and most dominant, they were renowned for eating the toughest remains, able to gouge deep inside at even the strongest tendon or ligament. The vultures would feast for days on the wretched hulk, jettisoning their white excrement all over what had once been such a proud, regal specimen.

Later hyenas would arrive, as would the occasional wild dog, sneaking a snatch of flesh between the larger, more aggressive animals. Hyenas, Africa's must proficient big carnivore, the only mammal able to eat and digest bone crushed in its fearsome jaws, were recognised by conservationists as being vital to the ecology of nature, seeking out sick or weak targets and efficiently disposing of carcasses to control diseases like anthrax in a natural way.

What had once been a rhino soon reeked, casting an increasingly obnoxious pall over the vicinity, flies buzzing, flesh disappearing, maggots gobbling at the intestines until eventually it would be just a gaunt shell of bones drying and turning grey-white as the sun beat mercilessly down.

'Rhino genocide,' Mkhize labelled it when he finally arrived at the scene, disconsolate yet also determined, a cold fury beginning to burn inside him. But how on earth had it happened? Zama Zama's security was so tight – or so they had thought. It seemed so clinical. Why? How?

'Must be an inside job,' he muttered to his ranger partner, an equally depressed and furious Steve Brown, as they scouted around the carcass.

They discovered the dead guard and immediately radioed in to the camp headquarters to send out searchers and trackers for the guard's partner and the poachers, whose footprints they could see disappearing into the scrub.

In the days that followed, Zama Zama staff visited the family of the missing guard in the village nearby, down a dirt road, barefoot kids, dogs and cattle swirling around. But his wife and mother pleaded ignorance. He had come home, dumped more cash than they had ever seen and simply disappeared. The women's eyes darted with fear – both for their man and for their own future, now that he was being hunted. Flies buzzed around his small children, barefoot and badly clothed, chickens pecking about, a dog slouching in the shade of a creaky shed.

After local police officers also visited the family to no avail, Zama Zama managers and rangers met for a war council. The charismatic Owner went through the options. Different incentives for the guards? Maybe. But you could never outbid the poacher syndicates. Rhino poachers could earn anything from R15,000 to R80,000 for just one consignment of horn – between five and twenty five times the normal pay of guards.

Extra guards? Maybe, but that also increased the chances of having a bad one. Hiring a private security company? Out of the question, because his budget would not stretch to the huge extra cost: the priority was new fencing for the vast enlargement he'd recently negotiated with local chiefs, especially to cope with new babies in the elephant herd and get access to a new river tributary, because water was getting scarcer with climate change.

Mkhize was clear, insisting to his colleagues: 'We must have specialist reinforcement, maybe a sniper, something like that.'

'A sniper?' the Owner pondered the pros and cons with the group of guards and rangers. 'You're all trained to shoot. What would a sniper add?' he asked.

'We are trained to protect animals and guests on foot. Of course we have wounded and sometimes killed poachers. But killing people is not our profession. You need a specialist in that. Someone cold and calculated for the job,' Mkhize insisted.

The Owner consulted each one of his people in turn. 'Although I see Isaac's point, I'm not convinced. Let's instead redouble our existing efforts.'

As the group dispersed, their mood sombre, the Owner quietly beckoned Mkhize to his office in the old colonial farmhouse, which stood high, overlooking the reserve. Flowers and vegetables ringed the grass outside, its garden surrounded by a strong fence designed to keep out animal intruders but which had been easily flattened years before when the new, then difficult, elephant herd had come visiting. The Owner had spent months, even years, wooing the herd until it finally became fully and contentedly assimilated.

Now he closed the door and offered a curious Mkhize a glass of water as they both sat down around the huge old mahogany desk that had come with the house but had seen better days. Mkhize thought he was to be mollified by his boss after his suggestion had been spurned, and wasn't in a positive frame of mind; in fact, he was inwardly seething. They all seemed like a bunch of amateurs ready for the taking by the sophisticated armed syndicates running the rhino-horn trade. What the hell had been the point of the meeting?

'I wanted a private word – strictly private, between us only for now, please. Okay?' the Owner said.

Mkhize nodded, still sullen – though respectful as always.

'When we recruit staff – from rangers to cleaners for our lodges – we try to vet them, especially the rangers. But I know from my membership of South African National Parks that the smuggler syndicates have penetrated everywhere – park rangers, SANParks officers, the lot.'

Mkhize nodded, more attentive now.

'We have to assume the same is true for Zama Zama. It isn't just about bribing a guard or recruiting an unemployed local villager. Yes – we know that goes on all the time, and appears to have happened to us this time with the missing guard. But we know that anyone can be bribed for a price, and that means we could have somebody more senior implicated.'

Mkhize leaned forward. 'But we are all dedicated to our work – it's a life duty for us, rangers like me and our managers.'

'Yah, of course, I know that. But how many would you really trust with your life? How many of your colleagues do you really know?'

Mkhize replied stubbornly. 'Brown. Steve Brown, he'd lay down his life for me. So would I for him. We've come through so many difficult situations together in Zama Zama. We know each other inside out – our girlfriend troubles, our finances, our families, our weaknesses, our strengths, everything.'

The Owner nodded, saying nothing, encouraging Mkhize to go on.

'As for the others, well, we are all Zama Zama comrades' –Mkhize found himself using the Veteran's lingo – 'They all seem good blokes in a good team. But do I know them inside out in the same way as Steve? No, I can't say I do.'

The Owner smiled, as if pleased at the answer. 'Good. Because I think we may have a rotten apple. That rhino killing was just too slick. The missing guard coming on duty would have known where the rhino was when he had left for his break, but when he arrived for his shift, the rhino would have moved on. As you know, we monitor our rhinos from camp command. Only a few of our rangers and managers involved know of their exact whereabouts day to day.'

He paused, leaning over the desk. 'Isaac, I want you to undertake a personal task for me, reporting to me alone. Nobody else. Nobody else. If I'm away, you phone me on my cell. Otherwise you come and see me. Understood? Where you have to inform Brown, you do so only on a need-to-know basis. Work out a strategy. When you guys on my team are round the *braai* with the guests at night and chatting among yourselves, as you do, find out more about each of your colleagues. Reveal your worries over security like you did out there. Even imply you think I'm being complacent. See where that leads, who responds. But watch your back. These people stop at nothing. Assault, intimidation of your family, murder – the lot: *die hele boksendais.*'

He paused. 'Are you up for this?'

'Of course! In fact, I am deeply honoured, sir,' Mkhize replied.

They shook hands, the Owner coming round the desk, clapping him on the shoulder as Mkhize stood up, then gesturing him to sit again.

'I'm not finished yet!' he smiled conspiratorially.

'Your suggestion of a sniper. Brilliant idea. I didn't want to say so because I don't trust everyone in that room. But I happen to know just the person from when we were together in the army a couple of decades ago. Not sure if he's still up to it, though! And if I can bring him in, it may be as a guest or as some sort of inspector, from SANParks possibly, or maybe even the Customs Border Control Unit. We will work out some cover story.

'And I want somebody on the Zama Zama payroll living in the village, not working in the camp – an informer to give us eyes and ears on locally recruited poachers. An *impimpi*. You handle him directly. Nobody else knows. You pay him the cash that you get from me and me alone. Probably best to phone me rather than coming to see me too often, which might arouse suspicion. We have to assume someone inside is watching everything.

'That's it. The future of our rhino herd is in your hands,' he said staring pointedly at Mkhize with a seriousness that seemed humbling to the ranger, 'Now, when you return to duty, tell them all that I tried and succeeded in persuading you about my decision and that you accepted my reassurances. Don't lie, but don't reveal our new arrangements.'

Mkhize left the house with a new spring in his step, deep in thought.

81

He would find the right moments to bring Brown selectively into the picture; otherwise he was on his own, and the responsibility both exhilarated and scared the shit out of him.

He had deliberately decided not to inform the Owner about his conversations with the Veteran. But in due course he had to find a way of bringing the Veteran into the new Zama Zama picture.

And another reason to see Thandi, of course.

A few days later Mkhize was in the camp, pottering about, chatting to guests over early evening drinks while dinner was being prepared, other rangers joining in, setting tables and serving at the bar.

He urged the guests to be silent, to listen to the magic of the bush as it settled down, ready for the fast-arriving night. A heron, silhouetted against the deep orange and yellow sky flew overhead, with cries of jackals, the bustle of nestling guinea fowl and the call of a fish eagle echoing away, and a hypnotic sunset of changing colours, orange, red, purple, pink and yellow blending successively.

His phone rang piercingly, and the guests laughed that it was he, not they, who had transgressed. It was the Owner, and Mkhize sheepishly stepped immediately away from the sudden chatter to be out of earshot.

'We've had the post-mortem report on our dead rhino. The bullet was from an R1 rifle, you know the South African–made semi–automatic combat rifle similar to the AK-47. I was told informally it was of a calibre and a type that means it was almost certainly South African army issue, maybe from the apartheid days fighting ANC guerrillas. Could well be one of the Boere mafia guys. Not just a local poacher outfit. So all the more reason to be careful. Stay closely in touch.' The Owner ended the call.

Mkhize stood looking at the sunset. When European guests were present they were always struck by how very different and rapid the Zululand transition was between day and night from what they were used to in the northern hemisphere, where it was long and slow. Here the dusk was almost over before it started. A sudden scarlet-to-pink blazing sky with mauve and purple edges as the light fell like a stone to deep black darkness.

Now he had to be in touch with the Veteran as soon as possible.

'Hey, Isaac!' Brown called, 'No slouching, these guys and girls are bladdy thirsty.' He gave a raucous laugh, the easy rapport and banter between the two obvious, a good advertisement for post-apartheid, and often lightening the atmosphere for guests.

'He's probably chatting up his new girlfriend again,' Brown winked, handing over a cold Windhoek lager in a frozen glass to a guest. 'She's a real stunner. Came on safari like you guys a couple of months ago.'

Mkhize arrived, looking uncomfortable at overhearing this bit. 'Don't listen to him, always full of bullshit. I know because I taught him all he knows.' Both rangers bellowed with mirth.

'Who's the boss between you?' one of the newly arrived guests asked, as someone in a new group invariably did.

'Him,' Brown would point self-deprecatingly. 'I'm just his chauffeur.'

'Him,' Mkhize would reply. 'I'm just a poor Zulu boy.'

However, after the last guests had turned in for the night and the two rangers headed for their quarters, Mkhize's in a hut with outside shower and toilet overlooking the camp, he rang the special phone number, not listed under the Veteran's name, and only to be called sparingly. He and Thandi had both been given it for their exclusive use.

At home in Kalk Bay, the Veteran was reading in bed, about to switch off the light, and didn't answer immediately. When he did there were no greetings between the two, simply clipped, purposeful conversation.

'We've just had another rhino killed. Post-mortem showed the gun used probably ex-SA army issue, maybe a Boere mafia operative, our Zama Zama owner reckons,' Mkhize told him, 'and he's asked me confidentially to be his eyes and ears; he thinks we have an informant among our senior team.'

'Hmm,' the Veteran replied, pondering the significance. 'Good that you're on his inner team and that he trusts you.'

'There's something else,' Mkhize added. 'Our Owner's bringing in a sniper, someone from his past. I haven't told him about you. But now things are getting more serious at our end, should I do so?'

'No, not yet, maybe not ever. But when you know it, I'd like the name of the sniper. Very interesting, especially if the same people try again – you might catch them. Then we can follow the trail, see where it leads. I appreciate your call. Keep in touch.'

The rhino horn had been placed in a cloth sack and moved systematically away from Zama Zama by the poaching gang.

Within hours of the kill, the burly, bearded gunman and his two

African collaborators – the missing guard and the *panga* man – had climbed through a fresh gap they had cut in the perimeter fence and begun hiking fast to the nearest road. The gunman, not as fit as in the old days, puffed to keep up, especially with the guard, who was terrified.

When they eventually reached the safety of a waiting four-wheel drive, the group arranged to separate. The Africans were paid off in cash, driven away and dropped off, each at a different point. The horn remained in the back of the vehicle. Later it would be left to dry out to expunge the putrid stench of rotting flesh at its base where it had been hacked off.

In 1973, aged twenty-five and having served his full ten years' incarceration on Robben Island, Samuel Makojaene was released, having been transported back to Pretoria Central Prison, where he was collected by his family.

It was a strange reunion for them all, the ecstasy somehow anticlimactic as father and mother savoured the young man they had last seen as a boy. The wide-eyed ten-year-old brother he had never met, and the sense of open space and the bustle of the city all unsettling to Makojaene.

As they embraced, his mother crying and worried at how skinny her son was and his father misty-eyed, their joy became bittersweet as burly Special Branch officers forcefully served him with a five-year banning order which, among other things, stopped him being politically active and meant he could not meet more than one other person at a time.

Which is why, when they all returned to their small home in Atteridgeville township, he was only able to see the waiting group of relatives and friends one at a time as they were ushered into the kitchen, leaving everyone else to party without him in the living room through the closed door. If he had stepped through the door, he could have been rearrested.

And also why, several years later, at his engagement party, his teenage brother awkwardly placed Makojaene's engagement ring on his future wife's finger on his behalf and delivered the groom's speech, because his banning order prevented him from attending.

In the meantime his mother had fussed over Makojaene, overfeeding him at mealtimes as he continued his law studies, sometimes through the night.

Once he began practising, he established his own African law firm,

84

rather as Nelson Mandela had done with Oliver Tambo a quarter of a century before. He took on cases of persecuted Africans, including ANC activists after the resistance started again after the 1976 Soweto uprising. His career at the bar began to sparkle as he ably represented freedom fighters and businesspeople alike.

So it came as no surprise that subsequently – of course only after apartheid's abolition – he was appointed to the bench. Soon his meticulously crafted judgements filled law reports, to be avidly studied and cited. As he was promoted to the Constitutional Court, his reputation grew for favouring the weak, the powerless and the vulnerable while remaining rigidly within the country's new and evolving constitutional jurisprudence.

His workaholic grit was combined with an unbending integrity – nobody could buy or influence him against that yardstick, no force, however potent, could deflect him, however unpopular he became among the rich and powerful. At one point some shady operators in the ANC governing elite spread rumours that he was a 'counter-revolutionary'. That hurt, but he consoled himself that Mandela and his fellow leaders would never have agreed.

The poachers on the ground may not have been aware of the latest scientific developments to combat the rhino trade, but Piet van der Merwe was. It was his business to keep up.

He was especially anxious that the Zama Zama horn dried out properly to reduce the chances of detection by pure accident. He also knew that it was possible through DNA profiling to trace the horn back to its origins. Several years before, a Vietnamese security guard had been arrested after rhino horns were found by staff in his luggage as he was preparing to fly out from Johannesburg at O. R. Tambo International Airport. DNA tests on the horn's cells proved a link to a particular poaching incident several days earlier, and this forensic evidence helped convict and sentence him to ten years' imprisonment.

Van der Merwe had read up on the case, including how the calcium and melanin horns grew and hardened upwards from the nose of rhinos, the cells unique to a particular animal. That was producing a growing database of rhino DNA which could be a threat to his operations and those of others like him in the poaching trade.

*

85

The Sniper kept in close touch with his elderly mother. She was physically less mobile these days but mentally still sharp. He had ensured she had a cell phone and tutored her on its basics. Where many elderly people wouldn't touch the 'newfangled' technology, she became a serial texter, keeping in touch with her large family of children and grandchildren, her phone key to her matriarchal role.

But he always called her, never the other way around. So when his phone rang and 'Mom' came up on his screen, he was immediately worried. Maybe she had had an accident?

'Something wrong, Mom?' he asked.

'No, not to worry, my boy,' she replied; she had referred to him as 'my boy' ever since his toddler days. 'Just an old friend from your army days. Called on the home phone. Said he'd found it in the directory and needed to speak to you urgently. Wouldn't say what about. Here's his name and number.'

She read out the details slowly as he grabbed a pen.

'Thanks, Mom. I'll give him a ring. See what he wants.'

She suddenly sounded concerned. 'Now don't let him get you into trouble, my boy. I never liked it when you were in the army. I used to worry all the time you were away, and about that gun stuff.'

'Mom! I'm not a kid any more!' he chided. But he knew only too well that, while she may have been a serial texter, she was also a serial worrier, the more so since she had been alone after his dad had died suddenly from a heart attack.

He pondered the message. What could it mean? Although he remembered the name of the fellow young army conscript, they'd not been in touch since their late teens in military service. Slowly he dialled the number.

His call was picked up immediately with a gruff, 'Yah?'

'I'm returning your call to my mom.'

'Aah, thanks man. Very good of you to call back. I'm really grateful,' the Owner responded enthusiastically. 'It's been a long time. How are you doing?'

'I'm good,' the Sniper replied cautiously.

'What are you up to these days?'

'I run my own IT consultancy.'

'Still got your eye in?'

'Yah, I do a bit at weekends. But I'm not as practised as I used to be in the old days, obviously.'

86

'Fancy a weekend in my game reserve in KZN? On me. I want to ask a favour,' the Owner replied.

'That's really nice of you,' the Sniper replied, 'but why me?'

'I'd prefer to talk in person, if that's okay. We'll show you around and look after you. The beers are also on me!'

The mystery deepened for the Sniper. At the same time he was intrigued and flattered to be asked and had always considered the Owner dead straight.

The Owner continued. 'Actually, I've got a spare guest place on a plane from Joburg flying into to Richards Bay this coming Friday late afternoon. Someone's dropped out late. I could book you on it if you like. We can pick you up at the airport with the other guests and get you back on the Sunday-evening flight.'

The Sniper checked his smartphone diary. 'Yah, as it happens. I'm not looking after the kids this weekend. They're with their mother. We're divorced.'

'Great. Sorry! I mean great you're free, not you're divorced,' the Owner apologised profusely.

'No problem,' the Sniper replied coolly.

'I will fix it all up,' the Owner continued, 'just give me your email and ID number, please, for check-in. Any issues, just call me.'

They exchanged a few pleasantries and then the Owner added: 'By the way, please don't mention anything at all – anything at all – about this to anybody else. Friends, relatives or my staff or fellow guests. As far as they're concerned you are just taking a safari. Actually, better still, you are looking to advise me on IT stuff. I will explain all when you get here.'

'Okay,' the Sniper replied hesitantly.

'One other thing. Do you have a permit to fly with your equipment?'

'Yah,' said the Sniper, wondering where the hell all this was leading.

When Thandi had been briefed by the Veteran, one of the things he had instructed her on was counter-surveillance, as he had done with his London Recruits decades before. She found that part particularly exciting. Always check your car or taxi mirror. But if on foot, never turn around to scout for a possible follower: that would be too obvious. Instead find a way of stopping, querying directions with a stranger in a manner where you could easily look around; pretend to take a phone call or sit on a bench and idly scan the scene. Be careful of people fiddling with their car or motorcycle engines, people window shopping, people loitering with intent or people refusing to make eye contact.

'Look, you can't expect to be a professional,' the Veteran said. 'In fact, you mustn't try to, because you won't succeed and you will only reveal yourself by looking furtive. All I am advising is: take elementary precautions. If they ever send a team of professionals you won't spot them. One will drop back, a second will be on the other side of the road, maybe level with you. And they will probably change for another couple, then change back again. I am not talking about that sort of large professional resource. Just basic counter-surveillance. For instance, if you are carrying out a task for me, don't ever go directly to your destination, find as circuitous a route as possible, enabling you to check if you're being followed.'

She was on a task for him now, after following a convoluted route that included popping in one entrance of a department store and leaving by another. She walked along Church Street heading for Church Square. There she was to perch at the foot of the bronze statue of Paul Kruger, the old Boer leader. She would have a plastic bag from a supermarket chain containing a small package. An older white woman wearing sunglasses and carrying a similar Pick n Pay bag would stop, ask her the time, and they would switch bags.

Or at least that was the plan. But at the allotted time for the rendezvous nothing happened. Thandi started to get nervous. A couple of young African men in reflective shades sauntered along, eyeing her up.

That's all she needed, Thandi thought. Morons.

'Hi chick,' one said.

'Hi,' she smiled synthetically. 'Now piss off and leave me alone.'

They looked first startled, then angry, their pride injured. 'Okay, you dyke,' they sneered.

On a normal day Thandi's temper would have flared and the young chancers would have had the full treatment from her. But this time she checked herself.

Almost at that moment, a Pick n Pay woman walked up as if out of nowhere. 'I'm looking for the main court,' she said. 'Can you please direct me?'

Thandi stood up and gave directions, feeling her bag being effortlessly switched as she pointed the way, the woman looking around, the bored youths sauntering off.

Just as suddenly she was gone, walking across and away as directed.

Thandi's heart was pounding. 'Don't be so ridiculous,' she scolded herself, it was only something simple. She took out her phone and pretended to be calling someone, swinging idly around as she did so. The Square was bustling busily. Nobody appeared to be the slightest bit interested in her. She loped off, sticking her phone in her pocket.

But a minute later it rang. Christ! A problem? Nervously she peered at the screen before answering. To her utter relief 'Isaac' came up. He was free to fly up in a week and see her in Pretoria. This time she sounded enthusiastic, especially when he told her they had lots to catch up on, intuitively implying news that would interest her. She also sounded unusually flustered, he thought. Odd.

He was desperate to see her again. No longer were his roster breaks a bit of a pain.

As for Thandi, contemplating his call as she continued walking, she didn't mind seeing him again in the slightest.

When the Sniper arrived at Zama Zama, after an hour's drive from the airport with the other weekend guests, it was pitch dark already.

The air was cool, deep elephant rumbles, throaty, hoarse lion calls and hyena laughs all around him.

He checked his luggage and a long outsize bag into his spacious tent, normally meant for two, without any real sense of what was around him. He used the toilet and washed his face before readying for the bar and the *braai* that awaited.

There was a clearing of the throat outside. 'Excuse me, sir,' a slim young woman called. 'Please can you come now, sir?'

He followed her as her torch picked out a small path and he caught a glimpse of her swaying hips. Escorted to a waiting Land Cruiser, its engine running, he was introduced to the driver, ranger Isaac Mkhize.

'Aren't I heading for the bar?' he asked.

'Don't worry,' Mkhize smiled, 'there will be a beer or more awaiting you at the Owner's house.'

It was a ten-minute drive through the dark, the vehicle bouncing on the rutted road, its headlights periodically reflecting off the watching eyes of animals in the bush. As he drove with one hand, the ranger shone a bright searchlight around, slowing to pick out a buffalo or a group of springbok. The Sniper breathed in the air – so clean, so refreshing – a contrast to Johannesburg, like all African cities these days dank with vehicle emissions.

Mkhize chatted amiably about the terrain and the wildlife, not revealing he knew exactly the purpose of the Sniper's invitation until they were waved through the gate of a large house, its outline barely visible against the ink-black moonless sky.

The Owner was on his verandah, a big barrel-chested man with wide muscled shoulders, as the Sniper had remembered him, but now with an untidy beard and a rather large paunch, which protruded well down over his shorts.

'Hey, man! Good to see you, man! Such a long time. I'm so glad and so very grateful you could come. Really good of you to do so.'

'No problem – thanks for the invite. Quite a place you have here,' the Sniper replied, a little subdued. He had never been one for hale and hearty chatter and remained cautious about the purpose.

The Owner eyed him up, noting the same tall, slim frame he remembered, the same muscles, though the face and frame had filled out a bit. 'You have hardly put on any weight, man,' he patted his paunch. 'Not like me, hey! How about a beer for you? Or will you first join me in my bush evening favourite, a single malt?' There was a glass in his hand, the Sniper noticed, with a golden brown two fingers poured in it.

'Thanks, a beer's good for me,' the Sniper replied.

The Owner returned with a cold can, clicked open the tag and handed it over. 'Isaac here is joining us – he's a beer man too. But far more abstemious than me! Someone has to keep order around here.'

Chortling, they all sat down in the large living room festooned with paintings of animals and photographs of the Owner alongside wildlife.

The Sniper sipped from his can, coming straight to the point. 'So what's this all about?'

The Owner filled in the background, explaining the reason for the invitation.

'The time has come to hit back against the rhino barbarity. These people have to understand that if they come for Zama Zama, there's no messing. They're dead. I've got good men, like ranger Isaac here, the best. Brave guards too, though one of them's gone rogue. They can all shoot, of course. But they are not professional shooters like you. I need someone who can kill from a distance, unknown, out of sight.'

'Kill?' The Sniper was shocked. 'I'm not an assassin, man! And I don't want to end up in prison, thanks very much.'

'Don't worry, I am not going to ask you to do anything illegal. But we're fighting a war. A just war against ruthless killers who will stop at nothing, spare no human – not my rangers, not my guards – to get the horn,' the Owner replied. 'It's self-defence, protection of our people and our rhinos.'

The Sniper nodded, understanding, finding himself agreeing – even warming to the idea of testing his old skills again. He knew he was still sharp, but how would he actually feel come the moment? Shooting a man, not a guinea fowl?

Sensing the Sniper's mood, the Owner said: 'Let me describe what it's all about. Rhino poaching is horrifying beyond belief. If the rhino is shot and wounded but alive, they hack its spine or Achilles tendons so it can't move – and only then hack off the horns. They sometimes poison the rhino's carcass so the vultures are killed and don't attract rangers by circling overhead.'

'The disgusting stench of decomposing flesh pollutes your lungs. Within twenty-four hours, the carcases are crawling with flies and maggots, wonderful two-ton animals turned into hideous remnants, their hacked-out horns becoming phoney cures for hangovers and cancer, or proffered as cocaine substitutes at parties for the decadent.'

The Sniper said nothing, numb, just nodding.

During the rest of the evening the three discussed logistics while they enjoyed a steak with veg and sweet potato washed down with a couple of bottles of lusciously smooth, deep-red Fairview Mourvèdre. The Sniper raised an eyebrow that Mkhize confined himself to just a single glass. 'We rangers are never off duty when in the reserve,' came the rueful explanation.

A plan was agreed. The Sniper couldn't be permanently based in Zama Zama. Both his own work demands and the costs to the Owner negated that. But he voluntarily cut his costs to a modest daily stipend to cover expenses, paid in cash. He would try to come as and when he could without any fixed pattern so as not to create suspicion. His spare rifle would remain locked up in the Owner's house so that he could arrive and leave without anybody noticing the strange case. It was pure chance whether he happened to be in the reserve when the next attack occurred – when, not if, the Owner predicted full of foreboding. It was only a matter of time, he was certain. Once successful, the syndicates came back for more.

When the Sniper was in the reserve he would tend to sleep and relax by day and be taken at night to where any rhinos were located. The guards would never know when he was joining them until Mkhize or Brown turned up with the Sniper. And they would never be told about his exact role or his skill. That he was armed would not be a surprise: nobody went on walkies in the bush at night without a gun.

The Sniper worked out his own modus operandi. He would communicate only as needed with the guards once he was dropped off with them. Then he would disappear, always ensuring the animals were in direct sight.

It would be exhilarating, out alone in the dark, with his night-vision glasses, rifle scope and binoculars. There was nothing like getting so close to nature.

Mkhize briefed the Sniper on nightlife in the reserve.

'Remember, there's a whole new world when the sun disappears – the nocturnal world. Some Africa lovers insist our bush really comes to life at night. Be especially careful of our hippos as they lumber up out of their pools to graze. Watch out for the big cats shrugging off daytime laziness as they ready themselves for hunting. Listen for the haunting hoots of owls, the singing of jackals, and the loud guffawing of francolin.'

Mkhize grinned. 'Don't worry, you are more likely to be troubled by annoying biting insects than these nocturnal animals, but you need to watch out for them.'

Then he cheekily added: 'By the way, never forget crocodiles are mainly nocturnal. You certainly don't want to bump into one of them.'

The first couple of times Mkhize came with the Sniper, giving him refresher exercises in bushcraft once almost instinctive to him, but which had grown rusty over the years. Mkhize had warned him to be especially careful with elephants. They had almost telepathic intuition, the largest brains of any animal and an uncanny ability to hear and sense sounds from many kilometres away through ground vibrations picked up through their feet, their long trunks deployed as sensory organs.

'If you respect elephants, they will give you space. But if you mess with them, invade their territory, or get near their babies, watch out!' Mkhize explained. 'Rhinos are not nearly as intelligent and their eyesight

92

is also poor. They won't bother you if you don't bother them and they are much more solitary. You see them more in pairs rather than in herds like elephants.'

The Sniper made several visits without incident. But each time he had an uncomfortable feeling that the calm could not last.

When Mkhize's rostered break came and he prepared to travel up to Pretoria, he asked Steve Brown to take the Sniper to the rhinos and pick him up just before dawn. Brown wasn't fully briefed, but was instructed by his close friend not to disclose the Sniper's whereabouts, activities or even existence in the reserve to anybody.

Once in Pretoria, Mkhize quickly checked into his usual B&B and sought out Thandi. They spent hours ardently updating each other. But before that Mkhize was thrilled, yet even somewhat flustered, to be given an enthusiastic embrace and a warm kiss, carefully reciprocating and pleasantly finding he wasn't rebuffed.

The next day however, their so-far deepening relationship came near to breaking point over sex. Or, rather, cultural attitudes to it. And, as usual, it was Thandi's impulsive feistiness that provoked the clash.

It all arose over his home area of KwaZulu-Natal, where Zama Zama was located. Mkhize had no idea it had become the HIV-AIDS capital of the world, with one in three people HIV infected, and Thandi was incredulous.

'It is horrendous,' she insisted. 'In KZN, nearly two-thirds of women aged under thirty are HIV-positive and in many areas, a fifteen-year-old girl today has an eighty per cent chance of being infected in her lifetime. Half of pregnant women are HIV-positive.'

She jabbed her finger at him. 'And it's you men who are the guilty ones. The so-called "sugar daddies" or "blessers" – the older men in jobs, the ones who give smartphones, gifts and money to poor young girls for sex.'

'But I've *never* done that!' Mkhize protested. 'I am not responsible for all men! Why are you attacking *me*?'

He felt personally insulted, his reputation trashed by the very woman he felt desperately, deeply drawn to and in wonder of. He didn't comprehend why she had gone for him like this. He was angry and deeply wounded.

He glared at her, then got up. 'I'm going for a walk. You suit yourself.'

Thandi was both furious and shocked. Furious because he seemed so ignorant about something as basic as the AIDs epidemic in his back yard and the responsibility of men for it. Shocked, because, over the preceding months she had gradually come closer to him than any other man since her dad had cared for her as a child. She felt betrayed, tears welling in her eyes, making her even angrier with herself, as if she was being weak.

She sat on his bed moping.

He wandered around outside on the pavement, mind in a whirl, then squatted down morosely on the kerb.

A stand-off.

Thandi thought about what she knew and what she had read. Of the strong possibility AIDs would re-emerge as the mass killer it was at the turn of the century, when Nelson Mandela and activists in the Treatment Action Campaign bravely stood up against President Mbeki's denial over AIDS. Of the progress made since then by forcing down the cost of anti-retroviral drugs to just a fraction of their former level.

But also how treatment programmes were now being thwarted by fast-accelerating infection levels and burgeoning drug resistance. Of how men in rural KZN almost never attended clinics to receive treatment, seeing it as stigmatising to do so. And of how male behaviour obdurately refused to alter. Of how sex was about power. Of how she had witnessed her school friends being infected by men much older than themselves. Of the sulphurous cocktail of poverty and machismo.

Outside the B&B, Mkhize thought about what she had said. It was indeed appalling. He knew, of course, about the dangers of AIDs, and had always taken precautions, used condoms and so on.

The infection level in girls was unbelievably horrific. What Thandi had said also made him think as he had never done before about the culture of his upbringing. She was right, he had to admit: it was male-dominated. Women were apparently cherished but simultaneously abused and treated as chattels – he had to admit that too. Maybe she was correct: it was his fault, like all other men from KZN, even if he hadn't appreciated that before.

Thandi, too, began to reconsider. Maybe she had got carried away. She knew she had a tendency to get on her soapbox in a way that could give offence. She couldn't help herself – she cared so much. But she had never seen him so emotionally hurt, as if she had hit him. And – rather more than she had so far admitted to herself – she cared for him. Two people so close yet so far apart. Two people both stubborn and proud.

Two people with important missions in their lives. Two people recruited by the Veteran on a task to help save their rainbow nation, but now at loggerheads.

The Veteran suspected something like this would probably happen. But when it did it was still a complete shock.

The morning was fresh, the birds in song, the stroll his routine one to get a paper along the tree-lined pavement and down the hill to the Kalk Bay shopfront. There was nobody about near his home.

Or so he thought – until there was a blow to his kidneys from behind, as sudden as it was excruciating.

'As jy nie ophou met jou bladdy ondermyning nie sal dit volgende keer baie erger wees,' someone sneered in Afrikaans – 'If you don't stop your subversion, next time will be much worse.'

He fell to the pavement, doubling up with pain, grazing his knees, which these days were giving him a bit of arthritic aggravation anyway. His head spun as he wrapped his hands around his midriff and lay on the pavement writhing in agony, feeling at once foolish and helpless.

Time seemed to freeze.

There was a sound of running footsteps.

Someone was helping him up as he wheezed and groaned. A young black man, smiling and concerned, peered through his blurred, confused vision. 'Are you okay?' he asked.

'Not sure,' the Veteran panted, trying to get his balance, feeling thoroughly embarrassed and still wracked with a throbbing, shooting pain.

'What on earth happened?' the young man asked, 'I walked around the corner and there you were, crumpled on the pavement.'

'Don't really know,' the Veteran muttered, 'got hit. Did you see anyone?'

The stranger shook his head, asked if he could help any more, was told no thanks very much, and bid farewell. Unless there'd been a witness – which there wasn't – nobody, least of all the Veteran, would have had the slightest inkling it was the very same young man who'd crept up and thumped him.

When the number came up on Thandi's phone, her mind was in a whirl from the stand-off with Mkhize.

But, recognising the Veteran's unlisted phone, she answered

95

immediately. The Veteran hadn't yet been able to give them their own anonymous pay-as-you-go phones as he had planned.

Again, no pleasantries, no names used. But there was something wrong with his voice, she could tell. 'A problem. I was attacked this morning and warned off.'

'Bloody hell!' she exclaimed. 'Are you all right?'

'Badly bruised. Blow to the kidneys from behind. Never saw or heard the attacker. The local doc tells me I'm okay. I told him I'd been mugged.'

He paused, then continued. 'Is Isaac with you, by any chance? I need to speak to him too. You've both got to be extra careful now.'

'Err, sort of . . . I will get him for you.' She opened the door and spotted him sitting at the kerb looking thoroughly miserable, head in his hands, making her feel guilty.

'Isaac, come quickly, phone call for you,' she motioned him forward.

He looked at her blankly, then took the phone as she gave him an affectionate squeeze.

Again, standard procedure: no named greetings, no pleasantries. The Veteran repeated his conversation with Thandi.

'You must both assume you will be identified at some point.' He paused. 'And we both know she can be a little impetuous.'

Mkhize felt himself bristle, instinctively protective of Thandi.

The Veteran pretended not to notice, but he had. 'Please ensure she understands. I won't be deflected, but I have to be one step ahead the whole time. Any mistake by either of you could endanger us all.'

'Yah, sir,' Mkhize muttered.

'Never mind the bloody "sir"! Now, any news from your end?'

Mkhize brought him up to date on the Sniper. 'Joburg-based. Apparently he was on protection duty for Mandela on the day of his prison release. Seems a nice guy. Clearly knows his trade, though professes to be a bit rusty.'

'Mandela? Really?' The Veteran pondered this titbit, which was news to him. 'Interesting. I'd better try to meet him. Please text me his details. We may need him ourselves.'

After he had ended the call, the Veteran poured himself a cold beer and sat on his verandah. The pain was still killing him – it would do so for quite a while – and the doctor had prescribed painkillers at night to help him sleep.

Engaging the Sniper was a quantum shift. But the stakes were being raised, and he hadn't expected retaliation so relatively soon after his out-spoken and candid speech.

It was ironic. The guttural warning in Afrikaans was exactly like the old apartheid days. What came around . . .

Diffidently, Mkhize handed the phone back to Thandi.

They stood there looking at each other, wondering what to say.

Thandi made the first move. Although she didn't feel like hugging him – their earlier mutual affection having dissipated during the raw emotion of the argument – she squeezed his arm and smiled weakly.

'Come, let's have a walk,' she said. 'We can return to our disagreement later. But we need to talk about his phone call.'

Mkhize sullenly locked up his room and they walked over to a nearby park, which badly showed signs of neglect, the brown grass unkempt with sandy patches, and the flower beds untidy with far too many weeds. Litter was strewn around. Typical of public parks all over the city. Such a contrast to the finely kept hotel grounds and gated residential areas with their kaleidoscope of flowers, luscious bushes and mown, watered lawns.

'Look at this park, what a mess!' Thandi exclaimed, '"Private opulence and public squalor" – the description given by J. K. Galbraith to societies like ours where public spaces and services suffer and the rich prosper in their fenced-off spaces, while the politicians at the top loot.'

She never lets go, Mkhize thought glumly to himself. *Everything is political for her. Everything.*

Animatedly the two considered the implications of the attack, and resolved what extra precautions they had to take, like only phoning each other on new, anonymous phones. Their conversation was businesslike; they agreed to meet up next morning after breakfast and that was how their encounter that afternoon ended.

She went home, he to grab some fast food on his way to his lodgings, both purposeful but each miserable too.

Thandi's diatribe had so stunned Mkhize that when he returned to his B&B he immediately went online, and the more he read late into the night, the more horrified he became. He learned about the epidemic of tuberculosis and how, especially when the immune system was damaged by HIV-AIDS infection, it became almost became impossible to treat. Medication could last several years and wasn't always successful. Patients died because they missed the required daily dose of pills, or because their immune system was simply too shattered to recover. They easily infected close relatives with TB by coughing or sneezing. Mkhize was shocked to read that South Africans were contracting TB at a higher rate than any other country in the world, with around 400,000 people infected. Congested living conditions in squatter camps, a lack of cleanliness and shared toilets made TB rampant. Co-infection of TB with HIV became particularly common in young girls fond of drinking or frequenting nightclubs, when alcohol raised the risk of unsafe sexual choices.

'Unsafe sexual choices', as if the girls were alone culpable, he pondered. He knew what Thandi would say: what about the boys? And he knew she would be right.

When they met up next morning on the pavement outside their usual café, where Mkhize had arrived early, as he always did for her, he was awkwardly diffident, she subdued; neither had slept much.

Mkhize had thought long and hard. Usually Thandi took the initiative, but now it was up to him. If he wanted her – and he most definitely still did – he would have to make the first move, he had decided.

'I'm sorry if I sounded petulant yesterday,' he began. Then, not waiting for a response, he ploughed on quickly, his eyes avoiding hers.

'I was up most of the night on the internet, learning about HIV-TB co-infection. About the annihilation of people. The twisting of young girls' lives. It appalled me. I knew, of course, there was a problem and I'd always used condoms myself for that very reason. But I had no idea about the way it was just devouring our people and especially our women. Suppose I was too buried in my work. I was just appalled – and deeply ashamed to be a man.'

He stopped and looked up at her. There were tears dribbling down from her eyes. But, he noticed, confused, that she looked happy, not despondent. He didn't know what to do.

Thandi leaned forward and kissed him. Not pecking affectionately as before. But kissing him passionately, hugging him almost desperately.

For a moment his arms hung limply in sheer astonishment. Then, exhilarated, he gingerly reached out, holding her tight, feeling her tongue exploring his, her taut breasts against his powerfully muscled chest. He had dreamed this might happen, but wondered if it ever would. She seemed so strong, so alive, so tender – all at once. She was even lovelier than he had imagined.

Then Thandi wriggled herself free. 'That wasn't too bad!' she smiled playfully.

She stood in front of him, reaching for both his hands. 'Thank you so much, so very, very much for what you've just said. It means such a lot to me – you have no idea. I felt so conflicted last night after we parted. Still angry with you, yes, but also angry with myself for getting so angry with you. I just felt so empty and so frustrated. If I hadn't cared for you I wouldn't have minded. But it was the fact that I did care that made it worse. I am sorry that I hurt you, of all people.'

Now it was Mkhize's turn to reach for her and hold her tight. 'Let's go and get ourselves a coffee,' he said, holding her hand as he led her into the café.

'Only a coffee? Is that all I am getting?' She grinned impishly.

The Veteran winced in pain, cogitating on the bruising yet clinical assault.

He had not been robbed. The purpose was clear in the threat: it was a security services job, which precise part he couldn't be certain. They had been accountable under Mandela, when the Veteran was a minister. Now they were this president's personal political instrument – as indeed they had been for apartheid presidents.

The whole intelligence services set-up was now polluted by politicisation, presidential manipulation and factionalism. The rot had set in earlier: President Mbeki had often complained about substandard intelligence reports sent to him. Some of the factionalism dated from the ANC's intelligence network at the time of the liberation struggle and the President exploited this to serve his nefarious ends.

Even by 2008, the Matthews Commission found that the intelligence agencies were not respecting either the rule of law or the rights of opposition parties and critics. They had been politicised, undermining rights entrenched in the Constitution, and were not anything like accountable enough. But that was manna from heaven for this president who, on taking office, set about shaping the police force and the security services to serve him and him alone.

First to fall was the Directorate for Special Operations – popularly known as the Scorpions – the country's own FBI, formed to fight organised crime and advised by partner countries like Britain. Admired abroad as a model of its kind, and at home feared by criminals, it was disbanded and replaced by a unit known as the Hawks, easily manipulated by the President and his crony ministers.

The Police Crime Litigation Unit, instead of pursuing major criminals, was twisted from its original mission and used to plot against the President's opponents, including his own internationally respected finance minister.

Crime Intelligence (CI) – its mission to protect citizens from serious threats – became a shadow of its former self. Instead of delivering on its mission, it became an accomplice to serious crime, a virtual private criminal syndicate. Hundreds of millions were looted from a secret police slush fund as CI acted as a protective fiefdom for the President and his corrupt cronies.

Perhaps the most notorious instance was one CI officer arrested for masterminding a R50-million slush fund of cash dished out at the ANC's elective conference to buy the votes of delegates to back the President. He was exposed as a convicted armed robber who had escaped from prison and had begun working for the CI without being vetted.

Meanwhile the police service – transformed under Mandela from apartheid shock troops into human rights protectors – morphed quickly into an incompetent and corrupt organisation with a reputation for repressive brutality.

The ANC had allowed the police service to slip back towards apartheid days, when it had been a political arm of the white ruling elite, targeting political opponents rather than criminals and, indeed, with a record of complicity with criminal thugs, racketeers and murderers. The colour of the government had changed, apartheid had gone, but a corrupt police service had been reincarnated.

It was both a relief and a credit to its independence and integrity, the Veteran believed, that the judiciary stood up admirably against unrelenting attacks, the ANC-blessed Constitution standing firm against the forces of darkness, buttressed by vocal civil society groups, fearless investigative journalists and the odd incorruptible politician.

Now he was one of them. A rebel again.

CHAPTER 9

Just under eighty kilometres north of Durban, off the N3 motorway to Pretoria, lies the small city of Pietermaritzburg, founded by the Voortrekkers after the defeat of king of the Zulu Kingdom, Dingane, at the Battle of Blood River in 1838. It was the capital of the short-lived Boer republic, known as Natalia. When the British seized control of Pietermaritzburg from the Afrikaners in 1843, they established it as the administrative capital of their new Colony of Natal. And the city still retained its English feel and colonial origins.

It was also noteworthy for an incident early in the life of the Indian independence leader Mahatma Gandhi, who had lived in Natal as a young man. In 1893, while Gandhi was travelling in a train to Pretoria, a white man objected to his presence in a first-class carriage. He was ordered to move to the luggage section at the end of the train. Gandhi, who had paid for a first-class ticket, refused, and was thrown off the train at Pietermaritzburg.

Shivering through the winter night in the waiting room of the station, Gandhi made the momentous decision to stay on in South Africa and fight racial discrimination against Indians there. During that struggle he developed his own vision of non-violent direct action, known as Satyagraha, which he was later to apply in his homeland in the campaign to end British colonial rule.

In Church Street in the city's centre, a bronze statue of Gandhi has one hand raised strikingly in peace, the other holding a staff and wearing his traditional *dhoti*. That statue had become a personal shrine for a similarly diminutive figure, a man in his mid-seventies. Nearby, but off the main road, in his modest but spotless workshop, which doubled as a customer showroom, Solly Naidoo worked most days of the year in a labour of love, his wife hovering over the reception desk and answering the phone, which also rang in their house behind and above the workshop.

Solly Naidoo, whose grandfather, like many of his compatriots, emigrated in the late nineteenth century from India to work in the Natal sugar plantations, had come to regard himself as an inventive artist more than an artisan. He could make almost anything – carve and shape ornaments and home adornments, take worn family heirlooms and turn them into shiny smart originals, touch up or remove stains from paintings, turn battered old furniture into gleaming antiques. His skill was self-taught from a boyhood fascination with making and fixing things.

Much in demand, he didn't need to market or advertise – all his work came through word of mouth. If anything unusual needed creating or fixing, Solly Naidoo was the go-to man. Neither cheap nor expensive, he made a comfortable living for his family, enough to see his children proudly into professional adulthoods and to acquire his property from the previous owners, a white family business in what used to be a white part of town.

If Solly Naidoo was known for anything else, it was his passion for cricket. In his youth he had played to a good standard, might even have made the Natal provincial team – possibly the national side too – had it not been for whites-only sports policy under apartheid. He was a leg spinner, showing a mastery of probably the most difficult bowling art of all: turning the ball out of the back of his hand, sometimes so concealing his action that it would emerge as a 'googly' and spin the other way, completely flummoxing batsmen.

But his specialist skills had also been used by the Veteran in the liberation struggle: to forge passports, create hidden compartments in suitcases or secret linings in briefcases. Solly was the Veteran's man; almost nobody else in the underground struggle knew of his invaluable contribution. If they had heard his name at all, it would only have been for his reputation in Pietermaritzburg as an artisan par excellence.

After the transformation he still hadn't wanted recognition. An unassuming and shy person, he was happy to let his artistry speak for itself, and for him. He got on with his work seven days a week, when he wasn't nurturing his family as the Naidoo patriarch. Which is why the Veteran felt completely certain about contacting his old comrade now: Solly was another 'clean skin', like Thandi.

When his wife handed Naidoo the portable office phone, she was puzzled. Usually she sifted the calls so as not to disturb his concentration. But this time the caller had insisted there was no introduction – merely to speak to 'an old friend'.

There was indeed no need for an introduction. The voice and a phrase he had not heard for several decades got Naidoo's immediate and undivided attention. 'A mutual friend will call by for a small job; I trust you can help him out as usual,' was all the Veteran needed to say. There was only the briefest small talk about family and health.

No sooner, it seemed to her, had he taken the call than Naidoo handed the phone back inscrutably to his wife. She shrugged her shoulders. Theirs was a traditional marital relationship and she had long learned to bury her frustration when he became uncommunicative – because it never lasted long, and she trusted him totally.

Next, and again on his pay-as-you-go phone, the Veteran called Mkhize, also on his new, anonymous phone.

'Isaac, you know those horns we discussed, the ones you mentioned the Owner keeps from rhinos that have long died of old age? I want you to take one to a friend of mine. All you need to say is "a mutual friend asked for a small job". He will be expecting you.'

The Veteran explained the purpose to an attentive Mkhize. 'We need a small cavity to be created in the horn, capable of containing a micro-transmitter, so that the horn's movements can be tracked remotely.'

'But what am I going to say to the Owner?' Isaac asked. 'I know him well. He won't accept a lie or an excuse, and I wouldn't try to mislead him: that would completely destroy our trust. Nor can I just take one: they are kept securely; they are too prized.'

The Veteran paused. Always complications, always obstacles in any plan. The trick was to overcome them without compromising the mission. And he had learned from bitter experience how valid the saying of the ANC underground chief, Joe Slovo was: 'Never tell anyone anything'. One extra person to share a secret meant one extra chink in security – and maybe a fatal one.

'How much do you trust the Owner?' he asked the ranger.

'With my life.'

'Are you absolutely certain?'

'Of course – I wouldn't have said so otherwise!' Mkhize replied, indignant.

'How many others do you "trust with your life", then?'

Mkhize thought quickly. 'Not many. Him. Steve, my ranger partner. Thandi. You – probably.'

The Veteran chuckled, liking Mkhize's bristling parting shot. It encouraged him. The man was straight as a die – also increasingly impressive the more deeply involved he become.

'Okay. This is on your head. If anything leaks that's us blown – our total operation finished. Tell the Owner about me and our mission. But no more, only the barest detail and why we need just one tusk. If he presses you, tell him this from me: "What you don't know, you can't tell."'

He dictated Naidoo's name and address, leaving no text to store and be traced on a server in the Cloud somewhere, then rang off.

Mkhize listened to the familiar sounds of Zama Zama: cicadas' constant buzzing, champagne frogs popping amidst bird squawks, antelope shuffles and buffalo snorts.

Suddenly, he felt a burden of responsibility, the Veteran's ominous words running round and round in his mind.

The Sniper cradled his Precision Sniper Rifle (PSR), which had been launched in 2009 as part of a US programme to support army, navy, air and marine Special Operations Forces.

It was a Remington PSR 86642 and he had bought it from a Johannesburg gun shop, the man behind the counter a fount of knowledge. It came with a kit in a hard case, and he treated it like a baby. In special slots in the hard case were three cartridges: a .338 Lapua Magnum, a .300 Win Mag, and a 7.62 NATO. It also came with a variety of different but essential gadgets, including precision wrenches and drives, a bipod assembly, twenty magazines, a recoil pad with two spacers, and, most importantly, a cleaning kit.

He had two of them and they were both kept lovingly oiled and cleaned before and after use: his lethal pride and joy.

When a senior army officer had spotted that he had the skills to be a sniper, he had taken a lot of persuading. The snipers he'd bumped into seemed a special breed, mostly loners, often brooders. He was one of the boys – or thought of himself that way. And, actually, he remained one after the senior officer finally twisted his arm.

But over the years, especially after seeing action, and even more especially after his first kill – an unsuspecting ANC guerrilla in the Angolan bush – he was a changed man. He knew he was. Not obviously on the outside, where he seemed the considerate, affable, phlegmatic person he had always been. But inside – he wasn't sure exactly who he was any more. And that's really when things began going wrong with his relationships. Always short term. It must be the wrong girls, he convinced himself. So when he got involved with his wife-to-be, he was intensely relieved. And for a number of years they were happy together, their two kids slipping joyously into their lives.

He had been proud to be a dad – until gradually, and before he really understood what was happening, a gap opened up with his wife. There was nobody else in their lives. But she kept complaining he had 'disappeared into his cave' and she couldn't reach him any more.

For a while the all-consuming nature of responsible parenthood kept them in reasonable harmony. Until the arguments became more frequent and the irritations grew. There was no animosity, certainly no hate, just a sad but inevitable drifting apart. Suddenly one evening he arrived back home lateish, the kids already in bed. But instead of the usual welcome peck, she was standing in the kitchen, tense, arms folded.

'I cannot continue like this,' she said, eyes moistening. 'I still care lots for you. The kids are happy. You're a great dad. That side of our family life is okay. But you've drifted apart from me somehow and I don't know why. All I do know is this cannot continue or it will end up in hostility between us. And I would never want that. For either the kids or for us.'

Her head dipped. She seemed to grip herself even more tightly, then looked up at him and blurted out: 'So I want you to move out, please.'

That's exactly how it had happened. He'd been numb. Not just with shock but with emptiness. Which clung clammily to the Sniper as he moved out from their warm family home in Johannesburg's Mondeor suburb, across the city and into a flat in Rosebank, taking his clothes and two gun-kit cases and not much else of the happy life they'd been building together.

Maybe, he asked himself, he'd become more of a sniper than husband, father or friend? He didn't know any more. So he increasingly threw himself into building his business.

But now he had a new mission. It was his fifth visit to Zama Zama, and so far nothing, not a sniff of a rhino poacher.

Frustrating, but the Sniper had found solace in his growing enjoyment of the reserve. He hadn't had much of a social life since his divorce two years earlier, buried in work and looking after his teenage son and daughter on alternate weekends. But increasingly they seemed to want to be more with their friends than their dad.

Weekend guinea-fowl-shooting trips had also fallen away as his friends found him less available and less sociable when he was able to join them. Ironic, really – he should have had more time for that sort of thing as a single man. Instead he had drifted into an introverted life.

But Zama Zama was becoming a fixation. Although he slept up during the day as best he could, he would also cadge a lift with the rangers taking out a party when there was a spare seat going on a game drive, and found himself increasingly charmed by the experiences, learning all the time.

Mkhize had pointed out a bird the Sniper had never heard of – a fork-tailed drongo, a feisty little creature, which he witnessed astonishingly chase away from its territory a martial eagle ten or more times larger, by pecking at its head.

On the same afternoon drive he also saw two male giraffes fighting over a female. Bulls, Mkhize explained, tend to wander between groups. They have a loose social structure and no real leadership. Males will spar during mating season, characteristically swinging their necks, using their heads and horns as clubs – known as 'necking'.

That evening the Sniper resumed his now familiar routine of being dropped off by Mkhize to rendezvous with the rhino security guards near a pair of the animals who both snorted and stamped as they sensed his presence a hundred metres away, then resumed their munching mission, scouring the grass.

He had long been trained in waiting up, in hiding silently and observing, 'keeping his head-an'-eyes-a-moving' as his army trainer had described it. It wasn't as easy as it once had been over twenty years ago when he was a lot fresher. The Sniper had to work at his concentration where once it had come naturally, automatically. He pinched his eyes and focused hard, trying to ignore the grunts, the snorts, the shuffles of the wildlife around him. There was no wind, the moon high, translucent light offering a faint reprieve as he looked and listened.

Time dragged interminably. He felt himself tiring, a devilishly nagging pull on his mind to think about anything but the task in hand, his eyes drooping. Just in time he managed to wrench himself back. Focus, focus, focus, he cursed himself.

His task wasn't made easier by the behaviour of rhinos at night, when they tended to move around because it was cooler and therefore more tolerable. Which meant he had to follow them and find new vantage points, each time trusting he had avoided detection from prying poacher eyes.

When the sun came up the rhinos tried to rest in the shade or find mud in which to wallow and cool, and also protect their skin against parasites and the sun. The Sniper wished it were the other way around, but poachers rarely attacked reserves like Zama Zama during the daytime, when the rhinos would sleep either standing up or lying down, sometimes for eight hours daily in bursts punctuated by periods awake. Mkhize had explained how they might doze under a tree to avoid the heat, but if they fell into a deep sleep, they could be observed lying down, feet curled up and leaning over a little. So deeply could they sleep, they could even be safely approached.

By now the Sniper was more familiar with certain night sounds; all the time he listened and waited for his human prey.

That night, just as he was jerking himself into full concentration there was an alien rustle. He squinted around. Nothing — except two rhinos mooching in the moonlight. He strained into the night, using all his senses.

Another rustle.

But no sign.

What was it?

The barest shadow flitting to his left, not even a glimpse. He trained his rifle in the general direction.

Suddenly, movement. A man crouching down, a barrel lifting. Although the reticle in his infrared scope was ideal for the low light, he knew very well he would have only one shot. Just the vaguest outline of the poacher was in his sights. He aimed for the chest and squeezed the trigger. Aiming for the head was too tricky in the poor light.

There was a volcanic whoosh of his silencer as he used all his power to hold the gun steady.

The poacher keeled sideways, a suppressed scream of shock turning almost into a whimper. Then he lurched slowly up and off into the dark, a shout from the security guards hounding him.

Instead of following, the Sniper remained absolutely still. Typically poachers operated in pairs. He looked for the mate, careful not to reveal his position, for now it was he who was the most vulnerable of all.

There was a rustle, and the sense of a shadow slipping away in the general direction of the stricken poacher. He tried to get a fix on it, but the shadow quickly disappeared into the bush and the Sniper could not detect anything else.

He called the Owner, waking him from a deep, snoring sleep, to report what had happened, grabbing the Owner's immediate attention.

'Great job,' the Owner replied. 'The guards will have reported in already. I will scramble some men to give chase. Meanwhile, will you please melt into the background? Call Isaac and get him to collect you as soon as possible. I don't want you around when we notify the authorities and they come investigating.'

The Sniper woke Isaac, who promised to collect him as soon as he could, arriving by vehicle thirty minutes later. They drove back to the camp in the darkness, spotting animal eyes and shapes all around them, Mkhize congratulating him and quizzing about the shooting.

'Well done,' he said, marvelling at the Sniper's expertise in the dark, then pulling his leg. 'So you haven't lost your touch after all these years, man!'

'Hopefully not,' the Sniper smiled back, 'but I don't know how badly I wounded the man. I should have killed him.'

Later that day, and after the Sniper had been awoken from a deep sleep, Mkhize reported back. 'We trailed him easily, as he was bleeding heavily all the way. A few hundred metres from the fence he finally collapsed and was dead when our guys reached him. But there was no ID on him, and his gun wasn't there either. Some footprints at the spot showed his partner was there, probably taking away anything useful to us. Still, the police and the SANParks guys will get his DNA; who knows if they turn anything up.'

Then Mkhize paused. 'Hope you don't mind the change of plan, but the Owner and I think it's best if you don't go out again tonight. Just join in the safari activity before you are scheduled to head home. The rhino guards will have reported the shooting and one of them is claiming responsibility under our instruction. They are obviously always aware when you are around, but they don't know who you are. Nor do the other rangers – just the Owner, Steve and me. Let's keep it that way for as long as we can.'

Justice Samuel Makojaene looked carefully over the court's draft judgement, for it went to a question at the very core of what an African country should be about, he felt.

108

But first he began reading up on the background. The South African government wanted to legalise the sale of legitimately sourced elephant ivory and rhino horns, and there had been a judicial challenge by wildlife groups on which the court had to adjudicate. They cited Botswana, with more elephants than any other country and around a third of Africa's, which was at odds with South Africa and its other southern African neighbours in refusing to allow sales of ivory. Botswana's president was emphatically opposed to loosening restrictions on the trade, insisting that if ivory or other material from the horns could be traded, even from stockpiles on a one-off basis, it would legitimise the trade and prompt even more poaching.

Interesting, mused Makojaene, especially since in 2008 China and Japan were allowed to pay millions of dollars for over a hundred tonnes of ivory amassed and stored from African elephants that had died naturally. Although the aim had been to flood the market, to cause prices to collapse and thereby make poaching unprofitable, researchers at the University of California, Berkeley and Princeton University had discovered quite the opposite. The sale was followed by 'an abrupt, significant, permanent, robust and geographically widespread increase' in elephant poaching, the researchers stated. Their report concluded that selling the ivory legally in this way actually reduced the associated public stigma the trade had attracted and therefore boosted demand; it also acted as a smokescreen for smuggling illegal ivory, so boosting supply. The price of ivory may have fallen after the legal sale, but there was an increase in poaching, which could be directly linked, they reported.

There had been a jump of fully seventy per cent in the seizures of illegal ivory after the 2008 sale. That conclusion was backed up by separate research at the London School of Economics and the University of Queensland in Australia.

It seemed clear to Makojaene that, on precedent, a big legal sale of ivory or rhino horn intended to cut elephant poaching could well backfire by dramatically increasing elephant and rhino deaths. The statistics were horrifying, he read. More African elephants were being poached and killed than being born. Before the 1940s, estimates put the number of African elephants at between three and five million. Now, he read, there were less than half a million, with a hundred African elephants being poached and killed each day – at a rate that would lead to extinction within twenty years.

And whereas there had been an estimated 65,000 black rhinos in Africa, by the mid-1990s the number had fallen to just 2,400. One conservationist had said in 1982 that over the previous 160 years, ninety-five per cent of the continent's entire rhino population had been lost – killed by man.

Moreover, international criminal gangs were now driving the illegal global wildlife trade, which was worth $20 billion annually – the fourth largest illegal activity after drugs, counterfeiting and human trafficking. And the victims were not only wild animals. This organised crime destabilised many African countries, infected their administration with corrupt bribes and helped block any prospect of a sustainable future for poverty-stricken rural communities surrounding Africa's vast wildlife reserves.

In Zimbabwe's Zambezi Valley in 1993, sheer carnage and ruthlessness was evident in a fierce and protracted war, which continued until there were no rhino left – about 1,000 were killed along with 170 poachers and four rangers.

The case before Makojaene had been brought after the biggest rhino breeder in the world had wanted to sell about three hundred horns, or about a tenth of his five-ton stockpile on his farm west of Johannesburg. His practice was to saw the horns from the live animals he farmed, citing in his support the fact that the horns regrew around an inch each year. His case was that the auction would help to redirect resources to the reserves and therefore reduce poaching.

Some rangers and wildlife officials argued that criminals and poachers gained a lot more by keeping the trade illegal. They suggested that trading legally with rhino-related products would channel much-needed funds down to the units on the ground, to better equip and pay them. Rural economies would be boosted, creating jobs, enabling better protection of wildlife, and ensuring that generations to come would still be able to experience these the magnificent creatures.

Many conservationists were implacably opposed, however. They insisted the sale appeased consumer demand and also made it more difficult to enforce bans on smuggled wildlife memorabilia across Africa's borders. There were just thirty thousand white rhinos left in the wild, the number shrinking annually, and the international trade was illegal.

The more he read, the more Makojaene became compelled towards one conclusion. It was part of his professional discipline that he could not become emotional. His judgements had to be legally sound and certainly not socially or politically partisan. The Constitutional Court was the highest in the land and he and his fellow justices carried a huge responsibility.

He had long deduced that no judge could be absolutely objective or impartial – after all, the law was a human instrument and therefore intrinsically affected by the prevailing cultural and political mores; he noted, for instance, the impact of political appointments by US presidents on the rulings of US Supreme Court judges. Nevertheless, his touchstone was always the integrity of the law, interpreting probably the finest constitution in the world, building upon precedent and case law, carefully constructing a judgement able to withstand the harshest scrutiny. In his heart still burned the passion that had led him as a teenager to protest against apartheid's injustice, setting him on a path that took him to that cold cell on Robben Island. But in his head there was the cool logic and the precision of the law to which he was dedicated.

Sitting back in his chambers, lined with legal books but with a sense of comfort brought by African carvings on the shelves and framed certificates and photographs charting his illustrious legal career, Makojaene looked down over the atrium in the Constitutional Court's modern building in Kotze Street in Johannesburg's Braamfontein suburb. It had been described by one of the Constitution's architects and then judge, former anti-apartheid activist Albie Sachs, as 'a place for everybody'.

On the proposed government sanction for the sale of stockpiled ivory and rhino horn, Makojaene had reached his conclusion. He would finesse the draft judgement, discuss it further with fellow justices, and deliver it the following week.

Piet van der Merwe was perturbed.

He had just received the news that they had lost a man. In itself that didn't matter, for poachers knew the life was precarious and they were disposable. No, what concerned him was the report from the surviving accomplice. That, although he couldn't be absolutely sure, the shooter wasn't one of the guards. He appeared to be someone else. And someone else very good, it seemed. Who was he? A staffer or an outsider?

Van der Merwe had sleepers inside a number of the game reserves with rhinos. Each was on a retainer, handed over irregularly, always in cash. He texted his man inside Zama Zama.

It was a while before the man who received the text was free from his

111

duties and alone to call back. Van der Merwe explained the problem and asked: 'Anybody acting extra-normally on the reserve staff? Anything unusual going on? Anything different going on?'

The Ranger was nonplussed. 'Can't think of anything for now,' he replied slowly, thinking furiously, 'but let me scout around and come back to you.'

The cash from van der Merwe wasn't much, but came in very handy for his kids' school fees and the like. So far he hadn't been asked to do anything he considered unprofessional. He didn't consider he was betraying the drive to conserve wildlife with which he had always been imbued since boyhood. But now he felt under pressure. He had better find some answers – and quickly, or those handy cash payments, which up to now had seemed to come without obligation, might stop. And that would be difficult because he had got used to the additional income.

With the help of his assiduously attendant personal assistant, a large white Afrikaner woman, Samuel Makojaene carefully pulled on his judicial robes. There was no fancy wig, British-style, no implication of being set quaintly above citizens; instead the robes gave a sense of the status, which he welcomed – and truth be told, rather enjoyed, befitting the precious authority bestowed on him and his fellow justices.

He wasn't a vain man, rather a proud man, carrying himself with some dignity and import, his accent and grammar carefully tailored to the vital role with which he had been entrusted.

Makojaene stepped out of his chambers, one of fourteen set on three storeys with open spaces and ponds at ground level offering convenient access to the courtroom and to the library in the northern wing of the Constitutional Court building.

Makojaene was only too aware that the stakes were again high. The court did not lightly overrule a president as it had already done several times: it couldn't substitute judges for legislators, still less for a president directly elected by the people. Whatever his private resentment at being deliberately passed over by the President for the Chief Justice's job, he couldn't allow that to cloud the judgement in this case. It would be cool, clinical and legally rock solid, as he always strove for. Equally however, no insinuating, insidious political pressure and rumour-mongering of the kind all too familiar under this president would shift him from his abiding dictum: how ever high you were, the law was above you.

As Justice Makojaene made his way to the anteroom through which he would enter the courtroom, nagging at the back of his mind was the image of a fellow ex-Robben Island prisoner who had stared at him from the well of the court every day of the hearings in this case.

Actually, they hadn't overlapped on the island. His own ten-year term in the desolate prison had been completed several years before the other's had begun. But both had undergone a shared experience: the privations, the humiliations, the warder bullying, the attempted sexual abuse and the gnawing isolation from family and human warmth. Angry young men on arrival, both had knuckled down, both had studied for degrees, both had matured under Madiba's genial wisdom.

Yet even then it was apparent their paths would diverge. Samuel Makojaene had immersed himself in legal studies, Moses Khoza in philosophy and history. Makojaene's activism and youthful idealism was channelled into the law, to practice as best he could in the 1970s and 1980s, and after the change to become one of the few black corporate lawyers, where he enjoyed an undreamed-of income. Then, restless and bored with the valueless nature of commercial law, he accepted a cut in his salary and returned to his first love by being appointed initially a judge of the High Court in Pretoria, then, two years later a judge in the Constitutional Court.

Although Moses Khoza's trajectory into the higher reaches of the ANC was very different, both men moved in the parallel public circles of the new South African establishment. Occasionally they bumped into each other at public events, where they made small talk about family and country. Or chatted about the museum that had been so lovingly established on Robben Island from 1994 by Professor André Odendaal under the directions of Nelson Mandela and his close colleague Ahmed Kathrada.

But they were wary of each other. Makojaene wasn't an ANC loyalist or insider like Khoza. His youthful roots were in the rival PAC, and that always engendered a certain reserve in the ANC, at least in its higher echelons. For his part, Makojaene could be prickly if he sensed any challenge to the independence of his important role: nobody, but nobody could intimidate him or challenge his duty to uphold the sanctity of the law.

Now they were contestants in a case about the authority of the presidency. Khoza's presence each and every day of the hearings was a deliberate signal of that.

If so, it made no difference to Makojaene – except perhaps to stiffen his resolve. From those days long ago when he had stood alone as a teenager on trial in Pretoria, only the solitary white woman stranger signalling support and bringing him food and chocolates, he had steeled himself to be strong, not to flinch under intimidation.

This woman had fundamentally changed his youthful antagonism to whites. She did not recoil before the baleful hostility of the white police officers, who viewed her as a traitor. She simply ignored them, diminutive and determined: they didn't know quite what to do with her as she went about her mission of finding out the names of the young defendants, telling parents who wouldn't otherwise have known what had happened to the boys who had disappeared into the clutches of the feared police state.

The puzzle was that for nearly fifty years he hadn't known who she was, just that she had made an amazing impression on him. Only recently, by chance, he discovered she was a prominent anti-apartheid activist and they made moving contact; she tearfully thrilled at how high the teenager she recalled standing in the dock dishevelled in short trousers had risen.

In that harsh, intimidating Pretoria courtroom, so very much a world ago, she had never shied away – and he wouldn't now. That irritated all the President's men and women, who deployed his infamous sneer about 'clever blacks' – bright, educated, the country's new middle class, fellow Africans who couldn't be bought off, wouldn't clamber aboard his gravy train of state largesse and cronyism.

Makojaene was quintessentially a 'clever black' all right and, on occasion perhaps just a little too proud of it.

The Constitutional Court chamber is rather plain, even austere, its design flooded with light, expressly accentuating the transparency of its proceedings.

The wider building is also strikingly different from the forbidding character of most courts, being welcoming and warm, encouraging no deference. Gracefully styled in wood, concrete, steel, glass and black slate, it has an evidently African feel. Its ethos was summed up by one of its architects and founder justices, Albie Sachs: 'Public buildings normally shut off the outside world. Normally you get swallowed up in the power of the state or corporate entity, but here the building is saying, "I belong to you, you belong to me."'

As a symbol of the country's new democracy, the court was built nearby Johannesburg's notorious prison from the apartheid era, known as the Old Fort, where hundreds of thousands had been detained, including Nelson Mandela, Mahatma Gandhi – and the Veteran.

When he formally opened the new court in February 1995, President Nelson Mandela said: 'The last time I appeared in court was to hear whether or not I was going to be sentenced to death. Fortunately for myself and my colleagues, we were not. Today I rise not as an accused, but on behalf of the people of South Africa, to inaugurate a court South Africa has never had, a court on which hinges the future of our democracy.'

At the inauguration Mandela unveiled in the foyer a commemorative plaque depicting the court's logo – an artistic representation of a crowd of people standing in a circle beneath a tree, encapsulating the African tradition of dispensing justice. The logo displays people sheltering under a canopy of branches to illustrate the Constitution's protective role and a reference to a theme that runs through the court– the meeting place to resolve disputes, the tree, like the Constitution, offering shelter and protection.

That concept is also on display in the foyer's overall design: spacious and light-filled with slanting columns decorated by mosaics of blue, green, orange and red meant to depict a tree, with a concrete roof containing slots to enable an effect of dappled sunlight filtering through leaves.

Above and adorning the entrance, are the values of the court set in concrete in the handwriting of its very first judges, notably the almost childlike script of Albie Sachs, who was forced to learn all over again to write with his left hand after the apartheid security services ignited a bomb in his car in Maputo that blew off his favoured right arm, leaving only a stump.

Although he delighted in observing the wonder of visitors as they looked around the building, it was Justice Makojaene's office, his daily place of work and so had a certain routine familiarity, which he consciously had to push aside when he showed personal guests around.

He entered the courtroom with six of his justice colleagues in support. The legal teams, the law clerks, media and members of the public stood and bowed as Makojaene and his fellow justices seated themselves on the judges' podium, shaped in a half-moon and decorated in a cow-hide pattern – brown with splashes of white, each judge's name printed just below the rim of the surface.

As he gathered his papers and looked out over the court, there was Moses Khoza again with his intense stare. To the surprise of nobody who

115

had followed the detailed legal arguments during the case, except perhaps Khoza, Makojaene was about to disappoint his fellow Robben Islander.

Meanwhile, the Ranger had been ferreting about, probing the story of the dead poacher.

He asked everyone, including his colleagues Steve Brown and Isaac Mkhize as they gossiped in the evening, watching and interacting with the visitors eating their evening meals around the campfire.

But nobody seemed to know anything. An enigma. He didn't relish telling van der Merwe he hadn't come up with the goods: that he hadn't delivered on his very first task.

But if the Ranger was worried, so was Mkhize, who had been struck by the persistence of his colleague's questions. And had vowed to keep an eye on him.

Now, however, Mkhize faced a more immediate problem: snares.

Often set by local people, they could be lethal. With wire wrapped into several strands to make them stronger, they were attached to a noose and placed at different heights for different animals. Virtually all animals – even elephants – could be endangered by these snares, limping around for days or weeks until an infection spread and either killed or disabled them. If badly injured, their constant search for food could be seriously compromised and they would die anyway. Usually the targets were antelope, smaller ones like impala – a favourite for poachers – and bushbuck, or much larger ones like zebra and wildebeest. Occasionally a buffalo, maybe even a lion, could be inadvertently snared.

If an animal deemed precious enough was snared, it had to be tracked through telltale distorted footprints, then sedated with a dart, the wire snare unwound and maybe the infection treated. It was painstaking and enormously time-consuming work for rangers. Smaller animals like a scrub hare or a common duiker had to be sacrificed – unless a ranger came upon them.

Expert poachers returned to their snares to retrieve trapped animals, writhing and weakened, to kill and take them off. Which meant rangers had constantly to be vigilant for signs of poachers and remove any snares spotted. It was an endless battle.

The President was furious.

The Constitutional Court had ruled against the government's objective of legalising the sale of stockpiled elephant ivory and rhino horns, and in favour of the wildlife groups. Although the President's daughter would have been a beneficiary, having a business stake in the scheme, which attracted inevitably critical media headlines, the court hadn't been interested in that.

He berated Moses Khoza in frustration. Justice Makojaene was a bloody menace. But what could he do? The President paced the room, staring out of the wide windows but not seeing the expansive view over the hills beyond Pretoria's suburbs. Khoza and several other senior advisers were slumped in chairs.

Critics said the President ran the country as if it were his personal fiefdom, rather than in the national interest. But they were all the usual suspects. Journalists – self-seeking apostles of fake news. NGOs – bloody NGOs, full of professional agitators. The opposition parties – always out to have a go, regardless. But he was the President, for goodness' sake! Elected last time with a big mandate, he had totally convinced himself that he, not they, spoke for the masses. He ignored the community protests against poor service delivery and local corruption, and the loss of key cities to opposition parties for the first time in recent municipal elections.

He didn't seem to mind that the rand had slumped; that business confidence had plummeted to a low not seen since the dog days of apartheid in the late 1980s; or that international investors feared another Zimbabwe and wouldn't touch South Africa despite its huge potential, good infrastructure and renowned reputation for sound commercial governance and regulation.

He had sorted the National Prosecuting Authority. He had sorted the leadership of the police service. He had sorted the state security agencies to spy more on his party opponents than enemies of the country. He had done all that.

But his problem, which Khoza had patiently explained, though anxious not to cause offence – because the President never liked being told things he didn't want to hear – was that the Constitution specified the procedures for appointing judges. First, the Judicial Service Commission drew up a list of candidates, with three more names than the number of vacancies. It did so after calling publicly for nominations and holding public interviews.

Then the President, after consultation with the Chief Justice and the leaders of political parties represented in Parliament, chose the judges

117

from this selection, who normally served for non-renewable terms of between twelve and fifteen years. But this process meant he could not always get his way – which was of course the whole point of the Constitution: to ensure presidents were not autocratic.

Even when he had appointed the new Chief Justice of the Republic of South Africa because he knew him personally, not because he was the best lawyer, it was said the man had somehow become the creature of Makojaene. Whatever the President did, Makojaene seemed one step ahead.

The President stopped pacing about the room. He turned to Khoza: 'Check out Makojaene. Any indiscretions? Any girlfriends? Any financial weaknesses?'

He seemed blissfully unaware – though his aides certainly were – that those very same attributes described him to perfection.

The Ranger braced himself. He didn't like bearing bad news. Especially to van der Merwe. The man dangled him like a puppet on a string.

Having found a spot at the edge of the main camp where he could be alone, he dialled van der Merwe.

'Yah?' No courtesies – ever – from van der Merwe. No expressions of interest in his kids or himself. Just a trade in information.

The Ranger paused. How to put this? He took a deep breath and plucked up courage. 'I can't find anything more about who killed our man.'

'What do I bladdy pay you for? Every bladdy month? For Christ's sake, man!'

'Sorry,' the Ranger mumbled. Then he said it, what he had thought long and hard about saying, but did not want to: 'If I am not doing my job well enough, maybe you had better stop paying me?'

Van der Merwe pretended not to notice. He despised the Ranger for being so weak, so desperate for the cash. But he needed him. Especially now. It took too long to recruit an insider after having checked them out – and even then you couldn't always be certain that they weren't playing both ends off against the middle, weren't feeding you duff info. And this was a live problem. There were enough rhinos in Zama Zama to go back again, and they might have to.

Quite soon. Because van der Merwe was under pressure to produce.

'I need the information – soon. I'm suspicious they have someone

professional to help. We've got to know. You are on notice, my man.'
He killed the call abruptly.

The choice of 'my man' was calculated. Never let the Ranger forget
that was exactly what he was: van der Merwe's man, pure and simple.
Relieved in one way, yet hating himself in another, the Ranger brooded
over the call.

Back to work – a game drive was due soon – his mind in a flurry.

Moses Khoza was another who sometimes detested himself. He yearned
for the simplicity, the purity of his struggle days. Even, yes even, he
yearned for the island where – of course – there was intense, grinding
privation. But there was also comradeship.

He had no mortgage on the island, no bills to meet, no obligations
other than to his comrades. And no temptations. Instead, nurtured by
Madiba, he had only the determination not to be beaten. Even better
than that – much better – to emerge one day, head held high, at Madiba's
side in triumph.

But today there were bills to pay. His wife's ostentatious clothing and
ladies' lunches to support. His children's worship of the trivial to fund.
The house to maintain. The African servants to pay. The wine to buy.
The ballooning phone bills for the lot of them to settle monthly. The
relatives to look after. It was one never-ending treadmill.

And what did they know? His family. What did they even care? Had
they any idea what he'd been through? What it was like to be beaten in a
cold cell from hell? What it was like to be male raped by the black police
officer brought in to do his white master's bidding – then despatched back
to the township frontline?

Had they any idea at all?

Sometimes he wanted to call a halt. To tell his president. To tell van der
Merwe. To tell his wife. To tell his children. The bloody lot of them. To
sod off. To set him free. Free again. Respected again. As he once was . . .

Moses Khoza jerked himself back to reality, to the task in hand. No
time for self-moralising. No time for nostalgia. There was the president's
work to do. He began to think about the latest presidential obsession:
Makojaene. And what exactly to do about that immensely irritating
obstruction.

Khoza resolved to call again on the assistance of iPhone Man. For he
was both discreet and efficient.

119

CHAPTER 10

Solly Naidoo had completed his work of art.

Using stiletto-like drills and surgical-type knives, he had meticulously carved out a small cavity near the middle of the old rhino horn.

That had been the relatively easy bit.

More difficult was the first part of the surgical-type procedure: delicately to prise away a small panel from the surface of the horn, which would serve as a lid for the cavity. First he selected a spot where he could more easily conceal the new lid amidst the grooves on the surface. Then he marked out a semi-rectangular shape and gradually levered underneath it, prising a thickish slice away.

Even for someone with his micro-skills and long experience, it required enormous concentration and absolute precision. The room was air-conditioned, but he was sweating with both tension and effort.

He inspected the small panel and, satisfied, laid it carefully to one side. Then he began delicately spooning out a cavity below to the dimensions he'd been given by the Veteran's emissary, Isaac Mkhize. As he did so, he smiled: no doubt the bits he swept onto the floor would be worth a small fortune! He would later hoover them up with the other debris. Not even his wife, a little irritated at his very unusual plea for absolute privacy, knew the purpose of this piece of work. It simply reminded her nostalgically of the struggle days and of her pride in his status as a supremely trusted craftsman.

Isaac Mkhize was known for his placidity. His fellow rangers constantly pulled his leg about it. Whatever the problems – and there were always problems, always, on a game reserve – he just kept going, quietly and methodically. He seldom, if ever, got angry.

But one of his colleagues was really bugging him – irritating the hell out of him.

Why? Because the bugger kept asking, snooping – something the man had never done before in Zama Zama. Who exactly had killed the poacher? In past incidents poachers had always died messily, but this one died from a clean shot. Why? How?

The problem was that the Sniper was due back that evening. However, this time he wouldn't blend in with the guests as he had always done before. This time he would come quietly, do his business, and hopefully go quietly.

Mkhize ensured his irritating colleague was well out of the way repairing broken fencing right on the far side of Zama Zama, a good hour's drive or more away from the rhino herd when the Sniper was due to arrive. And then allocated to a dawn walk, which would take him well away at the time the Sniper was due to leave the reserve.

The Ranger rose at 05:00 hrs to get the coffee and biscuits ready for the early morning bushwalk.

He switched on his mobile radio and immediately listened hard. There was some excited chatter about an incident in the night, but he couldn't piece it all together.

After pulling on a fresh uniform, he made his way swiftly towards the lodge. All was quiet. His task was to fill and switch on the boilers, which stood on a table waiting, mugs turned upside down on trays left by the night staff. He collected the biscuits and rusks and laid them out for the bushwalk guests, turning around as Steve Brown rolled up, sleepy-eyed, ready for some caffeine and nicotine to kick-start his busy day.

'What was the fuss on the handsets all about?' the Ranger asked as casually as he could.

'No idea, *boetie*,' Brown replied indifferently, yawning – though remembering Mkhize's suspicions and, almost as an afterthought while rolling a cigarette, asking, 'Why does it matter? We'll find out in due course.'

'Suppose so,' the Ranger muttered, disappointed, adding: 'I will ask Isaac when I see him.'

But that wouldn't be for quite a while because, Steve Brown knew, Mkhize was at that very moment driving the Sniper to catch the early morning flight from Richards Bay to Johannesburg.

*

121

For the Sniper however, it had been a close call.

The moon had been high, the *veld* shimmering, the shadows dancing around the grazing rhinos.

He had tried to conceal himself in a nearby vantage point, upwind from the animals – the direction he surmised from which any poachers would come. They wouldn't want the peacefully chomping rhinos to smell or sense them. But that meant he would be between them and their targets. A vulnerable position, he was well aware.

The Sniper tried to put himself in the minds of the poachers. He imagined their fears and their tactics. Yes, they would be worried about the bright moonlight – obviously. At the same time it offered transparency – where the guards might be holed up, where any mantraps lay in waiting.

Mkhize had told him the Owner was convinced they would come back again after having been repelled once by the Sniper. Poachers had a recklessness about them, the money so important that the danger was secondary. As for their ringleaders, none of them cared a damn about the risks to their charges on the ground. Although their own safety was rarely jeopardised, the ringleaders had no compunction about sending fresh bodies into action. Losing a man – as the week before at Zama Zama – you simply recruited another. There was a long queue of ready replacements. That was always van der Merwe's dispassionate calculation.

The Sniper had moved into position at nightfall. He doubted the poachers – if indeed they were actually coming that night – would have entered the reserve the night before and remained hiding, resting up during the day, as often happened. They would know after the last debacle that security would be heavy, that the danger was heightened. Better to go in, grab the horns and scarper all in one night.

The Sniper had a clear view of the rhinos as they wandered innocently around, chewing continuously, Mkhize having explained how rhino spent fully half their time feeding. Their long, cone-like ears, situated on top of their enormous heads for maximum effect, were constantly moving. They seemed to rotate independently in just about every direction, straining for every sound. If they sensed anything important, both ears tilted in the same direction. Their sense of smell, through a low-hanging muzzle at the end of a huge powerful neck, was also very strong and sharp, both smell and hearing nature's compensation for poor eyesight.

Before moving into position, the Sniper had slept in the camp in the late afternoon to early evening, eyeshades on, and therefore felt sharp and fit. His old training clicked back in almost mechanically, almost subliminally. Don't let your mind wander. Never allow tedium to triumph. Always remain on edge, ready for the unexpected.

He had been taught that to be a sniper was to be a nomad. Try to pop up where least expected; never remain for very long in a single position, risking observation. Never mistake quietness for safety: it's the very opposite, because it can easily mean lethal danger. Never rush, always be slow, cautious, meticulous, methodical.

Be as still as a rock, constantly observing, trying always to be completely invisible, even to the trained eye. A sniper when in combat mode is always in a war of nerves, a war of concentration, a war of endurance.

Control of breathing throughout your shot was critical. Discover your best breathing technique and master it so your breathing doesn't interfere with your accuracy. It was amazing how much the process of breathing could disturb the rock-solid control needed over the rifle. Pull the trigger in a smooth, squeezing motion and never jerk – or poor trigger control would cause the weapon to kick or recoil.

He'd also been schooled to create distractions, exasperate the enemy with diversions, try to wear him down with exhaustion, breaking his concentration. The sniper craft was as much psychological as physical. Above all, never fire until you are absolutely certain of a kill or you will expose your own position and risk being killed yourself: impatience is death.

The whoosh of a silenced bullet pinging off a rock right next to him broke the background rumbling of the bush. He rolled away, frantically seeking protection from the line of fire. Another bullet screamed close.

Now he had a fix, he could just about spot the source, a shadowed figure crouching just above and to the side of him, about a hundred metres away. He levelled his infrared scope, identifying the poacher much more clearly. He had the gunman's head in his cross hairs.

In that split second the Sniper squeezed his trigger and almost simultaneously the man's head exploded in a mass of spurting blood, spongy bone tissue and brain cells.

But there was no time for either triumph or guilt. One threat eliminated, the Sniper anxiously scanned the vicinity for the gunman's mate. Because there would be at least one, of that he was certain. Birds had begun shrieking. The rhinos stamped and bristled, their ears swivelling, striving to make sense of the pandemonium.

123

The Sniper stayed cool and concentrated as he slithered slightly to one side, conscious he had betrayed his position, searching for new cover while peering intently into the scrubby bush. At that moment, more than any other in his life, he wished he possessed an owl's eyes. Not more powerful than human eyes, but able to collect much more light, allowing heightened vision at night.

He felt a gnawing itchiness between his thighs. Some termite must have crawled up his jeans. But he blanked that out, and waited. Seconds etched into minutes and then into an age. But still he waited, his night scope inching around, probing each rock, each bush. Nothing. No movement. No telltale human sound.

Then, just as he had swung his rifle around and over a small outcrop, well to the right of the dead poacher, his attention was caught by a shape foreign to the immediate vicinity. Meticulously and almost painfully slowly he swung the night sight back, settling over the shape, almost penetrating the image.

A man, crouching low, gripping a rifle, had lost patience with his waiting game and moved up into a more attacking posture.

In that moment the Sniper had him. Once again he squeezed hard and once again heard the whoosh of a silencer as a skull burst open and the figure abruptly collapsed. No scream, hardly a sound. Just a life brutally expired without even a split second to dissent.

But as if nothing had happened, the Sniper retained his iron concentration, scrambling away a little. He had been tutored hard in the art of silently avoiding a retaliatory fix from the enemy. All the time he was searching hard into the undergrowth. Ignoring the rhinos tramping feverishly. Not listening to the birds shrieking agitatedly. Blanking the monkeys scampering boisterously. Just scanning everything and everywhere.

Abruptly, away behind the second mangled figure, he spotted another one rise in panic and begin running hysterically, weaving through the straight, upright tamboti trees, moonshine playing havoc with the surviving poacher's image among the shadows. Without his infrared scope it would have been almost impossible for the Sniper to achieve a clear shot. He aimed for the middle of the back and squeezed twice in rapid succession, the man crashing, flailing to the ground.

But still the Sniper stayed hidden, not betraying his position. Aged nineteen he had seen a fellow sniper killed for his exuberance after downing what he thought was the only assailant left, but was fatally mistaken. A lesson burned into his professional psyche.

He waited for five long minutes. Then, still prone behind a rock, pulled out his phone, which he'd earlier put in vibrate-only mode, and texted Mkhize: *3 poachers dead get me out now please.*

A few seconds later and his phone vibrated: *Copy that. Soon on my way to meet.*

The Sniper started to creep away, crouching low, as silently as he could, peering continuously and, as he retreated, catching a glimpse of the rhinos circling around as they tried to fathom what the hell was happening, the creatures unsettled but nevertheless majestic in the African moonlight.

He tried not to think about the dead men's expired lives, or the impact upon their families, with the main breadwinners lost. Or his expended shell casings at a 'crime scene', if the police bothered to investigate. Instead he focused only upon the rhinos. A satisfying moment for them, indeed.

The rhino security guards, who had hardly taken in the detail of the blurred action around them, and hadn't even spotted the Sniper's meticulous retreat, checked out the three dead poachers in wonderment.

Their instructions were to claim the kills themselves. Under no circumstances ever – ever – to reveal the Sniper's presence. A special bonus worth their monthly salary awaited if they kept rigidly to that instruction.

After three hours of careful scanning for hyenas, which might have got an early sniff of the corpses, the two guards waited for the rangers to drive up in their *bakkie*, scoop up and load the corpses onto the back – and for the day shift to take over shielding the royal herd.

But one of the guards shivered in the encroaching warmth of the dawn, for he knew the poacher gangs were all-powerful and would see their rebuff as a threat to be mercilessly eliminated. And of that, the Sniper – gliding away through the bush under the dappled light, scrutinising everything, everywhere he could, gun held and cocked – was in absolutely no doubt at all.

Speeding along under the moonlight, the Land Cruiser bucked and lurched over the rutted tracks in Zama Zama.

The bright eyes of buck glinted from the bush as Isaac Mkhize swept around bends. Once, as he turned the vehicle sharply, headlights swinging around, they caught a buffalo glowering menacingly from the gloom.

125

With a foul temper, it was one of the most dangerous of all the animals to encounter, Mkhize knew only too well.

He glanced at the digital dashboard clock. 04:30 hrs. Just about time to collect the Sniper, drive the hour or so through the reserve and then the additional hour to Richards Bay airport in time for him check in and to grab a coffee before the 08:05 South African Airways flight to Johannesburg.

Mkhize was anxious. Although a booking had been made, it hadn't been confirmed online because they couldn't be sure of being there, and the flight was often full, with rumours of passengers being bumped off even from pre-booked flights. He had to drive with speed and care.

He stopped at the exact point where he'd dropped the Sniper seven hours earlier, and switched off the engine. All quiet now, save for the muffled sounds of the bush, all the eyes of the nearby wildlife, both curious and concerned, fixed on him. Even at night the bush never slept.

Mkhize pulled out a handgun from the compartment under his seat and cradled it on his lap, listening intently. Nothing for ten long minutes, during which he was uncomfortable, only too aware he was a sitting duck. Normally he was just as relaxed out at night as during daytime in Zama Zama. But not now. You could never be sure what might happen with poachers around and whether they had any back-up.

But, although professionally irritated with himself, he had to admire the sublime skill with which the Sniper eased the door open and slid into the front passenger seat without Mkhize even being aware he'd silently arrived.

The Sniper wrapped a heavy cloth around his gun and stowed it in the special security box, which would be placed by Mkhize under the Owner's bed.

'The poachers may not have been professional gunmen, but they were still more proficient than the first time. Three of them. And I'm still really pissed off that one got a shot at me before I spotted him,' the Sniper muttered. 'By the way, what's going to happen to the bodies?'

'Steve Brown and another ranger will collect them in a little while, take them to the camp and call the police. It shouldn't be a problem. The local officers are very supportive of us. They live locally and know the value of the reserve to the local community's income, so they hate poachers, would happily murder them on sight. They will understand why we couldn't leave the bodies out at the scene, or first the hyenas, then the dogs, and certainly the vultures would have eaten them.'

'So no trace of me, then?' the Sniper queried.

'None at all. The rhino guards won't talk. And we don't think anybody saw you arrive and hopefully nobody will see you leave. I'm stopping shortly before we get to the main gate so you can lie down in one of the back seats well under the guest blankets, like when you came in. None of the security on the gate will spot you as they wave me through.'

Reassured, the Sniper leaned back on the seat and closed his eyes. Although he couldn't sleep, he didn't feel like chatting. Now that he felt safe, it was slowly sinking in that he had killed three men. He hadn't done anything like this for decades, and then only in open combat. He felt no remorse because he believed entirely in the mission. Instead he felt a sense of chilling emptiness. He might have to get used to that, because Mkhize had said they would need him to return.

The sun was already bright and rising as they drove into the airport. Mkhize stopped – not at the main drop-off point for passengers but near the car park, away from prying eyes interested in the Zama Zama livery on the vehicle.

He watched the Sniper collect the backpack deposited before his night venture and swing it over his shoulder, wave goodbye and lope off towards the airport building. *A cool customer*, Mkhize thought, *but a decent guy all the same. And definitely one to have on your side, not your opponent's.*

Around the same time, about hundred kilometres away, a man of Thai origin waited at a roadside, increasingly fretful.

He had a special case for the rhino horns. His mobile signal was strong. There was no doubt he was parked up at the correct spot, just off the main road in the shade of a yellowwood tree.

The man waited and waited.

The hours ticked by, and it was getting hot. He went for a pee out of sight of passing motorists.

Still nothing. He was getting hungry. But his instructions were to wait.

Finally around midday, his phone rang. Thank God. But then he froze. Piet van der Merwe's number was registering.

'All okay?'

The man stammered. 'Uh, uh, not sure.'

'What do you mean?' van der Merwe asked.

'No sign of the guys or the cargo.'

'What?'

'I've been here for six hours since dawn, and nothing at all.'

'Fuck it!' van der Merwe screamed. 'I will make some calls.'

He ended the conversation as abruptly and curtly as he had begun.

Then, just as van der Merwe was considering the options, a familiar number called. The Ranger – his Ranger. But it was certainly not what he wanted to hear.

'Sorry boss.' The man seemed a little short of breath. 'Bad news. Local police have just arrived with us. Seems to collect three bodies. Can't find out the detail, but the word is three dead poachers brought in earlier this morning from near the rhinos.'

Van der Merwe's tone was ominous. 'What the fuck happened?'

'Nobody's saying very much except that the rhino guards got lucky.'

'Hmmm ...' van der Merwe pondered. Got lucky? Twice in a row? Twice?

'Keep your ears to the ground. I need to know exactly what happened,' he barked.

The hapless Ranger felt depressed. Once again, he had failed his paymaster. But professionally and emotionally he also felt relieved, for he had worshipped rhinos since boyhood: they were his favourite animal.

Van der Merwe toyed with his phone. He now had two calls to make. The first by far the easier: instructing the man of Thai origin to clear off. The second much more awkward: to Moses Khoza, bearing the bad news and requesting an early meet.

A sense of anticlimax had overcome the Sniper as the plane took off, and he closed his eyes for the hour's flight to ORT Airport.

And also a sense of foreboding. He had now killed four men, the last three in clear sight (the first having managed to run away before dying). He didn't know them, had no sense of who they were or what the personal consequences would have been for any wives or children.

The first time he had shot anyone he'd been eighteen, and hadn't given much thought to the victim amidst the adrenaline and excitement of success. It had been a professional job by a professional soldier targeting an enemy soldier. There hadn't seemed anything personal in it at all, apart from the exhilaration and pride in congratulations from his seniors and peers.

A couple of years later, after being assigned to protect Madiba, he'd had a complete rethink – like many white South Africans – and began to question the system of apartheid which, until then, he had never thought about that much. The plight of the African majority hadn't really registered with him before; he hadn't known about the hardship of their lives in the townships.

But now he had killed four Africans at much closer quarters. And been shot at himself. It was all much more personal, and he wasn't quite sure what he felt. Conflicting emotions and thoughts flashed through his mind.

But of one thing he was certain. He wasn't a natural-born killer. He took no pleasure in the death of the poachers. Only a sense of a job done. His mission accomplished: the rhinos protected from what would have been certain mutilation after being hacked to death if he hadn't been there. That at least was of comfort.

The Sniper dozed off, until fifteen minutes later when the pilot announced they would be landing shortly, and when an entirely different thought struck him. Next time – and there would be a next time – they would come even more heavily armed, probably with AK-47s, and likely in greater numbers. Then he would be their prey, probably equally with the rhinos.

Back at the camp, Isaac Mkhize had exactly the same thought as he clocked the same colleague once again.

Although everyone at the camp – staff and guest alike – was understandably agog and keen to hear the full story of the dead poachers, high fives all round in the team, one ranger seemed strangely subdued.

He kept asking about the detail, but little was forthcoming. The security guards had shot the three was all that was known. The police had taken the corpses away. Nobody at the camp recognised them, and they didn't seem local.

Mkhize noticed also that the Ranger furtively slipped away and he watched as the man stood apart and made a call. Rather, Mkhize observed, as he did when taking a call from or phoning the Veteran and Thandi – on his own, not wanting to be overheard.

Time for a serious chat with the Owner. Because, even with the Sniper in the right place at the right time – and that in itself was a lottery – if the enemy came with greater firepower and better planning, the Sniper might not stand a chance.

Zama Zama had taken their rhino war to their foes without knowing who they were or what they were. Without knowing what sort of organisation stood behind the poachers on the frontline or how powerful and resourceful it was.

Until now, Isaac Mkhize hadn't considered for a moment that his life might be in danger. He decided to phone both the Veteran and Thandi and update them.

After the Sniper had cleared arrivals at Joburg and picked up his car, his phone rang.

'Fantastic job, man,' the Owner's voice boomed, 'you were awesome!'

'No problem,' the Sniper muttered. A shy man, he had always been outwardly embarrassed by praise, even if inwardly buoyant.

The Owner seemed not to notice, however. 'I'm in Joburg myself today and overnight. Camp business, squaring off our bloody investors. How about dinner in the Rosebank Mall? Lots of nice eateries there.'

'Thanks very much, very kind of you,' the Sniper replied. 'Actually, I was thinking on the flight back that our success could mean an escalation as the enemy start targeting us more on their way to the rhinos.'

'Absolutely, I've just talked to Isaac about exactly that. What time's best for you? Seven p.m.?'

'Fine,' the Sniper replied. 'I may be a little late: after work I've got to call by my mom first, as she's on her own; see how she is.'

Details of the venue were fixed, and a discreet table reserved by the Owner.

CHAPTER 11

The Veteran poured himself a single malt whisky – plain, no water – and sat on his verandah looking out over his sweeping view of False Bay, majestic in the evening sun.

Isaac's phone call posed a dilemma. Another one. He knew the stakes were getting remorselessly higher. Trouble was, in the old days when he'd been up against the state, it was as a member of a formidable organisation, not with just a few amateurs, albeit well-intentioned ones.

Time to call in some favours from trusted and similarly disillusioned comrades from the struggle days, including those hanging on by their fingertips inside the administration. But approaching the latter comrades would have to be done with the utmost discretion.

By coincidence he had read online in the UK *Guardian* that very morning a detailed news analysis of an attack in a Paris zoo, when criminals broke in and shot its rhino three times in the head before hacking off its eight-inch horn with a chainsaw. The attack, the paper reported, marked a shocking new development in a crisis hitherto impacting mainly upon southern Africa.

But the Veteran's trained eye had been caught by another series of points in the long article.

Hundreds of poachers had been killed in the last seven years and a much smaller but significant number of rangers, soldiers and policemen had also died. 'Shooting and jailing the poachers is not a long term solution,' wildlife expert Julian Rademeyer said. 'They are very easy for the crime syndicates to find and very easy to exploit. Whether they get killed or arrested means very little to the syndicates, and the same applies to the couriers. The kingpins who are making the big money are getting away with it.'

With the prices high and penalties low, international organised crime networks had grabbed the illegal but multi-billion-dollar trade in wildlife trafficking.

And what about his predicament, the Veteran wondered?

Taking another sip of single malt, he started thinking about his plans ... But then came one of his periodic freedom-struggle flashbacks: memory snapshots, sometimes traumatic, sometimes joyous, but in recent times increasingly the former.

It was the flush toilet in his prison cell, pretty unusual from what he subsequently understood from consulting other comrades also detained at the time. That toilet. You not only defecated and peed in it. You also washed your face, your private parts, under your arms – whatever you could – in it. Including brushing your teeth. It was amazing what you could do – if you really had to.

He remembered always closing his eyes as he lowered his head into the basin, feeling bile rising in his throat, and somehow ashamed of himself. He used to flush it several times before plucking up enough willpower to start cleaning himself, but still the smell of shit and urine was palpable, because the toilet was only cleaned once weekly.

Every time he tried to control the anger that welled up, because that meant the authorities were getting to him. But it did nevertheless, especially when, escorted for daily exercise, he passed the shower room with hot water and basins, which was always spotlessly clean. Not for the prisoners, however. Prison inspectors were never informed that the shower room was out of bounds for use by political prisoners ...

... The Veteran jerked himself back to the present. Time to start mobilising his forces, the ones whom he had systematically contacted these past few weeks.

As instructed by the Owner, Mkhize had identified a suitable local villager. He was the father of the excellent masseur for guests at the camp – a woman in her early thirties who did back and shoulder massage on a portable bench she brought and set up on the verandah of each cabin.

He was a handyman, well known and popular in the village, and Mkhize had easily obtained his cooperation for a modest but welcome cash retainer – only on the basis he never disclosed to his daughter or anyone else that he was keeping an ear to the ground for any local men involved in poaching.

The ostensible reason for Mkhize's visit to the family home was the possibility of odd jobs in Zama Zama, but thereafter their communication would be by phone alone.

Van der Merwe sat by his wife Sarie's bed, as he did whenever he had a spare moment and whenever he was at home. He held her hand and she smiled wistfully, dreamily – and emptily. It gave him comfort that he could still give her some pleasure, if indeed that was really what it was.

They slept in separate bedrooms – had done so for years since she had slipped remorselessly from him into her present condition – but he remained devoted to her. As he studied her face he could see still the fine bones and cheeky eyes that had captivated him as a young, testosterone-filled man all those decades ago.

He didn't really know what she was any more. A person – no. How could she be? She didn't engage with anybody. A vegetable – no, not that either. She seemed caught in some vacant transit zone.

But she seemed at peace. At least he could be thankful for that.

Your whole personality is rooted in your memory, he had realised, trying desperately to cope with his wife's cruel, debilitating condition. Without your memory you are a blank. Your memory shapes who you are – everything little thing about you. From early childhood – maybe even earlier than that – your learned experience imprints upon your very being what you are. Lose your memory and you are no more. Never were a child, nor a teenager, nor a lover, nor a wife, nor a mother. Nothing of the real you exists any more, gone into the ether, leaving a sad, empty vessel without personality, without humanity, in fact.

What was the point of existing? Van der Merwe asked himself.

Yet he had ensured his wife was fed, showered, dressed and toileted by a quartet of twenty-four-hour African carers. They did pretty well – did everything that a normal independent person would do on their own. They got her up, fed her, wheeled her around the garden, and sat her on the terrace to soak up the warmth and vitamin D of the sun. They put her in front of the television to stare vacantly at the moving pictures. (The only time she seemed to react being when there was old-time dancing on. In her heyday, she had been proficient at the waltz, the jive and rock and roll. He had followed her around the dance floor, would have been dysfunctional on his own, but appeared proficient with her.)

The carers were lovely with her.

One was lovely with him too, as he sought solace, effectively a single man now.

He felt no guilt, because Sarie had gone from him. And having sex with a black woman gave him a secret thrill. Into his very DNA had been bred the ethos of apartheid – the supremacy of whites and the subordination of blacks. But he'd always had a hankering to sleep with a black woman – just to experience what it was like. And he hadn't been disappointed. He had come to enjoy her impish company in bed, not just to use her.

He knew of the fiendishly complicated history of centuries of inter-breeding in South Africa. It was rather like the history of slavery in America or the Caribbean or Latin America. Racism was common to all those countries. The subordination of black people was common to all. But white South African men, from the time of the first settlers in the late seventeenth century, had taken Africans to bed whether the women liked it or not, just as slave owners across the Atlantic had done.

Apartheid had banned interracial sex under the Immorality Act, but even then there were transgressions and, where these were discovered, prosecutions followed, which shamed the white men involved, including Afrikaners. There were also emotionally wrenching stories of children of parents on both sides of the racial divide being born either too black or too white as a result of genetic surfacing from ancestral 'misbehaviour'.

Although the black nurse's companion sharing the care of van der Merwe's wife disapproved of the relationship, she didn't seem to. They had enjoyed their illicit mutual comfort together. Or so, at least, it seemed to him after he had ejaculated into the condom, lain back in exhausted satisfaction – and then despatched her back to his wife's bedside. He had always strenuously avoided asking himself the really hard question that lurked tantalisingly in the back of his mind: what if she felt obligated, what if she felt she had to gratify him to keep her precious job? The job that with the other three carers was costing him R25,000 each and every month. And one reason, but not the only reason, why he remained a driven man.

Next on his list was a quite different tactic for Zama Zama.

The Sniper found the Owner sitting at a table slightly apart from others in the restaurant, a bottle of red wine open, his glass nearly empty already, the other filled.

134

'Good to see you, man,' the Owner stood, banging his hand on the Sniper's shoulder. 'Have a seat and a drink, let's quickly scan the menu, order, and then get down to business.'

He summoned a waiter – they all seemed to be from Zimbabwe, polite, attentive, and well educated. Some had professional qualifications but couldn't get jobs in the ruins of the Zimbabwe economy under Robert Mugabe's malevolently destructive rule.

'Good guys', the Owner remarked of the Zimbabweans. 'They're in all our restaurants. Problem is, despite very high unemployment, the locals couldn't be bothered to do these sorts of service jobs. There's a work-ethic problem, not just a jobs problem in our country.'

The Sniper raised his eyebrows, but the Owner abruptly changed the subject, and they quickly begun to strategise over their rhino predicament.

Thandi wanted to carry a placard, but the Veteran had imposed a strict ban on high-profile political activity.

'You are a clean skin and you have to remain a clean skin if at all possible,' he had instructed.

So she buried herself in the crowds thronging the pavements, watching the marchers from Church Square, singing and chanting as they went through Pretoria city centre, a buoyant bubbling mass of humanity demanding change. The Pretoria People's March was huge and peaceful, representing all races and all social classes, and eventually 100,000 converged on the wide lawns below the Union Buildings to hear speeches from opposition leaders, with star turns from trade union and ANC figures hostile to the President.

Referring to rating agencies downgrading South Africa's economy to speculative status, one speaker, wearing a bulletproof vest after receiving credible threats, said to deafening cheers: 'We're not a junk county, we just have a junk president.'

In the same spot over two decades before, watching crowds had been spellbound as Nelson Mandela was sworn in as president.

But now they were demanding the President go.

Police helicopters were thrumming overhead. Slightly apart on the pavements and then to the side of the large gathering on the lawns, Thandi spotted pro-President groups calling themselves 'MK Veterans', but many, she also noted, were too young to have participated in the ANC's underground struggle. 'White capitalist regime changers,' they chanted.

They must have been conscripted, she felt. The government was behaving like all those authoritarian regimes across the world, which mobilised supporter groups; these ones were often bussed in from afar, from poor areas like Mpumalanga, North-West, Limpopo, Free State and KwaZulu-Natal provinces. There were suggestions they'd been paid for the day. Many were carrying sticks, bricks and *sjamboks*. Some among them began grabbing and tearing up protest placards.

Is this what the rainbow democracy had come to, Thandi wondered?

Her own Veteran had better be planning something significant, she resolved.

It was neat, very neat, Makojaene had to acknowledge.

The South African subsidiary of a renowned British-based public affairs company commissioned by the President's richest confidantes, had come up with a new message: that the President's critics were 'agents of white monopoly capital'. It was an Alice-in-Wonderland twist of the truth, since the Business Brothers who looted with the President were themselves the very epitome of monopoly capital.

The President was himself in hock to crony capitalists and was the recipient of their largesse to his family and circle of closest friends. The message was indeed Orwellian, but it gave a strong line for his supporters to preach. It had to be a strong line because the public affiars company was being paid £100,000 a month. Their prolific social media was also racist: whites were all to blame, whereas the corruption known as 'state capture' crossed race boundaries.

Most of the morning papers carried briefings against Makojaene. One headline read: 'Senior Judge Investigated For Business Links'. There was only one hard, irrefutable set of facts in the whole story. The rest was speculative rumour-mongered invention by the 'security sources' quoted.

Makojaene had indeed been part of the corporate world after democracy in 1994, when he had been asked to chair a new black-empowerment legal services company set up as part of the economic transformation the Mandela government had initiated to accompany democratic transformation. But he had soon tired of the business world, cut his links completely, including cashing in several million rand in share bonuses – ignoring financial advice that he would lose out – and resumed his legal career. Before joining as a justice of the Constitutional Court, he had become a High Court judge in Pretoria, where his work had been highly acclaimed.

Widely regarded as a figure of shining integrity in the service of his country, the stories about him were extensively derided and disbelieved. But there they were, being parroted on Facebook, Instagram and Twitter by the President's supporters.

Seething, he pledged to his wife never to be beaten. But he couldn't prevent the stories eating into him because, whatever attacks he had faced in his life, they had been political. This was personal, undermining his integrity. Enduring Robben Island, defying apartheid or applying the principles of the Constitution in court against presidential intimidation were all easy by comparison. This was corroding his soul.

Which was, of course, the very intention.

The iPhone Man may have done his work well, but Moses Khoza couldn't bring himself to gloat.

There were times when he didn't like himself, and this was one. Mostly, however, he was okay. He could live in his parallel universes. Former Robben Island hero, but practitioner of the dark arts. Preacher of anti-colonialism who connived under his president with the new colonialists – the Russians or the Chinese.

Funny how they got away with it, the Chinese, he mused. Because they weren't the old imperial powers, Europe or America, they could buy up Africa's minerals, oil and gas in exchange for building often substandard but nevertheless very welcome power stations, roads, ports and hospitals. They brought in their own Chinese construction workforces, leaving no skills legacy. And the clincher, wherever they went, was that they left behind shops selling cheap manufactured goods made in China, staffed by Chinese immigrants who worked round the clock, and open all hours to grateful locals. Yet somehow they weren't stigmatised as the modern colonialists they undoubtedly were.

The Russians, of course, were once on the side of the anti-colonial struggles, funding the ANC, now plundering, conspiring and, where necessary, killing. Khoza knew all this. Whatever he had become, he was certainly no fool.

He had tried to intimidate Justice Makojaene by always being there in court. He had deeply resented the man's verdict on the rhino-horn trade. And yet he retained a grudging admiration, as if he recognised in the unbendable figure on the bench something of his former self, the character he had once been in his days defying the police in Soweto and joining the resistance.

In all honesty, and despite his cynical instructions to iPhone Man about the fake news against Makojaene, it made him feel dirty inside.

And also, in all honesty, he had felt like that for years.

When the Sniper wandered through arrivals at Richards Bay airport and spotted Mkhize waiting, he sensed immediately there was something wrong. The ranger's demeanour and greeting was unusually subdued.

'Something up?' the Sniper asked, clasping his hand on Mkhize's shoulder.

'Terrible. Absolutely terrible,' Mkhize shook his head, eyes moist, 'I never thought they would kill our babies. It's as if they have stabbed us in our very souls.'

During the night, Mkhize explained, a heavily armed poaching group had attacked Zama Zama's carefully guarded rhino orphanage, a refuge and rehabilitation centre for rhinos and other animals who had lost their families because of poaching. The armed men had assaulted and taken hostage of volunteer staff, ripped out the security cameras and then killed two eighteen-month-old orphan rhinos, tearing out their horns, discarding the small, precious, bloodied carcases. One was killed instantly, the other survived, only to expire within hours due to his brutal injuries.

The two babies had been found at their mothers' carcasses, having been there for a week, only walking a short distance away to eat and drink. They had arrived at the orphanage with their mothers' blood sprayed all over their bodies, their smell putrid. For months they had been fed by bottles and then gradually prepared for returning to nature.

It had been a brutally efficient, obviously meticulously pre-planned operation.

The irony was the two had been due to have their horns removed the following week to try to protect them from ivory gangs. The tragedy was also that they had been nurtured and fed over the previous year and gradually prepared for life on their own in the wild.

'Sacrilege,' Mkhize said, 'How evil can these people get?'

Over the previous hours since he had been jerked awake and asked to inspect the sad scene, his mind had been going round in circles. How? Who? He recalled the persistent questioner guest in that group when he had first met Thandi. What was his name again? He looked up his notes in his smartphone. Van der Merwe, that was it, the guy Thandi had found really creepy. Then he had thought of his ranger colleague, the one who had attracted his suspicions before.

'Change of plan, we're off to meet the Owner. He doesn't think there will be a repeat attack on the main rhino herd tonight. It's like one of those terrorist attacks in London or Paris or Berlin. There's so much heightened security immediately afterwards, that's probably the safest time.'

The Sniper nodded in understanding as they pulled up at the Owner's imposing house, its old Cape Dutch–like gables and solidity dating from its days as the main home on the nineteenth-century farm.

There were the usual pleasantries, but the Owner wasn't his normal garrulous self.

'Isaac filled you in?' The Sniper nodded. 'Any thoughts?'

'Actually I had been wanting to discuss a different approach before this horror. Because I've been thinking maybe my role is not sustainable in quite the way it has been. Over the past few months, I've shot – what? Four poachers? And each time they've been a little more prepared. From what you've told me, the orphanage attack was like a military one. Don't get me wrong: I am not backing off myself. It's just that I think soon they are going to come in such numbers that I will be overwhelmed.'

'I agree, totally,' the Owner replied, 'so what do you suggest?'

'Well look, if they send a small army we will be overwhelmed. So we've got to be realistic. First of all, have you looked at drone surveillance? There are some pretty smart machines these days. Through my IT consultancy, I've got to know a young guy who's a real expert. Drones won't stop you being overwhelmed by firepower if the bastards just throw more and more heavily armed men at us. But they could massively improve our surveillance security, enabling us to pinpoint when and where they enter, and move to intercept them.'

'The other thing we must do is get trained dogs,' Mkhize interjected. 'They can track poachers much faster than people. In the Kruger Park, they sometimes set them free in packs, followed overhead by helicopters. There's a new canine training unit at the Southern African Wildlife College, which you should talk to.'

'But how come these dogs can do the job?' the Owner asked.

'Because they're trained to track human scent. You know, like dogs are trained to smell out narcotics. Usually they are cross-breeds of English foxhounds. They can also be trained to detect poached horns and guns.

139

You also get Belgian Malinois in the chasing pack to bite and pull down poachers. These bite into arms and won't let go, even if the poacher tries to swing them free.'

'Okay,' the Owner responded, 'SANParks have mentioned drones to me before. They're heavily regulated over game reserves to stop poachers easily deploying them. But tell me more, because we've got to do something – and fast.'

The three of them remained talking, testing all the angles, Mkhize adding his suspicions about van der Merwe and the Ranger. He got agreement to ask the Veteran to track van der Merwe and for Brown and him to keep the Ranger under surveillance as best they could.

The Owner concluded: 'Right, Isaac, please get a map of the reserve. Will you two go up to Joburg soonest and meet up with this drone expert? See if you can make a plan for me with all logistics and costs, please. And I will contact the Wildlife College to see if they can help us with some dogs. Keep me posted on van der Merwe and our Ranger.'

Just as the two were leaving, the Owner called out, almost as an afterthought: 'For once we won't be desperately short of cash. I had a call right out of the blue from one of our new African billionaires: he was so outraged about the killing of the baby rhinos he's pledged a huge sum for upgrading our security.'

It had taken the Veteran longer than he would have preferred to meet the Sniper, both because it meant a flight up to Johannesburg, and because he wanted to ensure the Sniper met both his two young assistants as well.

They hadn't talked on the phone: Mkhize had made all the arrangements, and he had planned the rendezvous carefully.

The Veteran had to assume he would be under surveillance, just like old times. So he got a driver to welcome him at ORT Airport – the same one he always used: a former ANC combatant from Soweto called Marshall – to drop him off at Nelson Mandela Square in Sandton.

First he had a coffee at one of the eateries surrounding the square at the end of which a large statue of Mandela loomed. Twenty seconds later a young African woman and an older white man came in separately, the Veteran affecting not to notice, instead scanning the square for a third watcher because there probably would be one. As he did so he pretended to read his favourite weekly paper, the *Mail & Guardian*. Appropriately, it carried a front-page splash on another presidential

140

scandal. He clocked a man wandering aimlessly about, possibly a tourist, probably not.

The Sandton City mega mall offered the Veteran plenty of scope – which was why he had chosen it. Retail shops galore – Gucci, Bon Ami, Bell & Ross, Dechamps, Jacana, Shimansky. Their opulence was in stark contrast to the squalor of the former township of Alexandra just nearby.

He chose Hamleys first and wandered through the shelves of toys, and afterwards Woolworths, trying on some trousers in a cubicle, squinting and checking his watchers were following. He changed quickly into a hat and different clothes, pulled from a carrier bag.

Then the Veteran simply disappeared, taking a lift into the car park where Marshall waited, engine ticking over, the by now bored watchers oblivious until over five minutes later, when they realised in absolute frustration they had been duped.

Meanwhile the old combatants, checking they weren't being followed, drove quickly to an address in Rosebank in a comfortable block of flats that had seen better days, where the Veteran dialled in a flat number on the security intercom.

'Hello?' the Sniper said.

'Your appointment, as arranged,' the Veteran replied.

A buzzer sounded, the door clicked open and the Veteran headed for the lift, smiling at the bored security receptionist, who hailed from the Democratic Republic of Congo. Almost everyone on front desks or in restaurants seemed to be from anywhere else except South Africa.

The Sniper's flat was on the third floor and the Veteran walked along a corridor from the lift, counting the flat numbers. He looked around. There was a nice garden below, with well-tendered shrubs, bushes and trees, an empty turquoise swimming pool glistening in the sunshine, an African gardener toiling over a multi-coloured flower bed, an old white man wearing a soft hat resting in the shade.

The two strangers greeted each other politely, if warily, each knowing the other knew the stakes were high for both. Sensing this, the Veteran quickly put him at ease.

'So you're the guy who was Madiba's protector when he walked out of prison?'

The Sniper nodded.

'Fantastic, I never knew you were there with your cross hairs trained on us. Or I would have been a bit worried you might be tempted to take a pop at your old enemies!'

'No chance! I was on duty, obeying orders,' the Sniper replied with a smile.

The ice broken, they quickly got down to business.

'What sort of gun do you use?' the Veteran deliberately asked, trying to put the Sniper (still rather tense, he noticed) at ease. Soon the two were discussing their weapons – their common language.

'So yours was an AK-47? The same as most poachers, known as "the deadliest gun in the world"?' the Sniper mused. 'Funny, isn't it? I remember our army instructors scoffing at it for being ungainly. They said its ammunition wasn't as good as other rifle cartridges, its barrel was shorter than our infantry rifles and it didn't have their range.'

'Yah, all true, but the AK-47 is simple and practical, especially for guerrillas like us in the ANC, who didn't have the professional training infrastructure like you guys do in state armies. The AK-47 gave us a lethal power to rival proper militaries. It sort of rewrote the rules by giving groups of fighters with modest skills and resources the capability to confront much better-equipped armies.'

The Sniper nodded. 'They say there are a hundred million of them in the world. We called it the "terr gun" – the weapon of terrorists – because it seemed every bloody revolutionary in the world had one.'

'Hang on!' the Veteran exclaimed. 'I was one of your bloody "terrs"!'

'Sorry, man!' the Sniper laughed ruefully.

The Veteran clapped him on the shoulder, joining in his laughter. 'But you are right in a way. The AK-47 did become a global symbol for guerrillas. Our sister liberation movement in Mozambique, FRELIMO, ensured it was included in the new national flag on independence.'

'In MK we swore by it. When I was asked to help the Irish peace process, and addressed IRA groups about the need to set aside weapons when an opportunity for peaceful change arises, I got them chuckling and at ease by saying that in over thirty years of the armed struggle "I had slept with my AK-47 more times than with my wife".'

Gradually, as their conversation continued, the Sniper was amused to note that he was being quietly and persistently grilled. That hadn't really happened since his military training had prepared him for light interrogation should he ever be captured. Which fortunately he hadn't been.

It went on for half an hour before they both relaxed and discussed the way ahead.

Outside in his cab Marshall waited and watched. He never asked and he never knew. But he was energised to be part of something. Just like the old times.

Moses Khoza frowned at the news.

His watchers had lost the Veteran. 'For Christ's sake, man!' he shouted down the line, wondering what on earth the Veteran, who often visited Joburg for political meetings, was up to this time. What had caused him to drop a tail? Normally – especially when he had a public-speaking commitment – he didn't bother.

But Khoza had more important matters on his plate. There were now open challenges to the President, not just the usual opposition sniping from the Democratic Alliance or the EFF, but from powerful forces within the ANC.

The Veteran was more annoying than threatening – for now at least. Meanwhile what to do about the president's internal opponents? They seemed to be mobilising with a new momentum and determination. He needed his people to find their weak spots by combing through their bank accounts, checking out extramarital liaisons, anything – absolutely anything – that could cause embarrassment if exposed. For the party conference was due at the end of the year, and that was when matters would be decided.

Clouds of dust billowing behind him, Mkhize drove quickly through Zama Zama towards Richards Bay and then via the N2 and N3 main roads on the 290-kilometre journey to Pietermaritzburg and Solly Naidoo's showroom.

He had been told by the Veteran to collect the modified rhino horn he had dropped off weeks before, having persuaded the initially deeply sceptical Owner of the purpose in order to get him to part with it.

Naidoo ushered him into his anteroom, waving away his nervous wife and handed him the horn. 'Please check whether it suits your purpose,' he urged.

Mkhize grasped the precious cargo and turned it over and over in his hands, searching intently for a telltale mark.

He couldn't find one. 'Is this the correct horn?' he asked, confused.

The small, hunched Naidoo beamed. 'Absolutely,' he said, 'come, let me show you.'

Cradling the tusk, he moved his fingers gingerly to a spot about twenty-five centimetres from its base. Mkhize looked but saw nothing.

Naidoo beamed contentedly again. 'Here,' he pointed, 'a small mark I have left for you, put your fingernail on it and see if you can feel the incision. When you do so, prise it open.'

Mkhize did as he was told, and yes indeed, now he could feel something, a small protrusion perhaps? He ran his fingernail along it, and tried to lift. A small flap suddenly opened, and there it was: the cavity the Veteran had ordered, precise, concealed and potentially lethal for the poaching syndicate once it contained the transmitter to track its whereabouts.

Mkhize wasn't a demonstrative man. But he hugged the smiling Solly Naidoo: now there was a chance, just a chance, to turn the tables on the bastards. He placed the horn gingerly in the box the old craftsman handed him and drove it carefully back to deposit in the Owner's safe and await further instructions.

He also seized the moment to brief the Owner on an exciting additional option. Steve Brown had alerted him to it: 'Isaac, these guys are the real business. Awesome,' he had said, animatedly telling Mkhize that a tight group of former US marines had formed themselves into Veterans Empowered to Protect African Wildlife, or VETPAW, an American non-profit organisation funded by private donations. The ex-soldiers had all served in elite military units in Syria, Iraq and Afghanistan.

They weren't mercenaries, however, because they could be hired for free, exploiting skills and experience gained in expensive US government-funded training and deployment. They were equipped with vehicles, trail bikes, assault rifles, sniper suits and radios.

'Whether it is cold or hot, day or night, they will be out there,' Mkhize told the Owner. 'They use skills and experiences from the US military in conflict zones, and have been working on a dozen private game reserves in the north of the country. They also train local guides and security staff. Some are British ex-special forces.'

'So, these guys really come pretty well for free? And they're top notch?' the Owner asked.

'Seems so,' Mkhize replied, 'why don't you have a chat with them? We have been doing okay up to now, but if we need real firepower they could be our only answer.'

'Good point,' the Owner replied. 'I will track them down and sound them out.' He paused and clapped Isaac on the shoulder. 'And thanks, you are irreplaceable to me in our fight.'

Intriguing, the Veteran thought.

A credible challenger to the President's favoured successor had emerged. He was a senior ANC figure, a struggle hero, trade-union leader and close to Mandela during the transition to democracy. With business experience as a beneficiary of black economic empowerment, though untainted by corruption or cronyism, he was beginning to attract broad support from both the left and the centre.

It was very early days, and the President had always been victorious over previous challengers, holding strong cards by dishing out patronage on a prolific scale, and maintaining a tight grip on the party machine. Nevertheless there were growing rumblings of discontent and a shift of allegiance toward the Challenger, for instance by trade unions congregated under the Congress of South African Trade Unions federation.

In one way the Veteran regretted not still being a member of the ANC, able to play his part in the coming contest. But in another he was freer to exert pressure from the outside. Which is precisely what he was doing. And according to his socialist reading of history, big change never came solely from within the system, but from external forces as well. And in his own way he aspired to be one of those forces.

CHAPTER 12

Van der Merwe decided to up the ante.

He was under acute pressure to get some more horn. He needed the money, Khoza needed the money. Maybe they should target another game reserve, for there were rhinos in plenty of other reserves.

But his pride had been pricked and he was damned if Zama Zama was going to beat him. That's why he had gone for the babies in the orphanage. That's why he was going for some big horns on his next attack. He had a good network down to Richards Bay, and if absolutely necessary he could get the horns straight onto a cargo ship, but that wasn't his preferred option: he liked to have direct control.

This time he would go for five or six shooters.

He activated his chain of command, gave clipped instructions, and returned to check on his wife, dozing vacantly as usual. His affection for her was real and remained touchingly undiminished. And he had persuaded himself that, had she even some of her faculties left, she might possibly approve of his continuing and stimulating liaison with her one of carers.

Just as he was turning in for the night, Mkhize's phone jerked him back awake.

It was the village handyman, speaking in Zulu as the two always did. 'Two young men left the village yesterday. Wouldn't say why or where they were going. Took some clothes and essentials. The mother is worried, and confided in me. Says they will be away for a while; she cannot say how long. Except they will be paid very well. They seemed excited, she said. I smell something bad – maybe a big attack, I cannot be sure.'

Mkhize checked for flights and then phoned the Sniper, and got him out of the bathroom. 'I know it's short notice, but any chance you can visit tomorrow evening? There's an SAA flight leaving ORT at 16:55, arriving 18:10 and it will be dark by the time we get to the reserve, so easy to slip you in.'

'Give me a minute.' The Sniper looked at his diary. Enough time to fulfil his work requirements before heading to the airport by around four the next afternoon. No appointments until mid-afternoon the day afterwards; no kid-minding either.

'I'm good to go,' he said, 'so long as I can get out early morning as usual. I will be knackered, but what's new?'

'Thanks, man,' Mkhize said. 'But if they come the night afterwards, will you still be okay?'

'I'd prefer not to stay on, obviously. But if I really had to I can rearrange things.' The Sniper didn't mention that he had lost a few jobs because of Zama Zama. Nor that his business couldn't afford to gain a reputation for unreliability.

The Veteran had something else up his sleeve – or, rather, someone else. And, he mused, she was in a way a more senior version of Thandi Matjeke.

Just as the Soweto school-student uprising of 1976 had spawned a new wave of activists, including Moses Khoza, so the township uprisings linked to worker agitation that followed five years later had attracted new recruits to the struggle. Some were trade unionists, like the charismatic miners' leader Cyril Ramaphosa, subsequently a key figure in negotiating a new democratic and inclusive constitution for post-apartheid South Africa. Others were freshly blooded through new networks, the most crucial being the United Democratic Front (UDF), an anti-apartheid movement that helped power the growing resistance towards the transformation that saw Nelson Mandela and his comrades released from their long imprisonment.

One of the UDF's new bloods was a woman never comfortable in the limelight, someone who never sought position or platform, but who was indispensable to the resistance. A person who worked the networks, was on personal terms with almost everyone in the UDF leadership, but whose real value was in her close connection to the grassroots. Police informers would report back to their handlers, but without anything tangible on a woman who appeared then disappeared, leaving the security services puzzled.

147

She would surface without fanfare in black townships like Langa in the Western Cape, or Mamelodi in Pretoria, or New Brighton in Port Elizabeth, transmitting messages up and down the chain of command. Or, rather, the non-chain of command. Because the UDF's distinctive difference from the ANC was that it had no recognisable command structure, no identifiable organisational hierarchy. It was an amalgam of people from churches, civic organisations, trade unions, student organisations and sports bodies, such a powerful force because it was so very difficult for the government to act against. It had no property or formal leaders for the police either to seize or ban.

If its convenors were detained – as indeed many prominent speakers were after the inaugural meeting – the UDF continued in limbo until its member groups next decided to activate it. The only policy it adopted was a watered-down version of the ANC's Freedom Charter, so bland that not even the government could find an excuse to object to or ban it, like it had all other resistance groups – though it certainly tried.

But effectively it was a surrogate ANC, as many of its members both acknowledged and welcomed. It included the Veteran's comrade Yasmin Essop, a Muslim by upbringing in the District Six area of Cape Town, famed for its strong community bonds, culture, music and radical politics. She, like all her neighbours, had been uprooted as a small girl when her family house was knocked down by the government to clear the vicinity for a white suburb with a panoramic view of Table Bay below and Table Mountain above.

With a reputation for uncompromising feistiness, she was teetotal in line with her faith but had long ago left behind mosque attendance and was, she supposed, lapsed, though still respectful of her parents' culture and customs of worship. To her father, however, she was both a mystery and a disappointment. As a teenager she had refused to wear a headscarf. That was bad enough. But for him worse was to follow. Easily bright enough to top her class, she insisted on going to Western Cape University, which by then was taking increasing numbers of Coloureds, and even Africans.

Worse still for her father, Yasmin had got involved with a young white Afrikaner, also a struggle activist. And that meant the sort of big, big trouble his family could certainly do without, her father berated her, jabbing his finger. He might well not have bothered, for although she took no comfort at all from fighting with her dad, she was stubborn, rather like he was, her mother – much more emollient and, on the side, rather proud – noticed.

When Yasmin told her parents she was getting married, that seemed the end of the world to her dad. But at least she volunteered to have a Muslim wedding as well, which pleased him. As for her new husband's Afrikaner mother, she was mortally offended, and wouldn't have anything to do with them. Then they had their first baby and invited her to see her grandchild, booking into a hotel nearby his ma's home so that she wouldn't have to experience the opprobrium of her white neighbours at the curse visited upon her family; if only her deceased husband had been there to help her through this family crisis, she mourned.

His mother first refused to meet up at the hotel. There had been so much traumatic change to endure: for the very first time in her life a president who wasn't white, for goodness' sake – though to her absolute amazement he had proved a godsend. She could just about cope with that, because her daily routine hadn't changed. The sun came up, the sun went down, and she went on much as before. But a granddaughter who wasn't white: her very own flesh and blood? That affected her directly in the most personal way. She was traumatised by the intrusion of the societal change right into the heart of her own family life.

Then, on impulse, she suddenly appeared at the door of their hotel room. Brushing past the parents without acknowledging Yasmin, she spotted her granddaughter gurgling in a carrycot. At least the baby was light-skinned, she thought, finding herself involuntarily picking it up and cuddling it, tears streaming down her face.

Later, she began babysitting contentedly, staying with the family, even befriending her daughter-in-law Yasmin, welcoming two more babies, and finally moving in with her son's new family.

Many years before, the Veteran had spotted Yasmin as she flitted unnoticed behind the lines of the resistance and had recruited her to carry messages for the ANC's military wing, MK, responsible in May 1983 for exploding a car bomb outside the Air Force HQ in Pretoria, killing nineteen and injuring 200, both black and white. She hadn't been happy with the collateral fatalities of an attack at a military installation – and let the Veteran know this in no uncertain terms. But rather than resentful, he was impressed – not least because he knew only too well that his underground world of intelligence, secretiveness and suspicion encouraged a culture of Leninist authoritarianism in which a leadership

149

command was always correct – even when, as palpably in this instance, it wasn't.

Later that year, in a daring mission that shook the white community, MK also blew up a section of the Koeberg nuclear power station near Cape Town, delaying its commissioning by eighteen months. Again, Yasmin had performed a vital role, this time delivering a package containing the timer, and this time she was a lot happier because there were no deaths.

Now she held a senior officer position in the Military Special Police Division of the South African Defence Force (SADF). And, unlike others who had come through the freedom struggle to hold well-remunerated positions, she shared the Veteran's intense disenchantment with those in power. But in her anguished conversations with him, threatening to resign, the Veteran had urged her to stay inside the system, just in case she could one day be useful.

And for him that day had come. He sent Major Yasmin Essop the text she was not surprised to receive, given the national political turmoil, and, sitting at her desk in SANDF HQ, she responded as he had hoped and planned.

For her there was never any doubt that she would reply. They hadn't seen each other for some ten years, as she had risen steadily through the ranks, only her husband in the know about the Veteran's blessing. Her three children – from their mid-teens to early twenties – were oblivious, and that provoked considerable disquiet within her.

A quarter of a century and more ago she had thrown herself into the struggle without a second thought. But now she had responsibilities: her children, to whom she was devoted, a large mortgage to fund with her professor husband, not just on the Johannesburg house, but their holiday home on the Cape Peninsula too. And her mother-in-law, increasingly frail in her late eighties, but admirably independent, if frustratingly bossy about their house, to which she had moved some years ago.

Major Yasmin Essop swivelled her office chair around from her desk and stared out of the window, contemplating the operational resources she commanded in SANDF. They were quite considerable, from helicopters and armed officers to surveillance equipment. Of course, she couldn't just do what she liked. There were operational codes and procedures that had to be followed. But she had a certain amount of discretion too – especially if there was a perceived threat to the integrity of the armed forces or any subversion of the state's apparatus.

Within a few days she would know what the Veteran wanted. She would coolly and hard-headedly make an assessment. And then she would act decisively – but with the care for detail for which she was renowned, and which had bred within SANDF her devoted following up and down the ranks.

Long before, they had agreed where and how to meet, should they need to.

The Veteran would text something about the weather in Joburg, Yasmin would answer and ask what it was like in Cape Town.

Their long-agreed venue was Freedom Park, standing in over fifty hectares of tranquillity on Salvokop, a hill outside Pretoria, the city to one side, the national icon of the Afrikaner people, Voortrekker Monument, to the other. It had been carefully designed as an emblem of bringing a divided and diverse nation together in the common cause of honouring all who had sacrificed their lives to win freedom. President Nelson Mandela in 1999 had described it as 'a people's shrine, a Freedom Park, where we shall honour with all the dignity they deserve, those who endured pain so we should experience the joy of freedom'.

In testimony to the national inclusivity of the new rainbow nation, on a 700-metre curved wall of names are inscribed all those officially recorded as fallen in war, from pre-colonial wars to the South African War (colloquially known as the Boer Wars), the First and Second World Wars, to the liberation struggle. Including 150,000 names, it is a sombre edifice.

The exact spot they had chosen to rendezvous was where John Harris, the only white activist executed in the freedom struggle (as hundreds of blacks were), was listed. Better, the Veteran considered, to meet in a public space like that – which might be normal for him to visit – than in a café or restaurant, still less a friend's house. Nevertheless, he had taken his usual precautions. After landing at Joburg's ORT Airport, he caught the Gautrain to Pretoria, carefully sweeping the other passengers but knowing any followers could be in neighbouring carriages as well.

In Pretoria he picked up a cab and asked the young African driver, music thumping, to take him around the city, giving him an initial R500 and saying he was needed for the day, with more to come. First, they drove up to Union Buildings, where he got out to wander around, nostalgically remembering the excitement of Nelson Mandela's 1994 inauguration. Then it was back down to Church Square and a look into the Supreme Court where the Rivonia Six had been tried and sentenced to life imprisonment, forcing Mandela and his close comrades to spend decades on Robben Island.

Each time the cab driver waited outside, on each journey noting his passenger looking constantly behind. Curious, but what the hell, the fare was good, and the guy seemed a decent sort.

Then the Veteran asked him to drive off the N1 highway into a multi-storey car park at Menlyn Park, the second-largest mall in Africa, with over five hundred stores. It was ideal for the Veteran's purpose, having access to the mall at various points from four parking levels containing over eight thousand bays. He asked to be dropped off near one of the mall access doors, noting that no car was following, and sent the cabbie away, asking him to drive around for fifteen minutes, then pick him up again around the corner in Lois Avenue.

The Veteran walked through the mall, perusing behind and alongside as he window-shopped before going into Exclusive Books, picking up and flicking through one or two of the new books on politics, before walking into Woolworths, pretending to be interested in men's trousers. He bought some underpants and quickly moved outside and onto the roadside, jumping back into the waiting cab and telling the driver to speed off.

Nobody followed, nobody watched. Of that he was certain now.

The Veteran checked his watch. Good. He should be twenty minutes early for their rendezvous, giving him the opportunity to scout around even more before they met. On no account could Major Yasmin be compromised.

She walked along the curved wall listing the many thousands of names of the fallen in wars.

Major Yasmin was alone, it was a working day and there were hardly any other visitors. She was rather embarrassed that she had never visited before, her eye caught by the bright 'eternal flame', surrounded by water, a place of contemplation. Reading the visitors' guide, she saw the reed sculpture, around two hundred vertical metal reeds up to thirty metres in height and visible from across the city. There were a few small groups of people sprawling on rolling green lawns, taking in the view.

Her military driver had parked up outside, as she'd deliberately made no secret of her trip. It was in her diary: homage to the war dead. What was secret was the real purpose, and she knew that the Veteran would never compromise her.

So much sacrifice, so much heroism; it wasn't easy to find John Harris' name among the seemingly endless list of inscriptions.

'Just a few metres on and a little up.' She was startled to hear the familiar voice, as she hadn't noticed the Veteran sidle up.

Yasmin looked around, noting he was decidedly podgier than when they had last met – and older. Much older. Tired-looking too.

'You're looking good,' he beamed, giving her a hug. 'Nice uniform. Very sexy.'

She smiled. Such a cheeky charmer, just like the old days. No sexism, or she would have bridled immediately. Just provocative mischievousness from a senior gent. And despite her middle-aged midriff bulges.

'Nice to see you again,' Yasmin said. 'And how are you getting on alone?'

His face darkened. 'Okay, but I miss her all the time.'

They caught up on family then found a spot higher up to their left where they could sit looking down on the park towards the water and the eternal flame.

'How are you finding work?' he asked, scrutinising her carefully.

'Quite enjoying the job. Interesting being a woman in what is still such a male set-up. But the politics is crap.' Her brow furrowed. 'So much pressure from the presidency to appoint incompetents. And their security guys are bloody dreadful, always snooping around. I can't be sure who they have bought inside my team. But there will be at least one – as part of the chain reporting up and down to the President's inner circle. He's more preoccupied with security than with governing.'

'Nothing has changed,' the Veteran sighed, referring to the President's reputation during the liberation struggle, Major Yasmin nodding gloomily.

'How much autonomy do you have?' the Veteran asked.

'Quite a lot, but it all depends what the operation is and what logistics and people are needed for it.'

The Veteran explained his problem. The rhino carnage, the collusion, the mini-war going on. And the opportunity, not just to damage the criminal syndicates but their political masters. He told her specifically about Thandi and Mkhize, also about the Sniper. But he had no real logistical support. Could she help?

153

Yasmin nodded sympathetically. 'Let me think.' She wasn't impetuous or rash. Serious work needed a serious attitude was her motto.

She scanned the park, considering all the angles, trying to anticipate likely problems.

The Veteran waited. He didn't mind, for he knew her of old. If she took a risk, she would calculate all the options and angles carefully beforehand.

'Right,' she said after a few minutes. 'Let me explain what I can do and what I can't. The most important thing I need is a good reason to act without first getting permission from my boss, only keeping him generally in the loop. Although he trusts me totally, there is all sorts of bureaucracy and process involved at his level and you never know who in the state, especially the security state, will poke their nose in. Also, there must be a military angle and you and I have to square that together, but the game-park owner has to be the one to call on my help so that I and my people have a reason to act that can be corroborated if necessary.'

The Veteran nodded. 'Completely. But there is one immediate thing I need.'

He explained the plan to insert a transmitter in the rhino-horn cavity and why he needed it to be tracked and all the people involved to be monitored and, ideally, apprehended.

'Not a problem, that's easily done,' she replied. 'We have a monitoring and surveillance capability. I can get you the transmitter and I can allocate a team to it. That's pretty routine for me. More of a problem is if you need any of my military police involved in combat, but even that could be solved, depending upon the circumstances.'

The Veteran also asked if she could supply handguns and machine guns – but only if needed. 'More difficult, but not impossible, as long as I get them back,' she replied.

Then the Veteran mentioned a name: Piet van der Merwe. Could she find out who he was, what he was? He gave her the ID number Mkhize had retrieved from the Zama Zama booking records. 'I'll get back to you soonest,' she said.

Then, by agreement, she left first.

He had been keeping an eye open throughout their encounter, but it seemed nobody had taken the slightest interest in the two of them.

Nevertheless, he was taking no chances. The Veteran dawdled for a while, looking constantly around as he peered at the list of names in the section of the wall devoted to the Second World War. As the minister responsible for the monument and for war veterans, he had taken a special interest in the Italian campaign, where many South African soldiers had served with distinction. Visiting some of the Commonwealth War Graves Commission cemeteries, the South African one at the Apennine village of Castiglione dei Pepoli stood out, set in a beautiful glade, a kaleidoscope of green shades with a sprinkling of brightly coloured flowers, birds tweeting in the sunshine. It was peace and tranquillity personified and such a contrast with the blood, death and mayhem that had consigned those men to be buried at the long rows of light grey gravestones now commemorating them.

Deep in nostalgia, the Veteran turned to go, walking around the two thousand-seat amphitheatre, down the slope to the pond surrounding the eternal flame, past the *Gallery of Leaders*, an exhibition of inspirational international and local leaders, and to the exit, where his cabbie waited, snoozing in the car. He climbed in, feeling proud that the government for which he had struggled and in which he had served had commissioned such an imposing, moving and evocative memorial.

Thandi Matjeke sat transfixed at the research.
It was horrifying. Three children were dying every day, a third of them killed by their mothers, mostly lone parents and almost exclusively black. Every six hours a woman was killed by her current or former intimate partner, with a further one in four women suffering physical abuse. Authoritative estimates had a woman being raped every thirty seconds, with some reports suggesting South Africa was the 'rape capital' of the world.

She'd come across yet another startling – perhaps for its constitutional implications even more ominous – statistic: there had been at least one assassination of a politician every month for the five years up to 2013. That meant at least sixty over the period.

Then there were the regular deaths of white farmers, killed in the name of redistributing land. She believed passionately in that objective: after all, the land had been brutally stolen from her ancestors, often at the point of a gun, by white settlers. But she certainly did not agree with that violent method. Since Madiba walked from prison in 1990, over one thousand white commercial farmers had been murdered, the Transvaal Agricultural Union of South Africa claimed to one news agency.

155

What was happening to her society? Was this the better world her grandmother had craved as she talked on her death bed? What would Nelson Mandela have thought? Especially when one of his successors seemed more interested in lining his own pockets than running the country. It reinforced her determination to help the Veteran in whatever way she could.

But this time Thandi was ignoring the Veteran's dictum not to protest. And she was taking Mkhize with her. He had never joined a protest march before, and left to his own devices, he wasn't at all sure he really wanted to. But he either went with Thandi or she left him to go on her own. That was it and there was never a choice.

As for her, she was pretty certain they wouldn't attract any attention to themselves. The President's Praetorian Guard kept their beady interfering eyes on all political protests against him – that went without saying. But protests against the rape and murder of women – why, the President claimed he was even in favour of those.

Mkhize wasn't used to big crowds like this, for many thousands of men and women – he couldn't tell how many – surrounded the two of them marching against the abuse of women and children in Pretoria. It was a Saturday, and they had gathered at Church Square, then to make their way to the Union Buildings.

'Not in My Name' adorned banners held by the marchers; one was thrust into Mkhize's hand by someone. Feeling awkward, he offered it to Thandi.

'No, it's important for you men to be carrying the placards,' she replied. As they walked, she explained, leaning towards his ear to avoid deafening chants from the marchers, that the hashtag #MenAreTrash had been trending on Twitter, with scores of women sharing their stories of abuse at the hands of loved ones and strangers. 'There's a real anti–male anger among women's groups. The more men like you front the protest, the better for us all.'

Mkhize listened intently as he glanced about the multicoloured crowd, noting with approval the presence of many African men like him. But he also felt the anger of the women. One of them actually shouted at him, as if he was to blame. Thandi shrugged her shoulders. 'Don't take it personally. It's a male problem,' she said, squeezing his hand, 'women don't rape, but rape by men is like a disease in the very soul of our people. And the problem is in the home, not on the streets. Shamefully, South

156

Africa has one of the world's highest rates of female deaths at the hands of their intimate partners. It's our husbands, boyfriends, lovers that rape us, batter us, abuse us, and kill us.'

She sounded angry now because she was, Mkhize noted, and she was in full flow.

'This latest horror – it's getting huge attention in mainstream and social media. Good, that's why we are marching. But it's just the tip of the iceberg.'

Mkhize nodded; he had read about the gruesome details of a recent murder and what shocked him more than anything was the callous power the murderer had demonstrated, as if his girlfriend was disposable. He was a rich black kid too, not some poor unemployed, embittered, destitute and desperate male.

They had had a heated argument in a Sandton nightclub frequented by the wealthy that deteriorated into a fight, and they'd left early, she never to be seen alive again. The argument continued in his luxury apartment in Sandton, where he killed her. Mkhize couldn't comprehend what the man had done, stuffing her body in a wheelie bin to get it out of the flat, then loading it into the boot of his luxury Mercedes and driving to his family home, where he picked up a tyre, acid and a container to buy petrol, then proceeding to a deserted area in the *veld* outside the city, where he burned the body.

She was a beautiful student, found two days later by a passer-by, who at first thought the body was a burnt mannequin. Later the rich kid was arrested and charged with pre-meditated murder.

Thandi continued talking and Mkhize had to tilt his head to listen, surrounded by the din of the march. 'Some say high levels of sexual violence have a lot to do with a history and a tolerance of violence in general, which was what apartheid was all about, of course. They say that it generated a type of aggressively repressed masculinity, which is also to blame.'

He tried to take this all in, but it was a lot to digest. This lovely girl next to him, holding his hand, in an almost protective fashion was opening his eyes to things he had really never confronted properly. His ranger life seemed an awful lot simpler and purer. Part of him wanted to retreat back there, but then he would lose her and also, he had to concede to himself, lose something much worthier she had stirred in him.

*

While he was up in Pretoria, the Veteran had fixed to meet up with Thandi. The timing was propitious because Mkhize was with her that day, and he found them still flushed with the excitement about the demonstration the day before, reminding him of his youth.

When he challenged her, Thandi quickly explained her reasoning, adding: 'There were none of the self-styled "war vets", none of the presidential heavies; it was more of a social protest than a political one.'

'Everything is political, Thandi, especially in these times in our country with community and political protests happening almost every day. Anyway, you can't be sure they didn't have spies on the march.'

He could see her bridling, Mkhize, he noticed, tensing as if to defend her.

'Look, you guys, I totally understand the cause. I would have been there marching myself. But I cannot stress too highly how vital it is you remain anonymous if you are going to be of any use at all to me and our project. You are my "deniable operatives". I need you to remain that way. Things are coming to a head. Please, please keep under the radar. They have eyes and ears everywhere.'

Thandi nodded glumly.

'Now,' the Veteran smiled, relaxing. 'This is where we are.' He summarised how he saw it, mentioning the valuable additional help he had secured, but not referring at all to Major Essop, only to 'another struggle friend' with a senior security role.

Mkhize filled him in on developments in the reserve, including the extra support promised to the Owner by the African billionaire, Thandi observed, partly with pride, partly intrigued at how authoritative and decisive Mkhize seemed in dealing with matters on his own turf. In most of the things they had done together so far she had been leading him. Now it was the other way around – and, she realised, she didn't mind at all: they made a good team, but were they a good couple, she wondered?

The Veteran's next appointment before he flew back to Cape Town was to meet the Sniper again.

The purpose was twofold. To introduce Thandi and to ratchet up the Sniper's involvement in the wider project. Thandi drove them in her parents' battered old Toyota to the Sniper's flat in Rosebank.

After reaching Johannesburg and crawling slowly for an hour through the seemingly endless traffic, they passed Witwatersrand University campus, the scene of student protests against fee rises, the Veteran telling them that's where he had studied in the late 1950s. 'It was an exciting time. Lots of us who studied there formed lasting friendships, joining the ANC, and in the case of some of us, the Communist Party too. Mandela, who studied law there for a while, explained in his memoir that meeting white students involved in the struggle for the first time made a marked impression on him because they were sacrificing their privileged lifestyle, whereas blacks like him were campaigning out of necessity.'

The Sniper greeted them warily: he hadn't been at all sure about meeting the Veteran the last time after googling him and realising that at the beginning of his career they had been on opposite sides of what had been drummed into him was a war. Despite the country's transformation a quarter of a century before, the past clung on to everyone like a limpet. Nevertheless, they had got along just fine.

The Veteran explained how he saw it: the poaching predicament along with the political unrest was changing rapidly, and he gave an assessment on why they needed to change in tandem. Then he stopped talking, a sympathetic twinkle in his eye.

'Any questions of me?' he asked.

The Sniper shook his head, then paused as if he was thinking afresh, brow furrowed.

'You are asking me to join an insurrection against the government? That's against all my military discipline. And I'm not a politico like you guys.' He waved his hand around his living room, past the Veteran over towards Mkhize and Thandi sitting together on his sofa.

'I'm not a political person either! I'm just doing my duty protecting rhinos,' Mkhize interjected, bristling.

'Everything is "political"!' Thandi exclaimed. 'What you earn, the value, if any, of your house, what job you manage to get, whether your air and water are clean, school and health standards: everything. You know what the Greek translation is for "non-political"?' she asked, pausing momentarily. 'An idiot.'

'Come on!' It was the Sniper's turn to get heated, standing up, fists clenched.

Normally he seemed placid, phlegmatic, very hard to rile, rock solid, Mkhize thought; now he was like a coiled spring.

The Veteran smiled. 'Now, now, you guys! We don't need to fall out. We're on the same bloody side!'

159

He gave Thandi a fierce stare and turned to the Sniper, patting him on the shoulder, which irritated the ex-soldier no end because he had never liked his body space being invaded. He wasn't the tactile sort, and involuntarily shook his shoulder as if shrugging off the Veteran.

'You don't by any chance have a beer, do you?' the Veteran asked, deliberately changing the subject, 'I could do with one after all this bloody heat.'

The Sniper, a natural courtesy bred into him from childhood, felt embarrassed. 'Of course I do. Very sorry guys, I should have offered one earlier,' he mumbled.

The tension dropped like a stone.

'Anyone else for a drink? I've got cold Castles in the fridge.' The Sniper looked around.

'Yah, please,' said Mkhize.

Thandi felt sheepish. 'Me too please, and sorry for my outburst, I didn't mean to offend.'

'No probs,' the Sniper replied. 'But politics is a foreign world to me; I just get on with my life.'

They settled down again, each holding an icy bottle.

'Where were we? I'm supposed to become a sort of guerrilla in our new democracy, am I?' the Sniper asked with a mischievous smile.

'No way!' the Veteran replied. 'That's what I was in the old apartheid days.'

'I know, bloody subversive – lucky you never got in my sights!' the Sniper bantered.

He could warm to this guy, the Veteran thought. 'Actually, you are a defender of the new democracy, a defender of the Mandela vision, and I am asking you to help us cut out the cancer that's destroying it.'

The Sniper looked quizzical, sympathetic again.

Continuing his theme, the Veteran said, low-pitched and calm, looking the Sniper directly in the eye: 'We are up against a ruthless, corrupt and self-serving clique who have captured the state apparatus and the ANC party structures. They don't care about the country, still less about the people – just themselves. We have limited resources but plenty of friends, you included, I very much hope.'

The Veteran paused for effect, and then added: 'We simply cannot do without you. And I'm never going to ask you to assassinate people. Just to be willing and ready to help us take out the ringleaders of this rhino genocide. They go right up to the top, in my view, though we need proof.'

He sat back in his chair and took another swig of Castle. 'Does that make more sense, or do you want to suggest some more limitations on what we might expect of you, some more no-go areas for you?'

Always try to put the person you are seeking to persuade in a place where they think they have the initiative, they are the ones whose counsel is being sought, the Veteran had learned over the decades.

'Okay, I can see what you're expecting of me better now,' the Sniper replied. 'Instead of being a sitting duck in Zama Zama, taking out the poachers, we follow the command chain upward and take *them* out? Get to the source of the problem, in other words?'

'Exactly. Got it in one,' the Veteran smiled.

'I can see that logic. But I don't want to be manoeuvred into being a hired gun. That's not me. Besides, it's illegal. I'm not prepared to go to prison, destroy my reputation and harm my family,' the Sniper replied.

'Totally agree. That wasn't what I meant. We'd like you to perform the kind of role outside the game reserve that you do inside. Rather than waiting for them to attack and trying to kill them, we follow the trail and confront or block them higher up the chain. If we can get them arrested, that's what we want. But if they retaliate with gun power to stop that, we need you to be prepared to intervene, and only if absolutely necessary by shooting, preferably not killing. We want the bastards in courts, not coffins.'

The Veteran leaned back and sipped his beer again, waiting.

The Sniper stared out of the window for what seemed an age; in reality it was less than sixty seconds, with Thandi and Mkhize spellbound in silence, the tension rising again, but this time in anticipation.

He worked it through his mind. All the angles. All the consequences. It was moral, noble even, to block rhino killers by shooting them in the reserve. Of that he was sure. Especially when he could disappear afterwards undetected. Mind you, that might not last. He knew he was on borrowed time – of that he was also sure. And there was a logic to the Veteran's argument. Stop being a sitting target liable to be killed if the luck swung or superior forces overwhelmed. He had been on a run that couldn't last – that was the salutary reality. So, he supposed, the choice in his mind came down to this cold conclusion: kill or be killed. Unless, of course, he pulled right out. But his sense of duty wouldn't allow that.

And he had a grudging admiration for the Veteran for not hectoring him, just gently leading him to what was the only real conclusion consistent with his values and his loyalties. He wasn't the sort to abandon allies.

'Okay then, I'm in,' the Sniper finally said.

'I realise it's a huge, huge ask,' the Veteran said quietly, 'but I am deeply grateful. We all are.' Thandi and Mkhize nodded vigorously. 'And I promise you this: we will never, ever force you do something you don't want to. It's about defensive protection, not offensive action. Always.'

The Sniper nodded.

'One other thing,' the Veteran asked, 'can you use a handgun? And a machine gun?'

'Yah, but I am not nearly as experienced or familiar with those and I haven't used them in decades, unlike my rifle.'

As the Veteran sat chatting with Thandi and the Sniper, Mkhize looked up from his phone and interjected. 'What's this about a Canadian special forces sniper in Iraq breaking the record for the longest-distance confirmed kill?' he asked. 'I can't believe it! He actually shot dead an Islamic State fighter from more than three kilometres away. Over three Ks? That's incredible.'

Looking down at his phone again, the Veteran intrigued, Mkhize continued, 'The bullet, fired from a McMillan TAC-50 sniper rifle, took less than ten seconds to travel 3,540 metres before it hit its target!'

'Yah, I read that this morning too. It's quite unusual for any secretive military unit to confirm a kill, but I guess they wanted to claim the world record for their guy,' the Sniper replied. 'The fifty-calibre bullet travels at around two-and-a-half times the speed of sound. But because of the enormous distance he used a spotter lying in hiding right alongside him with a laser and also a Kestrel weather meter to calculate the wind speed and humidity. It's pretty scientific. But the guy must have been very lucky, because that's an incredible distance, a kilometre more than the previous record.'

The Veteran abruptly changed the subject. 'But what would have happened had the first shot missed?'

'His spotter would have helped him recalculate the range and other factors before he shot again. Your spotter is as vital to you as a navigator is to a rally car driver,' the Sniper explained. 'For instance, if you incorrectly estimate the distance as, say seven hundred metres when the target is eight hundred metres away, the bullet will be two hundred millimetres lower

162

than it should be by the time it reaches your target – and you miss. The calculations to be accurate can be pretty complex. Especially if you're shooting uphill or downhill because gravity – which drags the bullet directly downward in a perpendicular direction, of course – comes into play.'

'But you have been much closer, surely, in Zama Zama?' Mkhize asked.

'Yah absolutely. I am used to shooting from much greater distances than I have been protecting the rhinos. Military snipers like I was don't normally shoot targets at less than about three hundred meters. Over longer distances we usually aim at the chest because it's larger and there are key organs, heart, and stomach and so on. But police snipers usually operate at much shorter distances, So they can obviously get a more precise shot at the head or the heart – like I have been doing for you guys.'

'Also,' the Sniper continued hastily, 'sniper fire can cause panic, damaging morale in the enemy if they cannot locate the sniper. Armies use us to put the enemy under constant stress. They don't know whether to move or leave cover. We're a psychological weapon as well as a lethal one. One of my army officers instructed me always to kill the second man in the line of advancing soldiers or guerillas so nobody wanted to follow. They say during the American War of Independence, undercover snipers were considered uncivilised by the British army. I suppose we are.' There was a rueful smile, almost a grimace.

'So what do you actually feel like – at the moment when you kill those poachers?' Thandi asked.

The Sniper's face darkened. 'Don't even go there,' he said, 'or I will stop helping. Frankly, I have hated it every time. I wake up with nightmares, trying to stop myself wondering if they have kids, wives and parents to feed. The only thing keeping me coming back to do it is the cause. The rhinos. And doing my bit to stop those mafia. I try to convince myself I am a servant of good values, not a killer. But sometimes in the early hours, lying awake, I really don't know what I am any more.'

A grim silence enveloped the flat, as if the others were sharing his pain.

'Any chance of another beer? Mine's gone straight down the hatch,' the Veteran asked.

The Sniper jumped up, apologising for not offering one sooner. Thandi and Mkhize declined his offer; their bottles were not empty.

Before they left his flat, the Veteran handed the Sniper a secure phone, the SIM card to be topped up as usual. 'From now on we communicate only by these.' Thandi and Mkhize exchanged numbers as well.

163

The Sniper closed the door on them, deep in contemplation. Despite his confession just earlier, he'd had a real buzz inside ever since the Owner had first engaged him. Now he was on a mission again. Now he was really valued again. He rarely, if ever, drank alone, but just for once he'd have another beer, maybe even more. He put on some music – R.E.M. 'Losing My Religion' blared forth – very appropriate, he thought.

The three were on their own now, and Thandi was always fascinated talking to the Veteran.

Their relationship was not so much father to daughter, as one of mentoring, Mkhize observed with affection. She would soak up the Veteran's insights and experiences gleaned from fifty years of struggle activism, of transformation, of serving in government and its aftermath. Always attentive and respectful, she would question and challenge, which the Veteran enjoyed. A perfect pupil, he thought to himself, though he would never dream of patronising her by confessing that, knowing the instant stormy reaction that would provoke.

'How on earth did the ANC get into this dreadful predicament?' she asked. 'I mean, its values, its traditions, even the policies adopted at its recent conferences are an anathema to the venal web of corruption and cronyism it got entangled by.'

The Veteran paused, then spoke.

'I've thought continuously about this and delved back into our long years in exile, trying to understand how the noble values of the struggle have been so badly perverted, sometimes by the very same people who were jailed for their bravery.

'Certain freedom fighters justify taking money – not brazenly like the president and his clique – almost as their entitlement. Having sacrificed a great deal and suffered in the struggle, they ended up poor, with a belief their country owed them. Others felt it was "our time to eat". For some, getting money only prompted an urge to get still more. It became addictive.'

'Yes,' Thandi interjected, 'but that didn't happen to Nelson Mandela, to Walter Sisulu, to Ahmed Kathrada, Andrew Mlangeni, Mavuso Msimang, and many, many other struggle leaders and grassroots activists. It didn't happen to you!'

'I know. But I don't think it is just a question of character flaws. None of us are saints,' the Veteran said.

164

'Okay, but those involved receive "struggle pensions" from the state, don't they?'

'Yah, and that is a lifeline for many, especially those who weren't prominent. But I come back to the need for a deeper understanding.'

'I think it is worth reading an article written in 1991 by Rusty Bernstein, one of the ANC leaders accused at the Rivonia Trial. It was titled "The Corridors to Corruption". He analysed the shift in Eastern European nations from revolutionary socialist fervour to institutionalised corruption. He also talked of factors he described as being "in embryo" in our own South African liberation movement.'

Thandi observed: 'So it was published during the period *after* Mandela and the Rivonia comrades were freed but *before* the 1994 elections when the ANC won and got into government?'

'Exactly, that's why Bernstein is so interesting,' the Veteran replied. 'I knew Rusty well and he wrote about the subtle process by which the sort of power that corrupts creeps up on us unnoticed, and we ignore the warning signs at our peril. He argued that unless we identified and eliminated the factors corrupting good honest leaders and organisations elsewhere – Latin American liberationists, for instance – we could well repeat the experience of their decline and fall.'

'I suppose,' Thandi observed, 'the problem was that none of you acted on what he was anticipating?'

'Exactly,' the Veteran smiled ruefully, 'We were so engrossed in, first, the serious problems of transition, then the exhilaration of taking power and finally the incredibly complex pressures of delivering radical change in government, that we didn't confront what Rusty had warned us about. And just look at the terrible price the ANC is paying, and the country even more so.

'There was a similar phenomenon in newly independent African states, made worse by the way the former colonial powers resisted liberation movements fighting for majority rule until the last minute, and in some cases sabotaged it on transition – like the Portuguese as they pulled out of Angola's capital, Luanda, pouring concrete into lift shafts.'

'But I thought Mandela acted against corruption?' Thandi asked.

'Yes, to his great credit he made a speech at an ANC conference when he was still president, warning them of the dangers of corruption and greed, and against the "careerism" of politicians who use their positions to make money. So he was onto the problem quite early. But none of us anticipated the sheer extent of barefaced greed, which subsequently spread like a cancer throughout all systems of administration and governance, led from the very top under this president. The saying "a fish rots from the head" fits very well here.'

Thandi seemed reassured that her hero Mandela had been on to the problem. 'Didn't he allocate part of his presidential salary to charity?'

'Yah. Mandela gave a third of his salary to the charity he established, the Nelson Mandela Children's Fund, which is still doing great work. But Archbishop Desmond Tutu criticised the new ANC MPs for accepting big salary increases. He quipped: "The government stopped the gravy train long enough to get on it." After that, Mandela announced a cut in the salaries of MPs and of the president.'

'But weren't the apartheid governments notorious for taking bribes?' Thandi asked.

'Yah, our ANC tried to clean up the rotten apartheid networks of bribes and the treats from the government, and the Bantustan governments as well. We also faced the problem of white entrepreneurs dangling bribes in front of politicians to acquire business footholds.

'But what really gets me is how the whole movement has been corrupted – involving many who had served in the liberation struggle with real courage and dedication. So many betrayals, the cancer spreading, so many previously admired comrades becoming supplicants to patronage wielded by a deeply corrupt leader. Integrity and principles going out of the window. Ego and ambition triumphing over what was bred into us in the ANC – serving the people, not oneself.'

Thandi noticed how suddenly old and exhausted the Veteran looked after this passionate peroration.

CHAPTER 13

Moses Khoza escaped to his office in the presidential compound.

The demands from home had been incessant. His wife wanted the latest Audi coupé so she could be one step ahead of her girlfriends when they turned up for their regular lunches. His eldest daughter was fed up with her iPhone battery running out of juice, and wanted him to buy her the latest model, which Apple had promised would have longer battery life. *No bloody wonder it ran out so quickly*, he thought: she seemed to be on it twenty-four hours a day. WhatsApp, Snapchat, Facebook – they were her life. It was astonishing she managed to do tolerably well at school, though he worried about her looming Matric exams.

The problem was that his bank account was running dry and there had been no recent cash coming in from the rhino horns. That source had frustratingly stalled, and he must chase up van der Merwe once he had cleared his overnight emails on the security intranet, accessible only on his office PC.

It was 06:30 and the sun was already rising on another bright Pretoria day as the guards waved him through the barrier and he drove round to park next to his office. The President would still be asleep, snoring gently, one of his wives by his side. Which one, he had no idea. He wondered whether the President did. He had to hand it to the old man – his libido seemed insatiable. For his part, Khoza had lost the zest; he was overweight, his wife was overweight and both fell asleep immediately on reaching bed.

He grabbed an espresso from the coffee machine, greedily slurping down the stimulant as he booted up his computer. At work he lived on espresso, at home on wine – which reminded him, he must order a few more cases from Macro to top up his dwindling stock.

An email from iPhone Man pinged into his mailbox, forwarded from monitoring at ORT International airport. The Veteran had flown in from Cape Town yesterday and flown back on the last flight out. Nothing much to be noted – except, iPhone Man reported, he had obviously left his phone at his home in Kalk Bay, where it had apparently remained switched on all day, so they couldn't use his service provider to track his movements and they had no idea where he'd gone.

Odd. There'd been nothing reported on the Veteran since the mugging – no media outbursts, no suspicious activity. He seemed to have gone to ground. Oh well, maybe the mugging had done the business.

No. Anybody can leave their phone behind – of course they can. But he knew the Veteran of old. His struggle comrade may be growing elderly, but he doubted he had lost his capacity for being coldly, calculatedly meticulous too. Better tell iPhone Man to up the level of surveillance on the man.

This time there were five.

They were semi-walking, semi-crouching in a line as they gingerly circled closer.

And as he'd anticipated they were heavily armed. Or at least the first four were: bristling with AK–47s. From what he could see, the last poacher seemed to have only a machete – though you could never tell.

The third one was in his cross hairs and he shot him cleanly through the head. Then he swung his night scope gently round to focus on the fourth one, shooting him in the chest. Instinctively, the first two had swung around backwards, when what they should have done was concentrated on the line of fire – exactly why the Sniper had shot poacher number three first, then immediately afterwards poacher four.

The Sniper picked the others off in turn, the first a shot to the head, the other, as he fired off a round, in the chest. He had been lucky: all four framed perfectly for him in the half-moonlight, probably two hundred metres away.

But the fifth man with the machete had fled amidst the carnage – which is exactly what the Sniper wanted.

The poacher half staggered, half sprinted in small bursts, dodging between trees – tamboti, bushveld gardenia, and closer to the ground, magic guarri, known colloquially as the 'toothbrush tree' because its young twigs were used to clean teeth. He scurried through bushes of red spike-thorn, which tore at his trousers, trying to follow a wildlife trail barely evident in the moonlight.

He was terrified of a bullet in his back, stunned by the way his four colleagues had been cut down with such brutal efficiency. He couldn't understand it. His heart pounded, his chest heaved.

All the poacher heard was a constant churn of animal, bird and insect life, of crackles and grunts, of snaps and cries, shrill, deep, low and high. But never the alien hum above, its eye in the sky relentlessly watching him as he lurched about, a man driven by terror of the mysterious shooter.

The rhino firefight had been around five kilometres from the safari fence, to which he now raced, confident he had lost any pursuers. But he hadn't. Mkhize and the Sniper watched him on a laptop screen through the infrared night camera on the drone's base – or, rather, followed the white image of the running figure, its heat source magnet-like with similar glimpses of the wildlife around him.

The two men were also relieved that the fence was relatively close, because the drone's range was limited to around five kilometres.

Instead of their previous practice of immediately departing the scene of the shooting and rushing the Sniper out of Zama Zama, they remained in the Land Cruiser, Mkhize operating the drone while the Sniper spoke on his phone to the Owner, who had deployed two cars out on the road to which the man was heading. Not to intercept him, however: to follow him.

No point in capturing, still less killing, the desperately fleeing poacher, for there would be more. Better to track him to his handler, if that were possible. But doing so might take the man well beyond the drone's range – hence the cars on the road, in one of which sat Steve Brown at the controls of a second drone, seeking to take over from the first one as it turned back to stay within operator range. It was a tricky manoeuvre, but one Mkhize and Brown had practised several times since the Owner had purchased a couple of drones and sent the two rangers on an instruction course.

'Boys' toys,' Thandi had chided Mkhize playfully as he proudly told her about his new skill on one of their secure mobile chats.

The hazy white figure on the screen was obviously tiring and should soon be visible on Brown's drone as it sought to rendezvous. Brown picked him up as he neared the fence and scrambled through: it was a secure barrier to large wildlife, especially predators, but not to humans.

Slipping into foliage the other side, the man stopped for the first time and listened for any pursuers. None that he could identify. He turned, relieved, and began making for the road half a mile away, the bush now giving way to easier, more open terrain.

His heart gradually stopped pounding, his terror subsiding. He had escaped and his money awaited, even if he had no prize of horns to give the man of Thai origin who anxiously awaited him. Another failed attack at Zama Zama. Which probably meant he wouldn't get another pay packet. *Well, that may be a blessing in disguise*, he thought, remembering the killings around him, as everyone else in the poacher gang had been shockingly cut down by a frighteningly accurate but unknown assailant.

He was ambling rather than running now, physically and mentally drained, anxious that the road seemed ever-more distant. It seemed like an age before he finally stumbled through a clearing. He looked around nervously, but not a soul was in sight as he turned right and started to walk slowly forward, past oncoming traffic only intermittent in the early hour.

Brown's ranger colleague followed the poacher all the way as their vehicle pushed slowly forward several hundred metres behind and completely unknown to the poacher, sweat congealing in the early morning cool on his foul-smelling body, the drone hovered above and slightly behind him.

In well under an hour, light would start to creep over the land, but for now the poacher was only highlighted by the momentary headlamps of vehicles whooshing by, their drivers uninterested in the tired figure; black people walked these roads alone to and from work all the time.

It was just under an hour along the road that he saw the car parked, as it should have been, under the yellowwood tree standing in a small clearing on the edge of the bush. He walked over and knocked on the window, the figure slumped on the driver's seat jerking awake.

The man of Thai origin opened the door with a welcoming smile, which soon drained away as the lone poacher explained what had happened, the drone creeping slightly lower and videoing their encounter, as well as capturing the dusty Nissan's number plate.

Immediately, Brown phoned Mkhize, who in turn called Major Yasmin, who'd asked a trusted corporal to carry out a confidential mission reporting only to her. His understanding was the target could be involved in illicit arms deals of direct interest to their Military Special Police Division.

The Corporal, experienced in surveillance, was already on the high-way, parked up in the direction of Johannesburg ready to clock the car as and when it drove by, and follow it. Meanwhile Major Yasmin had instructed a search to be made for the car owner.

The man of Thai origin listened to the details and made a sketchy note or two on a pad in the Nissan. Then, pleading privacy, he asked the poacher to get out of the vehicle as he made a call.

Van der Merwe answered immediately. 'Yah?' He followed up with a few questions. 'Definitely all four dead? And they were carrying AK-47s, as I had asked?'

Affirmative.

'Ask our poacher, is he absolutely certain there was just one attacker?'

The Thai rolled down the window and pressed the poacher several times to be sure. Then he rolled it back up and repeated the answer: 'He thought it was just one attacker, but he was so shocked and terrified that he was next to be shot, he cannot be certain.'

'Hmm . . .' van der Merwe pondered.

'So, do I still give him his pay packet?'

'Yah, of course, man! Thank him very much, say we're sorry he had such a narrow escape and we will be in touch.'

The man of Thai origin did as instructed and was soon driving off back home to Johannesburg, oblivious that about fifty kilometres down the highway the Corporal was ready to pull out and follow him.

Still traumatised, clutching his money and thanking his lucky stars, the poacher started thumbing a lift back to his village.

Van der Merwe always took pains to ensure that nobody connected to his subterranean work ever came to his house. So as usual he rendez-voused with the man of Thai origin in a shopping-mall car park, taking additional care to ensure his own car was on a separate floor as he hung about waiting for the familiar Nissan.

It was late morning by the time they met up and he climbed into the Nissan. The car park was busy as usual and although he vaguely noticed the Corporal's vehicle pull in nearby, he thought nothing of it. Nor — after they had conferred for nearly half an hour and he had retrieved the four gunmen's cash and paid the man of Thai origin — did he clock the Corporal (who'd meanwhile photographed them both) following him on foot.

171

He hadn't the faintest idea his normal meticulous routine of covering up his tracks was so badly compromised this time.

The Corporal followed him to his car on the floor above, noted his number plate and then raced back to jump into his own vehicle, the two finding themselves a couple of cars apart caught in the same queue for the exit barriers.

A few minutes later and the Corporal began following van der Merwe's BMW 320d to his house, while also calling Major Yasmin on his Siri voice-activated hands-free. He read out the number plate of the new target for her to run a check and was instructed to tail him all day if necessary. She would send a relief if needed, but she'd prefer to keep the mission to him alone.

Having activated a trace on the second vehicle, and discovered the names of both owners, Major Yasmin phoned the Veteran to fill him in.

'We may have found a couple of key leads,' she said, explaining the background. 'One seems to be a Thai immigrant who's lived here for a while; the other may be even more interesting. Piet van der Merwe: he has some sort of connection to military business circles way back. I am seeking more detail, but I may not get much more because I have to be careful in case he's got friends in high places. Meanwhile, see if any of your people have come across him.'

'Van der Merwe is such a common Afrikaans name,' the Veteran responded, thanking her very much, 'but I seem to recall Mkhize or Thandi – cannot remember which – saying something about someone of that surname arousing their suspicion as a Zama Zama safari visitor. A long shot, but I guess they might have all his details on the booking and entry form, so I will get that checked for you.'

'That would be very helpful, because I imagine SANParks regulations require ID on all guests,' Major Yasmin replied, promising to keep him posted if anything further transpired.

The Corporal followed van der Merwe, who was deep in thought as he drove home to contemplate his next move, oblivious to his tail.

Noting the address as he drove past the BMW disappearing through a security gate, the Corporal pulled up in the tree-lined suburban street, all the ample houses surrounded by high security walls on which were pinned private security-patrol notices deterring intruders: the norm for most Johannesburg householders in that sort of spacious suburban property.

The hours dragged by and the Corporal began getting restless. He was also hungry and tired, having made a start before midnight on the drive down to pick up the tail. Then his phone rang: Major Yasmin asking for an update.

It was now mid-afternoon and, as she had promised, a relief was on its way. When that arrived, he must go home, grab something to eat, have a few hours' sleep and come back on duty please. Meanwhile, when the new officer arrived, he would have a vehicle tracker for the Corporal. He should try to get an opportunity to attach it somewhere to the underside of van der Merwe's car so its movements could always be monitored.

Inside his house, Piet van der Merwe checked on his wife, giving her a peck on the cheek, though she hardly stirred from her bedridden somnolence.

A deep, soulful sadness ate into him: increasingly it was as if she wasn't there any more, only her physical presence remaining. Yet they'd been so close and she'd been so supportive of his work, which in the prime of his career had often been 24/7, with days and days at a time away. Despite temptations for them both, neither had cheated on each other – and he didn't consider his liaison with the carer to be cheating on her now either.

He texted Moses Khoza, asking for an urgent meet. The response came almost right away. Since Khoza was in Joburg that day, they would do so in five hours' time for a coffee at Mike's Kitchen in Parktown. They'd done that before, and if the weather was okay they usually sat outside in the garden at one of the tables under the trees, where they could chat with discretion.

Van der Merwe had ample time for a catnap followed by a shower and a meal. Refreshed, he got into his BMW, pressed the remote to activate the sliding gate to open, and pulled out into the road.

A little way down, the Corporal had returned to wait and watch. His relief had arrived earlier and he'd been home to grab something to eat and freshen up, but couldn't sleep so had returned to his task, the tracking device now ready in his car.

The Corporal pulled out a little while after the BMW, following it. The journey wasn't long, despite the traffic, and he just spotted van der Merwe pulling into the underground car park in Killarney Mall,

173

following him in. There were numerous cars leaving and entering and he was confident he would be unnoticed.

That wasn't his problem, however. Van der Merwe locked his car and walked into the mall, the Corporal hastily tailing him on foot. But then, absolutely frustratingly, he lost him in the crowd. One minute van der Merwe's cropped grey hair was in clear view, the next nowhere to be seen.

Without knowing he was being followed but adopting his normal procedure, van der Merwe had given the Corporal the slip as he exited the mall and climbed into the waiting Uber he had previously been online to order. They always seemed to arrive semi-instantly.

The Corporal scurried about, checking in all the shops and eateries, but the man was nowhere to be seen, and despondently he mooched back to the cars. At least he had time to check nobody was taking any notice and attach the tracking device under the offside front mudguard of the BMW. Just a shame he couldn't tag the man himself.

Khoza's meeting with van der Merwe was animated.

The security chief was highly critical of the Zama Zama failure. 'Are your men no bloody good?' he asked, 'I get them AK-47s, I authorise payment for greater poacher numbers and still they get mashed. What's going on? You are not on a retainer to keep failing, man!'

'We didn't fail with the rhino orphans,' van der Merwe mumbled, 'but they've obviously got some crack shooters guarding the adult animals.'

Then another thought struck Khoza. 'We've got someone on the inside of the reserve, haven't we? Your payments cover his retainer.'

'Yah, and I am chasing him all the time. But he has been kept in the dark over the rhino security. He doesn't know what's going on, just that the poacher bodies pile up every time we attack.'

Khoza cogitated, sipping his cappuccino, looking around at the other customers eating and drinking. Nobody seemed interested, and both he and van der Merwe had taken precautions, were sure they hadn't been followed, their mobile phones switched off so they couldn't be tracked to the same spot together.

'It's uncanny. We've never had so many fatalities during our attacks in any other game reserve. Four dead this time? Four. On top of every other time recently? And just one escaped – and he didn't even have an AK-47, did he?'

'No,' van der Merwe mumbled glumly.

'Something's not right,' Khoza persisted, 'but what the sodding hell is it? They have serious, expert firepower. Make sure you find out – or we will have to switch to another reserve, but that means researching it from scratch, and I don't have time.'

Khoza stared vacantly into space. 'The President's on my back all the time. He doesn't want to know the detail, just that the revenue keeps flowing from his mates in China and Vietnam.'

'Surely the President doesn't need any more money?' van der Merwe exclaimed, exasperated. 'He's looted so much for him and his family already.'

Khoza looked thunderous, veins bulging on his forehead as they always did when he was angry. Then he checked himself. 'Look man, we're all in this to-fucking-gether. No need for us to fall out.'

He reached out, patting his white compatriot on the shoulder. 'I trust you, as always, to do your very best.'

Then he passed van der Merwe a copy of that morning's *Star* newspaper. Tucked inside was the usual bulging brown envelope of rand. Tens of thousands of rand, helping to pay for his wife's care and to pay off his poacher subordinates.

They bid farewell and left separately, van der Merwe walking along the road past Wits Business School campus and switching on his iPhone as he did so to order another Uber. It arrived quickly and ten minutes later he was back in the car park climbing into his car, the Corporal watching and following him home as he called Major Yasmin. From now onwards they would be able to track his BMW wherever it went, just as they would the car of the man of Thai origin, because he also had one attached to his Nissan.

But Major Yasmin was very concerned about whether she could conceal this covert mission entirely from the police – or, more especially, the Police Crime Intelligence Unit (PCIU), for it was headed by a looting presidential crony responsible also for irretrievably damaging the National Prosecuting Authority. He was protected by the highest office in the land and earned over eight million rand a year, despite being 'suspended'. What this demonstrated, after the multiple corruption charges against the President were dropped, is that due process and the law weren't important – it was political power that mattered.

That PCIU head had done immeasurable damage, Major Yasmin

175

mused – and not just by helping a man who was completely unsuitable to be president, and then protecting him to stay there. But so undermining the Crime Intelligence Unit that he disabled the police service at the very moment when the country started suffering from exorbitantly high levels of violent crime. The PCIU was failing completely both to prevent mostly violent criminal acts, and to help catch the perpetrators afterwards. Because its chief was prioritising protecting presidential corruption and cronyism rather than fighting serious crime, people died, and people were robbed.

But all that meant she had to be extra careful on top of being careful anyway. Or she would be taken out as well.

Thandi was also very aware of the corruption that had spread like a bushfire through the state and its various agencies, from security to prosecutors.

But when the Veteran spoke to her on their safe phones, it was the money-laundering dimension on which he now focused her attention, patiently explaining the background in a very long call.

'The criminal network is not localised to South Africa. It is part of their transnational money-laundering network, including bank accounts at global financial institutions. All this is known, but what we need is hard evidence,' the Veteran told her. 'And I want you to get that evidence for me.'

'How on earth can I do that?' Thandi interjected, bristling in her usual chippy way.

'Hang on! I'm about to tell you! Always so impatient, you are.'

'That's what you usually tell me,' she muttered sullenly, unwilling to acknowledge he was correct yet knowing he was.

Ignoring that, he ploughed on regardless. 'I have a very good contact who works in the Reserve Bank. Another struggle comrade. Good guy. Diligent but angry. He has had finance ministers sacked by the President for trying to rein in the corruption, and the new one won't let him do his job any more. So he has turned to me for help. Can you please contact him?'

'Of course,' replied Thandi, her earlier irritation forgotten: it always came in a hot rush then expired, sometimes as if it had never happened.

'Good. Now this is what I want you to do. He must be protected, or they will sack him or maybe even take him out. So, you only make contact via messaging on WhatsApp.'

'Because it's encrypted?' Thandi asked.

'Exactly. Never ever call or text in any other way. Only via WhatsApp.'

'I'm impressed you even know about WhatsApp at your advanced age!' Thandi replied impishly.

'Cheeky bugger!' he laughed, continuing. 'You will know him only by this nickname he and I have contrived: Baard. You don't need to know his full name unless for some reason he wants you to. He's a Muslim, quite devout, so be respectful, but he's also a modern person, so gender equality is important to him, you will be relieved to know. Please take down this cell number for him. He lives and works in Pretoria, so it should be easy for you to see him soon. You contact him right away, please.'

'Sure, but what exactly am I to do with any info he gives me?' she asked.

'I was about to come to that. Because he's senior in the Reserve Bank, he can give you detail on the money laundering. A little came out in those hundreds of leaked emails a while ago. But what we need from him is an analysis in a form that can be easily turned into a draft speech.'

'Draft speech?' Thandi looked nonplussed.

'Yah. I was about to come to that. I know a friendly MP in London who's agreed to fix a debate to expose the detail we need and press the London and European regulatory authorities to take action against this money laundering. Because if we do that, we could cut off the spoils of corruption being shipped out of South Africa by the billion. But it's really crucial you get the material you want in a digestible, deliverable form. Financial experts like Baard know so much detail that they miss the wood for the trees. He must explain it all and give you a draft speech that you could easily understand and deliver yourself. If we are going to make the impact we want, our MP comrade will need it served up to him that way.'

Thandi nodded.

'So be patient with Baard. But insist that's what you need. Otherwise he tends to give you a pile of stuff that is impenetrable to anyone except a finance guru like him.'

The Veteran paused. 'Any other points I need to explain?'

'No, that's clear. When do I start with him?'

'Yesterday would have been good, but as soon as possible will just have to do,' the Veteran replied, pulling her leg.

'Cheeky monkey!' Thandi bristled, laughing. 'I will contact him right away.'

*

Van der Merwe thought long and hard about the uncomfortable conversation with Moses Khoza on why his poacher teams kept getting mashed at Zama Zama.

What to do? His Ranger was just as flummoxed as him.

There must be a rational answer. They'd never had this anywhere else. Or indeed in Zama Zama – at least until recently.

He poured himself a stiff gin and tonic. Ice in the tall slim glass first, then the lemon slice, then the gin flowing through the lemon, followed by the tonic.

Settling down on his verandah, he went through practical options. One by one they were rejected. Until he had a novel thought. He'd enjoyed his brief safari in Zama Zama. So why not enjoy another? And have another nosey around to see what he could find out? It had been productive last time, maybe this time too?

Van der Merwe scrolled over the Zama Zama website, his head feeling a little fazed after the second very large gin and tonic – but not sufficiently to prevent him accomplishing a booking and then going to the fridge in search of some food.

Since his wife had so tragically fallen ill, his meals had been erratically jumbled. This evening there was only cheese and bread plus baked beans, which he washed down with several or more glasses of Cabernet Sauvignon. Always KWV. That was the main brand in the good old days. Now there were all sorts of brands in the rainbow nation. But van der Merwe in his personal life was a man of habit and pride.

CHAPTER 14

'Thought you'd be interested in this, boss,' his office clerk called to the Owner. 'Another repeat booking.'

'Oh yeah?' he replied politely, 'that's good, must be doing something right. Name?'

He was thinking about something else entirely: raising money for the new fence covering the extended territory he'd acquired for Zama Zama.

'Van der Merwe, Piet, booked in last night. He was here earlier in the year.' She continued allocating the new bookings to their accommodation.

Ten seconds passed.

'Say that again.' The Owner jerked to attention from his subconscious.

'Aagh, boss you never listen, do you?' she said playfully as she retrieved the information from her PC, having moved on meanwhile; she gave him the dates. Next week.

He left the office and called Mkhize immediately, explaining the situation. 'Get our man down for those dates. I smell something bad coming.' Pausing to think, he added: 'Our man had better stay for the entire time at my house. I don't want him mingling with guests and bumping into van der Merwe.'

'Okay,' Mkhize said. 'I will get straight onto it. What about those volunteers? The ex-US marines: VETPAW, they call themselves. Shall I see if they can come too, to complement our normal guards?'

'Good idea, Isaac, see if you can get them. But don't tell the guards until the last realistic time that they will have company. I don't want any gossip circulating.'

*

The newly booked-in guest was meanwhile arranging another attack.

It would happen during his stay and it would be led by two of his younger ex-colleagues. Real pros from the shadowy life he had long led. Proper gunmen. One a Benoni guy, the other a South African expat from Mozambique: Momberg and Botha.

No messing any more. Veterans of the last years of the anti-guerrilla action, young guys then who still kept themselves in good shape, he had been assured when he contacted them. But a lot pricier than his regular poachers from the local townships, and there would be a couple of those locals along as well.

He'd consulted Moses Khoza, who was willing to cough up the extra cost.

And he'd be on site to wait and watch.

There wasn't much time, but Mkhize and Brown made sure they prepared well.

The drones were on hand for them both to operate. The VETPAW guys were very happy to come and asked only for accommodation to be covered. They would arrive the day before van der Merwe in their home cars, not their Land Rovers, because the livery would give them away, and book in like other guests.

The Sniper was also willing to come when Mkhize called, expressing his relief that VETPAW would be joining in. 'Frankly, I was worried because I've increasingly felt I was living on borrowed time,' he said. 'Only one stipulation. I want to meet the guys beforehand. In the reserve is okay for me if the timing works, but well in advance, because we must coordinate carefully. My instinct is they should replace the regular security guys. On the other hand, we need lots of flexible firepower on the spot, so maybe keep them on their regular watch as usual.'

'Can you get here the day before with the VETPAW guys?'

The Sniper consulted his diary. He could make a late-afternoon flight work. 'Only arriving at the airport evening,' he said.

'We will have to make that work then,' Mkhize replied, hoping to hell their assumptions were correct and van der Merwe's presence in the camp would coincide with an attack.

The tension was escalating because he'd also been alerted by his informant in the local township that something was up.

180

And if their fears were right, there could be an almighty firefight this time.

In the Owner's living room, the Sniper shook hands warily with the VETPAW guys.

But he soon warmed to them. 'Rob Clinton, Pat Kennedy,' they said, 'but call us Clint and Ken, everyone else does.'

There was an awkward silence as the Sniper said nothing. Just smiled. Then he spoke. 'Just call me Sniper, please guys. I prefer the anonymity.'

Mkhize and Brown looked embarrassed. The VETPAW duo looked at each other quizzically, then shrugged. 'Fine by us.'

Then they got down to work, with food provided. But all of them rebuffed the Owner's usual offer of beer or wine. He was the only one to consume both as the planning went on late into the night. It had to, because van der Merwe was checking in around lunchtime the next day. Everything pointed to the attack being that same night: barely twenty-four hours to go.

They had a map of the reserve spread out before them and a computer with Google Earth on the desk. 'Show us where the rhinos are, please?' asked Clint.

'This is the spot today,' said Mkhize pointing. 'I don't expect they will move very far by tomorrow night, as it's good grazing scrub and there's water nearby.'

'How far from the main road?' asked Clint.

Brown looked at the map. 'About fifteen Ks.'

'Hmm, bit of a hike. Where would you approach the rhino from?' Clint turned to the Sniper, looking also at Botha.

The Sniper thought for fully a minute, surveying the map, looking at the access. He was a cautious man, reluctant to commit himself verbally despite being quick and decisive in action. 'If they've got real pros coming this time – and let's assume so, because they must be seriously pissed off at all their failed attempts and fatalities by now – then probably from the direction you least expect. But that doesn't mean they won't get into the reserve at its boundary point nearest to the road. They could be dropped off there, walk in to a point about one K from the rhinos, then circle around. Probably if I were them I would do that, and come from the opposite side to the path in from the road.'

'If that's the case we will need to put one drone up near the boundary to spot them if we can and follow them in, with the second circling round the rhino site,' interjected Brown.

The others nodded assent.

Ken got up and asked Mkhize to zoom in on Google Earth so they could study the terrain. But they couldn't see much in the dark, so resolved to look at it again in the morning. It was getting late anyway and they'd all need a decent night's sleep. If their assumptions were correct, they wouldn't get any the following night.

Thandi messaged Baard through WhatsApp, and he replied quickly: clearly, he'd been expecting the contact, and they arranged to meet that same evening.

Best in a neutral venue, he suggested, asking her to rendezvous at a cheerful bar/eatery off the main road up to Lynwood Ridge, barely a mile from where he lived.

It was packed with families and beer drinkers when she arrived carrying a copy of that week's *Mail & Guardian*, as he'd specifically asked.

She felt awkward and shy: a young black woman on her own quickly attracting looks from the mostly white blokes in the noisy bar area. She didn't like walking into a place like this to meet a total stranger. She stood about, attracting even more looks.

Bloody men! Always the same. She didn't like it: feeling as if they were undressing her, even the ones with their wives or girlfriends. She looked around, feeling as if she should disappear into a hole in the bare wooden floor. Then a young black waiter sidled up, smiling broadly. She stiffened, thinking he was on the make too.

But he wasn't. 'Your host is sitting by the window in the corner there. He's expecting you. I will take you over now,' he said courteously, though she sensed the ogling still around her. And curiosity too from the blokes: just who was the lucky man?

Baard – real name Iqbal Vallie – rose from his seat. Thin, austere and in his mid-fifties, she judged. Strong grey flecks in his black hair. Glasses. Stooping. Rather bookish-looking. But with an engaging smile and a sense of traditional courtesy, as he waved her to her seat and pushed it up behind her.

With a mild stutter, he introduced himself and they shook hands. 'What would you like to drink?' said the hovering waiter.

'Diet Coke,' said Thandi anxiously, 'is that okay?'

'Of course! Sure you don't want a beer or a wine? I'm very happy to get you one,' replied Baard.

Thandi wasn't sure. She was desperate for a Windhoek lager and he hadn't ordered himself yet. Also, he was Muslim, might take offence.

Sensing that, Baard reassured her: 'I don't drink myself but almost everyone else around me at work does and I really don't mind.'

'Okay. I'd love a Windhoek,' Thandi stammered uncertainly.

'Excellent! I will have a Diet Coke.' said Baard, fingering the menu. 'Can you bring us the drinks and we'll look at the food,' he said to the waiter.

'Are you sure?' asked Thandi.

'Absolutely. My wife knows I'm eating out. Let's decide what we want and then get down to business. It's important we appear like just two more diners.'

The waiter came back with their drinks and Thandi waited for Baard to order first so she could be sure hers wouldn't be more expensive. In fact, they had chosen the same thing: the standard South African fish, grilled kingclip, together with mashed potato and salad.

'Right,' he said, 'let me remind you of the background first. We start with the Business Brothers around the President. You probably know about them?'

Thandi nodded. And for the next fifteen minutes Baard talked non-stop about a vast criminal network facilitated by the President's family and his closest business cronies to launder their illicit looting of the state.

'This network is not localised to South Africa — indeed it has been enabled by transnational money laundering, including bank accounts at global financial institutions like Bank of Baroda, HSBC and Standard Chartered. As you know, several multinational companies, including McKinsey, Bain & Co, SAP and KPMG have recently been implicated in facilitating this criminal activity. KPMG has sacked its South African leadership, and McKinsey also had a clean-out.'

'I work in the Reserve Bank, liaising directly with the Treasury, and some of us have tried to get our country's prosecuting authorities to take action. But they too have been compromised.'

Their food arrived, they tucked in, and Baard continued talking.

'Lots of the background is well known.' Thandi nodded. Nothing he had told her so far was exactly a revelation. But it was his clarity that made it compelling.

'I've put all this as context in the draft speech. Now we get to the important bit where we need help from your friend in Westminster.'

The detail started flowing out of Baard like a river in flood and Thandi could barely absorb it. She kept interrupting for clarification, which he provided. Then he got onto the money-laundering aspect, which was the kernel of the case for pursuing corruption abroad.

'Where does the money go?' she asked.

'From what we know, mostly through Dubai and Hong Kong. I'm going to give you in print and on a memory stick a full analysis within the draft speech. Don't worry about the detail. But importantly it will contain the names and IDs of about thirty of the individuals and their front companies, which we want investigated by international financial institutions and the regulators.'

He paused: 'Our mutual comrade has assured me you can get it to the friendly MP in London to deliver it in Parliament?'

Thandi nodded, and he handed her sheets of A4 paper, closely typed. She skimmed it. There were the names of the President and his key family members. Also the Business Brothers and their family members and associates. Incredibly, also, each of their ID numbers. 'How on earth did you get those?' she asked.

'Aah,' Baard giggled, 'best not to ask, but bear in mind I work in the Reserve Bank. We can access everything financial about everyone. The IDs are vital because they can be the keys to open the lock for the investigators. The great thing about the digital financial system is you can follow the money. Money laundering is not really about suitcases full of dollar bills any more. It can move around the world digitally and if you have some clues, determined financial detectives can often, but not always, follow the footprint it leaves.'

He gave Thandi a memory stick. It's all on there. Please get it securely to your MP in Westminster.'

'Is it in a readable form?' Thandi asked nervously, glancing at the bundle of printed A4 papers.

'I think so,' Baard replied, 'but have another look while I order coffees.'

She did, and although it all made more sense, would it really do so to Bob Richards, the MP in London? He would be getting it cold. She asked Baard a few more questions and scribbled in the margins of the text.

Baard was quietly impressed with her. Sharp mind, focused on the big picture rather than his world, where every small detail mattered.

The Veteran had urged him to be self-disciplined when he drafted the speech: 'Don't get buried in your usual financial undergrowth, Baard. I want this speech to make a big impact. You're not writing a submission to fellow geeks. Don't use bank-speak. Try to write it so even I might understand – and you know what I'm like!'

Baard paid the bill and Thandi thanked him profusely, then as he had instructed, shook hands and left first, while Baard observed the rest of the diners and drinkers. Still nobody interested in them. Just envious young male eyes following her out, boring into Thandi's back.

Women have 'rear-view vision' about males fixated on them, Thandi had often gossiped to her girlfriends. But it was always uncomfortable – unless of course it was Isaac, in which case she felt a glow.

There was a knock on the Veteran's front door, which he wasn't expecting.

Before opening, he peered carefully through the concealed video security camera he'd had installed. A uniformed police officer stood waiting. She was Coloured – frequently the case for police in the Western Cape.

The Veteran opened the door and gave a genial smile: 'Hi, how can I help?' he asked, speaking deliberately in Afrikaans, likely her first language.

Knowing full well the Veteran's status as a struggle stalwart, the officer looked uncomfortable, shifting her legs crossed over at her ankles. 'Sorry to bother you, sir. I have a letter for you.' She handed it over, looking awkward, her eyes fastened firmly on the doorstep.

The Veteran took it, noting it was stamped *TO BE HANDED TO ADDRESSEE ONLY*, as the officer handed him a form and pen to sign for safe receipt.

'Signing my life away, am I?' The Veteran almost felt guilty at the officer's obvious deep embarrassment and bid her farewell.

She quickly swivelled to go, then turned back equally suddenly. 'This has nothing to do with me, sir,' she mumbled before shuffling off uneasily – then veritably fleeing down the short path to the pavement where her police vehicle awaited.

The Veteran closed the door and quickly opened the envelope, pulling out a letter from the head of the State Security Agency he had once overseen as a Mandela government minister.

There were no niceties. He was simply warned in writing to 'desist from ventilating matters in media in a manner that may transgress the

185

relevant intelligence statutes or any other legislation'. The Veteran smiled to himself. They must be rattled. Then he smiled again: exactly the sort of warning letters the old apartheid Minister of Police used to issue to anti-apartheid activists.

The letter would not deflect him, he resolved. Others like him had heard nothing further once their lawyers had responded to ask what precisely they had said or written to transgress 'the relevant intelligence statutes or any other legislation'.

As she drove home in her dad's old Toyota, Thandi's mind was abuzz.

She went straight to her room and logged onto her laptop. Her parents had fairly good internet and she was IT proficient. She had all she needed, including Bob Richards' personal email and his mobile number for WhatsApp.

But first she downloaded Baard's draft speech from the memory stick and read it carefully. It wasn't at all bad. She fiddled with some of the text, absorbing her clarifying scribbles and simplifying some of the arguments – she'd picked up some of how to do this from her university course and then as a radio-production assistant – which reminded her: she was on duty early the next morning.

She looked at her watch. Already 23:00 hrs. And her alarm was due to go off at 04:00, so she could Uber to work in time to prepare the programme. Tough. She worked for the next hour until she was satisfied, saved the document onto her personal memory stick – she couldn't risk putting it on to Dropbox or even her own hard drive, in case she was hacked. Then she emailed it to Richards, checked it had appeared in her 'sent items' and deleted it from there too. Of course, that could be discovered if she was ever targeted by state security. But it was worth taking the precaution in case of a casual search.

Quickly messaging Richards on WhatsApp that the strange email was genuine, and he therefore need not worry about opening the attachment, she flopped down into bed, her adrenaline still surging, as she tried to think of Isaac to calm her thoughts.

Bob Richards rose early as always and brewed a rooibos tea, which he liked for its naturally caffeine-free taste and antioxidant content.

He was an early-morning person, liked to read, write and do emails before the rest of the world took over his busy MP life.

As his rooibos infused for several minutes he glanced at his iPhone. There was a WhatsApp message, the opening line of which immediately caught his attention. 'The Veteran asked me to contact you.'

He read it and switched to his inbox. There it was from Thandi Matjeke. Safe to click on, otherwise he'd have despatched it straight to junk mail. Soon he was poring over the gripping attachment. So, the Veteran needed his help. He reflected briefly, then penned an email to the Speaker's office, applying for an adjournment debate, stressing the importance of the topic.

If he were successful, his speech was already drafted – but some personal tweaking was needed to make it his own. He'd asked for a Westminster Hall debate. That way it would occur mid-morning, good for media attention. His mind was already planning ahead as he had his morning shave and headed for the gym, which opened at 06:30 – the only time he could guarantee to get there, because the diary filled up for the rest of the day. He would tip off *The Daily Maverick*, the South African online newspaper, which had a fantastic record of fearless investigative journalism. They wouldn't know him from Adam, but would surely be interested in reporting his speech. Frankly, it was dramatic. He was delighted to be able to respond to the Veteran's request, mentioned months before when he had no idea what it might be about.

It simply wasn't the same for him any more.

Although he didn't like taking breaks from the game reserve, going home used to be special. Seeing his mom and giving her the slightest of hugs; slightest because he wasn't the tactile sort. She longed to see him, and he loved her – of course he did. But he wasn't very good at showing it. Or rather he hadn't been until the change with Thandi. He was different now, he knew it.

His mother had been pleased to see him again. But now the visit was over and Mkhize had to race back to work, and his mom, he thought, was more emotional than usual as she waved goodbye. Maybe she sensed she was losing him?

He turned out of the village in the direction of the main road along the familiar minor road – tarmac now where it had always been dirt-rutted and slippery when it rained heavily – if it rained heavily, which wasn't often enough.

He'd usually travel back to his village by bus, but this time Steve

Brown had loaned him his Nissan Micra, petite but with a souped-up engine and a specially fitted throaty exhaust. Steve was a bit of a boy racer, had pretensions to being in motor racing. But driving Steve's prized car wasn't why he felt different either.

He used to enjoy the pointed brighteyed looks of the local girls as he walked from the bus into the village, down the main road if that's what you could call it. They would stand outside the little square government-built houses that had once been mud huts and smile invitingly at him, call flirtingly, giggling among themselves. He used to relish that, he must admit, used to bask in their admiring, longing looks. A few he'd been with, just occasionally bedded, always condoms to hand.

Now he wasn't interested. He smiled back politely, broadly even, but no longer invitingly. They were nice enough, some well schooled yet with their lives seemingly on stop; no ambition, no sense of higher goal than to own and obsess over their smartphones, no wider interests except to gossip about catching a man. Probably they wouldn't bother to vote. And the freedom struggle? What was that about? they would have asked. Had any even bothered to wonder?

Then he corrected himself. Opportunities for jobs and a better life were so limited in the locality it wasn't right to denigrate the girls he'd once mixed with – or the boys, for that matter, who were in much the same predicament, and who often drifted into petty crime.

Mkhize had changed and he simply didn't feel like he used to. He was uncomfortably embarrassed about this, because he was the last man to be patronising or elitist and he didn't want to turn his back on his roots, of which he was proud in an undemonstrative manner. Proud especially of his late father, who'd taught Mkhize so much despite himself progressing no further than primary school, the deliberate ceiling for most blacks under apartheid. Proud also of his mother, so unbendingly dutiful in such difficult circumstances, and now with his dad gone, devoted to her gospel church.

It wasn't even the distraction weighing on his mind of new research he'd just read, and the finding that for those born after 2012 there were half the number of species alive compared with those born in 1970. Over just forty years fully half of the globe's species had become extinct. Half. Mkhize had weighed that devastating statistic in his mind throughout the two-hour drive into the foothills, where his boyhood home was.

Other facts had been imprinted in his head. Although humankind represented a miniscule 0.01 per cent of all living things, since the dawn of civilisation people had caused the loss of 83 per cent of all wild mammals for food or pleasure, and half of plants by culling or eradication, radically changing the natural world. Just one sixth of wild mammals, from mice to elephants, and just a fifth of marine mammals remained from the time before humans became farmers, whalers or fishers and the Industrial Revolution started in the West, and began spreading through colonialism.

The havoc created by humankind had been pretty staggering, Mkhize worried. Farming, logging, overfishing and development had destroyed wild habitats in a mass extinction of life.

Yet although that seemed much more important than the village parochialism of his past, it wasn't simply his vocational calling that made him feel different – because that had been his life for quite a while now. None of that was really why he felt, and indeed was, a very different person from only a year or so ago.

Thandi was the reason. He smiled, a hard-on straining at his trouser fly as he thought of her while he pulled onto the main road towards Zama Zama, his old village increasingly distant.

CHAPTER 15

In their room in Richards Bay's Protea Hotel, where Momberg and Botha had booked in for two nights, they were preparing, their laptop screen also zeroed on Google Earth.

Regular gym-goers, they were fitness fanatics, muscled and slim despite being in their late forties. They were also what was known in the trade as 'khaki-collar criminals': mainly white Afrikaners who'd worked, or still did, in wildlife as landowners or organisers for trophy hunts – even as wildlife vets.

The so-called 'kingpin' of the khaki-collar criminals was a man called Dawie Groenewald, who'd run a safari tour company until twenty rhino carcasses with their horns missing were found buried on his farm. In 2014 he was put on trial in North Gauteng High Court. The case was repeatedly postponed, but he was subsequently indicted by United States prosecutors.

Huge, formerly hunted areas in Africa were now emptied of wildlife and were returning to pastoralism, disproving protestations by hunters that their sport protected biodiversity and farmer encroachment. In any case, there were increasingly no trophy animals to kill in former hunting areas. Organising hunting to self-fund wildlife conservation, popular from 1970 to 2010, had therefore run out of road, and so Momberg and Botha shifted their focus.

The Ranger had tipped them off about the spot where the rhinos were likely to be. They'd enquired about the routes taken into the reserve by van der Merwe's earlier missions and consulted the poacher with his machete, who'd been the sole escapee on the previous one. He gave them local advice – though very much against all his instincts because he'd been

190

terrified out of his mind by the ruthless firepower they'd confronted last time. Only after his money had been doubled and paid in advance had he agreed to accompany them, together with several other local poachers.

They had also interrogated him repeatedly about what had happened that night. Initially he wasn't that helpful. He described how his heavily armed colleagues had all been killed.

'Exactly how?' they asked him. 'Just shot so they died immediately,' he replied.

'But tell us exactly what happened. We need to know precisely to stop it happening again,' Momberg probed gently, only too aware the man was sweating with terror at the memory of his own narrow escape.

He scratched his head, dredging for the memory, which he'd blanked out.

'First to die was the man third in our line. Then the fourth one, right in front of me, because I was last. I thought I was next. But then the first two died just as they turned around to look.'

'Are you absolutely certain that is what happened? That exact order of the deaths?' Momberg asked.

'Yah, boss, because I couldn't understand it. I thought the man in front was the bravest because he'd be first to be attacked. I thought: Why wasn't I killed too?'

Momberg and Botha looked at each other knowingly but said nothing. They didn't want to, didn't need to. Each just knew. Classic sniper tactics. Killing in a way precisely to bamboozle the enemy and sow maximum confusion in those precious split seconds before retaliation could occur.

So that's what they were facing. A professional. Maybe even one of their own. Someone they could even have served alongside. That upped the odds considerably.

Momberg and Botha calculated the options. Then they decided upon their plan.

The rhinos were munching peacefully in the sunshine.

Only weeks before there'd been an addition to their group – a tiny one. The mother had dropped it carefully and the newborn had slithered out gently. As his mom turned around, the red placenta tailing untidily from her, she began nuzzling and stroking him as he writhed almost comically on the ground, trying to make his legs work, trying to get up in his new life, his skin silky and moist. Eventually, gently prodded

191

by her horn, he had struggled upright. Well, sort of upright, flopping unsteadily, wobbling as she then turned and lay on her side, encouraging him to feed on her milk.

Mkhize had been a lucky man, the envy of the ranger team, because, spellbound, he'd witnessed the birth. And filmed it to place on Zama Zama's website for promotional purposes. It had gone viral on YouTube.

The baby weighed over sixty kilograms and would remain with his mother for two to four years until the next offspring was born. If it lived that long, though there was no purpose in a poacher killing it, because babies were born without a horn. That only become visible after about a year, and took some seven years to grow to its full length of between nearly a metre and under two metres.

Better to let it grow well into adulthood, then kill it for its horn.

This one flopped engagingly around its mother. White rhino females and their young associated in groups across their home ranges, with adult males territorial and essentially solitary. As the baby grew more confident over the next days, it wandered off, only to be cuffed by a gentle horn and brought back close. Her horn was multiskilled. Not just for maternal care. But for defending her territory. For defending her calf from other rhinos and, especially, predators. For foraging, digging for water and breaking tree or bush branches to reach food.

As the baby rhino began growing into a toddler, he was oblivious to the mortal danger his mother faced.

Two weeks after he'd had the email from Thandi, Bob Richards MP rose to speak. He had about fifteen minutes of the half hour allocated for the debate, leaving time for the government Treasury minister to reply.

There were few MPs in the Westminster Hall debating chamber that morning. Just him, the minister and the minister's dutiful private parliamentary secretary, also an MP. But the media section was packed because Richards had taken the precaution to speak to as many as he could and given them the text of his speech in advance.

The chamber was oval in shape, set in the old Grand Committee Room up the stairs in the corner of historic Westminster Hall, the oldest building in the Palace of Westminster, where Charles I had been tried for treason and sentenced to be hanged, his severed head mounted in the ancient ceiling, where tennis balls belonging to Henry VIII had reputedly been found wedged. Westminster Hall is huge with a magnificent roof.

Over nine hundred years old, around it gradually developed the rest of the British state: Parliament, the law courts and various government offices. It acted as the kingdom's legal and administrative centre for several centuries and is now the place where the lying-in-state of monarchs and consorts traditionally takes place.

In its Grand Committee Room, which could hold around one hundred people, Richards began with the usual courtesy praising the chair of the debate, a Conservative MP from the Speaker's Panel (though it could easily have been a Labour colleague), from which were allocated chairs of legislative committees and Westminster Hall debates. It was in some ways a tiresome ritual with an element of phoniness to it, but part of the etiquette of the occasion.

Then he turned to the subject. 'If I may begin by explaining my own interest in this topic for debate today: my parents were active in the British Anti-Apartheid Movement and as a teenager so was I for the few years before the system was overthrown and Nelson Mandela became president.

'He set very high standards. Maybe nobody could hope to live up to those. But what we have now in South Africa is totally traducing Nelson Mandela's legacy and the values for which so many of us fought in the anti-apartheid struggle.

'Running South Africa today is a vast criminal network, at the top of which is the President, his family and his closest cronies, the Business Brothers. They have been looting the state on a prodigious basis. But this criminal network is not confined to South Africa. Over one trillion rand have been illegally laundered by a transnational money network, through Dubai and Hong Kong, by British headquartered or located banks. Also London-based are the global corporates Bell Pottinger, McKinsey, Bain & Co and KPMG, all also implicated in facilitating this financial crime activity.

'The Business Brothers came from India and within fifteen years were among South Africa's very richest businessmen, with a huge empire. They employed the President's wife and his children, doing so in the name of "black economic empowerment". Actually, it was nothing of the sort: it was elite empowerment for themselves and all the President's cronies and relatives.

'They "captured" the South African state with corruption and crony-ism, plundering taxpayer resources on an industrial scale. In consequence, economic growth has plummeted, international investor confidence is rock bottom and state institutions have been hollowed out in that great country.

'I am therefore asking the Chancellor of the Exchequer to ensure UK law enforcement and regulatory authorities investigate this and also request all UK financial institutions to review their exposure for the following individuals and entities – though not limited to these.'

Richards then paused, the moment dramatic, and began reading out the thirty names he wanted investigated for money laundering. Then he turned to read out a list of fourteen enterprises (mostly 'shell' or front companies) linked to the Brothers, suspected to have been set up for the purposes of transnationally laundering their illicit proceeds.

'Can the government also please request the authorities responsible for proper financial regulation in Dubai and Hong Kong to stop this immediately? And refer this to the Serious Fraud Office for investigation and the Financial Conduct Authority too?'

His time up, Richards sat down and the minister responded with a mixture of the polite, the half-positive and the bland.

But Bob Richards wasn't worried. He'd got everything on the record. And it was indeed explosive. Soon both the UK and South African media were running the sensational revelations, able to repeat the names and institutions, safe in the knowledge they couldn't be sued because they were reporting what had been said under parliamentary privilege.

The Veteran, Thandi and Baard, each watching separately online in South Africa, were thrilled. Baard felt tears welling up. After years of them undermining the integrity of the state, to the point where they'd captured the Treasury, at last he'd been able to hit back at the bastards on a global stage.

Someone else glued to the PC on his desk was certainly not thrilled, however. Moses Khoza was furious.

He called in his subordinates, including iPhone Man. 'This MP obviously received insider information. Must have been somebody in the Reserve Bank. The detail is too precise and those names, too. The President wants us to find the mole and eliminate him.'

Khoza paused, thinking for a moment. 'And if we find the mole, try also to find out who else knows this MP. See if our IT security can hack the mole's system. See if anyone can get into the MP's IT and discover where he got the information.'

194

'But that's hacking the parliamentary IT of a friendly country, boss,' iPhone Man reminded him.

'Sod it! See what you can do anyway,' Khoza replied tartly.

The Sniper had an uncomfortable feeling about his latest assignment.

Yes, he had some real pros with him, for a change. The VETPAW guys were good, knew their stuff. No egos, just cool, matter-of-fact, expert.

But he'd felt for a while his time was running out. Maybe because – the zest of the Zama Zama missions apart – his life still wasn't going anywhere much. He pined after his previously settled family existence, yet realised he must have been a failure. The shock of his wife telling him – quite of the blue, at least as far as he was concerned – that she couldn't cope any more and he must move out, still haunted him in the small hours.

Yet, he wondered, would he really have been there for her with this rhino-protection work? The hours were brutal. The secrecy essential. And the buzz was obviously integral to his DNA: it gave him a real sense of purpose to his life for the first time since his army sniper days.

Something else weighed heavily on his mind, and he didn't much like to admit it. He was a trained killer. Not for satisfaction – not at all, but for the wildlife of his heritage, for humankind, for decent values, indeed, for his country or, rather, for what he yearned for his country again to be. The country of Madiba, whom he'd once feared as a 'terrorist'.

And here he was again, preparing to kill – or be killed. Once he was out there in the reserve – listening to the grunts and groans and shrieks and calls, sensing the stealth of the predator and the eternal vigilance of the prey, sweeping the vista with his special night-vision binoculars – it was him or it was them. It was binary.

But there was no contest in his mind who would win . . . Or was there?

A limited number of civil servants in the Reserve Bank had access to the kind of detail that Baard had supplied, and he knew he would be under scrutiny.

So he had deleted all email, even WhatsApp, contact with Thandi, the Veteran or anybody else involved in getting the information to the British Parliament. But on the President's instructions, the intelligence services were crawling all over everyone, including him, for he was known to be an associate of the sacked former finance minister.

A fastidious man, he decided to get his affairs in order and – without telling her exactly why, because he didn't want to make her vulnerable as well – to make his wife fully aware of the danger he might well be in. Just in case.

Clint and Ken had made their plans in close consultation with the Sniper. Despite a certain reserve about him, they had increasingly warmed to the man. He was serious. He was professional to his core. He was dedicated – and, because of all of those attributes, was much like them: prepared to risk their lives for the greater good, as they had done before in service of their country.

In a way they were all soldiers again together.

The Sniper had proposed that he change role from the one he'd adopted these past few months. The two of them should get as close to the rhinos as he'd always been, while he would draw back, try to get an overview, waiting for the unexpected, positioned to take out any attackers in a way they might not expect.

Previous clashes had always been pretty close to the rhinos. If, as the Sniper sensed, this attack was different – had to be different, because all the others had failed and the enemy, even if mercenary, certainly wasn't stupid – then he, indeed all three of them, had to be different as well.

The Sniper would hole up a couple of hours in advance of Clint and Ken at a vantage point. They would creep in afterwards, much nearer to the animals. All three would be in constant contact via special earpieces and microphones clipped close so that they could advise each other. The quality of the VETPAW equipment and the upgrade from his previous lone missions came as a welcome boost to the Sniper's morale.

On previous occasions, the poachers had entered by the same route, from more or less the same drop-off point on the main road to wherever the rhinos had migrated. On this occasion he was convinced they would try something different.

But, Clint responded, certain parameters were fixed. The road, for example. VETPAW had studied this carefully. Access was the key for poaching. Both access and egress. The advance and the retreat, equally important to any poacher mission. Clint explained: 'I read a 2012 report about poaching in the Tsavo National Parks in Kenya, and another about the Democratic Republic of Congo. Apart from obvious factors, like density of elephant or rhino, road access pretty well always tops the list for poachers. In our case these guys will come in from the usual main road and plan to leave that way too. Some experts say that as much as eighty-five per cent of poaching takes place within a hundred and fifty metres of roads.'

Therefore, they concluded, consulting Mkhize and Brown as well, they should put one drone up along the perimeter near the road, and the other up scouring the area over the rhinos.

'We'll have to be lucky with both these devices, because its hellish difficult using a drone for spotting guys in the bush at night unless you know roughly where they are,' Brown interjected, 'so don't rely entirely on us.'

'Explain more, please,' said the Sniper.

'Basically we scan live video from a thermal-imaging camera attached to the underside of the drone,' Brown said. 'It looks for the heat signatures of the poachers stalking through the bush. But it picks up heat signatures from animals too, and some of them are nocturnal, moving about. So I will be a bit like I am with a PlayStation, toggling a special video-gaming control, zooming and swivelling the drone's camera.'

Clint added: 'VETPAW uses a new drone system, Bat Hawk. It can operate up to forty kilometres from the command-and-control vehicle, so we can easily cover the whole area we need in Zama Zama. We've brought one and its operator in to assist us here, but, to maintain surprise, only later tonight. Inside the vehicle there are three large screens displaying moving maps and live video feeds. That's where our operator will be sitting.'

'And I will be operating our drone in the area between the road and the fence, the VETPAW guy the Bat Hawk nearer the rhinos,' said Brown, 'but remember ours has a much more limited range, much more limited.'

'That doesn't matter,' said Ken, 'having a big range like the Bat Hawk is only any good if you can spot the poacher. You've got to find him first. So your local drone will be vital too.'

'And if, as I suspect, we face some real professionals tonight, won't they hear our drones?' asked the Sniper.

'Probably not,' replied Clint, 'some are silent; others have whirring propellers that mimic the sound of bees. That can be a problem with elephants, by the way, because they are terrified of bees. So I'd be very surprised if any of the poachers heard or spotted them.'

'Yah, fantastic,' interjected Mkhize. 'But remember there's nothing to beat people on the ground. We must use this technology, of course we must. But you cannot ever replace humans. Also, drones aren't foolproof.

197

Gusty winds, hills can make them difficult to operate. In Australia about one in five drones, used by farmers and in mining, have been attacked by wedge-tailed eagles, which actually destroy the drones. Incredible, isn't it?'

Clint, Ken and the Sniper were taken with Mkhize's engaging wildlife passion and enthusiasm. But now they focused on the task in hand, making sure their guns were oiled, cleaned and checked one last time.

After testing their new communications gear, they were each ready to go. The Sniper's earlier uneasiness had diminished as the action drew nearer. They were better prepared, better equipped than ever.

But so would be the enemy.

Momberg and Botha were also finalising their plans.

They would separate and fan out, each with African poachers alongside them nearer to the rhino patch. Then make their approach from different directions – hoping both to spot the guards before they were spotted, and to confuse any sniper or gunmen of the kind they anticipated from the reports of previous failed attacks.

They had never failed before. Admittedly they weren't getting any younger, and they'd vaguely talked about retirement because all their training had taught them that ageing meant you were on borrowed time. Yes, the older you got, the more experience and canniness you acquired. But there was no getting away from it, you also lost that razor-sharpness of trained youth.

Yet success on this attack would bring their biggest fee yet. Paid always, they insisted, not in rand but in dollars.

Baard was immediately placed on a list of suspects in the reserve Bank.

It wasn't a long list, and when the security services stopped him at the entrance as he was leaving for home one evening, he was shuffled into a side room.

Their questions were aggressive and pointed. He was known to be a friend of the 'disgraced' former finance minister. Why had he leaked this information to the MP? Didn't he know it was an offence to disclose confidential personal information like that? It was treasonable to implicate the President and vicious to smear his family.

They'd accessed his office computer but found nothing incriminating there. They'd checked his personal phone texts and calls through his mobile provider Vodacom, on the pretext of a criminal investigation. Nothing there either. They now demanded he hand it over to look at his WhatsApp messages and calls. They flicked through. Nothing there either, because he'd deleted Thandi and the Veteran as contacts – indeed, anybody now considered a political dissident. His phone was handed back over.

Despite his steadfast denials, they pummelled him repeatedly with a barrage of allegations. But Baard stayed calm. He was by temperament a quiet, reserved man, studious even, and his placid response infuriated the security trio even more.

'You can leave now,' they said sullenly, then added menacingly, 'but behave yourself.'

Afterwards they called Moses Khoza.

'No joy. The officials we looked into with the kind of access needed had no apparent motive, no previous record of dissent. Only this guy is a known traitor. If it's anyone inside then it must be him. But we cannot find any fucking evidence.'

Khoza thought long and hard.

'You still there, boss?' asked iPhone Man.

'Yah, for Chrissake. Okay. First find out if he has had any contact with the Veteran, if he's worked with him. Meanwhile, get him sacked. Even if he hasn't done this, he's obviously an enemy of the state.'

Moses Khoza grimaced to himself. Yes, he was well aware he'd used exactly the same label apartheid security had applied to him: 'enemy of the state'. But this was different. This was a democratically elected major-ity African government, not an undemocratic, white-minority apartheid one. Very different, he convinced himself. Of course, it wasn't the same. Apartheid was an evil tyranny.

Nevertheless the motivations of the security services, albeit now black- rather than white-dominated, seemed remarkably similar. That discomforted him a little but it didn't dissuade him enough.

Baard had taken two other advance precautions.

First he'd kept a written list of key contacts, hidden at home, and when he got there he immediately WhatsApp-called the Veteran and Thandi. Second he'd spoken to an old associate from the accountancy firm in which he'd worked prior to joining the Reserve Bank in 1994 under the Mandela government, and was immediately offered a job should he need

199

it. Not least because his insider tax and regulatory knowledge could prove invaluable to clients, especially high-value ones.

Then he told his wife what had happened. Although she knew nothing about his material for the MP, she wasn't really surprised. Just so worried that she couldn't sleep at all that night.

He, by contrast, slept flat out. A man content with having done his duty – whatever the consequences.

As so often, the local poacher was essential to their task.

Momberg and Botha were equipped to the hilt with lightweight machine guns, handguns and knives. They had night-vision glasses. They had everything they needed – except the all-important, indispensable local knowledge.

The poacher from the local village was in the lead. Before the game reserve had been established, he'd known the terrain like the back of his hand. Where the main wildlife paths were. The dense bush to avoid. The water pools and the rivers. The dry gullies for shortcuts.

He loved the area, but resented being unable to get work in Zama Zama. Dozens from his village had done so. But he'd been unemployed for a while. Poaching was his breadbasket. He knew it was dangerous, but his life didn't count for much anyway. He was close to the wildlife, loved the animals, but if you couldn't feed your kids, what alternative did you have?

He'd met up with his fellow African poachers arriving from the Johannesburg area, and briefly got to know them. They'd then rendezvoused with Momberg and Botha, who'd quietly exited their hotel rooms, taking everything with them. They had prepaid so as not to draw attention to themselves by checking out after they'd day-slept for some hours. Their plastic key discs were on a desk in the room.

There hadn't been much of an opportunity to pre-plan properly, but the black poachers were just as impressed with the professionalism of the two whites as Momberg and Botha were with the black poachers' determination and the purposeful way they carried their AK-47s.

For the two hardened pros, the post-apartheid era meant entirely new relationships with blacks who were, under the new Constitution, their equals, whereas in their formative youth blacks were decidedly subordinate. Their racism, sense of racial superiority, wasn't consciously adopted – it was inbred. They had only known blacks as inferiors.

Their attitudes also reflected those of the majority of whites, who knew nothing about what was happening to their black compatriots right on their doorsteps, rather like the inhabitants of Dachau village right next to the Nazi concentration camp who claimed ignorance of the gas ovens. The great South African journalist Allister Sparks once wrote that whites 'lived inside a cocoon that apartheid had spun for them'.

But Momberg and Botha had adjusted to the new era without as much as a blink. So they had to show respect? No problem. Had a black president? What the hell – did it really matter? They still did the same jobs, lived in the same largely white suburbs and mixed in the same exclusively white circles of friends. Yes, they'd both been apprehensive about majority rule, but then they realised life for them went on pretty much as before.

They began carefully discussing their plan to advance together, then separate into two groups, getting nods of approval.

'Tell us a bit about the immediate area surrounding the rhinos,' they asked.

'I haven't been there for a while, but I think they are grazing slightly above and away from a pool of water where they go to drink and roll in the mud. There's a hill rising above the water on one side and on the other a flattish area, which then starts rising up as well,' the local man said.

'How much bush, trees and so on?' asked Botha.

'Quite dense, lots of tamboti trees, lots of thick bush everywhere up the hillside and also below, surrounding the flattish area, which contains some bushes and a few tamboti, as well as plenty of grassy patches.'

'Tamboti? Poisonous to man!' exclaimed Botha. He didn't like the sound of that one little bit.

'But not to rhinos. They thrive on tamboti leaves.'

The team were dropped off at dusk, slipping out of their vehicle, which had pulled well off the road and out of sight so as not to attract attention.

No talking if at all possible; just hand signals from now on. Their trek into Zama Zama began. Another human assault on wildlife in its natural habitat.

It was dark when Baard drove home from the bank in Helen Joseph Street and pulled up as usual outside the security gate which accessed his garage driveway in Lancia Street, situated in the comfortable but modest Pretoria suburb of Lynnwood Ridge.

He pressed the clicker to open the gate and it slid slowly sideways.

Navigating his way in, however, he missed a shadowy figure slipping in too. Baard switched off the engine. But before he had time to climb out of the car where he'd parked on the driveway, a man wearing a balaclava jumped roughly into the passenger seat and barked: 'Don't move!'

Wearing rubber gloves, he grabbed Baard's arm and pulled him around in the seat, levelling a squat gun at him. 'Your future is in your hands. We know you were the source for the MP. Just tell us the names of your intermediaries and we will leave you alone.'

Shocked and terrified by the gun, Baard tried to collect himself: 'Don't know what you are talking about.' Say nothing, he told himself inwardly. Say nothing.

The intruder was beside himself, battering Baard with accusations, threatening to reveal all. But somehow, the more he was threatened, the more an inner serenity subsumed Baard's terror. That infuriated balaclava man. Shouting, 'Answer, answer!' he waved the gun wildly at Baard, who'd never faced a lethal weapon before.

Baard lifted his arm as if to wave the gun away. In the heat of the encounter, balaclava man, misinterpreting the gesture as an attempt to grab the gun, pulled the trigger.

The silencer masked the sound of the bullet, which tore into Baard's heart, killing him almost immediately.

Balaclava man was aghast. It wasn't meant to be like that. He felt Baard's pulse, scrabbled around in panic for the clicker to activate the gate and slipped away unnoticed.

His wife had cooked a nice roast lamb, and he'd opened a Cabernet Sauvignon from one of the vineyards above Hermanus along the coast, two hundred kilometres to the east of Cape Town.

The girls had already gone to bed, though were probably still fiddling on their phones rather than going to sleep.

Moses Khoza took the call rather grumpily, and moved out to the verandah.

'What! You actually shot him?' Khoza was stunned. A relaxed evening had suddenly turned into a horror show.

His wife called: 'Don't let your dinner get cold!'

He got a grip of himself. 'Was your gun issued by our security?'

'Yah.'

'To you?'

'Yah.'

'Anybody see you waiting around the house or leaving?'

'Don't think so. It was dark already and I parked the other side of the block.'

'Apart from the bullet, did you leave any DNA?'

'Don't think so. I wore rubber gloves.'

'Right,' Khoza thought quickly, 'get rid of the clothes you were wearing and the gloves and shoes. Throw that gun somewhere it won't be found – a dam or river would be good. Hide the balaclava somewhere else entirely, or preferably destroy it. Get home after all that soonest. Just in case you ever need an alibi.'

What a bloody disaster. He slipped inside the house to join his wife, jerking his attention back to her. Well, sort of.

His mind was racing, but the Cabernet Sauvignon she'd already started on was good. Maybe they'd need another bottle of the same.

Momberg and Botha systematically, continuously scanned around, ahead and behind as their group followed the local poachers who'd estimated their trek at around three hours.

Working outside in the bush was their life. It was what made them tick, gave them their discipline, their purpose, their self-pride. Rhino horns and elephant tusks were their trade and eliminating anybody who tried – usually unsuccessfully – to get in their way was what they just had to do. They would never admit to being labelled 'poachers'. They were professionals – 'bush professionals' – and nobody was better.

The moon was bright enough to reveal their whereabouts, but not too bright to reveal them. Just about right, they smiled at each other, confident they would crack another attack just as they had so often before. It was routine for them. A job.

And they knew they were good at it, which was why, as van der Merwe had found out, their fee was near exorbitant. They never negotiated a rate, simply informed enquirers what it was in US dollars. The Chinese and the Vietnamese always tried to bargain, but Momberg and Botha never responded. If you want to hire us, you can – on our terms. If not, no problem, somebody else would – and always did: they were rarely out of work. Their problem was getting necessary breaks: necessary because the hours on a commission were onerous, the stress high, and they needed to recharge, sleep and rest in between to keep razor sharp.

But because they prided themselves on their professionalism, being repetitively, suspiciously alert was ingrained. Also ingrained was their sense of superiority, which others saw as arrogance and they saw as proficiency. It had worked for them, ensured they were always taken seriously, respectfully – sometimes even feared, which they considered wasn't a bad thing.

In company, over a beer during a *braai*, they would tell jokes, swear, and be one of the guys. They would chat up women who were drawn to them both, sometimes in turn. They even compared notes after sleeping with the same woman. Both divorced, single and childless, they were brothers in arms. Proud of being a team.

Momberg and Botha trusted each other with their lives – and there weren't many, if any, they could say that of.

Brown had nearly missed them.

He'd been toggling the drone for an hour and getting frustrated, patrolling the drone up and down a couple of hundred metres in from the roadside, when he spotted a strong thermal image – just caught a movement, not so much a flash as a smudge. He zeroed in, and there, to his relief, was the group. Five of them, as far as he could tell.

He relayed the information on to the team, the Sniper already long in position. Clint and Ken readied themselves to move in. They didn't know whether the poacher gang also had a drone, but they doubted it. The VETPAW Bat Hawk had been hovering above and around the rhinos for a while and there was no sign of another drone. Nor had Brown spotted one where he was.

The Bat Hawk was moved to try and link up with the oncoming gang. They reckoned around three hours before the poachers reached the vicinity.

For Momberg and Botha, the night was near perfect. Not much wind, in fact hardly any. Clear vision but the moon not too high. Dry. Cold – of course, it always was at night. They had lightweight thermal clothing, which didn't restrict their physical flexibility.

They were making pretty good progress, so far startled only by a warthog, which appeared suddenly in a small clearing and bolted like hell immediately it saw them.

Botha had worried about drones. He knew they were being increasingly used by game reserves, but neither of them could sense any. He still worried because drones weren't easily spotted. Still, their key source in the reserve had been specifically asked to check and had reported back he hadn't spotted any or picked up any gossip. That was encouraging, if not certain.

No problems – so far – as they traversed parched grass, scrubby bush and dry river gullies, the hard ground still a little warm and partially reflecting the pounding daytime heat.

Five hours earlier the Sniper had been brooding.

Although this time was very different, with the VETPAW guys and all their special gear, one thing at least was the same, he ruefully thought. You had made your plans meticulously, advanced painstakingly carefully towards the rhinos and had psyched yourself up. But the enemy might never show at all that night.

It was quite different from his soldiering tasks. There you were typically advancing on a known target. But this was the very opposite. The target was advancing on you.

Assassins could never hate their targets. He'd been tutored about that. Feelings, emotions, got in the way of the task, obstructed, distracted. Hate was a wild card; the Sniper remembered his instructor burning that into him. It must never be about whether you like or dislike the target – or targets, in this case.

The purpose was what mattered: to take him, her, them, out. It was a target, not a person. The enemy who had to be stopped, killed. Or else the mission would fail and the Sniper would be a failure when he had been ruthlessly, carefully, schooled never to fail. That was his benchmark, pure and simple. There was success – or there was failure. No in-between. And that was where it got personal. Not emotional. Just personal. For if he failed, he probably wouldn't survive.

He had found a place. It wasn't obvious, and that was why he'd chosen it. On every previous occasion before he'd been quite close to the fifteen-tonne rhinos. That had enabled him to cut down the advancing poachers before they had time to attack – though there had been that incident when he'd been fired on first.

This time his place was above the giant animals. He'd holed up the other side of the watering hole from them, on the hillock – *kopje* – that swept up from the pool. Anybody advancing from behind him would lack cover because there was hardly any concealment on the slopes, and in any case they might slither, so were unlikely to approach that way. He was within a clump of rocks with a slight overhang, which prevented any shot on him from above and behind. Also, the *kopje*'s surface was, where not rocky, for the most part quite loose. So he'd probably hear anybody trying to come down from above well before they spotted him.

Or so he hoped.

His position meant he was further away – perhaps two hundred metres from the rhinos instead of under one hundred as before. But that was nothing for the Sniper. He'd hardly have to calculate for any wind- or distance-induced swerve of the bullet. The main risk, he reckoned, was the incoming poachers getting in a shot on the rhinos before he'd spotted them. But hopefully Clint and Ken would have prevented that, because they were in the kind of close positions he'd adopted before.

The Sniper had grown fondly attached to the rhinos, almost as if they'd been his very own. The baby – toddler, really – was quite comical. It scurried and scampered mischievously like all little ones do, human or animal. Its mother kept trying to shepherd it with her tusk, prodding and pulling, but her child was a handful: inquisitive rather than naughty, exploring new boundaries continuously as she irritatedly tried her best to curb it.

Two hours walking without incident, and Momberg and Botha were into their groove.

Each one of these jobs – and they were veterans of scores – was different. Yet there was the same intense concentration throughout and the same adrenaline rush as the target neared.

They had fear – always. Fear was the guardian of life on dangerous missions like this. But doubts – never. They thought of themselves as invincible. Used to playfully labelling themselves 'the invincibles' over beers with admiring friends – especially girlfriends.

Earlier the same evening, the Ranger was frustrated and seething.

He knew something was going on. No question about it. Yet he hadn't a clue what it was. Mkhize seemed constantly preoccupied. Brown as well. And van der Merwe was on his back every other day, threatening to chop his retainer.

He never used to be asked to do the dawn safari walks, which were the preserve of Mkhize and Brown. Now it seemed every other day his manager called to say it was his responsibility, together with a back-up colleague, to escort the sleepy customers out.

Time to bring things to a head. He couldn't go on like this, not knowing where he stood – and not being on the inside track. The Ranger resolved to ask for a one-to-one with the Owner, but little did he know that's exactly what the Owner had also hoped for.

When their meeting happened a day later, he was astonished that the Owner was so supportive. Even offered him a beer, which he politely refused while the Owner sipped one, asking: 'How can I help you?'

'I'm puzzled, boss,' the Ranger said.

'Oh?' the Owner replied looking genuinely interested – as indeed he certainly was.

'Yah, I know something is going on. Other rangers seem so very busy. They must know. But I ask, and nobody tells me!'

The two men had a heart-to-heart for five minutes, and the Ranger was impressed at how suddenly valued he seemed. His moodiness had lifted. Then his morale went sky-high.

'I was so pleased you came to see me, because I had wanted to ask you to look after something rather special for me,' the Owner smiled conspiratorially, 'but you've just told me you are carrying too much on your shoulders, so should I task another ranger?'

The Ranger had never had a conversation like this with the reserve's chief. His pride brimmed. 'No, please boss,' he pleaded.

'But I can only tell you if you say in advance you will do it for me. I'm sorry if that seems unfair, because I suppose it is!' the Owner looked pleadingly at the Ranger. 'It's got to be completely confidential between me and whoever I task. But you've just told me in effect you're carrying too much for other rangers, Isaac and Steve especially?'

The Owner paused. The Ranger's mind was in a whirl. The Owner sipped his beer contentedly reading the mind of the Ranger like an open book.

'I will do whatever you wish me to, boss,' he mumbled.

'Good man!' the Owner leaned over and again patted him on the shoulder, 'I thought I might be able to rely upon you. But guaranteed confidentiality between us on this, hey?' he asked again, knowing full well he was wrapping the Ranger around his little finger.

'Of course, boss! Guaranteed. Totally and absolutely, boss.' Apartheid may have long gone but relationships of this kind between a white boss and a black staffer frequently remained paternalistic, to say the least.

The Owner stared at him for what seemed like ages but was only around ten seconds, as if wrestling with a decision – which in fact he had long made.

'Okay, then,' he said finally, beckoning the Ranger to follow as he got up and walked down the corridor from his office.

Stopping in front of a built-in cupboard, he showed the Ranger where the key was hidden on top of a strip of architrave, retrieved it and opened the door. Inside were numerous valuables, right in the centre of which was a familiar sight to the Ranger: a rhino tusk, this one in excellent condition.

The Owner lifted it gingerly, cradling it in his arms. 'From a rhino who died of old age,' he explained, 'a lovely specimen. And to think people will kill for this.'

He put it back, locking the door and inserting the key in its hiding place. 'Whenever I am away from the reserve on work, I want you to check up on this regularly, please. Be its guardian for me. Anything happens, anything suspicious, you let me know immediately.'

They swopped phone numbers, plumbing in each other's so that the number recognition would always occur.

The Ranger left with a spring in his step. In fact, he was buzzing.

He looked out from the Owner's headquarters. For the first time in months he could savour the beauty of Zama Zama. Its flat-topped acacias and vast-trunked yellowwood trees, its zebra and warthogs, impalas and wildebeest, kudus and waterbuck. Its springboks and hyenas, its elephants lumbering through the bush, a trail of destruction in their wake. Its giraffes sedately returning stares as around them monkeys frolicked in the trees and a magnificent martial eagle flew overhead, clutching a dassie in its talons. Lions, leopards and cheetahs lurked unseen.

The Ranger was entranced. What a marvellous job he had.

The family quickly gathered around Baard's traumatised wife to plan a funeral for the next day, in accordance with Muslim culture.

But news of his shock death spread like wildfire through civil society, with questions on Twitter and Facebook being raised about the murder and who was behind it.

It's the President.
It's the Business Brothers.
It's the state.
It's the security services.

Despite some of Baard's credit cards and money having been stolen, nobody believed he was a victim of a common criminal.

The online *Daily Maverick*, with its record of breaking news and exposures of state corruption, was first to link the murder to Bob Richards' sensational revelations in the British House of Commons. That quickly went viral on social media.

Baard's funeral was attended by a huge crowd, way, way beyond his circle of family, friends and workmates. The new finance minister, whom Baard despised, had invited himself – despite the family publicly humiliating him by saying he wouldn't be welcome. Instead the former finance minister, Baard's close colleague, was invited to speak.

Outside-broadcast TV vans with satellite dishes on top queued up outside the mosque, the BBC, ITN and Sky News among them. Baard's murder and the British parliamentary revelations were now international news.

When the former finance minister, an Indian whose family hailed from Durban, rose to speak, he expressed the sorrow and sympathies of all in attendance for the family. Then he gave thanks for Baard's exemplary public service. 'He was the epitome of a dedicated, expert official. Someone I was proud to call a both a professional colleague and comrade. I relied on his technical ability continuously. He was man of utmost integrity, appointed for his excellence under Madiba and murdered under this president.'

The former finance minister paused as the implications of that last sentence sunk in. There were gasps. Then, in a moment of hushed tension among the crowd, he raised his voice to a crescendo and said: 'Nobody believes he was the victim of a chance robbery. He was deliberately murdered.' The congregation rose to its feet and clapped long and hard.

There were chants among some, which gradually spread to almost all: 'Our comrade was murdered by the state. Our comrade was murdered by the state.' It was repeated a dozen times.

The former finance minister held out his arms and indicated silence. 'So, in honouring the memory of our wonderful friend, we say this: "He will not be forgotten. We pledge today to get to the truth. We demand that those responsible are brought to justice, all of them, however high they may be.'"

He bowed to Baard's wife, who had tears streaming down her face, but a proud smile breaking out too. She came forward to embrace him and the congregation rose again, clapping tumultuously, emotions running high, his dramatic words carried live on many TV and radio channels.

Thandi watched at home, sobbing uncontrollably. She felt terrible. She knew exactly what had happened before Baard's murder. She was the conduit and maybe also therefore complicit in his death.

She had called the Veteran to pour her heart out. But although he was comforting and sympathetic, he instructed her not to go to the funeral under any circumstances. She was effective only so long as she stayed anonymous. In fact, he was concerned that any police investigation might uncover her meeting in the diner, thence exposing her wider role acting for him.

Immediately after Baard's murder, the Veteran WhatsApp-called Bob Richards.

He explained how Baard had researched and supplied the original speech draft, how they were convinced he had been murdered by the state. 'Yes, that's what the media are starting to report here too,' Richards said.

They discussed what to do. 'Better not to admit he drafted your speech,' the Veteran advised, 'but do link his murder to a cover-up over the money laundering you exposed in Parliament.'

So that's what Richards did.

Typically on a Thursday morning, the Leader of the House of Commons makes a statement about forthcoming business, listing bills and debates for the coming week, and usually the following one too. It affords an opportunity for backbench MPs to ask about anything they wish, provided they preface it with: 'Would the government find time for a debate on [whatever topic concerned them].'

Richards was called towards the end of the Business Questions session, a couple of dozen MPs having raised issues on the crisis in the National Health Service and other topical matters, before it was his turn.

'Would the Leader of the House find time for an emergency debate on a murky murder by the South African security state? I do not believe Iqbal Vallie, known to his friends as "Baard", was murdered by a thief.

He was murdered by South African security sources acting on behalf of the President to cover up and prevent him exposing their corruption.'

On the Veteran's advice, Richards had tipped off the *Daily Maverick* and the British Press Association news agency of his intention. Both ran his words immediately after he had sat down, and a startled Leader of the Commons had given a non-commital but superficially sympathetic reply.

Soon his intervention began trending in South African social media and the clamour started for an inquiry into Baard's death, with the former finance minister especially vocal.

CHAPTER 16

A sniper's mantra is patience, patience, patience.

Boredom is never tolerated. Boredom blunts alertness, diverts attention, accelerates tiredness. Boredom is also a deathtrap for a Sniper.

So he kept himself interested. Watching the rhino family, especially the comical little one. Scanning the bush. Listening, listening, always listening and looking. He had one other advantage over the attackers — the VETPAW drone. He knew the attackers were on their way, and their trajectory, because his earpiece kept him updated.

Of course they would be expecting their attack would be repelled, just as it had been before. But did they suspect his role?

The VETPAW drone hovered stealthy and unheard above the poachers down below.

It followed them as they marched towards their target, most of their journey completed. The operator watched the stealthy figures moving as a fuzzy white gaggle, noting the rhythm and the professional purpose. He could tell the way the front two led that they knew this bush, seemed always to traverse the terrain with ease, whether gullies and thickets or open *veld*, never seemingly losing momentum unless they huddled for what he supposed was a sip of liquid.

He had to admire their steadfast progress. Pros, no doubt. Formidable, no doubt either. He couldn't help shivering.

Suddenly there was a change. He strained to establish exactly what. There were now two fuzzy images of movement. They must have separated. Which group should he follow, he wondered.

He spoke into his microphone, relaying the news of a pincer attack, and an ETA of about twenty to thirty minutes.

Clint and Ken swiftly took stock.

The rhinos were in front of them, and beyond lay the pool glimmering in the moonlight, with the *kopje* behind, on which the Sniper had secreted himself. An interesting character, the Sniper, they'd mused. Decent, courteous, but deep – hard to reach. Like snipers invariably were, they'd discovered in their previous military lives, people burdened with heavy responsibility. How good was he? They didn't know, but had been impressed by the reports of his clinical-sounding kills.

Clint spoke softly. 'We have four: us two, Isaac and his colleague. But they're rangers, not military-trained. I will take Isaac, you the other guy – what was his name?'

'Bonang,' Ken replied.

'Okay, let's assume for now the two groups come in either side of the *kopje* and water. You move over to our right with Bonang; we'll be here on the left.'

'Cool,' Ken muttered, gesturing to Bonang to go with him.

The VETPAW duo had worked so long together that they operated with an umbilical understanding and minimal talking.

Before them, the rhinos stirred, sensing movement, innocent in the darkness of the danger but instinctively twitchy in the breeze, straining, sniffing, listening.

Clint slipped off with Mkhize to find a new vantage spot, putting himself ahead of the Ranger, the first in the firing line; the same order for their colleagues.

Mkhize's stomach knotted, his shoulders tensed. This really was not his scene. As a ranger he was frequently endangered by wildlife. But this was war and he was a soldier on the frontline, with two priorities of life protection: first the rhinos, then his own – in that order.

He had indicated to a worried Thandi that there was an imminent threat, but not explained the details. He crouched down, thinking of her bubbling, stubborn, impish, determined personality, the soft curves and hidden treasures.

Then he swept these thoughts out of his mind and jerked himself back to the task in hand, forcing himself to focus. This was his territory. This was his mission. These were his rhinos. The advancing bastards must

213

not win, must not be allowed to win. Mkhize surveyed the scene before him, giving Clint a cheery thumbs-up but feeling decidedly shaky inside.

Momberg went with one of the local poachers to the right, Botha with the other to the left. Not long to go now. He moved purposely forward, the local man just ahead. He had discussed going in over the top of the *kopje* but then immediately rejected it – tempting, but too many unknowns in the terrain: steepness, rocks, treacherous crevices, all with the capacity to trigger a noisy slippage in the dark and potentially lethal falls.

He and Botha had carefully calculated the odds. They expected a fire-fight, had been in plenty before, had always come out on top, had only once in fifty or more incidents suffered an injury, and that just a minor flesh wound from a bullet.

Then again, they hadn't before encountered anything with such a fierce record of successful resistance as Zama Zama.

The Sniper was firmly in the groove. No more idle swirling thoughts about his son and daughter, his life and where it was all going. They were banished – along with the gnawing sciatica that had recently beset him in his right leg. Although not crippling, it was deeply frustrating. He'd never had anything like it before – the odd sprain or ache, but not this, not an ailment that stopped him sleeping properly: he must be getting old.

He could see exactly where Clint and Ken had repositioned themselves after the message that the attackers had separated. And he thoroughly approved. These guys certainly nailed it, which was reassuring, to say the least, because he'd worried even more than usual about this particular assignment: that the threat might have escalated beyond their ability to combat it.

If, as the drone operator had just signalled, the attack was two-pronged, coming from behind him down either side of the *kopje*, then the Sniper wouldn't see them before the VETPAW guys did. His was a backup role, a relief in some ways, but even more of a responsibility in others.

The breeze had picked up, probably not enough to disturb his shot because the distance was too short for that, but a distraction nevertheless.

Hours ago van der Merwe had turned in for the night. But he couldn't sleep properly because he kept wondering how the expensive new guys were faring with the attack.

He'd hoped that, booked into the reserve, he might have picked up some intelligence. But there was nothing. Nothing at all. Not even from his 'own' Ranger, who had taken them out on walks and game drives. They'd only managed a few snatched conversations while he was escorted to his tent in the dark after the evening *braais* and, irritatingly, the man seemed to know very little.

Except for one important new development.

Van der Merwe's long, cautious experience might have prompted warning bells when the Ranger excitedly briefed him about his new status as the Owner's 'personal protector', and his access to the stored rhino horn. But van der Merwe was distracted by other pressures, mainly Khoza and the imminent attack, so the two instead talked about possible opportunities rather than possible complications.

'Let me consider this,' he told the Ranger, 'provided you think it's safe, one option is to exchange the horn in the cupboard for a replica, hoping nobody will actually notice. Risky, but practical.'

Practical, he didn't explain, because Moses Khoza had commissioned an expert to create a few. Compared with the price of a typical three-kilogram horn at $100,000 a kilogram, getting an authentic-looking replica made wasn't a bad deal at all. In fact, it was a bloody brilliant one.

Momberg tensed, totally focused behind the local poacher, who had paused and crouched in the tamboti thicket, gesticulating that the rhinos were just ahead.

He fanned slightly away from the local man so that they presented two separate targets, straining to hear movement. There were resonances of snorting, shuffling, chomping, meaning the rhinos might be around a hundred metres away he guessed, though he still couldn't see them. His night-vision glasses – the very latest on the market – were a tremendous help. He bent low, scuttling, his AK-47 cocked, eyes roving constantly, ears straining for any sound, especially human sound – for human assailants; animals he wasn't worried about.

The Bat Hawk operator, watching the drone screen, alerted them the attackers were very near.

From his hide, level with and close to the rhinos, Clint was the first to spot movement.

As he had anticipated, with Brown's guidance, the attack was coming from in front, around the side of the hillock. Then the local poacher came into view, creeping clumsily, his movement obviously instinctive rather than trained. But he couldn't see the other guy, and that worried him: although he had the first poacher in his sights, he didn't want to betray his position.

Yet he had no alternative, for they were too close to the rhinos. Clint fired, shooting the poacher cleanly through the head, the body instantly a corpse, crumpling.

An instant later he had to duck away as a stream of bullets from Momberg came within centimetres of him, one piercing the outer flesh of his upper right arm, which he grabbed to staunch the blood flow, unable now to hold his weapon.

From his vantage point, the Sniper saw everything – including the second poacher.

He had him in his night sight, the man's military-like posture some-how naggingly familiar. That distracted him for a split second as the man turned, his face coming clearly into the Sniper's sights. As he started squeezing the trigger, he was astonished to recognise Momberg from his army unit. The bullet powered away, the Sniper cursing himself.

Momberg took the hit in the back of his left shoulder, consumed by a searing, pounding pain, but simultaneously confused – this shouldn't have happened, had never happened to him before. What on earth was going on?

He slumped, his machine gun clattering to the ground.

Mkhize was transfixed. Clint, wounded, was somewhere to his left, the stricken poacher ahead as he crept forward. In his earpiece the Sniper directed him: 'Forty, now thirty metres ahead to your left, I shot the guy but he is not dead, maybe dangerous. He's a pro, so don't take any chances. Any chances. Or he will kill you. Take him out.'

Suddenly Mkhize could see the man, blood spouting – must be from an artery – clutching his shoulder, trying to stem the flow, on his knees.

Mkhize almost felt sorry for him.

'Take him out,' the Sniper urged.

Mkhize froze.

'Take him out! Or he will kill you!'

The Sniper's repeated command numbed him. He couldn't do it – couldn't shoot a person just like that, could he?

Then the wounded Momberg spotted Mkhize, and the two stared at each other, time suspended. Momberg was in such pain and was so preoccupied with the blood he was losing, he could hardly focus on the threat.

The Sniper, now rigid with fear, repeated his instruction, gently this time: 'Isaac, unless you finish him he will kill you, sure as hell. Please do it now.'

Mkhize was almost paralysed.

Then from nowhere into his mind flashed an image from a television documentary. In March 1994, weeks before the country's first ever democratic election, some six hundred members of the Nazi-like AWB drove into Bophuthatswana as part of an attempt to wreck the election. Rampaging through in their farm trucks and cars, yelling racial abuse, they took pot shots with hunting rifles, shotguns and pistols, killing and wounding several people.

Outraged Bophuthatswana soldiers fired back, shouting ANC slogans. One AWB car burst firing through a police roadblock and was halted by police gunfire. Two wounded men fell out of the car onto the road, begging for medical help and mercy. But, depicted on live TV, a young black policeman angrily screamed at them: 'Who do you think you are? What are you doing in my country?' Minutes later they were both shot dead.

The dramatic moment blew away the ancient myth that the white race, with its superior arms and training, could always dominate blacks. It also destroyed the folklore that whites would always fight to the last to preserve their supremacy. Here they had indeed fought – and lost, their most fanatical militarists actually gunned down by a black, live on television.

It was as if Mkhize had been jolted.

Empowered, he levelled his rifle, steeling himself to do something he had never ever contemplated: to kill a rogue human, rather than a rogue animal.

Time stopped.

He had the man in his sights, barely fifteen metres away, but could he pull the trigger? Then he thought of the baby rhino, its innocence and its potential magnificence. He squeezed and suddenly there was a gaping hole in Momberg's forehead. Momberg collapsed, lifeless – but not before his very last thought: surely he had always been indomitable; a black guy shooting a white like him, surely this was only a bad dream?

Mkhize gaped, mortified, transfixed. What had he done?

*

'Top job, Isaac,' the Sniper muttered into his VETPAW microphone, 'but take care, check very carefully that both of them are dead.' He worried the Ranger might drop his guard, inviting a counter-attack.

Then he cleared his mind to focus on the other poachers, just as the Bat Hawk operator was trying to find them. But the operator couldn't find the second group. He manipulated the Bat Hawk as methodically as he could, getting more and more frantic, for now the pressure was on him. He was the eyes for the ground team. It was all down to him. Where the hell were the bastards?

Botha had heard the shots with foreboding – the familiar sound of Momberg's machine gun was there at the beginning, but it was missing in the last exchanges.

He turned, trying to identify the single shot that had come from his right, but seemingly behind and above him, catching instead the laser-like eyes of an owl concealed in the foliage.

No movement, no sound other than the scratching of the wind in the bush. He searched for the rhinos, scouting forward, following the local poacher just ahead, the pool of water now vaguely visible to his right. They were getting close, but of Momberg there was no response to promptings, increasingly desperate, through their usual lapel microphone-earpiece link.

Botha gesticulated to his companion. Freeze. Size things up. Wait. Listen. Always the hardest thing to do for an action man like him, doing nothing. But maybe a lifeline. See what the enemy did next, wait for them to make a move. He looked at his watch. Not much time left to get the kill, yank off the horns and retreat before the sun would inch above the horizon and spray its intrusive light.

Ken and Bonang stared through the gloom as if their lives were at stake. Which they probably were.

Neither moved, because Ken was certain the attackers would have to cross their field of vision to get from where the two poachers had last been sighted, circling around the *kopje* to his right.

Mkhize had relayed the bare story of the other group, Ken relieved that Clint had only a flesh wound, temporarily disabling but apparently manageable. It was the first time either of them had been injured with VETPAW – and that was discombobulating enough.

218

The threat they faced was obviously deadly, but still nothing definite from the Bat Hawk operator on the exact location of the two remaining poachers.

The Sniper peered through his night scope.

He swung systematically, slowly in an arc starting with the rhinos shuffling uneasily, the mother clearly deeply disturbed, pushing her baby underneath her giant frame. He went over every metre of bush, searching for human movement, around from right to left and almost behind him to his left.

Nothing.

Then he traversed the same movement back towards the rhinos.

Van der Merwe had tossed and turned for ages, after an initial several hours of deep sleep from the moment his head hit the pillow.

What was happening out there? How was the operation going?

Round and round his thoughts circled. His arthritic knees were giving him gyp. Here he was, in his late sixties, lying on his own in a game reserve. Most of his circle of friends – to the extent he had any friends any more, for he hardly saw them – were enjoying retirement, playing golf, having *braais*, swigging cold Castles and moaning about the state of the country when they weren't moaning about the state of the Springboks, who had fallen from their perch at the top of world rugby. When they went home, their wives cooked nice meals, kept the house tidy, walked the dog, all the time keeping watchful eyes on their personal security.

And him? He was busy – but alone. Although he still felt intensely about his wife, and was widely admired by his circle for so doing, she was a vegetable: he had to admit now, there was no other word for it. As for the vicarious pleasures he enjoyed from her carer, those were no substitute for what he had lost when his wife had slid remorselessly away into her claustrophobic dream world.

He looked at his watch. The dawn game walk would begin in two hours; he'd better get up in an hour and get ready to join the other guests.

But what was happening to his team?

The Bat Hawk spotted them – at long last. 'Christ what a relief!' the operator gasped.

219

He'd become despairing. But there they were, two grey-white luminous figures crouching as they moved toward their prey – barely two hundred metres away.

They had to be stopped – had to be.

He spoke into his mouthpiece, giving the coordinates of the two poachers. But he also tried to explain where they were, because although the guys on the ground had GPS, precision was absolutely vital.

Still stationed near the fence, Brown heard the guttural words on his earpiece, worrying like hell.

What the hell was happening? He should be there, alongside his compatriot Isaac – not stuck here in case the poachers managed to succeed or make a getaway, ready to pick them up on his flickering screen.

The Sniper swung his rifle towards the spot, trying to identify the poachers' exact whereabouts from the Bat Hawk operator's clipped message.

It took him over ninety long seconds to get a fix. He took a deep breath, slowing his pulse, which had been racing away with tension compounded by the guilt of missing a clean kill earlier.

He cleansed his mind of the Momberg image, cleared away all the memories, and forced himself to focus.

Then he found them.

Botha led.

They'd rehearsed their hand signals before the operation. Danger was an aphrodisiac for him, propelling him forward.

Before, as they crouched, uncertain, vexed doubt had overwhelmed him. Now he forced himself to clear away his anxiety over Momberg, and that took some doing.

Trying to wipe his mind clean, Botha moved forward. But not where he was expected to go.

He dropped to all fours, beckoning his colleague to do the same, slithering to the side in the bush and away from the rhinos, intending to move around in an arc, hoping to confuse whomever was out there waiting for the two of them – as he knew would be the case.

The operator swore. The Bat Hawk had lost them again.

The Sniper cursed silently. The bastards had faded clean away. One moment they were focused in his cross hairs, the next they were gone.

Botha was in his own world, cold and calculating.

There were no guarantees left, he knew.

No guarantee he would reach and de-horn the rhinos. No guarantee he would find Momberg. No guarantee he would make it out afterwards.

He could have pulled back and tried to escape. But there was no guarantee that would work either. The thought of failure nagged at him. Momberg and he had never failed before. Why was failure even entering his mind?

The answer was obvious. Momberg wasn't with him, maybe never would be again. The question nagged at him.

Botha resolutely scampered and slid through the dense undergrowth, thankful his boots, thick socks and trousers were protecting him, but never once giving thought to the well-being of the black poacher now following him – fodder for the mission, not an umbilical comrade like Momberg.

The Sniper searched, the operator's eye in the sky too.

Both were getting desperate. So the Sniper tried to put himself in the mind of his target. The guy must be an ex-army pro like him. What would I do, he wondered?

The unexpected – obviously.

He swung his scope carefully away from the spot where he'd had a momentary fix, and away from the direct route there to the rhinos. Maybe that was too obvious a path for the surviving poachers?

Five, ten minutes ticked by. Then fifteen. The Sniper started to feel different in himself. Less frustrated, more panicky, and it wasn't a comfortable sensation. He wasn't used to panicky.

Maybe the target was now targeting him? Maybe trying to take him out before the rhinos? That could make sense, for the target would have a feel for where the Sniper was.

Ken wasn't sure at all, but he thought there was something there, something sort of moving, a kind of sound. He and Bonang had been peering ahead, but the faintest of sounds and movement seemed to come from behind and to his right. Or was he imagining it?

He gesticulated and whispered to the man swivelling silently, searching, listening and frantically using all his bushcraft.

But Bonang wasn't sure at all. Ken wasn't sure either. The night wind rustled through the tamboti trees, caressing the scrubby bush below. They heard the rhinos stamping, bustling.

But still they heard nothing definitive about the enemy.

Ken thought that this was more petrifying than even the IED that had blown up their military transporter in Helmand Province during his service in Afghanistan. Because that was sudden and vicious – and he'd been miraculously unharmed except for a few scrapes as he scrambled out.

But this wasn't sudden. This was quite predictable: a game of chess in the bush with one outcome: a killing following the checkmate.

His killing or that of the enemy? Scarily, he hadn't a clue.

Botha put his mind in that of his assailants.

They would be thrown – of that at least he was sure. They'd have expected him to go straight to the rhinos. But now he was circling – painfully slowly, admittedly – around and probably behind them.

Them? He wasn't at all certain, but had to assume the plural.

Botha's uncertainty was banished. He was again in his element among the elements. Conquest would be his – as it always had been before with Momberg.

The very thought of his buddy angered Botha. How bloody dare they harm Momberg, his invincible partner? If he'd been hurt – banish the thought, if he'd been killed – Botha would avenge that, make them all pay. Sod the rhinos – that was now second order for Botha. Vengeance was the priority. Never mind the dawn that would creep over in less than three hours. Never mind the rising odds against his escape – once taken for granted, now receding. Botha was focused on one thing: finding Momberg and taking out the enemy.

He checked his weapon. It was loaded and ready for the combat he knew was to come.

It was Ken's mistake, and he knew it too.

Scouring the bush for an hour, finding nothing, he'd beckoned Bonang and started moving, inching, crouching toward the rhinos. Better to put themselves in the way of any advance behind them or even to either side.

*

222

Botha spotted them.

Quickly, he positioned and fired. Bonang fell, screaming – and the bush went mad with a cacophony of sound. Ken went instantly to ground, and Botha lost him, rising just a little, but not too much, to search with his night sight.

It was perhaps the hardest shot he'd ever taken. Or so he told himself afterwards. Alerted by the gunfire, the Sniper had swung around and suddenly had the man in his night scope.

No need to steady himself or to focus. He had done all that. He was icy. Nothing else in his consciousness. No estranged wife, no increasingly distant kids, no meaning-of-life speculation. Just the target, the man in front: a white man, he thought, but couldn't be sure. He squeezed, caressing the trigger, then immediately he squeezed again. Two shots. Almost certainly into a fellow army old-timer.

Botha collapsed, writhing in agony yet shouting a defiant last 'No!' before all breath was sucked deliriously from him.

His poacher scampered, but wasn't going anywhere. The Sniper coolly focused and shot twice again, the man stumbling to his death.

Ken heard first the shot that had downed Bonang followed in short order by another two. Then still another two.

He was dazed. It was pandemonium.

Then silence. Total silence – at least from man-made intrusion. The bush was as silent as it could ever be, while the inhabitants took stock at the human carnage before them: only a distant chatter of monkeys, and birdcalls.

Ken crept towards Bonang, who was badly injured and clutching at his chest wounds, desperately trying to bind them, looking terrible. Then Ken turned, creeping towards Clint and Mkhise, keeping alert. He found Mkhise semi-shell-shocked, going through the motions of getting stretchers to carry the dead poachers to his vehicle. Clint fortunately wasn't too bad, holding his injured arm wrapped in a temporary bandage to staunch the blood flow. But he needed a doctor or hospital soon to stitch the wound.

Bonang never made it.

In silence they retrieved stretchers and lifted the five bodies into the back of their two Land Cruisers.

223

Minutes later the three clambered aboard, swinging around to collect the Sniper in order to smuggle him out of the reserve.

Despite saving the rhinos, a melancholy mood enveloped the group, with the Sniper reflective as he peered closely at Mkhize, driving but stone silent.

Sensing his turmoil, the Sniper said quietly to Mkhize: 'It's pretty usual to find your mind is bent by killing somebody for the first time. But you know it was only self-defence. You know it was to stop a bad guy doing evil. But it will probably haunt you, for a while at least. When it does, think not so much of the man, think of why. What would have happened if he'd lived? For a start, the rhinos would have been massacred for their horns, and you would have been killed. That's the truth: keep reminding yourself of this.'

Mkhize nodded, and drove. But his mind was still disoriented. How would Thandi take it? He'd become a killer. Yet had he really? His mind spun. And Bonang's death was a numbing blow.

He thought of the baby rhino, doubtless still cavorting with his mum. But his mind still spun.

Van der Merwe was splashing water on his bleary face, almost stumbling across the tent bathroom, when he heard the roar of engines rushing past the camp.

His tent was quite near the entrance and he thought he heard at least one vehicle stop, its engine idling. He pulled the tent flap back and lurched out, peering in the darkness, the camp lights bright enough to deter animals but eerie in the gloom; it was almost impossible to see.

Then he heard a voice – Zulu maybe, certainly African: 'We must carry the five bodies on stretchers and stow them safely in the secure shed for the police. Keep our colleague separate from the four poachers.'

There was a bustle and movement that went on for around five minutes, engines – actually there might be two, he thought – idling.

The same voice again: 'I'm off to the hospital, you go to the airport – see you later.'

Van der Merwe strained to listen. Nothing more. Airport? Hospital? The engines roared again. He turned back into his tent, searching in vain for explanations, changing for the bushwalk.

Remembering to grab his hat and binoculars, he closed the tent flap and headed for the lounge area, a construction open to the sides on a wooden platform and covered with a thatched roof, sitting raised upon

224

wooden poles and amidst surrounding trees, a swimming pool below glistening under the moonlight. It had a comfortable, easy feel about it, blending with the bush surrounding the camp.

His Ranger was there, coffee and Ouma rusks ready, waiting for the dawn bushwalk guests, fidgeting as he read the Ouma carton: *The story of Ouma rusks started in 1939 in the small North-Eastern Cape town of Molteno. The Great Depression spurred Ouma Greyvensteyn and her friends to find ways of helping the community. She started by baking a batch of rusks . . .*

The Ranger seemed awkward as van der Merwe loped up, looking furtively around, checking they were alone.

'Five bodies delivered to the camp this morning: four dead poachers, and one of my ranger colleagues.'

'Definitely all four poachers?' van der Merwe snarled. 'No room for doubt – all fucking four?'

'Yah, sir,' the Ranger mumbled.

'Come and see me when we can be alone,' van der Merwe ordered, the Ranger nodding morosely.

There was a rustle behind them. Other guests were beginning the walk into the lounge area, the Ranger turning to attend to them.

Van der Merwe mumbled good mornings and moved off to the edge of the lounge, leaning on a banister as he sipped his coffee in the cold. All four of his men dead, including the professionals, who had never failed before. He swore to himself: Christ almighty! What the hell was it about Zama Zama? Was the place sodding spooked?

Another operation failure, another bloody failure. Khoza would be on his back. Only one consolation – the exorbitant fee demanded by Momberg and Botha would now no longer need paying. And at least there was the replica.

Van der Merwe made a decision there and then. No more attempts on Zama Zama. There were plenty of other game reserves to target, though not always ones with similar ease of road access. He resolved to research new poaching venues. Meanwhile, he would prioritise stealing the Owner's horn, replacing it with the replica. That would fill the income gap, get him back into Khoza's good books.

Mkhize, more preoccupied than usual, drove fast, lurching along the rutted dirt tracks, his headlights sweeping the bush, searching out the prying eyes of animals as he rounded bends.

225

Clint, nursing his grazed arm, and the Sniper were on board. Nobody said very much. The Sniper kept counting his luck: a dozen successful poacher kills now; he winced, proud yet also discomfited at his prowess.

Deep in thought throughout the journey, Mkhize dropped the Sniper off at Richards Bay airport in time to catch the morning flight, before getting Clint's arm cleaned and bandaged at the local hospital, where doctors were used to dealing with game-reserve injuries of one kind or another.

Late that morning Mkhize was back in Zama Zama reporting to the Owner about the night's events, including his own role. The police had been and quickly identified the two white poachers, who had ID on them; the two blacks they would have to check out. Identifying the dead ranger was straightforward. Momberg and Botha were well known to the police as guns for hire, but had never been caught before. Now they never would be.

The Owner, a sensitive man despite his beery bravado, immediately cottoned onto Mkhize's utter desolation. 'Take a few days off Isaac, go and see your girl. I will change the rosters. Come back and start afresh.'

Mkhize nodded, grateful, saying little.

The Owner clapped him on the shoulder, then spontaneously gave him a bear hug, Mkhize stiffened, embarrassed: real blokes like the two of them didn't hug each other like that. He felt immediately better, nevertheless.

'You've done brilliantly!' the Owner said. 'Each time you think about the killing of that poacher, just think what he would have done to our rhinos — and certainly you too. What have we both said to each other? What have I heard you say yourself? "Poaching has become war out there." And what happens in war? You kill or you get killed. We stop them or they wipe out our rhinos, our rangers — and many others. This is our mission. We must not fail.'

The Owner paused. 'That's what you've always argued to doubtful guests, haven't you?'

Mkhize reluctantly nodded, and they shook hands.

'See you when you return next week,' the Owner said, squeezing him reassuringly on the shoulder.

CHAPTER 17

Sitting in the production studio where she was working on the mid-morning programme, Thandi had been concentrating on sorting a transport problem with the next guest, hardly registering anything else.

Then she sat bolt upright, listening to the newsreader.

'. . . the killing of two professional white poachers in KwaZulu-Natal's Zama Zama Game Reserve marks a step change in the war against rhinos. Usually it is black poachers or black game rangers who die. The identity of the men is being kept secret until their families have been notified . . . And now to the bankruptcy threat hanging over South African Airways. A former finance minister said again that it was a consequence of "state capture by highly placed corrupt individuals" . . .'

Thandi was only half concentrating on her studio duties. Before her was the familiar assortment of microphones, outside lines for phone and ISDN connections, digital playout systems and cart players, used to play clips such as stings, trails and jingles, plus CD players for feeding into the wide sound desk with its bewildering number of movable tabs and buttons for controlling the various levels of the output.

She pulled her iPhone out of her jeans pocket and WhatsApp messaged Mkhize: *Just heard news poacher deaths r u ok?*

He was just about to climb into his car when he got her message, quickly replying: *Sort of ok, on way to c u.*

What on earth could that mean, Thandi wondered? She flashed back a text: *Big hugs when I c u.*

But Mkhize was constantly on her mind as she went into autopilot for her morning shift.

*

The previous day something had happened to Bob Richards' email system – or, rather, his publicly available parliamentary one.

It seemed jammed up, his constituency secretary reported from the local office through which his constituents could access him. She couldn't do her work monitoring, processing, replying to, or simply deleting spam from the three hundred to four hundred emails that poured in daily. And that was a normal day. If he did something in the news like the South African stuff, the number ballooned. So she had immediately contacted the parliamentary IT team, available almost 24/7 to deal with problems on the vast network for the seven thousand or so who used it: MPs, their staff, peers and all the Palace of Westminster staff.

Russian, Chinese and other foreign and domestic hackers had already attacked it, so an IT-system problem was not new. What was curious, however, was that her own personal parliamentary email and those of other MPs and Westminster staff she knew were unaffected.

Richards checked his second, personal and undisclosed parliamentary email, and it appeared to be fine.

Odd.

As he drove out of Zama Zama, Mkhize stopped at the gates and called the Veteran, outlining what had happened and explaining he was on his way to see Thandi. He was elliptical about how he had shot a poacher, but the Veteran – experienced from the guerrilla struggle with young recruits to MK, and handling their trauma – could tell immediately Mkhize was holding something back.

'Explain the sequence again, exactly what happened, how each of them were killed, so I can understand,' he said gently, pausing to give Mkhize some space.

Mkhize grimaced, swallowing hard, thinking – then decided he'd better not hold anything back any more.

He spelled out details of the first attack: how the Sniper's shot had badly wounded, rather than killed; how Clint had been caught by a machine-gun spray after having killed one poacher.

'And the wounded poacher, tell me about him,' the Veteran said softly.

'Clint was disabled, couldn't do anything, so I crept towards where we'd seen the poachers both fall.' Mkhize stopped, gulping and then blurted out: 'One was lying there, a white guy, alive but sort of disabled, blood spurting and staring at me. I didn't know what to do – never been

228

in that situation before, and certainly never had to ... The Sniper was warning me he was very dangerous ...' He tailed off.

The Veteran waited, intuitively sensing what had happened, then prompted, 'Yah?'

Mkhize drew breath. 'I killed him right there; he died straight away. Clint had urged me to finish him off. But I don't know ...'

'Imagine what would have happened if the guy – you say he was a pro – had recovered and shot you, then had come back with even more firepower, with the backing of the criminal syndicate that hired him? Imagine if he had not been wounded – he would have murdered your rhinos, wouldn't he, including the baby? He would maybe also have murdered other rhinos, probably had done so before – and elephants too ... Am I right?'

Mkhize drew an even deeper breath, feeling emotions he wasn't used to welling up inside him. 'Yah, of course, I suppose so.'

'You're a decent, honest, honourable man, Isaac. It would be very odd if you weren't upset – in fact traumatised – wouldn't it?'

'Yah, maybe ... Yah, suppose you're right, it's just, well—'

'You've still got the image of the poacher trapped in your mind, haven't you?'

'Yah, can't get it out of my mind.'

'I suppose you didn't shoot him instantly, just like that. You weighed it up, didn't you?'

'Yah – but that makes it even worse. It wasn't like we were both shooting at each other. He was lying there stricken, trying to move his weapon. At first I couldn't decide what the right thing was. The Sniper was constantly in my earphone urging me to kill. Then I shot him – in cold blood.'

'Not exactly cold blood, was it – he might have died anyway.'

'But it's like shooting a captured prisoner in a war.'

'No it is not – definitely not. There are rules in war – the Geneva Convention and all that stuff, what you do with prisoners of war – not always observed, but they should be and mostly are. There are no rules in poaching. It's primeval, isn't it – kill or be killed, shoot the bastards or they wipe out the rhinos and elephants to extinction, don't they – taking many rangers with them too.'

'Yah,' Mkhize said sullenly. Intellectually he knew the Veteran was correct. Emotionally he was still battered.

229

They chewed it over a bit more, Mkhize feeling better afterwards, he had to admit. But what would Thandi think, would she cut him dead? With exactly the same thought, the Veteran resolved to phone Thandi and warn her. He couldn't have them falling out – not over this: more important tasks lay ahead.

'I was flying up to Pretoria tomorrow anyway. See you both there – with the usual precautions.' He hadn't intended to travel – but he was certainly going to do so now. Anyway, he had another task in mind.

He'd hardly ended the call when his phone rang – Bob Richards on WhatsApp. 'Hi.'

Richards wasted no time. The Parliamentary IT team had reported his public email hacked by a foreign source, somewhere in Africa – they were trying to identify where exactly.

'That's retaliation for your work exposing Baard's murder,' the Veteran said.

'Yes, they must have been stung,' Richards replied. 'What they don't know is we communicate via my personal email and WhatsApp, so if they're searching for my source, they won't find it.'

'Won't find it – yet,' the Veteran said brusquely, anxious his friend was too casual about it. 'This shows they're on to us – or at least strongly suspect us. I am using a friend's email, but sometimes pressures mean we both cut corners, so let's try to avoid that at all costs.'

Thandi hugged him close.

He had spilled his heart out to her, fearing she would have a go at him. But, far from being critical, she told Mkhize she was proud of him. He had become a 'new-age freedom fighter' she told him. Rather over-the-top perhaps – and he wasn't at all sure he liked the label – but he was surprised at how elated he suddenly felt.

They went for a late café lunch-snack. Mkhize always insisted on paying because he was in full-time work, and she wasn't, Thandi initially grumpy but over the months reluctantly accepting.

The Veteran was due to meet them later, mid-evening, and they snatched a couple of hours making passionate love in Mkhize's B&B bedroom, the same one he always managed to book, the others in the abode occupied overwhelmingly by whites.

Despite their increasing physical and emotional intimacy, however, Thandi was reluctant to commit to them becoming an item. Mkhize was achingly keen. He was besotted with her. He couldn't take his hands off her when they were together. He'd never met anybody like her. She was impish, beautiful, sexy and intelligent. Despite her sometimes waspish assertiveness, she was full of empathy. He discovered she also had a vulnerability she would not ordinarily allow herself to reveal.

They would talk around the houses about his ranger life and then about hers, their separate missions, how they rarely intersected, the limited time she had for a life outside political activism, and what this meant for their future.

But they never resolved the conundrum. In a way, they didn't need to – they were getting closer all the time, albeit in a manner that didn't compromise each other's professional (and in Thandi's case primarily political) lives.

At least for now.

Meanwhile, the Veteran had done his usual to shake off a probable tail, in and out of Pretoria's Menlyn car park, before they rendezvoused at the friend's house where they had first met after the public meeting where he had spoken.

To his relief, it was very obvious Mkhize was in a better place emotionally – time with Thandi had obviously done him some good.

Khoza was not a happy bunny – very far from it. In fact, he was furious.

Incompetence! What a total, sodding failure! He raged at van der Merwe. Why was the outcome always the bloody same? His team always taking fatalities at Zama Zama. Time and again.

'They obviously have something special there. I am identifying other reserves with rhinos to target,' said van der Merwe, trying to soothe Khoza who, by this point in their conversation, was hardly listening; he was thinking more about what he would tell the President. His President, who had a habit of firing those who did not deliver on his orders – from finance ministers who refused to cover up corruption in state-owned enterprises, to apparatchiks like Khoza.

The *Daily Maverick* was the first to report it in depth. Running a piece from their Scorpio investigative unit, they carried a background report on the Zama Zama poacher deaths, outing Momberg and Botha as experienced poachers with military service in the days of apartheid rule. But the report mainly highlighted the role of VETPAW, attributing

231

the poacher deaths to what it described as 'their feared proficiency'. It analysed VETPAW's history, together with their NGO and institutional funding.

The story popped up on Thandi's Twitter feed; she caught sight of the notification in the middle of the meeting with the Veteran, irritating him – he couldn't stand the youth's itinerant attention span, governed by social media – until she explained its nature.

'Very significant – absolutely no mention of the Sniper's role,' the Veteran observed. 'Long may that last. We could need him ourselves in future. But VETPAW will have to take extra care.'

Mkhize then filled in the Veteran on the implanted horn and the plan should it be taken, asking that he arrange for it to be tracked, and handing over the necessary receiver for doing so.

The Veteran withdrew from the two and made a call to Major Yasmin, explaining the project. 'I have the receiver on me and I'm in Pretoria now; it would be good for you to have it immediately, if at all possible.'

Major Yasmin paused, considering. 'Cannot collect it tonight, sorry.'

'No problem, except it could be moved anytime,' the Veteran replied. 'I will leave it with my comrade Thandi Matjeke – completely trustworthy even if young and green.' He read out her safe phone number.

'Right, tell her I will call later to make a plan,' she said cryptically.

The Veteran briefed his two protégés on the plan.

When the horn with its hidden transmitter was moved, it would be tracked by Major Yasmin's team and she would keep Thandi directly informed. He didn't want to risk too many direct communications between himself and her. Thandi would now be in the lead on this one, especially as it was likely, going on past practice, that the horn would be moved to Johannesburg or Pretoria.

The Veteran noted with paternal approval how Thandi and Mkhize were now an item, and he waved them off before his hosts arrived back home to prepare dinner. They headed for the nearby Aroma Coffee Roastery and Bistro in Lynnwood, arriving just in time to order something to eat.

They were being shown to their table, the waiter hovering to take their food order before the kitchen closed and Thandi having made her choice, when her phone burbled with a WhatsApp call. She pointed at a vegetarian option: 'Order this for me, Isaac. I need to take this.'

She answered – 'Give me a few seconds please, don't hang up' – and edged away to a quiet spot.

Major Yasmin gave directions for their meet at Pretoria Boys' High School while she was dropping off her son at 07:45. Lots of parents would be doing the same, she explained all in a rush, and they could bump into each other without being noticed. Thandi needed to be holding a copy of that morning's *Business Day*, which she would hand over with the device tucked into an envelope inside the newspaper.

'We should greet each other and hug like familiar friends. You then slip the newspaper to me.'

'Right,' Thandi replied, thinking she'd be late for her shift preparing for the mid-morning radio programme, but so what? She was always early and would cite bad traffic. They would understand – or better had. Her job was okay, but that was all. A job, not a vocation like Isaac's.

Next morning Thandi was there as agreed.

There was a bustle of cars arriving and dropping the boys off at the main entrance gate on Roper Street, to walk from there to the main buildings for school assembly or their classrooms. Some boys had left plenty of time to chat to their mates, others were in a mad panic to avoid being censured for lateness. Some parents jumped out to gossip as the few Matric-level boys fortunate to have their own cars drove through the gates to park. Boys cycling in locked up at the school bike sheds.

Unusually for her, Thandi was rather in awe. The school was a legend in the city. Even her grandmother had told her about it, when she used to listen enraptured by all her stories from a dim and distant apartheid past. How the white family she used to work for had two boys at the school. How, when their father was issued with a banning order preventing him (among a long list of other restrictions) from being on school premises, he used to watch his elder son play cricket from the other side of the school fence.

In those days, of course, it was whites-only; now it was bubbling with multi-racialism, the boys neatly turned out in distinctive dark green blazers with red-and-white stripes, similarly coloured ties hanging over crisp white shirts and grey trousers. She caught a glimpse of rugby and cricket fields stretching away into the distance. Out of her sight was the first team's manicured green cricket field with its small white pavilion. Football was also played at the school these days – an anathema for generations gone past, who'd gloried in it being a rugby school.

233

Thandi was deliberately a little early, waiting with the morning's *Business Day* she'd bought on the way, deliberately trying to be at ease, smiling at those her caught her eye, including some of the black Matric-aged boys, who stared at her longingly. She had no real idea what Major Yasmin looked like.

At 07:45 precisely, as the bustle of cars arriving, stopping, parking up and leaving now seemingly reached a crescendo, a voice called, 'Oh, Thandi, so good to see you!' She turned slightly as a rounded woman of Indian appearance, with short dark hair, wearing dark, modern clothes beamed, clasped her in a hug and gave her a peck as she slid the newspaper from under her arm and stepped seamlessly back, saying, 'Sorry, in a rush, must go now, let's catch up soon.' Then she disappeared.

Thandi was a little lost, but nobody, to her great relief, seemed to take a blind bit of notice. She headed off though the rush-hour traffic.

At almost the same time, sixty kilometres away down the N1 highway in a hotel room in Johannesburg's Rosebank suburb, a man died very suddenly.

He was in his sixties and was due to deliver an investor presentation. The previous night he'd enjoyed a rowdy time with old friends in a local steak house, knocking back the red wine and KWV brandy, chewing on a juicy cut of beef sirloin with roast potato; it came with veg, but that had been left uneaten on his plate. Afterwards he collapsed into a deep, snore-riddled sleep, oblivious to the covert entry of a man into his room, who methodically injected succinylcholine into him.

Later, confirming a collapse of his body system, possibly from asphyxia, a doctor acting for the coroner noted a life lived to the full, a body which, though overweight, had been fit and strong, but with furred-up arteries to the heart, which could easily have been relieved by stents had his health problems been properly diagnosed at a much earlier stage.

The doctor didn't spot the faint trace of the poison succinylcholine, which was virtually undetectable.

Uncannily, at the precise time he died, Zama Zama's elephant herd began moving for about ten hours in a stately procession to the man's home, gathering silently outside, then loitering for two days. Those who knew the ways of elephants said they were mourning, as if one of their own had died.

One expert later commented: 'A good man died suddenly, and from miles away the wild elephants he had nurtured from an aggressive rogue

234

herd to a normal contented one sensed that they had lost a beloved human friend, and began walking almost as if in funeral procession to make a call on the bereaved family at the deceased man's home. He had healed these elephants, so they came to pay tribute to their friend. Truly, an example of the interconnectedness of all beings.'

Van der Merwe had made arrangements for the Ranger to receive a replica horn.

When it was handed over, the Ranger was astounded to see how authentic it looked. Rough, with the usual markings, discoloured dingy beige-grey. It would take expert scrutiny to confirm it was a fake.

He'd been making regular visits to the Owner's home and had got on good terms with the staff as well as his vivacious wife. He'd almost become part of the furniture, unusual for the ranger team, whose duties kept them busy out in the two camps or within the reserve, not in the Owner's house or the nearby administrative office.

He always had his small backpack with him, slung over his shoulder.

The Ranger had chosen his time, when the Owner and Mkhize were away. But he hadn't counted on making his move the same day as the Owner's death, and there were huddles of staff talking together, shocked at the news.

He waved a 'ciao' to proceed through at ease, as if he was expected, then realised something was wrong, paused and made small talk until he was informed of the news, joining in the commiserations and speculation about the future. Zama Zama was the Owner's loving creation, with its widely known story of the rogue elephant herd enticed to normality. How could it possibly survive without him? Where would they all be? Round and round the conversation went, until the Ranger found an opportune moment to detach himself.

This time the replica was in his backpack, and he was surprised at how easy it was to exchange and slip the original horn into his bag unnoticed. Before he closed the cupboard door, he checked and was reassured that the replica looked just the same, snuggled at the back of the shelf.

What he didn't know was that, from the moment he had moved the horn, an alarm had triggered from the transmitter inside it. Major Yasmin Essop was almost immediately alerted, and allocated her trusted corporal to monitor its movements.

*

235

Later in the day Mkhize was stunned to be called by the Owner's distraught Swedish wife Elise, giving him the news and asking him to return to Zama Zama just as soon as he could.

'You were his favourite ranger, Isaac. I need you with me, please, so we can decide what to do.'

His mind was in a whirl as he checked out of his B&B, calling Thandi to update her. 'I must return immediately,' he apologised.

'Of course,' she replied, 'but will you be okay?'

'Yah,' he said firmly, knowing what she meant. 'I've cleared my mind. Now I'm thinking not about the killing any more but whether we can save Zama Zama. What we must do. It's scary. He was our visionary, our fundraiser, our ambassador. He made us into what we are: a special game reserve among all the many others available for people to visit.'

Thandi could tell he was focused, back on his mission, this time with even more purpose. She was left relieved, but also wondering what that meant for them. Meanwhile, of course, she had her own mission – except she didn't realise just how soon it would materialise.

The Sniper took Mkhize's call, dumbfounded as everyone was at the Owner's sudden death. What did this mean for his role in Zama Zama? But maybe that was over anyway?

Later, he took another call, this time from the Veteran, who wanted to meet urgently – as before at his flat in the Johannesburg suburb of Rosebank. The Veteran had one other request: did he have a spare bed for the night? 'Yes, of course,' he replied, wondering why. They agreed a time. And could the Sniper get in some food and wine, please? The Veteran insisted on paying – he was on a ministerial pension, after all – because he didn't want to eat out: there was a risk of being recognised in public, and he didn't want his presence to alert the President's ubiquitously prying security service. It wasn't as bad as the old apartheid era when he was underground, but it was still pretty bad.

There was a moment of awkwardness when the Veteran arrived.

The two men had only met once before, and although the Veteran felt embarrassed, he was used to asking favours of people and getting these readily accepted: he was never arrogant, simply authoritative with the sort of personality that encouraged people to feel it was an honour to be asked.

'Apologies for gatecrashing you like this; thanks very much for having

236

me to stay,' the Veteran said as he stepped through the doorway. From the moment he had been picked up by his trusty cab driver, Marshall, in Pretoria well over an hour before, he'd taken steps to check very carefully that he wasn't being followed, ensuring the cab doubled back on itself before he was finally dropped several hundred metres from the Sniper's flat.

'No worries, I was free anyway,' the Sniper replied as they shook hands, intrigued at the Veteran's purpose and showing him to the spare bedroom his daughter sometimes used and decorated with her things. 'White or red wine?'

'White to start with please, if that's okay,' the Veteran replied.

The Sniper pulled a bottle of Chenin Blanc from the freezer where he had stashed it when he'd got in after shopping an hour before, and poured them both full glasses.

'So?' he asked.

The Veteran filled him in. 'I am under continuous surveillance and it's not safe for me to stay in hotels or eat out. I'm pretty sure I am living on borrowed time.'

'You mean for your life?' the Sniper interjected, startled.

He knew all about the Veteran's background – when he was in the army the Veteran had been one of the bogeymen his unit had been briefed upon: labelled a 'terr' – short for terrorist. But the Sniper wasn't the political sort, didn't follow the ins and outs of politics, though he was disgusted by the rampant corruption under the President – which put him firmly on the Veteran's side.

'I assume they might knock me off.'

'Really?' the Sniper said sceptically.

'These guys are a mafia,' the Veteran explained. 'They have the security resources. They are ruthless. There's lots of money at stake because the President and his crony elite are determined to keep the gravy train flowing their way. But it would cause such a huge fuss, so they won't kill me unless they absolutely feel they have to.'

'Why don't you draw back, then? Is what you are doing really worth being killed?'

'Without being presumptuous in quoting him, Steve Biko once put it very well: "It is better to die for an idea that will live than to live for an idea that will die,"' the Veteran said, then paused. 'Why did you risk your life protecting the rhinos in Zama Zama?' the Veteran asked.

The Sniper smiled. 'Point taken . . .'

'For now I'm more worried that they will dismantle our network, which is very small and pretty thin, frankly,' the Veteran continued. 'They don't know about you, Thandi or Mkhize: you three are deniable combatants. We have to keep it that way – or at least for as long as we possibly can.'

'So where do I fit in, then?' the Sniper asked cautiously. 'I've been clear about my role in Zama Zama, but as you will remember when we last talked with Mkhize and Thandi, I don't want to be drawn into something that would see me doing something illegal in the community.'

The Veteran nodded as if accepting the point. 'Of course.' Then he proceeded to explain about the horn with the transmitter, how the operation was live, that he had a former comrade high in security – whom he trusted fully and who was providing necessary logistical support, but only within strict parameters and at considerable, though calculated, risk.

The Sniper was listening intently as the Veteran continued: 'You are the only one of our trio who has a military operational training and experience, and I am asking whether you would be prepared to provide some back-up, especially for Thandi, who will be active tracing the movements of the horn.'

'What sort of back-up?'

'Armed,' the Veteran murmured, as if it were a minor detail.

'Thought so!' the Sniper responded testily. 'But you've just accepted that's off limits for me.'

'Off limits for something illegal – yah, completely. But I'm not asking you to act illegally, merely in self-defence, or to protect Thandi or Mkhize, for that matter. A protective, not an offensive role.'

'So when does defending become attacking? The one can slide into the other. To protect the two of them I may have to take pre-emptive action and shoot, even kill someone.'

'Understood. But what were you doing in the reserve? Killing poachers before they killed you or, particularly, killed the rhinos.'

'That was quite different,' the Sniper insisted irritatedly.

Nevertheless, he had to admit to himself, he could follow the Veteran's logic. He just wasn't ready to concede – yet. He got the bottle out of the fridge and topped their glasses up. 'Have some more wine and please open the red. I'm going to heat up the pre-cooked meals I got for us in Pick n Pay.'

The Veteran let the argument lie and asked him where he could find the cutlery and crockery. Then he asked about the Sniper's IT consultancy before they tucked into the stewed beef and veg, the conversation ranging widely as the Veteran probed into the Sniper's military training, where he had been deployed, and how he felt about his role the day Mandela was released.

'I was partly in awe of my task, partly incredibly nervous – much more so than on any Sniper job I did for the military – because if there was an attempt on Mandela's life and I failed to stop it, violence could have erupted on a massive scale.'

The Veteran nodded understandingly, as the Sniper in turn asked about the experience of being stationed in the ANC camps in Tanzania and Zambia. They were two white South Africans who'd once been daggers drawn – could have killed each other if their paths had ever crossed during the liberation struggle – but now had common cause. The Veteran: politics, ideology in his DNA. The Sniper: who didn't see himself as at all 'political'. Thirty years apart in age – the Veteran could have been his dad – and a world apart in background. But in values? Were they still poles part?

The bottle of Cabernet Sauvignon was going down very nicely and the evening was getting late when the Veteran raised the subject again. 'Any further thoughts on how you might help us? Or would you prefer me to leave it? Your choice entirely.'

The Sniper grinned conspiratorially. 'I wondered when you'd raise it again! Let me sleep on it. We'll talk over toast and coffee in the morning.'

He knew he would say yes. But only if there were strict rules of engagement agreed in advance. He wasn't going to be manipulated or pushed into doing something he didn't agree with – or rather, he hoped not to be.

Next day, having alerted van der Merwe, the Ranger was sweating nervously as he drove from his lodgings away and out along the dusty track on the pretext of getting provisions from a nearby shop. Before stocking up he needed to entrust the implanted horn safely into the hands of van der Merwe's courier, fifteen minutes up the main road. There, the man of Thai origin was parked up at the expected spot, just off the highway in the shade of a yellowwood tree. The Ranger found it and pulled in, handing the horn over.

Studying the beeping screen from the horn's transmitter, Major Yasmin's corporal tracked the Thai's car as it drove away and later linked up with the main N3 highway to Johannesburg. Within an hour the car was passing through the picturesque KwaZulu-Natal Midlands and – still following remotely – the Corporal had worked out where and roughly when he should try to latch on to it on the outskirts of the city.

Nearly five hours later his instincts were confirmed. It was the same car with the same driver he had followed before, heading for the same house owned by Piet van der Merwe. This time the Corporal stuck his long Canon lens through the window and photographed the man of Thai origin carrying what he assumed must be the horn wrapped in a package into the house, its GPS coordinates confirmed by the hidden transmitter.

The question that remained was: where would it be moved next?

Van der Merwe accepted the package almost greedily, then checked it out gingerly. No question: it was the real thing, he found to his great relief. He stored it safely and was about to call Moses Khoza when the carer shouted for him. He hurried into his wife's room. She was hallucinating, and it was painful to watch – indeed, almost every time he saw her these days it was painful. He held her hand but couldn't do anything to stem her convulsions – better call the doctor.

It was late afternoon, but the doctor was delayed until early evening by the choking rush-hour traffic, by which time his wife was weak, her condition deteriorating, it seemed, by the hour. The doctor, a wiry Indian with a polite but formal manner made a quick diagnosis and told van der Merwe she needed hospital treatment urgently. An ambulance was called for and van der Merwe followed it in his car with a sense of foreboding, the watching corporal wondering whether this was a ruse to smuggle out the stolen horn until he realised from his receiver screen that it was still in the house.

The Corporal decided it was safe to clock off for the night to get some food and kip, but notified Major Yasmin the receiver would be by his bed because it bleeped if the horn was moved.

Major Yasmin decided this was the moment when she would have to activate Plan B.

She had relied upon the trusted corporal for her surveillance on the poaching trail. But she and therefore he were freelancing in a security world manipulated by the President, his cronies and acolytes. She never knew whom she could trust. She was treading a very thin line, risking exposure and censure, which could both prejudice the operation and her position.

It offended her professional integrity that the security services, including her military one, could be so blatantly manipulated for partisan political advantage, compromising the neutrality of the services and endangering the rule of law. Also betraying the values of the freedom struggle in which she had been a key activist in her youth.

She only continued in her job because she could at least do some good – like helping the Veteran – and because it paid for her family's lifestyle. But she was extremely uncomfortable, waiting and hoping for a change in the leadership of the ANC.

For instance, she was appalled at how the director-general of the State Security Agency used official secrecy laws to set up a parallel and unaccountable intelligence structure which expropriated R1.5 billion of taxpayer funds on nefarious covert projects to enforce the President's shadow state. Major Yasmin knew only too well how the presidency was underpinned by a powerful network of agents reporting ultimately to the President and not to the democratically accountable bodies the Constitution required.

She had started off under President Nelson Mandela, when the country's intelligence services had been reformed and switched from defending apartheid into protecting the national interests of the new rainbow democracy. In her own way she had helped accomplish that transformation – and it was difficult stuff. Preserving institutional memory that enabled basic administration to continue to function smoothly while radically re-orientating the very purpose of the whole country's security system was, to say the least, a formidable task. But it was becoming increasingly difficult to continue with that missionary assignment, so badly had the security world been prostituted to presidential malevolence.

She focused upon her immediate task – monitoring the stolen rhino horn. What she wasn't so sure of was whether Thandi was up to it. The girl seemed plucky and intelligent, and since the Veteran rated her highly, recommendations came no better than that: there was no savvier judge of character and ability. But it was still asking a lot of Thandi.

*

241

Piet van der Merwe sobbed like a child.

Sarie had convulsed one last time while he was holding her hand, and then simply faded away right there on the bed in front of him.

Relatives and friends would later console him, saying it was 'a mercy' or 'for the better', at least he could 'get a life of his own now' – and so on. All well meaning, van der Merwe knew that. But he couldn't help feeling such deep loss. It was as if he had been emptied out. The limp, lifeless body before him was of a woman he had cherished, once effervescent, a true companion who was always there for him whether in their intimate moments or in building a warm and welcoming home to which he could retreat from the edgy life he chose to lead and which furnished them with all-inclusive safaris, beach breaks, trips overseas – five-star destination holidays she lived for. They'd both desperately wanted children but couldn't have them.

All he had now was the bureaucratic rigmarole of probate and her funeral – followed by a future on his own; even his favoured carer would no longer be there for her – and therefore no longer for him either. She probably wouldn't mind – but he would, he was forced to admit.

He returned home to reflect on a long void stretching forward, snatching a look at her empty bedroom before downing a very large glass of KWV brandy and eventually falling into bed, immediately slumping fast asleep.

A surge of adrenaline pumped through Thandi in response to Major Yasmin's request when she answered her safe phone.

Could she come to Major Yasmin's house in Pretoria's Waterkloof suburb after dark? Yes, of course. But could she please park two blocks away and walk, phoning on her safe phone before she arrived, so that the security gate could be released to avoid her dawdling while pressing the intercom button and allowing her to come straight in as if she was part of the household? Yes, of course.

The Sniper phoned Elise to express shock, give condolences and offer to help in any way he could.

Although she was very appreciative, she explained she couldn't think straight at this time; she was still in emotional turmoil and overwhelmed by grappling with running the whole business – but would bear his kindness in mind and get back to him.

He wondered if she would. People often said things like that more out of courtesy than real intent – just like people who offered help as he had just done. If so, that would be a real shame: she was a fascinating woman and he really meant what he had told her.

Mkhize had arrived back in Zama Zama, noting the elephant herd shuffling silently, respectfully outside the Owner's imposing home. It was incredibly moving and not for the first time he marvelled at their regal empathy and deep intuition. They seemed like funeral mourners.

He went straight inside the house to see Elise, who seemed in control, but immediately he gave her a hug it triggered wrenching sobs.

'Sorry,' she said. 'I'm okay most of the time but when anybody shows me any affection I just lose it.'

'Almost certainly that will keep happening,' Mkhize replied, hugging her tight then gently releasing her to allow her to wipe her eyes and gather herself together.

She was a striking, mature woman with a soft husky Swedish accent that men especially found alluring. Her blonde hair now had faint grey streaks, and she presented an image of being in her prime. A woman until now at least very much in charge of her life, she may have periodically given her husband plenty of space to be a beery bloke, but there had been no doubt she was in charge of their relationship.

Elise sighed. 'I feel swamped. So much to get on top of. So much to learn.'

'But you were always involved in the business side of the reserve – in fact, in most parts of it,' Mkhize said gently.

'Yes, but that's not the same as running it.' Elise took a deep breath. 'Since he died we have had loads of cancellations, as if Zama Zama doesn't matter any more without him. Cash has completely dried up. I'm frightened, Isaac.'

Then, abruptly she straightened herself. 'Right, let's get down to business.'

They went through the wildlife side of the reserve, discussed the strategy the Owner had left in place, went over the security precautions. Mkhize filled her in on the Sniper's exact role – she already knew about him and about the rogue ranger with whom she made herself a note to establish a similar relationship to the one he'd had with her late husband.

'I cannot believe any ranger could conspire with poaching.' Mkhize

243

paused, searching for an analogy. 'It's like inviting a rapist to molest your child.'

Elise was startled at his ferocity, his deep sense of betrayal. 'Everyone has their price, they say, don't they?' she mumbled.

'He's a traitor. I could kill him myself,' Mkhize said, his manner thunderous.

She changed the subject. 'Can you ask around about an IT person? The admin people here tell me our system needs an upgrade, and we need to do much more on social media, but the consultant who's been working with us has moved to Britain. I have asked admin to consider it, but have you any ideas?'

Mkhize looked doubtful. Then he had a sudden thought: 'The Sniper is an IT guy, runs his own business.'

Elise looked interested. 'Aah, the friend who knows us, who's put his life on the line for us. He called me to offer sympathies, very kind of him, sounded a nice man. Can you see what he says?'

Mkhize nodded.

'There's another problem the rangers have brought to me and I don't know what to do. I thought our problem was poaching of our elephants, not just rhinos?'

Mkhize looked sympathetic.

'But now they tell me we are approaching an over-breeding elephant problem in Zama Zama. So, we're either losing too many through poaching or we're breeding too many. Can't win!'

Mkhize paused to explain. 'In Africa a poacher's bullet kills an elephant every fifteen minutes. But in reserves like ours they can breed like rabbits, doubling every ten to fifteen years. And because bull elephants must leave their family and find a new home range, as well as unrelated females to mate with, they often destroy fences in their way. Although all sorts of alternatives have been implemented, you cannot just let them breed as fast as they can naturally, or they will get out of control.'

Elise felt and looked dazed. She was having to cope with enough as it was. Now this.

Mkhize sensed her desperation. 'Let me discuss it with the ranger team and come back to you.'

She nodded her thanks, barely managing her usual warm smile.

More than ever, what Elise needed was solutions not, oh God, still further problems.

CHAPTER 18

Thandi had borrowed her dad's Toyota again. Though scratched and scruffy, it did the job and got her smoothly to Major Yasmin's home using the Google GPS app on her iPhone. There, she was let in, as arranged, and briefed on relieving the Corporal on surveillance duty.

Major Yasmin hadn't realised Thandi had met van der Merwe at Zama Zama when they had by chance been in the same safari group a while back. 'So that means he might recognise you?' she said, looking concerned.

'I'm not sure,' Thandi replied tartly. 'We blacks all look the same, don't we?'

Major Yasmin gave a knowing squeaky giggle. 'Look, here are some tips.'

Thandi readied herself with her tablet open to take notes and listened intently, just as when the Veteran had first briefed her on a covert role.

'First, it's good you've got a boring, old, dishevelled car nobody will notice. If you had a new van or a flashy sports car, they most definitely would. Second, check out the area, maybe on Google Earth, certainly on Google Maps, so you know all the ways to and from his house or which-ever route he goes. Take a physical map of the city with you just in case.'

'Map?' Thandi interjected. 'I just go online.'

'No, always have a back-up map so you get a more panoramic perspec-tive that you can glance down at on the seat rather than fiddle with your phone. Third, fit in as best you can to the immediate area. Try to feel at home, that you belong there – much better than trying to hide, especially in a residential area like that where the neighbours will probably notice, even if the target doesn't.

'Fourth, as part of the fitting in, try never to show your face directly to van der Merwe. And avoid eye contact. Remember, he has met you before, and is experienced at clandestine work. But remember also that, even if he glances at you, he may not actually "see you"; he may be thinking about something else, just sweeping his eyes around. And never react if you suspect he may have clocked you. Carry on as before, doing what you were doing: ignore him. But at the same time don't walk past his house too often. Limit yourself: unless you really have to do more walking by, make it once daily and that's it.'

'But,' Thandi said, 'most of the time I will be in my car parked up; you said a hundred to two hundred metres away, because I will have a receiver for the transmitter in the horn so I – and you back in your office – know if he's moving it.'

'Yah, right. But you cannot – and should not – sit in it all the time. That could make you an object of curiosity. Which brings me to the fifth point. If someone asks, especially if you get chatting, you need to be able to explain why you're there, so I suggest take a plastic laundry basket with some of your clothes piled in it. And keep the long-range camera and binoculars my corporal will give you hidden away.

'Sixth, I recommend arriving there in the early morning hours, so you aren't seen pulling up. And something else to bear in mind. You often won't be noticed unless you move. If you're static there's less chance of attracting attention. Also vary your arrival time if that's possible, so the same people don't notice you. And occasionally park your car pointed in the opposite direction to his house. Your headrests can conceal you and then you simply adjust the rear-view mirror for observation. But remember, it's a quiet neighbourhood, and if your car is always in the same spot it's like a fixture, though you are obviously more noticeable than if you were parked on a busy street.'

Major Yasmin paused. 'Sorry, this is a lot to take in all at once. You okay?'

'Absolutely,' Thandi replied, tapping away, making notes on her tablet, 'it's really interesting. So what next?'

'Right, where did we get to?'

'Seventh is next,' she said.

'Okay, seventh. Make sure you wear ordinary, casual and above all comfortable clothing, not bright or smart, which would again risk catching attention. And since he has seen you before, maybe wear sunglasses and a baseball cap to disguise your face and hair. Pack at least one extra set of clothes and plan for all weather conditions.'

'Eighth, make sure your petrol tank is full just in case you have to follow over a distance, and try to spot something distinctive on his car that you can fix on as you're following, because if there's traffic and especially at night, it's much easier than you may think to lose the car. And try your best to think ahead about upcoming turns, stop lights and other traffic, watching carefully what lane you're in. Anticipation is the key, because even if he doesn't know he's being followed, someone like him is bound to take precautionary diversionary measures to throw off any tail. You've always got the monitor linked to the horn's transmitter as a fallback of course, but that won't necessarily tell you the exact destination – if, for instance, it's in a built-up area or a block of apartments. Also, keep all your car windows and mirrors clean for photos or video.

'Ninth – and this one you're going to find difficult, I predict!' Major Yasmin smiled mischievously. 'If you really must look at WhatsApp, Facebook and Twitter et cetera, then please do lift your phone to eye level so that you can keep the target in your peripheral vision. Preferably don't use it at all, but that's a lot to ask from your generation, I know.'

She'd intended the remark as a leg-pull but Thandi looked indignant. 'I am not like that,' she insisted, 'but I do want to keep an eye on text or WhatsApp messages on my secret phone at least because that's often the way the Veteran keeps in touch.'

Major Yasmin nodded understandingly.

'Tenth, make sure you take food and a bottle of water.' She paused, looking embarrassed. 'And take some sort of container to have a pee in if needed; it's much easier for a bloke to do it outside somewhere. I took my baby's old potty when I was staking someone out. The thing is, the longer you can stay put in your car, the less likely it is you will be noticed. Immediately you move – drive away, come back, get in and out of your car, the more likely people will be curious.'

'Finally,' she said, 'dictate chronological audio notes on your phone; it's much easier to keep looking while speaking your notes than writing them.'

'Fascinating,' Thandi said, 'let's hope I don't drop a bollock.'

The Major winced at her vernacular. Quite a spiky young woman, she thought – rather like she'd once been when active in the struggle decades before: other activists used to claim they were 'terrified' of her.

247

But, encouragingly, Thandi was willing to learn. She'd be okay if everything went to plan.

Trouble is, it never did.

Mkhize rang the Sniper and asked if he could look over Zama Zama's IT system and website for guest booking and interaction.

'Of course, be delighted to.'

'This would be on a professional basis,' Mkhize explained, 'though we run a tight ship.'

'No problem, I'd be pleased to help,' the Sniper replied, 'what about social media?'

'That too, please. We have lots of engagement over the rhinos especially. When there was that attack on our rhino orphanage it went viral on Twitter and Facebook – also Instagram and SnapChat I am told – don't use any social media myself. But there's a big potential audience out there we haven't mobilised fully.'

'I've got a young staffer who's hot on social media and doesn't need to visit the reserve: he can do all you need remotely or via Skype conversations.' The Sniper paused, thinking. 'No risk I would be clocked and get outed as your sniper?'

'Don't think so,' Mkhize replied, 'because nobody ever really saw you in that role. Maybe one of the staff might recognise you as having visited before from when you first came, but that's not an issue.'

When they met up via the door in his garage as usual, Khoza offered van der Merwe condolences over his wife, which were gratefully received. They then spent some time discussing how to facilitate the deal over the stolen horn. Finally, a plan of action was determined and both men set off to undertake their respective tasks.

The tracker, still stuck under the mudguard of van der Merwe's car, alerted Major Yasmin to the meeting at Khoza's house, but not the purpose – though it was hardly difficult for her to hazard an accurate guess.

The Ranger was so preoccupied he was hardly focusing on the early morning bushwalk.

'What on earth is happening there?' an incredulous guest asked.

A group of impalas, normally fairly placid unless disturbed or alerted to a predator, were in a hyped-up state. It was the rutting season, lasting about three weeks, normally around full moon in May.

A male impala, emitting a guttural rasping sound, chased a group of females, mating with one, then chasing her away to mate in sequence with another, then another.

'Aah!' said the Ranger, focusing now. 'The initial roaring and guttural grunts are for territorial advertising, but can also be produced while in motion, for example, chasing intruder males or, as we can see now in front of us, driving the females, as this one is doing.'

The courtship was intriguing to witness, and the guests were glued to it. Initially the dominant male walked towards his herd, head low and flicking his tongue.

'The dominant male is testing urine from females to check their reproductive status. It's a process called "flehmen" by us rangers. If the female is ready to mate she allows the male to lick her ear, termed the "mating match".'

'How often does this happen?' one woman asked.

'After the rutting season, male impalas don't mate for a whole year, until the season comes around again,' the Ranger replied.

'Definitely not like human males, then!' a woman tourist interjected, laughing merrily.

Despite his depressed mood, even the Ranger laughed at that.

Her father had been grumpy about Thandi borrowing the car 'yet again', especially overnight. Her radio station had been grumpy too that she couldn't do the usual morning shift.

Tough. She was set on her task; it had absolute priority.

Thandi had rendezvoused with the Corporal in a shopping area near to, but not within sight of, van der Merwe's home to exchange equipment. He also downloaded some software to make sure the monitor was synchronised with her iPhone, so that a small red-coloured oval shape showed over van der Merwe's home on her screen. If the horn was moved there would be an immediate audio bleep and the red dot would move too.

She asked a few questions, her demeanour matter-of-fact. But the adrenaline was surging through her, as it had before when on a different mission for the Veteran.

The Corporal added as he headed off into the evening: 'You have my number – call me if there's an emergency, please. Don't hesitate, because I don't mind being woken up if it means catching these corrupt bastards.'

Thandi was startled by his vehemence. As with Major Yasmin, this was more than just another security job, she sensed. They both felt passionately about the task – indeed were risking their careers to undertake it because the President's crony spies were everywhere, including within the military security service.

Nervous as hell, she drove carefully to the spot he had advised and pulled up there on the grass verge: there were no pavements – there hardly ever were in these mostly white suburbs. A basket of dirty laundry lay on the back seat. Her heart was thumping as she settled back in the threadbare, bumpy front seat. It might be a long night.

Thandi, slumped sleepily in her dad's car, had seen van der Merwe exit his garage, then return, but the stolen horn had not moved, so she was unconcerned. Just bored. The early surge of excitement was long gone as the monotony set in.

She found her mind circulating around always on one theme: Isaac. She'd opened herself up to him in a way she'd never done before – emotionally and physically. It was simultaneously exhilarating and deeply disconcerting. Why? she asked herself. But she knew that she was simply avoiding the question. Fact was, she had fallen in love. So had he: she knew that for certain. What she liked especially was the respect he showed. That is how she had first begun to see him in a different way from the testosterone-laden males with their clumsy, lurching advances, who always seemed to swirl around her like flies.

But how could their relationship sustain itself when they were apart for such long periods? Was that a blessing, giving her the space for the independence she cherished? Or was it a prescription for a relationship that simply couldn't last? Isaac's life as a ranger was in his DNA. He thrived outdoors, and she could never imagine him transferring to work, like her, in a city, perhaps on policy or wildlife regulation – certainly not while he was young and fit, perhaps not ever.

For herself, she couldn't imagine relocating away from the metropolitanism of her own life, or the political activism that had taken it over, to live in a reserve, perhaps as an administrator. What would be the point anyway – as he would be on duty 24/7?

Perhaps they should both face up to that reality and go their separate ways. Trouble was, she didn't want to do that. In any case, their priority was to stop the political corruption driving the poaching syndicates. Everything else had to come second. Including their relationship and their mutual love.

Hundreds of miles away in his hut in the bush compound, Mkhize tossed and turned in his sleep as his thoughts churned away to exactly the same unhappily sombre conclusion.

The Veteran was anxious – indeed he was habitually anxious these days, he reflected ruefully; he must be losing it. In the struggle days, he'd frequently been tense, but there was no time to worry unnecessarily. You made a decision and moved on to the next tough one. You couldn't afford to be anxious.

He was concerned that on his command Thandi had emerged partially out of the shadows by undertaking this surveillance task – only 'partially' he emphasised, then quickly corrected himself. In this game, there was no 'partial' – you were either covert or you were out in the open; you couldn't be half-covert – there was no in-between.

But he knew the stakes were getting higher all the time. The President was under growing pressure from some fearlessly investigative journalists – the amaBhungane and Scorpio units leading the way on corruption exposés. Billions of rand in looted money from state coffers was at stake, along with the lavish lifestyles and the money for buying off the operatives it funded. It was not about politics. It was about money. And they would take no prisoners when it came to eliminating threats, of that he was absolutely clear. The 'Gangster State' as one commentator had termed it, was as ruthless as it was powerful.

A report by the Public Protector on state capture detailed the relationships between the President, his family and the Business Brothers, and the way they ruthlessly purged and replaced with cronies any government minister or public official blocking their looting spree, from the finance minister down to provincial and municipal levels.

He'd lost all faith in his old party, the ANC. Yet former comrades told him they were determined to defeat the President's favoured successor when the conference to make a choice came around. The Veteran didn't believe them. He wished he could, but the whole party was just too corrupted from top to bottom. The President had to be got rid of by popular uprising and, in his own way, that was what he was trying to promote. Not through an insurrection – any such thought was pure illusion – more like a spark that could light a fire.

251

The Veteran fretted about Thandi, but there was nothing more he could do. He had committed her, and she had gone willingly into action. Now he must just wait – and get on with something else, for Christ's sake. That 'something else' was a speech, drafted by another old struggle comrade highly placed in the South African Treasury, which the Veteran had emailed securely to Bob Richards a week ago.

The MP had come back shortly afterwards to report he'd found a suitable opportunity to deliver the speech in Parliament, and the Veteran decided to watch it online. It was due on shortly.

Thandi stirred uncomfortably on the car seat, stiff and bored.

It was six in the morning, non-residential domestic staff arriving after being packed like sardines into commuter trains from the townships. Not much had changed from apartheid on that score, she mused.

Street security gates swung back and professionals began driving out of their ample houses surrounded by high brick walls topped with stiff metal spikes to head for work. Some had teenage girls in the back to be dropped off in the accelerating rush hour at Roedean School, founded in the early 1900s by two English women graduates of Cambridge University, still the city's elite high school for girls – once whites-only, though with many black faces now.

Thandi wasn't due to be relieved until ten in the morning, because the Corporal would be trying to jam in the domestic chores and shopping trips his surveillance duties had precluded. If someone took any notice of her that might at least relieve the tedium, but of course the last thing she wanted to attract was any interest. Far better to be bored and ignored.

Suddenly she was jerked out of her somnolence by a bleep on her phone.

The horn was on the move.

Thandi grabbed the long-range digital camera from under the passenger seat, removed the lens cap and switched it on. Her eyes on van der Merwe's house, she turned the key and the car spluttered into life, engine idling.

Minutes later, the horn still on the move, his car pulled out of the garage. Thandi snapped a couple of photos of the car, anxiously hoping they were okay – she wasn't used to proper cameras. Her own camera was her iPhone, her pride and joy, the one bit of luxury she permitted herself.

She gave van der Merwe space, then lurched off the verge and settled in at a distance behind him. Her nerves taught, she hunched, concentrating at the wheel.

The Corporal's smartphone also bleeped. He cursed his bad luck, dropped off the food he'd bought while shopping for the maid to stick in the fridge, and headed fast to see if he could catch up on Thandi's tail.

Piet van der Merwe was on high alert as he pulled out of his electrically powered gates, and they closed seamlessly behind him. He always took care to glance back until the gates were securely locked up, for there were a good few moments for criminals to slip into the premises. And there were plenty of street criminals about, that was for sure.

Van der Merwe scanned his rear-view mirror for a tail but focused mainly on the traffic about him, especially as he turned into the busy nearby shopping street; the last thing he needed with the horn on board was a shunt.

Perhaps because of that his usual antennae didn't pick up the young black woman in her rusty old white car following him past his house, and then frantically weaving to keep up.

Thandi was edgy and stressed.

She'd comforted herself nothing was likely to happen on her night shift — and it hadn't. Until this in the morning. On the other hand, the excitement surged through her as she felt she was doing something really positive, making a difference.

What was it Madiba had so memorably said? 'What counts in life is not the mere fact that we have lived. It is what difference we have made to the lives of others.' She had memorised it word for word, could recite it in her sleep; it had become her own personal mantra.

She clung grimly to the steering wheel, hunched forward, catching glimpses of van der Merwe's bright metallic-blue BMW — thank God it was so very visible — in between a forest of hooting minibus taxis darting about to pick up and squeeze in yet another black passenger standing randomly at a kerbside. Johannesburg's traffic was dreadful, even now the rush hour had passed. During rush hours, it was impossible.

At least she had her beeping iPhone tracking the BMW — and the horn. But she had to be on the scene when the BMW stopped, in order to photograph him carrying in the horn, if at all possible. Major Yasmin had drummed into her the vital importance of hard evidence to be sure

253

of nailing the buggers: circumstantial witness evidence was not sufficient; it had to be concrete, which meant photographic.

She must not let Major Yasmin down.

Her heart pounding, Thandi drove on, revving, clutch screaming, gears crunching, then braking to duck and dive amidst the forest of vehicles and street vendors leaning out into the road or darting between waiting vehicles at traffic lights, selling just about everything from morning newspapers to contraceptives.

She'd pestered the Veteran to be right in the centre of the action. Now indeed she was – at last permitted to come out of the shadows.

And it was petrifying.

Van der Merwe drove onto the N1 highway for Pretoria.

He scanned his rear- and side-view mirrors regularly for pursuers, also for two cars, one passing him, the other hanging back, and then both switching roles in the regular tail routine. Nothing – at least nothing that caught his attention.

The journey to Pretoria he knew like the back of his hand – the landmarks that caught his eye: Kyalami motor racing circuit, once attracting a Formula 1 Grand Prix, now short of the necessary standards to qualify. Then Grand Central, where motor sport events used to take place before Kyalami was built. And of course, just before Pretoria's skyline came into view, the Voortrekker Monument off to the left, the enormous shrine to Afrikanerdom and his own spiritual icon.

As the city came into view, there up on the skyline was the ugly carbuncle of a building belonging to Pretoria University. Van der Merwe drove through the city and across to Khoza's home off Amos Street in Pretoria's Colbyn suburb; quite handy for the presidential quarters.

The transmitter hidden in the horn kept bleeping and Thandi followed, realising how tough it was to tail a car.

You had to keep up but not too near. You had to keep in sight but not be seen. For some reason the traffic in Pretoria was unusually heavy for that time of day, a godsend, she surmised – or rather, hoped. She could do with a pee, but there was absolutely no opportunity for that.

Suddenly she jolted as her phone rang. Her dad's car was too old for a built in hands-free; instead she had a Bluetooth-connected earpiece and reached down to answer.

It was the Corporal. 'We think he's heading for Khoza's home. It is number fifty-three. It's not far away now, possibly a couple of minutes. Suggest you catch him up – do it steadily, not in a rush, so hopefully he doesn't notice – then drive right past as he stops, pull in somewhere nearby not too obvious and try to take those photos of him carrying in the bag.'

No pressure, thought Thandi. *No pressure at all.* 'I'll do my best,' she muttered, cutting the call and screeching to a halt at traffic lights, almost bumping the car ahead, the BMW six cars further forward.

Van der Merwe turned left across the pavement up the short driveway to Khoza's double garage doors and stopped.

He looked left and right at the cars passing by on both sides of the road; nothing unusual. A battered small sedan with what looked like a cleaning maid wearing a shawl at the wheel swept past and pulled into a driveway a little way along on the opposite side of the road.

Cleaning maids had cars then, these days? Progress, he supposed, though the car seemed on its last legs. He climbed out and went to open his boot, scrabbling as he did so in his pocket for his keys to Khoza's doorway. He wasn't nervous – this was routine stuff. Grabbing the grip bag inside, he swung it out, closed the boot, locked his car, and then made for the doorway.

Van der Merwe didn't notice that the 'cleaning maid' had a long-lens camera poking out of the driver's window snapping away at him. Nor could he have known that once he was inside, her phone bleeper had stopped.

Away from prying eyes, the two of them alone in the cubbyhole in his garage, Moses Khoza greedily fondled the rhino horn.

It was a pristine specimen. Their prize consolation after all the Zama Zama frustrations.

They made a plan. Khoza would take over. Van der Merwe would move on to identify another game reserve and prepare another attack. It wouldn't be quick, Khoza knew that. Painstaking research would be necessary. A new target wouldn't have the defences Zama Zama had somehow established – he wished he knew what their secret was, but he'd already moved on.

There would be a cash transaction at a meeting with the trade attaché

255

alone in the embassy. A bloody lot of cash stashed inside a large package, that the man had agreed – provided he was satisfied with the horn. Which he would certainly be: no question in Khoza's mind.

Then the horn would soon be on its way out of the country. Job done and more of a bonus left for him, the President's son and van der Merwe, now that the poacher team were all dead and didn't need to be paid.

Khoza began to relax by scanning the news, his mood darkening as he noted a new report. The focus upon illegal wildlife trade was becoming increasingly unrelenting. Prohibited ivory had now been found on sale right across Europe including in Britain, contravening international bans aimed at stopping the poaching of elephants.

His Royal Highness Prince William called for an outright ban on any sales of objects containing ivory, insisting that the trade, even in antiques, provided a convenient cover for poaching syndicates to sell their elephant tusks and rhino horns. Of course the prince was correct, Khoza knew only too well – but no matter, he had a job to do.

CHAPTER 19

He had to admit it to himself: he was at a loose end.

Since the firefight vanquishing the biggest threat yet to Zama Zama's rhinos, the Sniper repeatedly self-questioned why a sense of zest was missing in his life. He was busy at work, he would have more time for his son and daughter and also his mother, and he'd committed to fitting in more time with his mates. But there was nonetheless a gaping hole that had been filled by his Zama Zama role.

Which is why he enthusiastically accepted Mkhize's invitation to upgrade IT security at the reserve. Supporting it had become a personal mission, except that this time he could travel down and book in openly, with only Mkhize, Brown and Elise aware of his killer role . . . hopefully.

An early visit was fixed, a bed reserved in the main house, Mkhize warning that Elise was still vulnerable and grieving, though coping by trying to bury herself in learning how to run the reserve. The Sniper was looking forward to seeing her again.

But Mkhize was preoccupied with another blow to the role of rangers and blurted out his anger, patiently explaining the background to the latest outrage. A Thai national, Chumlong Lemtongthai, one of Asia's most notorious wildlife traffickers, had been sentenced to forty years' imprisonment after confessing to organising the hunting of fifty rhinos and conspiring in the illegal killing of at least half of these. Lemtongthai's syndicate enlisted Thai prostitutes to pose as hunters in rhino 'trophy hunts' for whites, authorised by provincial conservation authorities, and then shipped the horns to Asia, with authentic permits that were obtained fraudulently under false pretences.

And now, despite all this, Lemtongthai was due for early release, serving a fraction of his sentence.

Mkhize sighed miserably: 'What the hell do we have to do?' he asked the Sniper in utter frustration.

They weren't brilliant, but Major Yasmin was satisfied that Thandi's photos would constitute the evidence she hoped would be needed. She called the young activist to congratulate her on a job well done.

Now they needed to see what happened next.

Their families had decided on a simple joint funeral for the brothers in arms.

Old Mrs Botha and old Mrs Momberg had both lost their husbands years before, and their sons had been the apple of their eyes. They were grief-stricken, unable to come to terms with their loss. Why? Why? The war against Mandela's 'terrorists' was long over and yet their sons had still been killed – 'serving their country', the mothers had been told, though not exactly how. They asked, but there was no answer. Better to keep it that way, it was decided by veterans they had served with in the South African Army's notorious 32 Battalion.

Van der Merwe joined the modest congregation at Johannesburg's Braamfontein Crematorium to pay his respects, noting that the short speeches were respectful rather than effusive. Afterwards, at the wake in a sports bar, the two men's friends and army veterans downed plenty of Castle beers and talked of old times. Apart from the waiter staff there was not a black face in sight.

Van der Merwe went back to his home, a lonely stillness about it now. He grabbed a drink, then another, then another. The country was a mess. Not just the corruption. But the dysfunctional layers of government: electricity black-outs, no proper sewerage maintanece – the bloody lot. The country was going to the dogs, he moaned to himself.

Time for another drink.

Meanwhile, the Veteran was driving on the Philip Kgosana Drive around the foothills of Table Mountain. As the traffic was heavy, he negotiated it carefully, looking as always in his mirror.

But the next few minutes were a blur. Before he knew it, his car had turned right over, rolling and tumbling down over the side of the elevated

258

carriageway. He had no time to think, except a flash as to whether this was indeed it? The end.

The car bounced onto a grass verge, luckily – miraculously – never hitting anyone. It settled, swaying, and he came to as steam burst from the cracked radiator.

What about the petrol tank? 'Get out, quick!' he thought.

Half dazed, he managed to crawl through the one of the electric windows, which had burst open upon impact. Passing cars had slowed, drivers and passengers gawping. One of the wheels had sheared right off in a really weird way, the tyre not burst. Stranger still, he was unhurt, just shaken with a few sore bits that would doubtless later turn into aching bruises. He looked at the wheel still hanging lopsided off the suspension; he knew about cars, but couldn't fathom exactly how the wheel had come off – except it had been expertly tampered with.

Still stunned, he had enough gumption to grab his essentials – his briefcase containing the vital effects of his missions: notes, laptop chargers and several phones. He stumbled away to safety, calling a cab, thinking hard once he had climbed in.

Had the time come to consider disappearing? To go underground as he had done during the 1960s, 1970s and 1980s?

The Sniper had discovered some information about interesting new IT kit that was being deployed to combat poaching at South Africa's Welgevonden Game Reserve. Now he was presenting his findings to Elise and Mkhize.

'The nub of the problem is that rhino wars are escalating,' he explained. 'Just as we found here, the more heavily armed the poachers are, the more we have to confront them with equally heavily armed defences. So far we've won – except for the baby rhinos so awfully murdered in the orphanage.'

He paused, noting the 'we' he had unconsciously adopted – for he felt it really was 'we' now.

'At Welgevonden they thought laterally and worked on smarter solutions: could data, instead of ever more guns, be the solution?' He explained it in detail.

Mkhize, brow furrowed, pondered. 'So instead of tracking animals, which conservationists have done for a while, this new method effectively tracks people or, more particularly, people who are poachers, without them knowing?'

The Sniper nodded. 'We get guns – poacher syndicates get more guns. We get drones – poacher syndicates get drones. Predictive IT is the next stage – and frankly it's not obvious how poachers can counter it.'

Mkhize was focused on him, Elise trying to keep up as the Sniper continued. 'We could learn from the Kruger National Park. As you know, it's got more rhinos than anywhere else, so gets attacked more than anywhere else. They introduced real state-of-the-art technology in their battle against the poachers, which they call "Postcode Meerkat".'

'What?' Elise asked, incredulous.

'Yah, because Britain's Postcode Lottery funded it and it's labelled "Meerkat" after the animal that stands upright and swivels its head as it looks for threats like people, especially poachers, who move in a more systematic way than wildlife. And when the operator clicks on a dot, the Meerkat immediately focuses there and apparently it's amazing – you can see really sharp black-and-white images of, say, rhinos, or springbok or giraffes or elephants or whatever wildlife is there. And of course, poachers too.'

The Sniper paused, letting it all sink in as Elise and Mkhize sat there spellbound.

'The problem is each Meerkat costs a cool one million dollars.'

'Out of the question,' Elise snapped.

'Can't we try to get donations from international agencies?' Mkhize persisted, 'Using Postcode Meerkats should help South Africa get to that vital crunch moment where rhino births top deaths.'

Tragically, the country was a very long way from that target.

Over her breakfast Major Yasmin was alerted by a bleep – the horn was on the move again.

She tracked it remotely in Khoza's car as she scrambled the Corporal to do his best to follow it. Fortunately, he was already in position outside Khoza's home, so that wasn't a problem.

Khoza had decided to take it into his office rather than leave it at home: more secure there, he considered. Also, he could make the necessary arrangements with the embassy trade attaché to ensure a smooth handover and negotiate the cash transaction with a 'danger' uprating because of the casualties the Zama Zama operation had suffered.

That would take time, he knew – it wasn't easy negotiating with East Asians because their culture was so different. The trade attaché could not be allowed to lose face. If Khoza was demanding extra payment, he most not do so as an ultimatum, but patiently explain the background, enabling the attaché to understand and – doubtless after an adjournment in which they might exchange a few words off the record – conclude (after consultation with his superiors back home) that it would be right to 'volunteer' an uprate as a gesture of goodwill.

The Corporal followed with his camera ready, recognising the likely destination and realising he would need to overtake and pull up in advance of Khoza's car before the security gates to the presidential compound.

That he did, anxious the guards at the security kiosks did not spot him. To his relief, they were preoccupied with checking and then waving Khoza through as the Corporal snapped away, the timing on the digital camera's image synchronising with the digital record of the horn's entry to the Compound.

It was heading right into the heart of the presidency.

Major Yasmin, receiving the Corporal's report, couldn't believe their good fortune. So far so good. Although how long they could remain in the clear, undetected, she had no idea – except that it was almost certainly within a narrow time limit. That, in her experience, could be taken for granted. Just as luck had been with them up until now, it could so easily swing the other way. So very easily.

The Sniper was in his element as an action man. Books and libraries he didn't really do. But as an IT professional he was good at online research.

The Kruger National Park, he discovered, needed the very newest technology to combat an army of 5,000 poachers regularly infiltrating its vast terrain covering nearly 20,000 square kilometres (well over 7,500 square miles). The Kruger had deployed every conceivable technique and technology in its rhino war. Its rangers got psychological counselling and had to take lie-detector tests because bribing by poacher syndicates was ubiquitous.

The park had four helicopters, two fixed-wing aircraft and three microlights. It also had fifty highly trained sniffer dogs, with two at each of the park's ten entrances, searching for concealed weapons in vehicles and also for animal parts. Apart from the Meerkat, they logged everything online from rotting carcasses to poacher incursions, routes and behaviour, weapons, trails and camps found in the park, allowing the rangers to build up a detailed picture of poacher practice, likely strike times and methods.

The Sniper noted the Kruger's switch from using drones to camera traps and sensors – for noise, weight and movement. Advanced number-plate-recognition systems and CCTV cameras were also deployed, not only to detect suspicious vehicles but to check numbers of passengers both leaving and entering to see if they were the same. An intelligence network in surrounding villages and areas with rewards for poacher convictions was another novelty.

The result, the Sniper saw to his satisfaction, was a decline in the rhino carnage and a sharp rise in poacher arrests inside Kruger. He was sure Elise would want all this for Zama Zama – if, and only if, the funds could be raised.

The news wasn't good and Mkhize was worried about his mother and her family.

In recent times KwaZulu-Natal had been scarred by dozens of unresolved, politically motivated murders, as ANC factions fought each other for control of the spoils that came with elected office, corruption starting from the very bottom, killing to maintain access to gravy trains. It was like drug-gang warfare in Mexico or Colombia, with the local police compromised and a culture of intimidation and paranoia allowing corruption to thrive. Politicians trying to escape it found others visiting their homes with AK-47-armed men in tow. 'Dante's Inferno,' was one description of a neighbourhood outside Durban where a hundred killings during ANC infighting resulted in only two convictions.

Mkhize wondered how long it would be before his mom and her village could no longer avoid the fallout. He'd better visit her soon – wondering momentarily if he should invite Thandi, then dismissing it. He was certain it would happen one day – but when, he wasn't exactly sure, and he certainly didn't want to excite village gossip.

Inside his office a relieved Khoza locked the horn safely into a secure cupboard.

So far, so good. But he'd been surprised at how tense he was. Although it was cool at this early hour, when he sat down for a breather he realised he had been sweating.

The whole thing was getting to him. He seemed to be on a treadmill.

The President – and especially the man's eldest son and daughter – wanted more. Always more. No sooner had he got more cash than they were asking after the next lump. And, to be fair, he needed his cut – then another cut, then another – to sustain his family's lifestyle. The pressure was never-ending, seemed to be taking centre stage, shoving his day job into the background.

Moses Khoza caught himself looking in the mirror on the wall behind his closed office door. He looked haggard, haunted. Because he was.

For quite another reason, Justice Samuel Makojaene was also troubled. Yet another legal hot potato had dropped on his lap. He seemed to attract them, his fellow justices knowing he was the most fearless – and the most legally sophisticated – among them, and therefore a safe repository for the controversial cases.

He was being asked to rule on whether the security unit called the Hawks was acting unconstitutionally; nobody could doubt that it had been far less effective in cracking down upon serious crime than its predecessor the Scorpions. Justice Makojaene knew the background but needed to familiarise himself with the detail. The track record of the Hawks was dismal compared with the impressive performance of the Scorpions, which had been deliberately dismantled by the President. Everyone knew why. It was blindingly obvious. Yet the President was shameless: he didn't care about the rising anger at the capture of the South African state by a tiny elite.

In their last year of operation, the Scorpions had seized R4 billion corruptly looted, compared with a miserable R35 million by the Hawks in their first year of operation – a catastrophic collapse. New investigations into corruption had also fallen by a massive eighty-five per cent, as the Hawks set about persecuting people in the ANC who still held Mandela's torch and opposed the President's faction and its bloated business cronies.

Makojaene began drafting his judgement for subsequent clearance with colleagues in the Constitutional Court. He would rule that the Hawks had been acting against the Constitution rather than being its protective arm on the ground.

His words began to flow: 'Corruption threatens to destroy virtually everything we hold dear and precious in our hard-won constitutional order. It blatantly undermines the democratic ethos, the institutions of

263

democracy, the rule of law and the foundational values of our nascent constitutional project. When the main police unit supposed to investigate and prosecute those responsible for corruption instead turns a blind eye and allows them to flourish, the very foundations of our society are mortally threatened.'

He researched the legal precedents, noting that his bête noire Moses Khoza was again the named defendant for the state, though the case would be argued by lawyers and Khoza would be a silent, brooding, baleful presence in court – as before.

Justice Makojaene was still smarting at the sophisticated smear campaign waged against him on social media – he was certain Khoza was behind it, even if it was the brainchild of Bell Pottinger.

It had been vicious and he'd had a crash course in modern digital methods from his teenage grandson, who'd tutored him about 'bots' and the other paraphernalia of Twitter, Instagram and Facebook, platforms he disdained himself but knew were now more powerful than traditional print or broadcast media. His grandson had tried to combat the bots on his behalf, but as soon as they were blocked or rebutted, a hundred more would be unleashed. His grandson had reckoned they were based in Dubai, through which the President's Business Brothers were thought to have laundered their ill-gotten billions.

Justice Samuel Makojaene had been roundly and systematically trashed. But he was still standing, upright and proud, his reputation among those who mattered – opinion formers and the ordinary citizens – just as high as it had been before. He adjusted his tie and brushed his jacket before once again reviewing the cases he relied upon to deliver his verdict, determined to leave no room for challenge. He may have been sore and bitter, but he remained cold and clinical about discharging his professional duty.

Major Yasmin called Thandi to update her on the horn's whereabouts, asking her to be on standby if it was moved, in case the Corporal was deployed on his normal duties.

At least it was now located in her hometown, Pretoria, which would make it easier for her, the Major reassured her. Could she park up near the presidential compound and alternate with the Corporal when he was unavailable?

'Yes,' Thandi said, thinking there would have to be some difficult conversations with her dad about commandeering his old Toyota on a semi-permanent basis, and another awkward conversation with her employer, her job now looking increasingly precarious.

Major Yasmin was still talking. 'I cannot imagine it will be all that long – a few days maybe – because they will want to get the money quickly. They always do.'

'Isaac will be up to see me tomorrow. Can he help me out?'

'Sure,' Major Yasmin replied to a relieved Thandi. He wasn't as familiar to the Major as Thandi, but because the Veteran rated him, that was fine by her.

There was another bonus for Thandi, because Mkhize had put her on the insurance of his newly bought car as a named driver, so she could use his car instead of her dad's, maintaining the peace at home.

Elise enthused about her new role, deliberately burying her loss by throwing herself into running the reserve.

Her new project was to keep alive the Owner's conservation vision. The Zama Zama Volunteer Academy would attract local and international volunteers to work on the reserve for up to six weeks, including patrolling fences, finding and removing poachers' traps and snares.

'If we mobilise the children, they will teach their parents,' she explained to the Sniper.

Elise looked radiant, he thought wistfully as she continued: 'We should involve them also in husbanding the reserve, activities that include quite a lot of physical work, so they realise what it takes to protect wildlife. But it's a community project. We've simply got to educate and inspire kids from local schools, and even older people from the local community, so that they too are involved and feel that wildlife conservation is part of their own proud heritage, not something whites have dumped on their doorstep.'

The Sniper looked doubtful. 'Great idea, but can you really achieve that? Lots of poacher recruits come from the village.'

'Yes! We've got to or, don't you see, we will fail!' she said, eyes blazing. 'It's their land too, after all. We've got to win them over, so they become converted to protecting their own wildlife and realise poaching by villagers is wrong and take them on,' she said.

In the dark early hours, they left a battered old van parked on the roadside a few metres along from the Veteran's house in Kalk Bay, its rear sealed from view.

It looked as if it had been abandoned, one flat tyre (which had been deliberately deflated) confirming first impressions. Dusty, the driver's compartment empty and dirty, it would soon provoke complaints to the local council. Kalk Bay's comfortable, mostly white, retirees were renowned for their nimbyism.

Inside the back, however, was a gleaming high-tech listening device powered by a gigantic battery with months of life and controlled by a special unit of the domestic branch of the State Security Agency (SSA) and reporting directly to Moses Khoza.

Even knowledge of the device's technology was carefully guarded within the SSA, though it had been available to MI5 and the CIA for over a decade. For it had the ability to scan, and then identify the number of, any telephonic communications from any property being targeted. It had been used in London against jihadi Islamists in 2006. On one occasion – celebrated by MI5 and GCHQ officers in the loop – operatives monitored a conversation from inside a south-west London property of an inmate shaving his bodily hair – presumed to be prior to a suicide-bombing mission. The house was quickly raided and the threat aborted.

The Veteran had noticed the van the very morning after it had arrived and, curious as always, had peered inside the front compartment, noting the rubbish strewn on the seats and floor. But the rear was sealed off and there was no way he could have known it was directed at all incoming or outgoing mobile phone conversations to his own home.

He simply assumed it had been stolen and dumped.

Major Yasmin Essop froze when she first took the call from a friend in the security services, whom she'd known since the resistance of the 1980s.

Then she moved coolly and clinically. From her office landline she rang a near neighbour of the Veteran, who wandered casually along the road and knocked on his door, handing over a copy of that morning's *Cape Times* containing a note he had scribbled, which he didn't really understand and didn't really want to. The two men chatted amiably for a few minutes about the latest Test Match score – South Africa's Hashim Amla had knocked a quick century – then bid each other a cheery 'so long'.

Ten minutes later, when he judged the two movements might not be connected, the Veteran trundled down to the Kalk Bay shopping front and went into the back of a craft shop where the owner was busy sorting new products to display. She nodded brightly and indicated the shop phone behind her, then immediately closed the connecting door after going through to serve a customer.

The Veteran rang the number he'd been given and Major Yasmin immediately picked up the phone on her desk. Their conversation was precise and brief, but it sent a chill through even the Veteran's hardened mind.

She'd just had a tip-off. There was a new surveillance system on his house. She wasn't specific. Only that while in the house he must never make or receive any calls on one of his unidentifiable phones. Never. And they must always be switched off in the house. Because the new system had the capability to suck the numbers from any incoming and outgoing mobile phone traffic to his home. Any calls he didn't want identified must be made well away from his home. But he should also perform routine ones as usual on his landline and his own known phone, because they would be monitored and must be observed to be operating normally.

The Veteran would have to find a new method of clandestine communication, both with her and any others in his network. He could still use the pay-as-you-go phones he had distributed to them all, but only well away from his home. Bloody inconvenient.

Emerging from the back of the craft shop, he nodded a thanks to the owner as she smiled in return and decided to get a drink in the Brass Bell over the road, watching the waves crashing against the boulders at its base and spraying the pub windows as they did so.

Sipping a large glass of Windhoek beer, he remained deep in contemplation for some time. First the near-fatal sabotage of his car, then Yasmin's call – a real shaker. Although he had had intelligence responsibilities in one of his roles as a minister, he wasn't up to date on this new system of surveillance. What had changed around his house, he wondered? Aah – maybe the battered black van?

Taking care to ensure nobody was nearby in the pub to overhear, he made calls to the Sniper, Thandi and Isaac, informing them of a new procedure for making safe contact. He had to protect them, to ensure they retained their status unknown to the enemy.

But there was no question. The captured state was closing in on him, waiting to pounce on the slightest slip.

It was now years after the Marikana miner massacre, yet not one police officer had been prosecuted. Despite government promises to do so, no compensation had yet been paid to the families of the workers killed. For

267

the new black elite joining the old white one, justice always happened. For the country's poor black majority, it never seemed to. The new democracy for which the Veteran had fought so hard remained badly flawed.

But the Veteran was encouraged that the resistance was building up. The ruling ANC had haemorrhaged support to opposition parties. The traditional trade-union alliance around the ANC had become fragmented, with new and more militant union formations. Students, always a bellwether for change, had revolted – in militant campaigns against the Cecil Rhodes Statue at the University of Cape Town in #RhodesMustFall and against high fees in #FeesMustFall. There had been big marches against presidential corruption and state capture, and vocal demands from ANC struggle stalwarts that the President must go.

The roots of popular discontent were deep. He couldn't lead campaigns any more. But he knew he was onto something very important through the poaching angle. It could be a real Achilles heel for the corrupt clique. Which was why his contribution now was even more important – even if by necessity more covert than before.

Khoza was preoccupied. It had been a long day of pressure. Pressure and still more pressure. He had been briefed on yet another case up before Justice Makojaene, and he wondered whether the media smears would have got to the judge. Bound to have done so. The man was incorruptible, but also prickly about his reputation. The smears would have needled him. Good. These people had to understand that there were consequences for taking on the President and his cronies.

He discussed strategy for the case with the smart advocate hired by the presidency – a prominent black man, urbane and senior in the profession, noted for his outspoken membership of the Economic Freedom Fighters party. If anyone could win it, he could, thought Khoza, recalling he swept up to courtrooms in his Mercedes sports car, the advocate's ostentatious personal lifestyle at odds with his fiery radical rhetoric.

Khoza's other irritant – the Veteran – seemed to have nine lives, though he was using them up fast. A shame about the unsuccessful car sabotage – but at least they would be able to monitor all phone calls with the Veteran none the wiser. That could be a real treasure trove. He smiled for the first time that day.

Then he realised it was already late – after seven in the evening, and his wife and kids would be waiting for him to come home and eat. He

268

was looking forward to a bottle of red – he had a nice vintage Boschendal that would be his tipple for the evening, as he listened to the fatuous celebrity tittle-tattle from his wife and girls. Maybe he would have to attack a second bottle to endure another dose of that. How was it that all his sacrifices in the freedom struggle had come to celebrityitis among his family? The values of both were so far apart.

But then what had happened to him, to his original values? He knew the answer all too well and, in darker moments of self-reflection, he no longer respected himself for it.

Khoza grimaced – next morning he would be up early for business as usual, this time moving the horn to its next destination.

Thandi drove into the position the Corporal had advised.

It was her first time outside the security-controlled entrance to the presidential compound, just along the road, not too near to attract interest, but near enough for a clear view and, more importantly, a clear long-lens photo of the car carrying the horn. Because once her system bleeped, showing the horn was on the move, there was only one way out and she'd have time to set up a surreptitious shot.

She was nervous, wondering if the armed guards might notice her. She could see them around the kiosk on the left of the entrance, where the barrier would be lifted on their say-so to allow cars to pass to and fro.

Isaac's car was a little easier to drive than her dad's. A newish Renault Clio, it even had air con: what a luxury. She sat hunched, ready to look like she was asleep should anybody take any interest.

Dawn had just broken and it was cold – very cold. She shivered, thinking – foreigners always associate South Africa with hot weather, but once the sun went down in the Highveld, it could be freezing. Just as well she'd brought a beanie.

An hour rolled by. She was bored. Later on, a vast blue sky would hang over the horizon, draped over one of those crisp, clean winter days – and the heat would rise dramatically.

She stirred. It was now 07:20 and cars started arriving for work, includ-ing, unbeknown to her, one driven by Moses Khoza.

He'd breakfasted early with the kids, his wife still slumbering, and dropped them off early at Pretoria Girls' High, proud they went to such a prestigious school.

Khoza went straight across the city to his office, waved through as usual by security after a perfunctory glance into his car; he was, after all, their boss.

He was annoyed. Not with his main task for the morning – to move the horn. But at having his attention diverted by yet more screaming headlines fomented by that infernal nuisance, the amaBhungane investigative unit. It was no consolation that their latest irritating exposé didn't concern his President – for once. Instead their target was the Deputy President.

The Deputy had risen to power as the head of one of the northern provinces, where he operated as a mafia boss, climbing right up the ladder to the top of national politics. He controlled all the province's patronage and tender networks. He and his cronies systematically inflated prices for new school projects, which were built shoddily. On his watch, his province even fabricated exam results to enable him, entirely falsely, to claim high pass rates and educational success.

He had millions stashed in a secure cupboard for pay-offs or to buy votes in ANC internal elections. He exacted cuts from corporates before they were awarded public contracts, and any that refused to participate never got any provincial work. He also had a hit squad to kill anybody who seriously crossed him. One brave whistle-blower was poisoned, an official pathologist confirmed.

Khoza studied the report with interest. It was a damned nuisance – of course it was. But at least there was one bonus. The President owed the Deputy for switching his province to back him in the last ANC elections, and that had always been a pain for Khoza, because the man insisted on getting a share of the looting largesse. Now he would be weakened.

He alerted the President's office of the need to see him right away, and twenty minutes later was shown in. Their meeting didn't last that long, and Khoza was smiling as he strolled back to his office. The President liked to have something on everyone – that had been his trademark since exile in Tanzania and had oiled his route to the very top.

Feeling cramped and uncomfortable, slumped in the car, Thandi flicked through the morning news on her phone to stop herself getting bored, idly looking up from time to time.

Her attention was drawn to one story because the Veteran had been fulminating about it to her last night when he called. There had

270

been another revelation, the Veteran explained: 'Monumental looting of state-owned enterprises uncovered by able investigators and brave whistle-blowers. Often it was through consultancies ostensibly established in the name of Black Economic Empowerment, the policy admirable when launched under Mandela, but which had been systematically perverted.'

Then Thandi jerked to attention. Her device had bleeped. She sat bolt upright, grabbing her camera, checking she wasn't under surveillance from presidential gate security: no, they were focused on the cars coming and going, not down the road where she was.

Thandi winched the window carefully down, steadied the huge lens of the Canon digital camera on the car-door ledge and focused the revolving tip carefully before withdrawing it, ready to return it back for the shot. She had been given a description of Khoza's racing-green Jaguar XF.

Thandi tensed, ready and waiting. The bleeping continued, but since there was no movement on the screen, the car couldn't have moved off yet.

She was distracted by a text: *Horn on the move.* Yes, she bloody knew that.

She tensed. This was a key moment and it was all down to her. Then she realised she'd almost forgotten an essential next step. She checked the gears were in neutral, turned the ignition key and fired up the engine for a quick getaway.

She could see the blue dot coming down what was depicted as an unmarked track on the screen. It was ten o'clock, the morning bright, the sun already sweeping up across the sky. Not bad for photography.

There wasn't much traffic now. The early bustle through the gates had ebbed. Her long lens was protruding like a great eyesore from the window and she worried again that it was so obvious. Several cars slid down the slope towards the barrier to the presidential compound and slowed to stop for the routine check before the barrier was raised.

Khoza's was second, its luxury metallic paint gleaming. The first car, smallish in anonymous white, paused before accelerating away. Khoza's was now in clear view, the barrier momentarily closing then lifting again. A perfect shot – if she could capture it in the bare few seconds she had.

Thandi clicked away. She must have got a dozen or so shots before Khoza was suddenly clear, the turbo on his powerful two-litre diesel surging. She quickly pulled the camera back inside, laying it on the floor in front of the passenger seat.

Surprising herself, she felt calm as the Jag swept past. She hastily snapped her seatbelt on and made ready to pull out to tail it.

Oblivious to the hesitantly tailing Renault Clio jerking in and out of the traffic well behind him, Khoza was concentrating hard on the Jaguar's satnav. He had set the destination before he switched off the engine on arriving for work early that morning: The Embassy of Vietnam, 87 Brooks Street, in the Pretoria suburb of Brooklyn near the university; not far, only about three kilometres from his presidency office.

It was a modern two-storey building, had been a large family home in the past, modest by embassy standards, set in gardens behind a light brown wall with a few cars pulled up between tall trees on a wide pavement area on the roadside. He had been there before and the trade attaché was expecting him. He knew the drill: call the guy from the car before arriving, park on the pavement, and the gate would open for him to walk through without any hanging about.

He made the call and it was quickly answered. The man had been waiting, sounded business–like rather than nervous.

The Jaguar was in Brooks Street now, slowing as Khoza searched for the right number, concentrating on the approach. He had done rudimentary security checks in his mirrors, but hadn't noticed anything unusual. Frankly, he was focused on the prize and it hadn't occurred to him he might be one himself.

Before she set off, Thandi had set her phone on speaker mode, and Major Yasmin was now talking. 'Looks like he may be heading for the Vietnamese Embassy. If so, get a photo of his car parked outside, please, as well as him entering and leaving if you can.'

Thandi hung well back, better to get a shot after he had walked in than risk being spotted going for one on arrival, though that would be perfect, of course.

She glimpsed Khoza turning in, perhaps three hundred metres ahead, and slowed right up, her adrenaline pumping, her mind whirling. She crept along, trying to judge where to stop close enough for a shot but far enough to avoid any risk. It wasn't easy. She'd forgotten to change down gears and the car started to stall: just in time she crunched it into second. (Sorry, Isaac!)

Khoza was climbing out of the car. She anxiously pulled over to the left and halted on someone's front drive, hoping nobody would use it soon. That aside, it was quite a good spot, unobtrusive to Khoza yet with a pretty clear view for photos.

Thandi grabbed the camera, fumbling to switch it on. 'Steady yourself, concentrate!' she muttered under her breath, trying to ignore Major Yasmin's eager prompts and increasingly fretful questions on her speakerphone.

Just as she steadied and focused, Khoza was lifting a grip bag out of his car boot. She snapped away as he closed the boot, pressed on the front-door handle to lock the keyless car and walked to the now opening gate, the embassy sign next to it. Thandi hoped she had caught him framed alongside it, but wasn't sure. The light was dappled at that point and the Corporal had explained the camera only took an average of the light at the point of focus. Her heart was thumping. She hoped to hell she had done it well enough.

The young clerk, well down the food chain in Khoza's security team, was performing her daily routine of scanning the CCTV video cameras.

It was pretty boring, but she was proud to be in the job and her family even more so. Fresh out of school after her Matric and already on presidential security duties: wow! Although she had obtained decent grades, so too had many of her friends and none could find jobs.

She was as diligent as possible, having clocked on at seven that morning as always: she took pride in being on time, even though it meant three journeys from Mamelodi outside the main city precincts squeezed into jam-packed minibus taxis. The problem was, one day was just like the next. Nothing around the perimeter, and at the gate just comings and goings, staff and visitors passing in and out.

Except this time, as she scanned through, something caught her attention. She scrolled back. What was it? A car parked up this morning down the road from the barrier-controlled entrance, just where she had spotted a different one last night, surely. Maybe a local resident?

She zoomed in to take a look. But the closer she got, the more blurred the image, as the vehicle was quite a distance away from the gate cameras. She froze on the car as best she could. Somebody was sitting inside. She noted the digital time coordinates and, thinking hard, rewound quite steadily to the early hours, pausing to see a different car similarly positioned also with someone inside. Curious. Or maybe just servants switching shifts?

She studied more closely. No! There was someone inside all the time! In both cars. It wasn't easy to pick out face features, but they seemed to have differently-shaped faces, to be different people. That would make sense, of course.

It took her hours to search through the recordings. Time slipped by. Then, startled, she froze the image again. She had already seen the second car arriving just before the first left, the two drivers getting out momentarily and exchanging a package. Now there was a cylindrical barrel of some sort pointing out of the window!

What on earth was going on? She zoomed in as closely as she could. The driver was at one end of the 'barrel', sitting hunched. But only for a couple of minutes. Then the implement was withdrawn and the car moved straight off and away out of sight. She wound back and looked more closely. Was it a camera?

Suddenly she was scared. Excited but scared. She spent some minutes checking over and over again. Yes! It must be a camera – but why? Again, noting the coordinates, she had another look at the departing car. The registration plate was vaguely visible, but frustratingly the letters and numbers were not distinct enough. The image might need to be looked at by the technical team.

She thought for a moment, then copied down the coordinates on a separate piece of notepaper, got up and hurried off to talk to her manager.

Major Yasmin had been on tenterhooks, but at least Thandi seemed to have got the photos of Khoza entering the embassy. She didn't like deploying amateurs, but had to admire the girl's tenacity and courage.

Now she had to wait for news on the quality of the photos.

She thought proudly of her youngest daughter, who'd been made head girl at her high school, seemingly running the whole place, from what she could gather: in and out of the head teacher's study to influence matters. A leader in the making, maybe? Rather like herself in her youth?

A security alert suddenly flashed up, jolting her back to focus on work: 'Two suspicious long-range photographers spotted outside presidential gates. Security heightened.'

She called Thandi immediately with a curt explanation. 'Move out now please, but slowly, normally. Don't arouse suspicion. They may be on to you. We need those photos safely deposited. There's no alert on number plates – yet. So maybe we have a little time. Whose car were you in?'

'Isaac's,' Thandi stammered, frightened for the first time. Her mind raced at the ramifications of implicating Isaac. 'I must protect him.'

'Right, we will work out a plan,' Major Yasmin said calmly, assuming control. 'Let me think.'

After just a few seconds, she spoke: 'First, exit the area. Then drive right away to meet me where we did last time. Except leave the car around the corner and come on foot. I will do the same. We can walk separately through the school gates – they're usually open – and into the grounds, rendezvousing under the trees nearby. Stick the gear in a plastic bag or something so it isn't obvious.'

What Major Yasmin didn't say was she also hoped to God the number plates didn't show, because that would link in the Corporal – and hence her. They'd all had a remarkably clear run – up to now. But she'd known all along it couldn't last.

She headed out of her office, leaving a message for the Veteran via their new circuitous link.

Khoza exchanged the horn for the bulging envelope with the excited embassy trade attaché, who explained it would be exiting in a few days via the diplomatic bag to Hanoi, thence to a trusted contact in Ho Chi Minh City.

Khoza wasn't worried about that. He had the cash – $150,000 of it in hard currency. As he left the building and made for his car, he noticed a WhatsApp message on his phone about the photographer outside the gates. Odd? He looked around him before climbing in. Nothing. He would investigate the incident when he got back. Meanwhile, he needed to distribute the booty. That was his priority – not some prying photographer: there were always paparazzi trying to make some trouble and cash.

The trade attaché had already made careful plans. The diplomatic bag to Hanoi was due out in two days.

Thandi drove, worried – desperately worried.

It was one thing for her to take risks. But to implicate Isaac was unacceptable. Her mind churned as she forced herself to concentrate on the driving. Yet surely he was implicated already – willingly, as one of the Veteran's co-conspirators?

Maybe – but only through her.

She pulled up, parking out of sight of the school gates and walked around and through them.

About a hundred metres up the drive was a clump of trees near a sports pavilion. She headed there into the shade, looked around to see if anyone was taking any notice – which appeared not to be the case. A cricket ground was being mowed and worked on, with a rope on short stilts providing rectangular protection around the batting pitch near the middle.

The birds were chirruping. The sun was shining over the green fields – rugby posts visible in the distance. There was a light breeze. A normal school day, and the classrooms well up the long drive were out of sight and full of school students.

She hung about and looked at her watch. A further ten minutes ticked by. It must have been half an hour or more since Major Yasmin had called her. Thandi was getting fidgety.

It could only have been a minute or two later when there was a tap on her shoulder. She jumped almost out of her skin and turned quickly. 'Hi,' Major Yasmin smiled.

'You scared me!' Thandi blurted.

'Sorry – necessary precautions.'

'How on earth did you creep up so quietly?' she asked, handing over the bag.

'Training,' she smiled then continued quickly. 'We now have to be doubly careful, especially if they trace Isaac's car. Then Khoza's security mafia will be all over you – and me, if the Corporal's car has also been found.'

Thandi looked terrified, not least by Major Yasmin's switch from warm friendly to cold security mode. *Welcome to my world*, Major Yasmin thought but didn't say.

'Look, no need to panic. Apparently the car numbers weren't clear on the CCTV and the technical guys are poring all over it now. Your car was in daytime, so is much more vulnerable. This must be your line and you stick to it, come what may: a journalist friend you had met through your job asked you to do this. You took photos of cars coming in and out on the off-chance. He wanted to get one of the Business Brothers he'd been tipped off was visiting that morning. Isaac knew nothing about this.

'If they ask you who the journalist is, you say you're in media yourself and professionally you will not reveal the name: no journalist divulges a source. That's Isaac's line too. Whatever they ask, stick resolutely to this line. They will be tempted to rough you both up, but they will be cautious because there's so much bad stuff in the public arena on the Brothers and the President, they won't want to risk fanning that even more by detaining journalists. If they believe you, that is.'

Thandi looked sombre. She was thinking about a difficult conversation to come with Isaac.

Good, Major Yasmin thought: the young woman had to get real. She looked at her watch. 'Right – you stay here for another fifteen minutes, out of the way but not hiding.' She looked around. 'Sit on that bench over there. Fiddle on your phone. Let me drive out and get well clear. And – be very, very careful. These people don't mess around. They will bury you and your man without any compunction if they think it is necessary.'

As she made to go, Major Yasmin turned. 'You did well. I will let you know what the photos look like and any news on the cars. My guess is they haven't been able to identify the numbers or I would have heard by now. But you never know.'

Buoyed by the praise, but lapsing quickly into worry, Thandi went to sit on the bench as the Major slipped away. A few minutes later she thought she heard a car start up, but if so it didn't come out of the entrance she'd used, because there were several to the school.

One careful lady, Major Yasmin, Thandi thought.

Mkhize was wondering why he had bothered to drive up to Pretoria in the first place, for Thandi had been away most of the time.

Was their relationship working for him any more? His place always seemed to be second. Yet he was infatuated with her. No, he checked himself, the wrong word. He loved her. That was both the thrill and the problem.

'Isaac! Are you there? He jerked awake from his catnap. She was knocking on his B&B room door.

Mkhize felt a rush of exhilaration, sad only that he had to drive back the next day.

They spent the next few hours in his bedroom – both in bed caressing each other, but also talking. Lots of talking. One way, mostly as Thandi poured out her experiences.

She was intoxicatingly effervescent when she talked animatedly, so seriously, at once thrilling him and worrying him deeply. Both about his car and whether he was really suited to this life as an appendage or not.

At least for now, he concluded, as she buzzed away, he probably was. He couldn't get enough of her – maybe never would? But he still wanted her.

The technical guys examined the key CCTV footage of the two cars and the camera lens. They zeroed in as best they could, but both cars were too far away to get a really sharp image of the number plates. The first one was at night, which made it even more difficult to identify.

The second was clearer, but the numbers were too blurred to be sure. The image was nevertheless stored, just in case it came up again, and also sent away to a laboratory with a request to the boffins to reconstruct it.

A report went to Moses Khoza.

CHAPTER 20

Much to their chagrin, the Veteran simply disappeared off the security services' radar one afternoon.

He had caught a Comair flight from Cape Town to ORT Airport in Joburg, having checked in two bags of clothes and other living essentials, with a distinctively luminous light-green strip binding both. His laptop, various phones, chargers and memory sticks he kept glued to him in a small bag throughout the journey. And, as he knew full well, he was watched to the gate, then picked up when the plane landed at ORT, and monitored to baggage reclaim, where he collected a trolley and wheeled it over to the gents, leaving it outside.

Amidst the bustling travellers searching for their suitcases, his watchers waited at a distance.

Big mistake.

As he walked into the toilet, a black cleaner gave a cheery grin: 'Welcome to my office, sir!' The Veteran reciprocated by pressing a R20 note into the young man's hand, and glanced at the cubicles, noting the only one that was full, walking into its immediate neighbour.

'Damn!' he muttered loudly. My fly was undone all through the flight!'

'Don't worry, often happens to blokes!' The Corporal muttered the reply code next door, sliding a bag underneath the dividing partition.

The Veteran retrieved the clothes, a hat, a long, straggly grey-haired wig, matching moustache and stick from the bag, put these on, and slid the leather bag back under to the Corporal, putting his own clothes into a Pick n Pay plastic bag.

The Corporal flushed the toilet, washed his hands and checked to see if anybody was loitering with intent. Nobody was. 'All clear,' he whispered as he walked out, giving the cleaner a R10 note, and headed to collect the Veteran's two bags with their distinctive band from the revolving carousel.

A few minutes later, a dishevelled old man shuffled clumsily out of the gents and, clinging precariously to his stick, slowly wobbled to the exit, attracting not the slightest interest from the watchers now getting agitated that their man had not yet appeared. By the time they swooped on the airport toilet and sounded the alert, the Veteran had been safely whisked away, reunited with his bags and driven by the Corporal to an old comrade's 'safe house' in Pretoria, where the disguise was taken off.

Quite like old times, he mused. He'd lived underground from the 1960s to 1980s, but in those days, of course, there were no mobile phones, and this time he was careful to keep his switched off, using only his untraceable phones and even then, calling or messaging invariably by WhatsApp because it was encrypted and therefore protected from the President's ubiquitous security mafia.

Just to sow confusion in the security circles desperate to find him, he had asked a favour of another old comrade who was properly retired – unlike the Veteran, who was very active despite living on a pension alone. The trusted friend was a normal retiree and travelled a lot with his wife: on holiday, sometimes abroad, sometimes taking breaks or visiting relatives and friends across the country. Ideal to be given the Veteran's phone.

Every so often (and strictly only if he was away from home and on the move, never in one place like someone's home or staying at a hotel), the Veteran instructed his friend to switch on the phone, check for any messages and relay these back to the Veteran. However, the main purpose of this subterfuge was to lay a false trail of the Veteran's movements for those monitoring the phone.

For an IT specialist like the Sniper, the task was a relative doddle. He had been presented with all the digital images and the digital tracking trail and asked to knit these together to form a compelling picture of the rhino horn's theft. His instructions were also to make absolutely certain there was no embedded digital footprint, either to his computer or, more important still, to Major Yasmin's official systems.

It was fascinating putting all this together, taking care of the details, ensuring that photos of the number plates of Khoza and van der Merwe – occasionally, but not always evident – were included. He hadn't been given their phone numbers because these weren't available, but he was able to build in, using the transmitter's GPS coordinates, the Ranger's movements from the time he had switched the horns in the Owner's home to the handover to van der Merwe. Thereafter the horn's signal largely did the job for him; it was just a question of arranging all the digital material into a recognisable report.

The only issue was the resulting file was huge – about twenty-nine gigs – which meant physical transfer via a memory stick was the most practical. With a file that huge, email was out of the question, Dropbox and even WeTransfer also awkward and probably security-risky. The Sniper copied the file onto twenty new sticks as requested.

He didn't charge for any of this work, happy to absorb it as a business cost.

Having discussed it with the Veteran, Major Yasmin decided to finesse her next step rather delicately.

She couldn't make an official request on behalf of military intelligence, because that would have been logged and there would have been awkward questions asked. So she decided instead to speak informally to a contact in Interpol about the horn, giving them the GPS coordinates to try and follow its movements still being signalled by the transmitter.

The Veteran had thought about informing VETPAW but decided against it. Preferable to alert them much later (and other NGOs concerned with protection of the rhino species) to Bob Richards' intervention for follow-up. Better that way than risk it leaking out in a messy manner before the story had broken in the terms he planned.

Stowed carefully in a diplomatic bag covered by the Geneva Convention and not subject to random search, the horn stopped transmitting after the Boeing 777 took off from ORT Airport at around two in the afternoon.

The Emirates plane flew eight hours nineteen minutes to Dubai and the diplomatic bag was transferred automatically to a new Emirates flight – again a 777 – which took off three and a half hours later, arriving in Hanoi at shortly after one o'clock in the afternoon the next day. As the plane was unloaded and the bag was handed to a waiting government official, the GPS signal was picked up again, to be tracked wherever the horn went in the Socialist Republic of Vietnam.

*

The Veteran was the very first person to whom the Sniper gave a memory stick, because his task was to write the story in the form of a speech Bob Richards could deliver.

He enjoyed the opportunity, for he was a good writer (his memoirs were a racy read) and wanted the political context and texture to be clear. He never made any apologies for trying to be readable – academic as well as most specialist writing was often so dense as to be unintelligible and failed to communicate anything to anyone beyond the cognoscenti. Speeches were often the same – utterly tedious.

His own test for a speech – which, when he was a minister, he impressed upon his officials – was always: 'Imagine sitting in the audience. Would you really want to listen to this stuff yourself?'

In the Veteran's view, far too many speakers liked the sound of their own voices. That was certainly true of politicians, often of vicars or priests, business leaders and trade unionists. For him a speech always needed to have a clear purpose and its entire contents had to be single-mindedly directed at that purpose. Communication was the name of the game. Not droning on.

Anecdotes were important to convey something unfamiliar or complex. Also, he tried to tell a story – not to recite loads of facts and figures that the audience probably knew anyway – building it up to the main conclusion. Above all, the Veteran believed, decide what your main purpose is – that may have sounded obvious, but in his experience was far too often neglected. Ask yourself in preparing a speech: what is the main thing you want the audience to remember? If you want to get people's attention, what in a few sentences (no more) is your speech all about? What's its essence? Some called it 'the elevator test', but it was astonishing how very few people – even those at the top of their profession – were able to answer that question.

Now he would have to apply the same verities to himself, as he began assembling the complex data and drafting the speech for Bob Richards. It would be, he knew, one of the most important he had ever written. It could even trigger the endgame for the President who, up to now, had consistently broken domestic law with impunity. But illicitly trading in rhino horns was in breach of international law and would cause not just a domestic outcry – they happened almost daily – but a global one too.

*

His Honour Justice Samuel Makojaene was professionally allergic to being dragged into battles that should have been resolved politically. Equally, however, he was proud that the Constitutional Court had demonstrated its resolve in confronting the most powerful person in the country, the President himself.

Makojaene despised the man, and was relentless in requiring him to fulfil his constitutional obligations. One of his coruscating but legally impeccable judgements went to the heart of power: 'He is a constitutional being by design, a national pathfinder, the quintessential commander-in-chief of state affairs and the personification of this nation's constitutional project. Yet the President fails to uphold, defend and respect the Constitution as the supreme law of the land.'

Now he had been asked to act again, but this time in a uniquely unusual way. And for once he wasn't sure what to do. The law had been broken. From the evidence he had been shown, there seemed no doubt about that. But no actual case had been brought before the Constitutional Court for him or his colleagues to adjudicate upon, simply because it was too dangerous for those in possession of the palpably incriminating evidence to do so. Instead he was being asked to use the gravitas of his great office to make a quasi-legal pronouncement that would ultimately become public. That was awkward – damned awkward, and would expose him to heavy criticism that he was no longer professionally impartial.

The whole saga had begun in a most disconcerting fashion, offending his sometimes pompous dedication to judicial protocol.

After work he had been driven by his usual Constitutional Court driver to his home in Waterkloof, Pretoria. Sitting in the back, he normally used the drive to catch up on reading or do his personal emails and messages; it always irritated him that too often he never had time to do the reading because the bloody phone consumed the entire hour the journey normally took. Trouble was, people expected an almost instant reply these days. Everything seemed to operate that way. They went so close to deadlines, whereas in the old days of pre-digital communication, that wasn't possible: you had to plan ahead and build in time.

As normal, his car had driven him into his drive, and the security gates began closing automatically behind him. But, with a million other things on his mind, he did not notice a figure slip silently and invisibly through to wait in the shadows as he climbed out of the car.

He began walking to his front door, his Zimbabwean servant already having opened it for him, when he nearly jumped out of his skin.

'Good evening, Comrade Justice!' a familiar voice said.

The Veteran was approaching him, smiling out of the darkness, a hand extended in greeting.

'How on earth did you get in? You startled me!' Justice Makojaene sounded aloofly grumpy. He didn't consider himself an arrogant man, but his high office as a custodian of the country's precious Constitution some-times made him appear too self-important to those who didn't know him.

'I apologise, but for reasons I will explain, I cannot approach you openly. I would be grateful for a bit of your time this evening to ask a vital favour,' the Veteran explained in a way that left Makojaene – who knew and respected him – little alternative.

'Very well then, come with me,' he replied huffily.

Directing the Veteran to his study, he confirmed the morning pick-up time with his driver and instructed him not to mention to a soul what had happened. The driver, expecting to incur some wrath for not having spotted the intruder entering behind the car – a favourite trick of muggers and criminals – was only too relieved to banish it from his mind.

Makojaene then instructed his house servant similarly and went off to find his wife, explaining they unexpectedly had an extra belly to fill for supper this evening. She wasn't happy either.

Soon the two men were huddled together in deep conversation.

Via a secure memory stick inserted in Makojaene's PC, the Veteran showed him the photos with their digitally timed records, together with the digital GPS records from the transmitter, tracking the movement of the horn all the way from the Owner's house in Zama Zama to Ho Chi Minh City.

'Here is the Ranger taking the rhino horn to Mr Piet van der Merwe; here is the latter taking it to Moses Khoza's house. Here is Khoza driv-ing to his office through the barrier to the presidential compound and here he is emerging back through the barrier and then later entering the Vietnamese Embassy. Everything matches: times from the transmitter coinciding with times on the photos,' the Veteran explained. 'Digitally it cannot be challenged.'

Makojaene sat back in his chair, a frown on his fine but increasingly lined face.

'So you want me to give my judicial imprimatur that this case is proven? That a crime has been committed in terms of illegal trade in rhino horn? To pronounce guilty without even charge or trial? When the whole foundation of my career, my profession, our judicial system, the whole presumption is "innocent until proven guilty"?'

'Yes,' the Veteran replied frankly. 'We go back together a long way. We trust each other. You are the only person I could approach on this, both certain that my identity and those of my colleagues will be protected, and hopeful because of the very high respect in which you are held for your integrity, your courage and your unrivalled legal acumen and experience.'

The Veteran knew he was appealing both to Makojaene's professional self-esteem and his high reputation for an unfailing commitment to justice and morality.

'And this will be exposed first under privilege in the British Parliament with my name and office associated as prosecution, judge and jury all at the same time?'

'Yah, Samuel, because you know that this will never be brought to trial here. The National Prosecuting Authority is manipulated through its corrupt crony head by the President and the Brothers.'

'Yes, yes,' Makojaene waved his hand in irritation. *As if he of all people needed to be reminded of that! For goodness' sake!*

The Veteran, playing his friend perfectly, added gently: 'I know this is incredibly difficult for you. If I had an alternative I wouldn't be troubling you, believe me! But it is so important, so vital. Cast-iron evidence implicating the President's security chief in high crime! Khoza is his right-hand, dirty-tricks man — he does his bidding all the time. The President has been Teflon Man up to now. Everything gets thrown at him and he is still there. Discredited and despised, yes. But still there! Looting with impunity despite your best efforts. This may be big enough to unseat him at the coming ANC conference. We have to seize it. Please!'

The trouble was, the Veteran was dead right, Makojaene had to admit to himself. Equally, that put Makojaene impossibly on the spot.

To the extent that this could ever be the case in a game reserve dedicated to the complex, constantly challenging, never-ending tasks of sustaining and managing groups of wild animals contesting for space, food and life, a sort of tranquillity descended upon Zama Zama.

VETPAW advised that serious follow-up rhino poaching attacks were unlikely, almost nil. The publicity given to the deaths of the white poachers – the black ones hardly rated a mention, never did, though scores died every year across the country – would have been a huge deterrent.

Khoza, anxious about where the trail might lead, instructed the Commissioner of Police and the National Prosecutor – two other presidential placemen – not to pursue the deaths. The local police were relieved. They couldn't cope as it was with rising daily crime waves and inter-ANC political assassinations.

Meanwhile, the Ranger was not a happy man. Van der Merwe had abruptly cut his regular payments, as he had no interest in Zama Zama any more. Instead van der Merwe had identified game reserves in the Bela-Bela area in the country's northern Limpopo province. There seemed to be less attention focused there. The road access wasn't too bad: in fact, some of the reserve boundaries ran right alongside tarmac roads, which led via others eventually to the main N1 highway to Pretoria and Johannesburg, just a couple of hours away. He booked a visit at one of the reserves, which had half a dozen rhinos.

Thandi didn't have a passport, so Major Yasmin had to fast-track her application.

It was risky because it linked her to the young activist for the first time – if anybody ever noticed. She also called in a favour with the British High Commissioner to get a quick visa for entry to the UK – the bane of South African citizens after new visa requirements had been imposed for the very first time in 2009 as part of wider security checks after concerns the country was being used as a staging post for terrorists and illegal migrants.

Thandi had never been abroad, let alone undertaken a mission as sensitive as this one. She was daunted but determined.

When she told him, Mkhize was worried. But what could he do? She was on his mind, distracting him as he guided a new bunch of guests around the wonders of Zama Zama.

When the further report came back to Khoza on the mystery CCTV images, it was a little more interesting, but still not conclusive.

Thinking back later, he should have focused more stringently on it at the time. But he didn't. He was too distracted. By the President's incessant demands. By the individuals and groups mounting increasing political and media attacks against the President and the Business Brothers. And

286

then last, but certainly not least, by the necessity to open up a new rhino-poaching target.

Khoza had fixed in his mind that the grainy photographer must be from the media, pursuing one of their prurient ventures against the President and his circle. Although he did notice momentarily that the last images outside the security barrier had been captured at a similar time to his departure with the rhino horn, he simply thought that a coincidence, even though the car that had pulled out had driven off at rather the same time as him.

However, the boffins had managed to identify possible permutations of the car registration. None seemed to have been of any interest to the police or security services before: one from Benoni, one from a village in KwaZulu-Natal, the third from Midrand. He asked them each to be checked out, but didn't place a high priority on the enquiries.

He had a more immediate problem: the deputy finance minister. The man was being decidedly uncooperative. He had been chauffeured to the palatial Sandton compound where the Business Brothers and their families had their homes, and had been offered a R600 million cash inducement on the spot – provided he complied with a list of their requirements. In particular, not to pursue banks that were a conduit for billions of rand in suspicious or shadowy transactions.

No ordinary citizen or businessperson could have got away with all this. But the Brothers now wanted the deputy minister to sign a pre-drafted, yet entirely false, statement to help kill the mounting complaints against them. On top of that, they wanted an assurance he would push through the astronomically expensive R1 trillion nuclear deal, from which the President, with the Brothers, was to get a R1 billon kickback.

And one other small matter. The minister was told by the eldest Brother he would be killed should he ever reveal publicly any details of this infamous meeting.

Despite all that – Khoza was astonished – not only had the minister gone straight to his immediate boss, the finance minister, and spilled the beans, he was also alleging that the Business Brothers, when they offered him the job, had explicitly said at the meeting: 'Be in no doubt that we control everything. We control the police, the National Prosecutor and National Intelligence.'

If all had gone well, the deputy could have had the finance minister's job in the near future and a pile of cash to boot. The problem was, the infernal deputy finance minister had said no.

Khoza knew exactly what the President's decision would be when put in the picture: the man had to go and be replaced by somebody malleable. He called the President's office and asked for an immediate meeting.

Then Khoza sat back and looked whimsically out through his office window in the bright sunshine at the meticulously maintained gardens, with their medley of contrasting colour from plumbago, agapanthus, cannas and spiky aloes, nestling alongside the jacarandas. He was given to philosophical spasms – indeed, more of them as time went on and as he was dragged deeper and deeper into the presidential mire. He realised he had become two characters in one. Not clinically, but morally. Half of him careered along, hoovering up the largesse and enjoying a lifestyle he could never have dreamed of on Robben Island or in Soweto. The other half – occasionally, though increasingly frequently he had to acknowledge – despised himself.

At one and the same time he could be angry with the deputy finance minister, methodically setting up his political assassination – and yet admire the man's character, his fearless unwillingness to be bought.

Moses Khoza thought back to the island, the example of Madiba, wondered if it was actually the highlight of his life, and whether his young self then would have approved of his older self now. The difficulty was, he knew the answer only too well. And it wasn't comfortable.

His phone rang, summoning him to see the President. His life lurched forward – as usual.

Justice Makojaene had asked the Veteran to leave the memory stick of material with him. He would look at it again, sleep on it, then make an early decision.

The thing that made up his mind was unconnected. An exposé of the manner in which the President's crony placemen at the top of the once globally admired South African Revenue Service (SARS) had not only corrupted it, but rendered it virtually dysfunctional. No surprise, then, that tax collection slumped dramatically.

Desperate to plug the gaps, all the President's men began to ensure SARS started withholding VAT refunds – except for the Business Brothers: they alone got theirs pronto. SARS became broke, and the public finances went into a downward spiral. That meant fewer houses built for the homeless, fewer schools repaired, worse health services, still higher unemployment – among many other signs of public decay under the President.

The crony appointed by the President to head SARS had no experience of revenue collection, but nevertheless immediately began denouncing and humiliating its senior executives, bypassing and ignoring their immense expertise and experience in a reign of terror and mistrust. A world-class organisation had been turned upside down, poisoned with intrigue, suspicion, distrust and fear of new senior management. All that had disabled revenue collection and opened the door for illicit financial activity to flourish.

What the hell, Justice Samuel Makojaene decided: go for it. Somebody had to make a stand.

He began drafting a short affidavit for the Veteran to use publicly. It stated, on the evidence he had seen, there was no question that the presidency, through its head of security, had acted criminally and that there may well be a prima facie case against the President: because of Khoza's close proximity to the President, it was inconceivable he wasn't implicated.

He would get it typed on his official notepaper by his faithful PA and sign it in front of a witness, then have it handed to the Veteran.

CHAPTER 21

It reminded Khoza uncannily of Nelson Mandela's 'Black Pimpernel' phase.

That had been during 1960 when the ANC had been banned and its leaders were on the run to avoid being arrested. Mandela had been forced to go underground to set up the resistance around the country, going to ANC leadership meetings, and popping up everywhere to talk to white newspaper editors. This produced countrywide news reports dubbing him 'The Black Pimpernel' as he eluded police roadblocks, with a warrant out for his arrest. He was often disguised as a chauffeur, chef or 'garden boy', finding the role of chauffeur (neat peaked cap included) ideal because it enabled him to drive around freely as black men often did under apartheid in their white masters' cars.

The security services had a fix on the Veteran's phone. But they might as well not have. For its signal popped up purely randomly, with no pattern at all. And, frustratingly, always when on the move, to be switched off before Khoza's people could zero in and pick him up. The man seemed to surface in all sorts of places, retrieving incoming texts and voicemails, but very seldom, if ever, replying. The other puzzling thing was the phone signal occasionally popped up abroad – once in Europe, another time in Mozambique – yet Khoza had checked and there was no record of the Veteran leaving the country.

He must indeed be operating underground and when travelling outside the country doing so illegally either on a false passport or somebody else's. Khoza resolved to make enquiries with passport and immigration.

*

Thandi didn't even tell her parents she was travelling to London.

Apart from the Veteran, only Mkhize was put in the picture. 'Don't worry, I will come straight back,' she told him.

He could tell she was nervous – yet excited too, both emotions colliding as she was constantly on edge. The Veteran – who had done the journey regularly over the decades – had tried to give reassurances as he briefed her, but was struck at the inner anxiety of this normally confident, sparky young woman, assessing it must be because she was leaving her comfort zone.

Then her conversation switched.

Mkhize also listened attentively – as he often did when Thandi was on one of her rants. This time she launched into yet more revelations about the President's corrupt rule. Hundreds of emails implicating the Business Brothers had been leaked to the *Daily Maverick*'s Scorpio investigative unit, which became known as the #BrotherLeaks. These proved their complicity in the looting that funded a multinational empire worth billions.

'Sickening! Absolutely bloody sickening!' Thandi said. 'But why should I be angry? After all, it is no surprise, is it?'

Mkhize put the phone down, musing in quiet delight at his spirited girl. She was his girl, wasn't she? He certainly hoped so – and thought so, though she could be so elusively preoccupied by what she termed 'the struggle' that sometimes he didn't know where he stood. Yet he wasn't even registering any other girl any more. She was definitely the one for him, he had decided, surprised at his conviction, and that his female wanderlust had ended.

Zama Zama was busy and Mkhize was due to take out a group on the afternoon game drive.

Since the poaching shootouts, there had been many other distractions from his daily work as a ranger. A baby hippo reared from very soon after birth in the orphanage didn't like water! It had to be trained before being released into the wild. The Reserve had opened a volunteer camp for young people from nearby villages, together with global volunteers. They could come and live in basic tents very close to wildlife to be tutored in the bush and its conservation. Mkhize especially enjoyed the one-to-one teaching and group interaction, which was entirely different from escorting guests.

Elise, though still privately in mourning, had devoted herself to continuing her husband's vision of building a massive conservation area to provide a legacy for future generations. She thought back often to the elephant herd's extraordinarily moving reaction to her husband's death. When he was alive the herd would suddenly appear by the fence surrounding their house and peacefully nudge a newborn baby to introduce it to him, or simply turn up for a friendly inspection that all was okay.

But when they had arrived immediately after his death hundreds of miles away in Johannesburg, they were deeply disturbed. Initially Mkhize wasn't sure, until he noticed signs of deep stress, even on the babies. There'd been no poaching attacks or other similar crises to produce the telltale marks of liquid secreted from temporal glands in wet streaks down their cheeks, almost like a human crying. Then he became transfixed as low-frequency rumbling came from the herd – as they had when they had stood communicating with the Owner – with the dominant bull pacing restlessly up and down as the matriarch stood silent and solemn, waiting for the Owner to reappear, yet, Mkhize conjectured, knowing he was never going to again.

The relationship with the elephant herd was deep but also complicated, as Mkhize well knew from having been deputed by the Owner to befriend an orphan male bull, who – in accordance with elephant custom – had been ejected from the herd when nearing adulthood to avoid his raging testosterone levels driving him to interfere with the teenage females. The aim a sensible one: to prevent inbreeding and distribute genes widely.

Although he was an orphan, the matriarch enforced the practice, and the young bull was left utterly bereft, having already lost his mother and now his foster mother and adopted family. He began starving himself, almost to death. So the Owner introduced Mkhize to the downcast bull. Gradually Mkhize built trust and friendship, tempting him with branches of alfalfa and thorny acacia, and soon the bull began lumbering up to the Land Cruiser whenever the ranger was driving nearby him, standing quietly and signalling comradeship, his life restored and adjusted to his new normality as a loner until a female from another herd was introduced to Zama Zama.

It was experiences like that which Mkhize knew meant he could never be torn away from his work in the bush – even by the new love of his life.

*

Thandi's instructions had been very clear.

She was to rendezvous with Bob Richards in a pub near Parliament, hand over ten of the memory sticks supplied by the Sniper, with all the data on the rhino horn, together with another one containing the draft speech. She was to read a hard copy on the flight over so that she could talk him through it and provide any background understanding needed.

She had been advised by the Veteran – an intrepid air traveller – to get to ORT Airport three hours before her flight and buy water once she was through security at the airport because she should drink lots of it in-flight to avoid dehydration.

Having caught the Gautrain there, she walked to check-in, the queue exasperatingly long for those, like her, in economy. Finally her suitcase sailed off on the conveyor belt and she made her way to security – another long delay as the queue wound its way towards the X-ray and other checks. Frustratingly, they chose to search her, a woman airport officer feeling over her body: 'Random check, madam,' she was told. Then she joined another long queue to show her passport at immigration.

It was all so fiddly, and took so long!

Her flight was scheduled to board in an hour and she bought a couple of half-litres of water in plastic bottles, sat down on a bench and waited, looking around as she did so at the great bustle of people walking determinedly about. Nobody was taking the slightest notice of her – except for a couple of young blokes she judged at roughly her age, who were giving her the look. Not something she ever encouraged.

She tried to avoid being nervous. *Treat the whole thing as a novelty, a learning experience*, she tried to urge herself.

But it didn't make much difference: she remained on edge.

Bob Richards did not know what exactly the material would constitute, but the Veteran had hinted at a big story when he WhatsApp called.

Richards was both intrigued and excited. Making a difference – that mantra of his again: Mandela's mantra. He also anticipated the media-fest that might follow. It gave him an adrenaline buzz, for he was known to be a good performer, an accessible backbencher who spoke his mind, but not in a gratuitously disruptive manner, to his party. He wasn't a rent-a-quote MP, always available with a ready line to garnish a political reporter's story, regardless of the subject – and he was respected for that by his colleagues and those journalists who were serious rather than spin-merchants, of whom there were far too many these days.

The Veteran had been very clear. Richards must tip off Westminster journalists in advance that there was a big story he would break. South African media would be taken care of by the Veteran.

Richards went personally to see Mr Speaker, with whom he got on well, and explained that he was putting in for another adjournment debate to expose corruption with international collusion in South Africa. It was duly granted – an hour-and-a-half debate in Westminster Hall, granted at that length because he'd rounded up a few of his fellow Labour MPs to put in for it too, with him as the lead speaker.

That ensured he would have a good half hour to speak, or roughly three thousand words.

A date was also agreed – several days after he was due to rendezvous in the Clarence pub with a young woman he didn't know, bright, brave but probably apprehensive, the Veteran had warned before he sent her photo by WhatsApp.

Very attractive, he thought, looking forward to meeting her.

Bob Richards was known at Westminster for having many female Labour MPs within his circle of friends, among them the strongest protagonists of women's equality and independent rights, who took no prisoners when encountering a straying hand or a lecherous approach – sadly too common in Parliament, with many well-known cases of exploitation of young female researchers or secretaries.

He thought himself as a 'male feminist'. Which triggered hilarity from his wife, who regularly pulled his leg about it. From the generation of women who had fought for equal opportunities in a very male world, she had a close and loving relationship with her husband, but she didn't think any man – certainly not him – was capable of being a feminist. That, she insisted – laughing whenever he made the claim in jest – would take a few generations, noting that their two sons were responsible for far more of the childcare of their kids than Richards had ever been – despite being regarded, for his era, as a progressive dad who nappy-changed and potty-trained.

Nevertheless he 'wasn't too bad', she conceded.

The meeting with Ms Thandi Matjeke was scheduled for 17:30 on Monday: a little tight, as there was an important three-line whip for a vote at seven o'clock, but he was busy earlier.

*

Van der Merwe was jolted by the news.

Police had arrested half a dozen rhino-poaching syndicate bosses in Limpopo province. Luxury vehicles, motorbikes, trucks, millions of rand and animal skins were all confiscated. Officers were coordinating with the Asset Forfeiture Unit to seize properties owned by them, two of whom were serving officers of the South African Police Service, another a former police officer. Now opposition MPs were demanding lifestyle audits of high-ranking police officers.

Van der Merwe would be have to be extra-cautious about how he set up his new planned operations in Limpopo.

The Veteran had worked hard on the speech Thandi carried with her in cabin luggage. It tried to tell a complex story very simply but powerfully. And it would be ready for the media to report, embargoed for when he was speaking at the time allotted.

The Veteran planned to alert Scorpio, which would write it up for the *Daily Maverick* to break the story online before anybody else. But Thandi was also to check that Richards would definitely alert the London media: very important that the global nature of the story – the criminality – was exposed in London, Washington, Paris and Berlin, indeed worldwide.

When Thandi boarded the plane and found her seat, she insisted on having the bag containing the memory sticks with her, not tucked into the overhead cupboard where the cabin staff indicated she should put other things. She had gone through security, immigration and the boarding-gate check anxious some state agent might grab it from her.

She was tense and hardly slept on the flight. The passenger noise – especially crying babies – and the bumps, together with the exhilaration, kept her awake. Focused on the flight path displayed on her seat screen, she couldn't get it out of her mind that she was traversing the whole African continent. Across the top of Zimbabwe, Zambia, the DRC, Sudan, Algeria – the lot. Millions and millions of people below her, dying, being born, laughing, eating, drinking, working, relaxing, loving, hating, fighting, playing; young, old, rulers and citizens, bosses and workers.

Humanity – with all its complexities and wonders, its frustrations and its achievements. Wondrous and despicable, generous and repellent, aggressive and caring, moral and depraved – sometimes all in one person.

She thought back to the long conversation she'd had with the Veteran before leaving.

'But why?' Thandi had asked him. 'Why did it go so wrong? Why do liberation movements and struggle leaders fall to the temptation of lining their pockets and robbing the very people they once fought for? Some jaundiced white South Africans have been making accusations of "corrupt black majority rule", as if it always was going to be corrupt, almost as if it's in the DNA of Africans.'

The Veteran had sighed. 'I agree with you. But there has been important research showing that the sort of naked corruption we have seen under the President, and links to the criminal networks underpinning it actually predate 1994 when we came to power – there was a deeply corrupt system in the apartheid state, specially around defence and sanctions-busting.'

'So are you saying that the President and his cronies just continued where the apartheid state had left off?' Thandi had queried.

'Yah – absolutely. But I'm certainly not saying that is any sort of excuse, because the ANC should have been better than that – and under Mandela then Mbeki we mostly were. But the apartheid state we inherited was shot through with corruption. So the channels and the businesses that made it happen were ready and waiting.

'They had so much to hide when Mandela was about to take over as president that the National Intelligence Agency destroyed over forty tonnes of incriminating documents. Who knows how many millions of other documents were also destroyed by military intelligence and the other security agencies?'

'How did they get to that point?' Thandi asked.

'Enforcing and propping up apartheid meant that the whole country was militarised from the 1960s, especially under President P. W. Botha. Before that, President Vorster's intelligence services had used every trick in the book – including bribery, and arms dealers got huge fees. But then power shifted from intelligence services to the military. The Defence budget rocketed.

'But the international arms embargo deprived white South Africa of various major weapons, and that led in 1988 to the South African army being defeated by Cuban soldiers in Angola at Cuito Cuanavale. It was a major blow – the white state had never been defeated before.'

'I remember reading about that as a real turning point,' Thandi mused, the Veteran nodding, then continuing.

'Under apartheid they built a war economy to get vital supplies, from

296

oil to arms, through sanctions. Defence expenditure ballooned, and private companies were involved in all sorts of dodgy deals and sanctions-busting – and made a pile of money too.'

Thandi remembered being startled by this revelation as the plane forged forward towards North Africa.

'Buying oil on the black market was cripplingly costly, with various front companies, also involving Craig Williamson they called the "master spy", a nasty piece of work.

'The apartheid regime even did military work for the Russians and obtained Chinese arms. There was so much duplicity.

'It is fashionable now for everyone to claim they were always against apartheid.

'But the truth is that only a minority ever did something about it. The majority expressed their distaste but got on with business as usual.

'The fight against apartheid was long and bitter. Pitches were invaded to stop all-white South African sports tours. There was pressure for a ban on arms sales and for economic sanctions. Grannies boycotted Outspan oranges. Students drove Barclays Bank off Britain's university campuses until it withdrew from South Africa.

'Although the anti-apartheid struggle was victorious, massive economic crime was normal in the apartheid years, and that persists today.'

As she recalled the vivid impact upon her of the Veteran's lesson in recent history, Thandi drifted off.

She had no idea how long she'd slept when she jerked awake as the captain announced half an hour to landing, leaping up and making for the sleepy-eyed queue outside the toilet before the instruction confining everyone to their seats.

A retired business friend of the Veteran, very comfortably off and living in Constantia on the Cape Peninsula had happily covered all the costs of Thandi's mission. To avoid the Veteran's digital fingerprints anywhere on the bookings, the friend had booked Thandi's return flight and stay at the Travelodge in Fulham Broadway. 'Close to Shangri-La,' the Veteran had twinkled, describing the location just along from Chelsea Football Club. Conveniently on the District Line straight to Westminster and just along from Earls Court, where she would transfer off the Piccadilly Line from London's Heathrow Airport.

The friend had generously booked an early check-in at the Travelodge because the overnight flight from Johannesburg was due in at 05:15, so Thandi would be able to go straight to her room. She was staying two nights – enough time to make the meeting but also to have a bit of a look around London.

But when she had stared at the city map, with the Veteran pointing things out to her, it seemed very peculiar. She would be well out of her comfort zone, never having stayed at a city hotel before, visiting a strange country on a strange mission to rendezvous with a strange man. The only relief was the generous bundle of pound notes provided by the retiree friend, so she shouldn't have any money worries. In fact, if she was careful where she ate – and there was a Sainsbury's supermarket at Fulham Broadway with cheap ready-made meals and drinks – she would probably have some spare cash on her return to keep. Useful, since she was losing about a week's pay and wasn't even sure she would have a job to return to, as the radio station wasn't at all happy at her unpredictable absences.

Sensing her unease, the Veteran had gone over the details again, giving her a reassuring hug as he did so. Buying an Oyster card for the Tube and buses. Taking the opportunity to receive an officially guided tour of Parliament – the friend had pre-booked one too. Popping in to see the Churchill War Rooms at the back of the Foreign Office, opposite St James's Park, where Winston Churchill's bed and desk were preserved. Visiting the National Gallery and having a look at South Africa House, both off Trafalgar Square.

She needed to seem like a regular tourist just in case anyone ever took any interest in her or her visit. Very unlikely, the Veteran calculated – but just in case. In any event, Thandi should broaden her experience, he had insisted.

Thandi had wanted to fly in, deliver the goods and fly out the same day. All perfectly possible, given the flight schedules. But no, the Veteran insisted, she had to behave as normally as possible. How many of her schoolmates would ever get an opportunity like this? She might as well make the most of it. Even then, a couple of nights (effectively the equivalent of three full days) wasn't exactly decadence, was it?

London was grey and drizzly as Thandi looked out of the Piccadilly Line train window on the overground stretch through London's suburbs before it went underground to the centre of the city. It looked drab and uninviting. Nothing like the royalty, celebrity, luxury, history of the greatest city in the world.

She was tired and rather stressed after a few little panics on the way. Worrying whether her bag would appear on the luggage carousel – it took ages. Purchasing a SIM card at an airport kiosk, the assistant bored and completely uninterested in reassuring Thandi it would work for both voice and data – which it did, of course: the Veteran had insisted she must have mobile reception for the visit, and must WhatsApp her temporary number just in case. Trying to buy the Oyster card from the machine, which was more interested in a credit or debit card and she didn't have one, until a friendly station attendant helped do it for her.

Then she fretted about the change of Tube lines at Earl's Court, which Tube train to catch to her hotel, where it would be and so on, continuously propelled forward in a daze by a bustle of people and still more people in the morning rush hour. She'd never encountered so many people, and it was overwhelming.

Eventually she got to the hotel and checked in, starting to worry about whether Richards would be at the rendezvous or not, whether she would get there on time, what he would be like. And so on, and so on . . .

Thandi slumped, exhausted, on her hotel bed.

She couldn't wait to get back home.

When she jolted awake a couple of hours later, she grabbed at her watch. To her relief there was still plenty of time before the MP rendezvous.

The room was fairly spartan but clean, with all the facilities she needed. She WhatsApp messaged the Veteran to confirm her safe arrival then jumped in the shower, allowing the hot water to pour all over her after she'd soaped herself clean, energy and purpose seeping back into her. Luxury, pure luxury; she didn't normally have time for a long, languid shower and in any case never wanted to waste her parents' meagre resources.

Wrapped in a towel, drying quickly in the warm but now damp bathroom she reached for her phone again and sent Mkhize a WhatsApp message with lots of heart emojis. She was missing him more than she would ever volunteer to anyone else.

Later, Thandi blinked her way down in the lift and out to find the supermarket in the Fulham Broadway mini-mall around the Tube station. There were coffee shops, mobile phone shops, fast-food outlets, a Boots chemist and upstairs more outlets and a cinema. A large opening to the supermarket drew her forward. She helped herself to prepared packaged convenience food – like salads and smoked salmon pieces, yogurt and fruit, some with small plastic forks and spoons. A cheap but good way to eat; the variety suggested lots of Londoners must eat that way too, she decided.

She took the bag upstairs to her room for a picnic lunch – a picnic dinner would come later, as she didn't fancy eating on her own in a café or restaurant somewhere.

Thandi planned a visit to the Churchill War Rooms before her meeting at 17:30; she would set off shortly and get to the pub a bit early.

She was apprehensive, checking over and over again that she had all the memory sticks and the hard copy of the speech safely stowed in the backpack habitually slung over her shoulder and a receptacle for all sorts of her stuff; she never managed to keep it tidy or get around to weeding out the debris.

The Deputy President's excuse was almost comically Orwellian.

'Yes,' he admitted, while answering questions from a parliamentary committee, 'while I was still premier of Mpumalanga I did meet with the President, but I did not intend on meeting with him, as a meeting is not necessarily a meeting to meet individuals but rather a meeting intended to meet with him in a capacity that we had already met.'

Reading about all this in the *Daily Maverick*, the Veteran shook his head. *Nothing should surprise me any more about these guys*, he thought, *but it still does, they are so nakedly blatant.*

Another story caught his eye. It revealed a multibillion-rand cigarette-smuggling operation headed by two self-confessed tax cheats who made huge donations to both the governing ANC and the opposition – the supposedly radical EFF – and exploited their covert links to the South African Revenue Service chief to avoid paying multimillion-rand tax bills.

The looting was insatiable, the criminality ubiquitous. Where would this all end, the Veteran wondered?

He had to try and block it.

Then Thandi's message popped into his phone with a notification alert. A relief – the meeting the Veteran had set up was the key to blowing the venal conspiracy wide open.

*

300

She was ten minutes early at the Clarence, having timed her exit from the War Rooms to be so.

Feeling awkward, Thandi pushed her way past the men around the bar (which at the end of the working day would soon be packed to the gunnels) and looked about her. There were only a couple of women and she was the only black.

Sitting in an alcove with a clear view of the main entrance, Bob Richards spotted her immediately, and rose to greet her as she made her way uncertainly forward, eyes darting about. Yes, she was indeed attractive, he thought. Then pushed it immediately and guiltily to the back of his mind as most certainly not the impulse of the 'male feminist' he liked to think himself.

'Thandi Matjeke?', he asked extending his hand. Amidst the swirl in her mind she was amused that he pronounced her first name as if he was saying 'hand' instead of 'hund'.

She nodded.

'Are Chelsea playing at home on Saturday?' he asked.

'No, they're away to the Springboks.'

Their opening exchange – absurd though it was mixing Premiership football with international rugby – had been carefully choreographed by the Veteran, each separately and securely briefed.

She relaxed a little as he pointed her to the seats he had commandeered, a pint of Abbot Ale in a straight glass standing on the small table already sipped. 'What would you like to drink?'

'Just a Diet Coke please – with ice,' she muttered, sitting down, still nervous, wedging the bulky envelope between her feet.

He returned a few minutes later and sat down smiling. 'Nice to meet you. I guess it's been a tense trip?'

'Very,' she grimaced, 'I have never flown anywhere internationally before.'

'Oh?' he looked surprised. 'I guess the sheer volume of people in the city, finding your way around the Tube network – all that stuff – is a bit strange and stressful?'

'Yes,' she smiled ruefully, still very tense, he noted.

So, he asked her about her parents, her job, where she lived.

She chattered happily, smiling now. Then stopped abruptly. 'How much time have you got?'

Richards looked awkward. 'I had hoped plenty. But at only a day's notice to catch the Tories out, they've scheduled a strong three-liner and I must be back in time.'

'Three-liner?'

'Sorry! It means a strong whipped vote. I must be there or they'll defenestrate me.'

Thandi roared with laughter, throwing her head back. 'Now that would be painful!'

It broke the ice. 'Now, down to business,' she said, reaching for her precious envelope.

He noticed that her nervousness had evaporated. Here was the young activist the Veteran rated highly, revealing her true self for the first time since she had walked in looking extremely unsure.

Handing him a copy, she took him through the draft speech, Richards seeking clarification now and then, scribbling in the margins.

Then she explained what was on the memory sticks: the incriminating photos with digital links to the tracking images giving locations.

They were so absorbed that Richards had forgotten the time rushing by, their drinks only sipped, when his phone buzzed: *Vote shortly.*

'Christ almighty!' be blurted, hastily gathering everything up.

Now he was the one panicking and looking flustered, Thandi noted, amused.

'Have I got everything?' he asked, as he stood and started moving.

'Hope so.'

'Sorry to rush,' he called over his shoulder, 'thanks for everything. You're very brave. I salute you.'

So, that was it, she thought, stuck on her own in a strange Whitehall establishment, quite unlike the cafés or eateries at home where most people went for a drink. She looked around, slowly drinking the rest of the Coke and people watching for a while, feeling somehow empty.

All the effort, all the tension, and her vital mission was over. Just like that.

Now came the wait to see what impact it had – if any.

Richards careered down Whitehall.

He had to get there on time. It was crucial. If he failed there would be all manner of repercussions. And he didn't want that. Although noted for his independence of spirit, he prided himself for being conscientious, and didn't take liberties with his obligations.

Although in much better shape than most of his colleagues, male or female, he wasn't used to running a distance and was soon panting. He kept glancing at his watch, worrying. The minutes ticked by, beads of sweat surfacing on his brow in the cool evening as he darted between startled pedestrians on their way home from surrounding government offices.

And all the time his mind was pulsating at Thandi's haunting briefing – and the responsibility he must discharge to honour the values, the traditions for which he had once campaigned.

Even if he could keep up this pace, he wasn't sure he would make the deadline. It seemed like ages before he started hearing the rasping parliamentary voting bell ringing, summoning him insistently, incessantly. Sweating like mad and spotting a few others ahead desperately running as well.

Then the dreaded command: 'Lock the doors!'

The Doorkeeper, catching sight of him but determined nevertheless to carry out her duty, began to wrench the doors closed. Richards just burst through the narrowing opening, catching his shoe and tumbling to the carpet of the Ayes Lobby, his precious envelope sliding away across the worn green carpet.

'Just bloody made it, then,' a booming Scottish accent reprimanded him. The Pairing Whip. Not a bad guy, really, Richards knew.

'Been drinking with some fancy woman, then?' the whip half-joked.

How true that was, Richards thought. But not for the usual Westminster reasons. Quite the opposite – and the whip would never know.

Grimacing in humiliation, he smiled at the whip, who twinkled back, picked himself up and grabbed the envelope, checking it was all there.

To his utter relief it was.

Mkhize was in a rage as he studied the latest report.

An elephant was being killed for its tusks every twenty-five minutes. The trade in animal parts amounted to an annihilation of wildlife by organised criminal gangs in a barbaric, corrupt and sinister war.

If only, he felt. If only people realised they were all losers as the creatures with which they shared this planet were pillaged to extinction. The massive decline in the size of wildlife populations since 1970 was the same as losing the entire human population of Asia from the world. What was the bloody point of negotiating more treaties or international agreements to protect wildlife? There were already plenty of mechanisms to halt the trade. China's closure of its domestic ivory market was welcome if very belated. But there was a war on the frontline – with rangers like him risking their lives to protect wildlife.

Action was needed. Action by governments to intervene militarily, if necessary, and halt this war.

Mkhize sighed, then smiled to himself. He was getting political – at least Thandi would approve!

Bleary-eyed and tired, Thandi got home safely, landing at ORT just after seven o'clock on a bright Joburg morning. It was a joy to hear the familiar African chatter and laughter of the airport staff as she made her way to immigration control, passing through without incident to her immense relief, and collecting her suitcase.

Arriving home via the Gautrain, she was greeted by her anxious parents, who hugged her, upset she wouldn't reveal where she had been or why she had left without explanation.

She was an adult, yet they still kept worrying. Some say a parent never stops worrying about a kid. Although she found it irritating, she forced herself to understand, explaining patiently she would be able to explain one day, but not now. That made them even more worried. They had no idea what she was up to, though her dad – the more politically conscious of the two – talking to his wife late at night, said he was proud of her; she must be up to something good, something important.

His daughter hated the President and so did they. He bet that was what it was all about. But then that made them even more worried, since they knew full well you didn't mess with the President or you'd find yourself tied to a rock at the bottom of Hartbeespoort Dam.

The Veteran had ensured his trustworthy media contacts were briefed in advance and under strict embargo about the imminent explosive revelations under parliamentary privilege in London. They had each been handed a memory stick by one of his comrades containing the digital images given to Bob Richards, together with the final text of his speech – which, the Veteran was quietly pleased to note, had hardly been changed from his draft – just a few parliamentary niceties added and some stylistic tweaks.

Richards, he noticed, had a habit of speaking in verb-less sentences when he was emphasising a sequential series of points. The Veteran knew why: it was punchier and more modern. But the grammar systematically instilled in him at his school, King Edward, would have had no truck with such a perversion.

'Mr Bob Richards!'

The committee chair's voice signalled the opening of his adjournment debate. Unusually for one held in Westminster Hall, the media were present in numbers because Richards had briefed them beforehand, distributing memory sticks to key reporters.

He began with the usual quaint House of Commons courtesy by paying respect to a fellow MP who was a member of the Speaker's Panel and thereby on the list to chair such adjournment debates, as well as the Standing Committees that met to consider legislation.

'Mrs Price, it is a pleasure to serve on this committee with you in the chair.'

He followed that by thanking four other colleagues who had put in to support his application for the debate, ensuring he was allocated a full ninety minutes rather than the usual thirty.

Then he launched into the meat of his speech virtually word for word as drafted by the Veteran. The President's bête noire, the *Daily Maverick*, stood ready to go online with the full text any minute, and South Africa's Radio 702 carried the speech live, one of the station's fiercest critics, Moses Khoza, listening intently.

Just as well, because the speech was about to change his life irrevocably.

'Honourable Members may be aware that I have spoken previously about corruption, money laundering and looting under the current President of South Africa. I have done so at the behest of brave militants and whistle-blowers, who are acting to uphold the legacy of the freedom struggle and Nelson Mandela. A legacy being trashed and betrayed by the current President and his cronies.'

Khoza winced. Half of him inwardly acknowledged the truth of this charge; half of him could not bring himself to do so. Richards was a difficult character to smear because his anti-apartheid heritage gave him real credibility – he was more than just another critic. Try as they may to label him a 'white monopoly capital' stooge, as the Business Brothers did using social-media bots from the British public affairs company, Khoza knew that there was no cut-through.

Richards was in full flow.

'Even by the standards to which South Africa under this president has degenerated, the latest revelation is pretty outrageous.'

Richards paused deliberately, looking around the chamber.

'Mrs Price, I now come to reveal an entirely new and – even by the squalid standards to which South African governance has sunk these last years – profoundly shocking act of international crime committed by a senior member of the President's close staff with his express authority.'

Khoza's attention had waxed and waned but now he was glued to the radio. What could this possibly mean?

Richards continued. 'Over the last few weeks brave investigators, led by a former struggle hero whose identity I shall not reveal because otherwise he might be killed, have tracked a criminal conspiracy to steal a rhino horn and export it internationally in direct contravention of international law, which bans the illegal trade in wildlife. I will now explain exactly how this was done. I have placed photographic and digital evidence in the House of Commons Library for all to examine and it has been provided under embargo to the media both here and in South Africa.

'Importantly, this evidence has been independently reviewed by a senior and globally respected judge, His Honour Justice Samuel Makojaene, who has corroborated everything I am explaining today, though these are my own words, not his.

'Perhaps most shocking of all, this conspiracy was organised inside South Africa from the President's office. I name Moses Khoza, his security chief, as the man responsible. There is photographic and digital evidence proving this beyond any doubt. Because what Mr Khoza did not, and could not, know was that this particular horn, stolen by a ranger – yes, a ranger – in Zama Zama Game Reserve in KwaZulu-Natal had inserted within it a tiny transmitter enabling it to be tracked wherever it went.'

Richards paused again and nodded to the chair: 'Mrs Price, I have provided you with a copy of the evidence proving that the horn was handed over to a member of one of the many criminal syndicates based in East Asia engaged in killing and poaching African rhino horns. It was then passed to a Mr Piet van der Merwe, who personally handed it to the President's security chief at his home.'

Moses Khoza was stunned. He could not believe what he was hearing. His whole life was being unravelled by this MP. Brushing aside the turmoil in his head, he forced himself to listen.

306

'Now we get to the next link in this conspiracy. Mr Khoza first of all took the horn from his home to the President's office, where he works, and later drove it to the Embassy of the Socialist Republic of Vietnam, entered the building and handed it over. He carried it in a grip bag and emerged a little later without it, instead carrying a bulky envelope. I am certain this must have contained cash − probably around 150,000 US dollars, because that's what these horns command in Far Eastern countries like Vietnam.

'The times on the digital photographic evidence coincides with the GPS evidence from the monitor tracking the device hidden in the horn to prove Khoza's culpability. And also, the culpability of the Vietnamese diplomat or diplomats involved.

'The evidence shows the movements of Khoza and his car as well as what then happened to the horn. GPS monitoring demonstrates that it was taken in a diplomatic bag from the embassy in Pretoria first to Johannesburg international airport and then on an Emirates Airlines flight via Dubai to Vietnam. It arrived in Hanoi and was then flown to Ho Chi Minh City, where it was taken to a private address for which I have the GPS coordinates.

'I am also today sending all the detailed evidence to 10 Downing Street, asking the prime minister to take the matter up with the President of Vietnam and to refer it to the International Criminal Court and Interpol to bring prosecutions of all those involved, including the President of South Africa and his security chief, Moses Khoza. I have also written to the Vietnamese Ambassador to Britain asking that his government brings to justice those of its citizens involved.'

Richards paused again. 'In conclusion, let us remember what is at stake here. Not just state-sponsored corruption and crime within South Africa, which must have Nelson Mandela turning in his grave. Not just the complicity of the Vietnamese government and criminals in that country. But also the very future of the rhino species. These majestic animals are hurtling towards extinction. Not because of climate change or natural disaster. But because of human greed and venality on an epic scale.

'Until all the citizens of the world demand that our governments act together globally to put a stop to this obscene criminality, then it will continue unabated. I hope that at least our government and our Parliament will act decisively, and that the people of South Africa will demand change from their president.'

His words were soon sweeping around the media in South Africa, in the UK and across the world.

The Veteran, Thandi, Mkhize, the Sniper and Elise, all listening to Radio 702 or watching the debate online, felt that at last there might be a breakthrough – at long last.

CHAPTER 22

Previously the President had been in the firing line, now it was Moses Khoza himself – and he didn't like that one little bit.

There were photos of him all over the media – some video footage as well, hovering in the background at various official events or, decades previously, in his prime speaking at ANC meetings as a popular militant.

Khoza knew without a doubt that everyone who did the President's bidding was ultimately expendable – and anyone becoming a liability would be ruthlessly cut loose or otherwise disposed of. In other words, anything went to protect the man. Why, he had done this countless times to others on presidential instructions.

The problem was he had now joined the ranks of expendables. He knew it, even though he would never ever have thought it. But from the moment that sodding MP, authenticated by the imprimatur of Justice Makojaene – them again – had exposed Khoza with all the digital evidence, the media had gone mad. So had opposition MPs, demanding the President sack him. That, perhaps, was his only salvation, for the President was renowned for refusing to bow to the opposition, indeed would go to almost any lengths to avoid that. The President was a stubbornly proud man, insisting that as a former liberation leader he was entitled to respect, almost regardless of the allegation.

Nevertheless, Khoza had to protect himself, and a lot of his time would now be devoted to doing so.

Earlier, the craftsman in Ho Chi Minh City had been both puzzled and startled.

He had been working carefully on the horn to ensure a maximum return on the material when he suddenly exposed the transmitter. In his small workshop at home, he had worked on countless rhino horns before and was a master at ensuring a rich reward for the Syndicate. As he stopped and stared at the electronic device, his mind began racing. And it was because he was in a panic that he failed to think through the consequences.

He put it gingerly in cotton wool and immediately drove to meet his contact with the Syndicate. Normally the man paid up promptly and their dealings were simply transactional. But this time the man reacted with cold fury. Why had the craftsman come to his office? Why hadn't he suggested meeting in the street somewhere?

The man had immediately clocked it was a transmitter, which meant that he would be under the cosh because the location could be traced to him. Icily he told the craftsman to take the tiny item into a nearby square in the city, crush it under foot, then retrieve the bits, stick them in an envelope and take them to a designated street stall among the thousands in the city and leave them with an old woman there. He should take all the elements he had carved out of the horn, including, of course, the powder, the man stressed, together with his tools, to a safe address. There he must complete the job. After which he would be paid handsomely as usual – but this time only after two weeks to see whether he could keep his mouth shut and profess ignorance to any enquirers, saying there must be some mistake.

The craftsman, jittery as hell, confided in his wife, telling her to take all the cash they had accumulated from previous horn jobs and disappear with it to the home of a friend in a small village on the coast nobody would ever trace them to. He would join her there and wait.

Except that never happened.

For, having handed over the finished product, he was silently strangled on the spot and his body stuffed into a crusher at a scrap-metal yard.

It couldn't have gone better, the Veteran thought, surveying the morning papers, listening to Radio 702, Kaya FM, SAfm and watching eNCA's main TV news channel.

There was saturation coverage, which developed over the following days, moving on from the graphic and sensational detail of the photos and images tracking the route of the horn, to demands on the President and international outrage. The Vietnamese government came under pressure at the United Nations to retrieve and return the horn. Bob Richards, having tipped off the Speaker and been called at Prime Minister's Questions, demanded action from Britain. South African ambassadors and high commissioners across the world were bombarded by animal rights activists and wildlife NGOs.

In South Africa an enterprising opposition MP demanded how much money had been received and that the President stop stonewalling and return it. There was absolutely no chance of that happening, as the MP and everyone else knew.

Although aware he had little time, Khoza thought long and hard.

Unquestionably, this was a make-or-break moment. He had to get it right or he would be history. When he was shown in to see the President, the atmosphere, as he had anticipated, was icy. But before the President's fusillade could be unleashed, Khoza presented him with his plan.

Explaining that the Veteran must be behind the whole plot – or why had he disappeared? – Khoza got grudging approval. The President knew the Veteran only too well, having worked with him for years in the ANC guerrilla base in Tanzania; they had even infiltrated South Africa together over the Mozambique border. In those days the President had been a South African Communist Party operative codenamed Emilio, who had been trained in Russia and rose to become head of ANC intelligence in exile. He was doubtful the plan would work, but it was worth trying anyway, for neither man could think of an alternative.

Mkhize had left Zama Zama reluctantly, as always.

The orphanage had new rhino calves, hornless, with soft faces, unable to survive alone in the bush, needing constant care, nursing and cuddling, supplies of coconut milk to hand in bottles. A year before, the mother had been butchered by poachers when her little ones were only five months old. When the poachers had come, the baby rhinos had known of the danger well before their human guards, their incredible smell alerting them to the threat. They started snorting and shrieking, distraught and stressed.

The poachers had arrived ruthlessly and rapidly in stormy weather, their intrusion concealed in the rain and thunder tearing through the bush in a cacophony of loudness, threat and confusion, and set about destroying the mother, leaving her prone on the ground, blood spreading into reddening puddles of water, the desperately distraught calves scampering in a confused frenzy as they tried to nuzzle her lifeless giant frame.

The sky had unleashed a waterfall, in seconds soaking anyone unlucky enough to be out and about. Having been bone dry, the reserve's roads and tracks were now like foaming streams, gullies like raging rivers, trees and bushes sagging under the weight of the water.

Over subsequent days the rain continued pelting down, the barren earth so dry it just swallowed it all up greedily – and kept swallowing, until it started leaping into life, wild flowers sprouting and greenery spreading, miraculously transforming both the grey-brown vista, and the wildlife – but not the mother of the calves long taken tenderly into care.

The comrade travelling with the Veteran's phone of course knew Moses Khoza by reputation.

So he was intrigued to pick up a text as he switched it on when his cruise ship called in at Mauritius mid-morning. *Can we meet and talk? I want to leave the President and come over to you. Moses Khoza.*

He immediately rang the Veteran and relayed the message. 'Let me think,' the Veteran replied. 'I'll come back to you soonest,' checking that the comrade would be in Port Louis until the ship sailed after dinner that night, and promising to call him before then.

It was either a trap or an opportunity, the Veteran thought – probably a trap, but you never knew. Maybe Khoza wanted to jump before he was pushed?

Deep in contemplation, he fixed to visit the Sniper, who readily agreed to leave work and head straight for his flat.

The Veteran was suspicious but intrigued. Khoza must suspect he might be behind the explosive revelations on the horn, which were still reverberating. If so, Khoza's purpose in meeting might well be to capture or kill him. Alternatively, he might want to throw in his lot with the Veteran if the President sacked him – but the more he considered that, the more far-fetched it seemed. There was no way he could sustain his income by coming out and joining the resistance; on the other hand, of course, if he lost his presidency job his income would disappear, and businesses or foreign foundations might be willing to employ him for his insider knowledge.

It was a conundrum and a big risk to agree to meet up.

*

The Sniper was also both intrigued and sceptical.

The Veteran had filled him in, then came straight to the point. 'Remember we had a discussion – and a bit of an argument – some months back when I explored whether you might be able to assist us, if needed, outside the reserve.'

The Sniper nodded. 'Yah, I was pretty hostile, but you sort of talked me around – depending upon the circumstances and what exactly it was you wanted me to do.'

'Well, now the moment has come, and I am afraid I cannot do without you,' the Veteran said.

The two men spent a couple of hours and a few beers talking through the plan in great detail, considering options, rejecting some, accepting others, until they were both satisfied.

'I still think you're mad going anywhere near it, but at least we have a chance of minimising the risk to you,' the Sniper said.

'Frankly, I am more concerned about the risk to you,' the Veteran replied. 'I really appreciate you putting yourself on the line in this way.'

Thandi and Mkhize were in a huddle with the Veteran and it was a sombre conversation – or, rather, an ominous one.

He briefed them on the plan and checked they were okay with their roles. They were, though desperately anxious at the dangerous predicament for him.

'I may well not survive this encounter and if not, I want you to take over my mission, Thandi.'

'How can I possibly do that?' she asked. 'I'm a nobody!'

'Everybody in the struggle starts as a "nobody" and some rise to become "somebodies", to use your language which, by the way, I don't like because we all have roles, however junior or senior in the movement. We are all important, whatever our rank. Leaders are nothing without the grassroots, who in turn need good leaders.'

The Veteran paused to let that sink in, then continued.

'Events have a way of finding key people who are in the right place at the right time and I am afraid this is just one such example. It happened to me that way. I was a keen young militant, an activist in the rank and file, and I found myself successively taking on new responsibilities. I never expected to be a leader, still less a government minister for eight years.

'When I talk at universities, students often ask me for advice on "how

313

to have a political career". That bothers me, and I always reply this way. "Politics isn't a career like others, it's a mission. It's not like any other job. It's your life. Start with what you believe, what are your values, what motivates you. Then get involved at the grassroots and see where it leads."

'Mandela didn't choose to be the ANC's leader. He was chosen and groomed by his mentor and subsequently close Rivonia trialist and Robben Island prisoner Walter Sisulu who, early on when Mandela wasn't even political, recognised key leadership potential and qualities in him.

'Anyway, this is all a bit academic, Thandi. You're here. There's nobody else, is there?'

She nodded slowly, reluctantly agreeing. It wasn't that she didn't want to contribute – hell, she was doing so already. Just that she doubted her own abilities and was overawed by the task.

Thandi looked at Mkhize, who nodded in encouragement. He was with her – which meant he was in it too.

'Right,' the Veteran said, and started going through each stage with them in great detail, starting with the Khoza plan and its sequences, agreed with the Sniper. Then he turned to his 'bible': a booklet with all his contacts, containing a brief description of each together with phone numbers. Some were old comrades, some were contemporary activists, some were media contacts. 'Burn it rather than surrender it to the enemy. Never betray those who trust you,' he instructed, telling them where it had been hidden.

'Now, if I am killed, you just leave me and escape. Just go and go fast, making sure you protect yourselves.'

Thandi couldn't believe how methodically sombre the Veteran seemed about his own possible demise. You could hear a pin drop.

'If I am hurt, you need to take me to this clinic and call this doctor in advance to tell her you're coming. Book me in under the name Fred du Plessis. Here is my ID card in that name. Do not use your own names under any circumstances.'

He looked hard at the two of them. 'You are Sithembele Nxumalo, Thandi. You are Elliot Mngadi, Isaac. If you have to call the doctor she will expect these names. You dump the van somewhere afterwards and you never come to the clinic for a visit except on foot, using a cab to drop you off – even the dreaded Uber, which I never use on principle.'

He went over it all again, step by step. When he had finished, the Veteran sat back and smiled. 'All clear? Any queries?'

Thandi shook her head. She was in a state of dumbfounded misery, neither frightened nor excited, just stoically solemn. Mkhize, she sensed, was exactly the same. The two of them were now so close, they didn't need to talk in order to know.

There was a silence that seemed long yet was only at most thirty seconds as the Veteran looked at them. He was satisfied.

'I want you to remember two other things, please. First, I was the future once. Now you are. Second, if transformation was easy it would've happened long time ago. What I mean by that is the struggle is always tough – it's a marathon, not a sprint. The push for justice and liberty and equality never ends. You have to keep fighting for it.'

He paused. 'And never, ever, ever give up.'

The Sniper had picked up the keys from an official in the Old Fort museum, another of the Veteran's network from the old days of the underground.

He had already scouted and selected an approximate position on the fort rampart, accessible only via an old – almost never opened – iron gate, though he hadn't had time to climb up there and so was uneasy: he would have preferred to check it out in advance, but there'd be no opportunity. Not to worry – no point anyway – he'd often had to adapt to a strange position.

Originally a prison for white male prisoners erected in 1892, the Old Fort in Braamfontein, Joburg, was built around it to help repel British invaders during the Anglo-Boer War.

Subsequently, however, Boer military leaders were incarcerated, and some executed there by the British. In the years that followed, cells to house black prisoners, and a women's jail were added.

Among the most famous prisoners were Mahatma Gandhi in 1906, and in the early 1960s, the Old Fort was dubbed 'The Robben Island of Johannesburg' for its infamy in holding political prisoners like Nelson Mandela, Robert Sobukwe, Joe Slovo, Bram Fischer, Winnie Mandela and Albertina Sisulu.

It was notorious for terrible, insanitary and overcrowded conditions for black prisoners, constant humiliations and beatings, with women stripped of their underclothes and dignity. Apartheid-era inmates also included those caught having sex across the colour bar or indulging in homosexual sex.

315

When he had chosen the Old Fort, the Veteran was conscious it was deeply evocative for himself and Khoza, who'd also been detained there.

The Sniper had arrived in the dark, an hour or so before dawn, the fort, its high walls and ramparts set in a rectangular shape, eerie in the moonlight. Not a soul was in sight. But within half an hour the city began coming to life, as early morning workers arrived from Soweto and other townships for the hotels, cafés, restaurants, and the other services the city provided.

The courtyard was always open to the public, and so it was straightforward for the Sniper to wander in. He found the gate in the corner. Although the lock was stiff and rusty, he'd taken the precaution of bringing a small tin of spray oil. After some attention and manipulation, the lock eased open and he slid through the entrance, looking around anxiously, relieved that only a stray dog seemed to have noticed.

He climbed gingerly up the twisted stone steps, conscious the city would be awakening within an hour.

But the Old Fort was not where Khoza had been told to head.

The rendezvous had been fixed late the previous evening, giving Khoza little time to prepare. The Veteran, joining his old comrade in a car being driven around the city – his phone intermittently switched to airplane mode to avoid identifying his location – had through successive text exchanges with Khoza, fixed to meet at ten in the morning in front of the Constitutional Court.

But if you bring your goons I won't come, the Veteran had texted, *my people will be watching out for me.*

That had necessitated some improvisation by Khoza, though there was still time for his Russian shooter to arrive at dawn and position himself on Constitution Hill, overlooking the Court.

There were now two men with long-range rifles in position about five hundred metres apart, oblivious to each other.

The day before, Thandi had chosen her spot carefully.

She parked the other side of Constitution Hill to the court, nearby the fort in Kotze Street, alongside a stop for the C3 or F11 buses. Carefully locking the rusty, dirty old van, long ago owned by Vodacom, its fading insignia just visible under an amateurish painting-over, Thandi had slipped away to grab some sleep.

Shortly after the Sniper had got himself into position, a taxi dropped her off nearby. It was still dark, though the moon would soon start to be edged out by the sun. As tutored by the Veteran, who had painstakingly briefed her, she walked to around a hundred metres from the van, stood and kept pirouetting slowly as she scanned the area. Nobody, nothing – at least that she could see. No reason for there to be, because the focus was on the Constitutional Court: that would be a target for covert surveillance.

Nevertheless, she was taking no chances.

Finally satisfied, her heart thumping, she made her way to the van and unlocked the back doors, slipping quickly into the dark interior. Now came the four hour-plus wait. She set her phone alarm and lay down on the hard, smelly steel floor, her head resting on a pillow she'd deposited there previously.

Mkhize drove, noticing that the Veteran seemed unusually tense and was perspiring heavily.

The night before he had told Thandi that he might not survive the Khoza encounter, adding that he had already put his affairs in order. His Kalk Bay house was in the name of his son and daughter living in England, who had power of attorney over both his financial affairs and his health.

Mkhize hadn't liked the drift of the conversation. Why was the Veteran putting himself in danger if he thought it was a trap, he challenged?

Because he had to, the Veteran grunted testily. The prize of a possible defector from the President's inner sanctum was too great. In any case, he had taken precautions, including the bulletproof vest Mkhize had helped him put on, much too large for his height, but necessary to accommodate his considerable girth.

'What if it's a head shot?' Mkhize had countered.

The Veteran had shrugged. 'Snipers normally go for the heart because the chest is a bigger target. Anyway, I have a Makarov – it's old, but in good condition. I oiled and cleaned it this morning.'

Mkhize gave a sceptical grimace, to which the Veteran responded quickly: 'It's a Russian semi-automatic pistol, compact, easy to use. From the Soviet era, but easy to get the cartridges, which fit into an eight-round magazine that sides into the handle. We had lots of them in MK. I kept mine, wouldn't be surprised if Khoza still has his.'

'Yeah, okay,' said Mkhize grumpily. 'You know you are going to your possible death, but you go there anyway?' He shook his head.

'In your life as a ranger, Isaac, have you never taken risks?'

Mkhize reluctantly nodded. 'Yah, of course, that happens regularly with wild animals. But this is not the same at all. You know you are going into an ambush, yet you are going anyway!'

'Sometimes in life you just have to do what you have to do,' the Veteran replied.

The car slowed to a crawl. Joburg traffic: bad usually, but there must have been an accident because it was even worse. *Why the hell don't growing African metropolises build metros*, the Veteran wondered? Lagos, Nairobi, Cairo and indeed Cape Town – they were all choked with cars, smothering their residents with harmful emissions and throttling economic activity.

The Veteran, looking out of the window at the hawkers and beggars on every traffic junction, focused on the Khoza meet ahead. An hour to go. Plenty of time – unless of course the traffic ground them to a permanent standstill. They crawled forward in fits and starts. At the allotted time of ten in the morning, his old comrade would text Khoza as he paused while driving near the city centre, with a venue change to the courtyard of the Old Fort, adding that if he wasn't there ten minutes later the Veteran wouldn't show. If there was any response, he would separately text the Veteran.

Fine – provided all the texts issued and were delivered as normal with no glitch on the servers, the Veteran fretted, acknowledging to himself, though not volunteering to his companion, a question: was he getting a bit too old for this sort of game? As he peered out of the car, headlines from his life flashed before him: was this the end of the story – or part of a new chapter?

His phone rang, jerking him back to the present. It was another old comrade reporting in. 'Cannot see any security lurking around, in fact, the place is pretty deserted.'

'Anybody inside the foyer of the Constitutional Court itself?' the Veteran asked.

'Not out of the ordinary that I can see. I'm now in here myself, looking out after walking around. There's a party of high-school kids and some ushers going about their business. Otherwise it seems quiet.'

'Okay, stay there please, tell me when he arrives.'

Mkhize meanwhile continued driving purposefully towards the Old Fort as the Veteran's thoughts drifted off towards Khoza, what he really felt about the man, how awkward it would be to speak again after a long interval of mutual hostility.

He remembered the lithe, brave militant of their struggle days, now an opulent passenger on the gravy train. What did they have in common any more? Would their conversation be purely transactional? Would he feel like shaking hands? It seemed such a long time since their paths had diverged so radically, but in fact it was under ten years. Maybe Khoza's trajectory had been in gestation before then?

Yet, he had to concede, decades of defiance to apartheid laws had eroded in many ANC activists a respect for the law. They had felt the weight of a police state that manipulated the law to enforce its oppression. They had served prison sentences, been detained without trial and tortured. They had fought the police on township streets and fought soldiers in the bush. And all the time they had seen businessmen lining their pockets with illicit profits from the apartheid war machine.

Perhaps it arose from something even deeper within the very foundations of the 'Mandela miracle'? The transformation, the Veteran considered, had been a 'Faustian pact' in which democratic majority rule had been conceded in return for maintaining the power of the predominantly white economic elite. Which had then, as part of the pact, co-opted a new black economic elite.

That, in turn, presented new opportunities for personal lifestyle enrichment to activists who had never dreamed of these, and found themselves almost unconsciously drawn in, initially quite legitimately to benefit their families – and what was wrong with that for any individual? – but then into a spider's web of intrigue and conspiracy to maintain and boost these privileges in increasingly nefarious and criminal ways, all the time eroding what was once a cardinal principle of service to the people, and replacing it with service to one's self.

The President's trajectory, on the other hand, could be traced way back to the exile days when he was known in the inner circles of the ANC to be on the take. Mandela had also advised that they needed a Zulu like him at the very top. The rest of the ANC high command were Xhosa, and dissident Zulus were capable of wrecking the whole transformation project.

The Veteran remembered a conversation in Lusaka with the ANC President Oliver Tambo and Thabo Mbeki. They'd concluded best to do nothing because the man was a senior operative, the head of intelligence, for goodness' sake, and there was no question of him being a traitor or

319

informer. In reality, Tambo and Mbeki were immobilised because he had built a powerful parallel network of his own, including to an Indian businessman in his home province of KwaZulu-Natal, who subsequently became a key fixer and personal financier.

But Khoza was different. He'd been clean, courageous and charismatic – until, that was, he'd been co-opted into the presidency.

A few minutes before the allotted rendezvous time, Khoza walked towards the ConCourt alone, having been dropped off in Hoofd Street near the corner with Joubert Street.

He was uncomfortably nervous. Yet, surely, he shouldn't be? His Russian shooter was in place protecting him, able also to take out the Veteran if Khoza hand-signalled as arranged by stroking his fingers through his hair. The man was a real pro, had flown in from Moscow via Dubai the previous day, collected his kit from a safe drop and gone to ground. Khoza also had a loaded Makarov in his holster under his suit jacket. And his security team was out of sight but nearby. He had an earpiece and wire microphone pinned under his shirt, both linked to the shooter. The whole of state security was behind him. The Veteran had nothing except doubtless a bunch of comrades.

What could go wrong? Logically, nothing. But. But. Although the Veteran was old and ailing, he was still a pro and had run rings around the presidency over the past months.

Khoza walked, tensing up more and more with each step.

Assuming Khoza might have his goons around the Constitutional Court, the Veteran had instructed Mkhize to approach the Old Fort from the other side, and drop him off in Hospital Street, after which the ranger would park up and go on foot to join Thandi in the back of the van.

Before the Veteran got out of the car, he checked carefully. Nothing untoward – at least that he could spot. It was 09:50 hrs, leaving comfortably enough time for him to stroll up and into the Old Fort.

Wearing a Panama hat to shield against the sun, his heart racing, out of puff and his face perspiring heavily, the Veteran walked into the courtyard, looking around, knowing the Sniper was up there somewhere, and finding a shady spot from where to watch the entrance.

It was deserted, his moment of truth fast approaching.

*

While Khoza was standing restlessly outside the Constitutional Court, thinking of his recent humiliations before Justice Makojaene, his phone buzzed and he grabbed at it hungrily.

'Shit!' he exclaimed after glancing at the text message. The bastard had switched the venue at the last moment. The Veteran had been too canny not to expect a trap. He texted back: *Don't like playing these games but will be there.*

He quickly spoke through their link to the Russian, who was watching over him, rifle ready, and told him to scramble over to the nearby Fort and climb into a vantage point. Trying to remember its details, Khoza gave him guidance, telling him to be very careful because the Veteran might well already be there and have watchers.

The Sniper was perfectly placed to see everything.

First the Veteran walking briskly in, looking restless.

Then the shooter climbing gingerly up from the outside and appearing slowly on the rampart opposite to where he was crouching.

He texted the Veteran. 'A shooter arrived. Want to abort?'

'No. Kill him. But only after Khoza arrives, not before,' came the immediate reply. Then an immediate follow-up text: *Kill Khoza too but only to protect me if he's up to no good.*

The shooter was setting up his sights as the Sniper framed him within his cross hairs. He had him. But it was worryingly dangerous: the Sniper couldn't take him out there and then, as he would have preferred. It would be an excruciatingly fine judgement when exactly to do so.

Leave it too late and the Veteran was toast. Too early and Khoza might scarper.

There were a few minutes of fidgety tranquillity before Khoza walked hesitantly through the open stone entrance, his eyes darting about suspiciously.

The two former freedom fighters spotted each other simultaneously and began to converge, leaving both the Sniper and the shooter with clear shots on both men.

They came to a halt. Neither stuck out a hand nor smiled.

'So you switched the venue,' Khoza blurted out, clearly angry.

The Veteran ignored the jibe. 'You asked for the meet, not me. What's it about?'

'As I said, I want to leave and spill the beans.'

'Really? Why?'

'Because I face the sack. The President believes I am now an embarrassment, even though I have loyally worked with him, covered for him, conspired for him.'

'So why hasn't he already got rid of you?' the Veteran asked bluntly.

'The President moves cunningly – always has done – in ways not easy to predict.'

'Okay, I understand that,' said the Veteran sympathetically, easing the tension between the two men a little.

Khoza smiled weakly, running his fingers through his hair.

Then all hell broke loose in the quiet courtyard, alerting Thandi and Mkhize in the van.

Having already lined up the Veteran in his scope, the shooter squeezed the trigger – twice.

Two bullets hammered into the Veteran's chest right over his heart, the force knocking him to the ground right in front of Khoza, who jerked and peered down in satisfaction, his thoughts turning immediately to making a hasty exit.

But something was wrong. The Veteran seemed to be moving as Khoza looked more closely, confused.

Two more shots rang out but sounded different to Khoza.

They were.

The Russian shooter had just begun to consider dismantling his gun when he slumped, blood pouring out of his temple and his chest; he wouldn't be going anywhere or doing anything ever again.

Khoza reached for his gun, beginning to panic, and managed to loosen off a bullet, which glanced off the Veteran's armoured vest into his neck.

But this was not Khoza's scene. Surely he instructed and others executed? What the hell was going on?

Just as a new and deeply disturbing thought began forming in Khoza's mind, the Sniper's two shots thudded into him. He would never have any more thoughts of any kind.

Tense and wary, the Sniper exited quickly, dropping off the keys as instructed near the gate and taking off his surgical gloves and the elasticised plastic coverings around his shoes, so as to leave no trace.

His instructions were crystal clear. Under no circumstances must he be discovered. The Veteran was emphatic. Protecting him was more important than the others, because he had killed.

His rifle and equipment folded and stowed away in an innocuous looking rucksack, he made his way out and into the bustling city, merging among the pedestrians.

The Sniper headed for the nearest mall at Newtown Junction. It was two and a half kilometres away, or forty minutes to walk; he covered the distance systematically, varying his direction, making it difficult to track him and disappeared into the mall, switching on his phone as he executed the next stage of his getaway. One of the Veteran's comrades who'd been on watch at the Constitutional Court was also inside the car park.

They made contact and the rucksack with his gun and its ancillaries was handed over, together with the old shoes and clothing he'd been wearing, which he had quickly changed in shadows among the cars. The clothes were to be disposed of – so there was no DNA trace left. The gun was to be secretly stored. Having paid for and collected his parking ticket, the comrade drove with the Sniper crouched in the back under a blanket. The barrier lifted and they were away.

Twenty minutes later they drove into another car park at Killarney Mall, where the Sniper got out, shook hands, found his car, and departed himself for the long drive to Zama Zama. He was looking forward to seeing Elise again.

But he couldn't get the Veteran out of his mind. He hated leaving him bleeding, comforted only marginally that Thandi and Mkhize would presumably have pounded into the courtyard immediately after they heard the shooting.

As indeed they had, reaching the stricken Veteran, blood pouring from his neck.

Thandi was transfixed. She didn't know what to do.

Equally appalled, Mkhize nevertheless went ice cold. This is what he had been trained for. He pulled out his ranger's knife and ripped a long piece of cloth off his shirt, quickly binding it around the Veteran's neck, noticing as he did so that it was a flesh wound, close to the surface, mercifully not the oesophagus.

The Veteran's glazed eyes looked at him appealingly, vacantly, but Mkhize took immediate charge.

323

'Grab his legs, Thandi!' he instructed, picking the Veteran up by the shoulders and hustling toward the van. There was nobody around, but it wouldn't be long before Khoza's security forces were swarming all over the place. Thandi panted, her back hurting all over. Mkhize walked, his broad shoulders and muscles making light of the Veteran's heavy load: this is what he did.

Together they levered the Veteran into the passenger seat of the van. Startled, they realised he was tugging Thandi close, struggling to speak. 'Call this reporter on the *Daily Maverick*. Tip her off about Khoza's death, but leave me out of it.' He tried to reach for his shirt pocket but couldn't – so Thandi did it for him, pulling out a note with a name and number. 'Do not elaborate: just tell her he had a shooter, who's now dead. Under no circumstances reveal who you are. She's a good professional, she will try to quiz you, don't take offence, just don't elaborate.'

The Veteran slumped back exhausted as Thandi drove the van to the private clinic he'd specified in advance just in case something went wrong. A senior medical friend there would look after him – and discreetly. Under no circumstances must he be traced.

Thandi, tense and gripping the van steering wheel as if her very life depended on it, dropped Mkhize off at his car and then waited until he pulled out behind her before roaring off, desperate to save the Veteran, who slumped in the seat, his whole neck excruciatingly painful, throbbing upward into his head.

Mkhize's attempt at a bandage had partially staunched the blood flow, but it was only a matter of time before there was an infection or worse. He had no idea how bad the wound really was. Hopefully a narrow escape rather than a permanent injury.

The Veteran's thoughts turned to the aftermath and the media/political reaction. Speculation would be fast and furious. The President's personally appointed national security chief, Khoza, named only a couple of weeks ago as a ringleader in the rhino crime, now shot dead. Who by? The dead shooter on the scene? Who was he, where did he come from? The story would dominate the headlines from the moment it broke which, he was sure, wouldn't be long – unless, that is, Khoza's team was at this very moment doing a very rapid and convincing clean-up without passer-by curiosity or social media interfering.

His thoughts turned to the Sniper. Unless Khoza's security goons were both very professional and very lucky with their clean-up, the

Sniper was probably okay. But if they had a trace, he was dangerously vulnerable.

The Veteran felt a pang of guilt – for he knew full well that he had manipulated the Sniper to ply his lethal skill on the street and not just in the game reserve. It reminded him of the way he had to send young men across the border into South Africa: raw guerrillas, the odds stacked massively against them.

In any case, the security authorities would have to explain away Khoza's death – and it would suit them right down to the ground to have a hysterical outburst at the resistance to the President.

As for the Veteran himself, he was vulnerable anyway. They would try to airbrush the shooter and find evidence to implicate him. The text exchange between him and Khoza would be enough to start a witch-hunt. He drifted into semi-consciousness remembering – way back in the early 1960s – when there'd been another witch-hunt.

Over five days in July 1964 many members of the African Resistance Movement (ARM) were arrested, including members of the South African Liberal Party, who felt that non-violent means had reached the end of the road against a repressive police state and that the sabotage of government installations such as electricity pylons – not killing or injuring people – was the only way forward; brave whites like Hugh Lewin and blacks like Eddie Daniels – the former ending up serving seven years in Pretoria prison, the latter ten years on Robben Island.

Liberal John Harris was another such ARM activist. On 24 July 1964 he placed a bomb in a suitcase, which exploded on the whites-only concourse of Johannesburg railway station, killing a seventy-seven-year-old woman, maiming her young granddaughter and injuring dozens of others.

Never intending such harm, simply a spectacular protest, he had telephoned a fifteen-minute warning to police and two newspapers, urging that the station concourse be cleared. But the security minister and head of security deliberately ignored the warnings – better to exploit the subsequent and inevitable furore, they cynically calculated, than to use the station loudspeaker system to clear travellers from the concourse.

And that, the Veteran, deliriously recalled, was exactly what happened. The Harris bomb became the pretext for the government to enforce an even more oppressive regime, paranoid whites willing them on, and Harris was hanged after his conviction.

Just as he recalled these details, another blurred memory, fading in and out: Bisho in 1992 when the negotiations between the ANC and the apartheid government had hit a crisis, with the government trying to cling onto power while unleashing 'third force' violence on the ANC: a 'campaign of terror' Mandela had called it.

In Bisho, just outside King William's Town in the Eastern Cape soldiers opened fire on eighty thousand peaceful ANC protestors, including the Veteran running low and weaving to dodge the bullets which killed twenty-eight marchers and wounded over two hundred. Captured on television, the shock of Bisho forced the negotiations between Mandela and President de Klerk to resume, eventually leading to agreement.

The Veteran was almost hallucinating now as he tried to recall the details before slumping either asleep or unconscious – Thandi couldn't tell which as, agitated and anxious, she peered at him between concentrating on the fast drive to the special clinic. Not far to go, fortunately.

She could see Mkhize in her rear-view mirror, hoping nobody had spotted their number plates. There might be some CCTV pictures because the Old Fort was a national monument, but what could you do?

She pulled up in front of the emergency entrance, spotting several people waiting.

Mkhize had parked around the corner so that his car could not be identified. He ran to join them, just as the Veteran was being lifted out on a stretcher and rushed inside, a doctor – he assumed it must be the one the Veteran had identified – already tending to him as she half ran alongside.

Thandi and Mkhize attached themselves to the medical group and were not challenged until they got to an operating theatre, when they were politely blocked. 'I will see you as soon as I can,' the doctor called over her shoulder as the doors shut.

They sat down on chairs and waited. And waited. All the time willing the Veteran on.

Thandi, meanwhile, had nearly forgotten. She called the *Daily Maverick* reporter, who promised to check the story out, disappointed that Thandi wouldn't give her name or number since hers was in no-identified caller mode.

CHAPTER 23

All the President's men were dumbfounded.

Khoza was dead. They found the Russian after scouting around, and he was dead too: that was going to take some explaining to Moscow. Of the Veteran there was no evidence at all. And no explanation of how the two had been killed.

Nothing. No trace.

They quickly removed both bodies, Khoza's handgun and the shooter's equipment, making sure nobody was snooping around. They would need to develop a cover story, because some journalist was already asking whether Khoza was dead. The only consolation was the journo didn't know much, if anything, about the circumstances.

The President's press team stalled as long as they could. But they knew that before long there would be media outside Khoza's house. And his family didn't even know yet.

The doctor came back out after nearly two hours.

'It's not looking great,' she said. 'He's alive and fighting, but the injury to his neck and his head is serious. We're doing our very best. He will probably come around in due course, but I don't know when or how long he will last. On the other hand, he's a tough old bugger and could recover.'

'What's his actual condition?' Thandi asked, worried stiff.

'He had a subdural bleed, meaning his blood vessels around the brain burst after he wounded his head when he collapsed on the ground,' the doctor replied. She looked stressed but was sympathetic as she elaborated. 'Although with a subdural you can be lucid for a bit, as he was with you, patients, especially elderly ones, then lapse into unconsciousness and can only be revived – if at all – through intensive care.

'The bullet hit his neck and damaged his spine, and that was compounded when it knocked him over, resulting in the subdural. Fortunately, you brought him in quite quickly and we were able to scan and discover the subdural and operate immediately, saving his life.'

'So, what's the prognosis for his future?' Thandi asked. The medical detail had made her even more fretful.

'He's not a young man, and the left-sided subdural haematoma he's suffered means he will probably always be weak and suffer partial paralysis on his right side,' the doctor replied. 'That means a wheelchair when he wants to get about, but he should be okay around the house with a few support grab-rails and grab handles, wheelchair access to the house, and so on.

'At least he should be fully in control of his faculties. He's just got to understand – and accept, because he won't want to, knowing him! – that his lifestyle must change and change fundamentally if he is to survive, let alone have any sort of quality of life. He will tire quickly, and his condition makes him vulnerable to overdoing it. You must make sure he understands that.'

The President was grim, but his instructions had been clear: call in the Russians.

They had a huge stake in sustaining his presidency because of the planned nuclear new build costing trillions – for Moscow both a treasure trove as well as facilitating a big strategic stake in South Africa's future. Khoza's deputy, Lynn Green, whom the President had lined up for when he planned to sideline Khoza, now took charge.

They were to request assistance from the Russian satellite to try to trace those responsible for Khoza's murder – after all, the Russians were particularly anxious to discover who had killed the shooter and to deal with that person. The other priority was to find the Veteran and, this time, eliminate him, if at all feasible.

The Sniper had plenty of time to collect his thoughts on the eight-hour drive to the game reserve. He hadn't flown as usual to Richards Bay because the Veteran was emphatic: one of the first things they would check was the passenger lists at ORT Airport; just disappear in the usual heavy traffic out of the city.

Also weighing heavily on the Sniper's mind was his dramatically changed status as a citizen. He was now a wanted man – and that had never happened to him before. As he had argued with the Veteran, killing poachers in a game reserve was one thing, so was killing people while on army duty. But killing people on South Africa's streets was something completely different. That could be murder; he could be a murderer.

He did not like that. But he had nevertheless been persuaded by the Veteran.

He had killed more men in the last year than ever before – many more, because in the army he'd been responsible for just one. What churned through his mind was that it had become almost routine: a quasi-mechanical process. Threat. Target in sights. Squeeze the trigger. Another life expunged. Another father, another lover, another partner, another uncle, another son, another grandson.

It troubled him that his killings were becoming too perfunctory. The white professional, Botha. The other white pro, Momberg, he'd been distracted by recognition of course. The shooter didn't bother him so much, to be honest, because it was stark: the shooter or the Veteran.

But the two pros did – because they were too like him for comfort. One he'd served with as a soldier, maybe the other one too, for all he knew. The two would have gone through similar training, been to similar white schools, come from similar families, lived in similar tree-lined white suburbs, played rugby and maybe cricket similarly, ogled at similar girls, had similar excited hopes on enlisting in the army, worried similarly about Mandela's impending release and what it meant for them.

The first difference in their paths, come to think of it, was he supposed when he'd been assigned to protect Mandela the day he walked out of Victor Verster prison. That day had changed him. From that day onward he had begun to see things differently from other whites from his background, like Momberg and Botha. They would have adapted to majority rule without really changing, he surmised.

But it didn't make it any easier for him to cope with being a killer. Because that is what he had become. Not just a retired sniper any more. Or even an active sniper. A reborn killer unwillingly cajoled into lethal action by the Veteran and let loose in the middle of Johannesburg.

It wasn't really him. Or was it?

He wasn't sure he liked what he'd become.

He drove on, because he was already driving on, his BMW diesel on a full tank so that he didn't need to get on some petrol station's CCTV on the main highway until he was in Richards Bay itself. Then it almost certainly wouldn't really matter.

Sitting in the corridor outside the Veteran's room, Thandi seethed – which Mkhize noted was happening all the time these days.

Two senior executives of Standard Bank had been bullied and threatened amid claims that they were agents of 'white monopoly capital' after the bank had shut down all its accounts for the Business Brothers.

'Outrageous!' Thandi blurted out as she looked up from her phone and summarised the latest state-capture revelation. 'They are using racist tactics to conceal their corruption and the Brothers are the epitome of monopoly capitalism – white, brown, black or colour-blind! And deeply corrupt venal capitalism at that.'

They were interrupted by a nurse in a very grumpy mood. 'He's come to and wants to see you both. But be very careful. He shouldn't be stressed. He should be resting. It is most irregular having visitors when his condition is so critical.'

As the two walked into the room, the Veteran smiled weakly, tubes sprouting from him, his heartbeat monitored and bleeping on a screen.

'You two must move out of here – right away. They might get satellite pictures and get a trace on us. There's nothing I can do about myself, but you have to be safe to carry on the fight. You know what to do,' he said, his voice straining, his breath wheezing with the effort. His eyes were closing involuntarily, but he had something else to say.

'Go by cab. Call one now. Get it to drive right into the nearest mall car park, pay for its ticket – that's what I do to escape the eye in the sky. Don't argue. If you get caught, we are done for. Go out of the mall by another route and get another cab. Isaac, leave your car parked where it is – go and get it another day.'

Thandi could see the logic. She nodded, unable to contain her tears as she bent down to give him a peck on his forehead. 'I hate leaving you,' she muttered.

'You cannot make an omelette without breaking eggs,' the Veteran replied weakly. Then he seemed to summon up a great effort: 'This country has a great future if you make it so. But always remember the edict of Antonio Gramsci, a Marxist I admire: "pessimism of the intellect but optimism of the will".'

330

They turned and went as the Veteran smiled wistfully, satisfied, and promptly fell into a very deep sleep again. Though in floods of tears, with Mkhize consoling her, Thandi thought of her granny again, thought of the tales she had heard while the old woman was also fading away. She resolved to carry the Veteran's torch.

As she did so, another thought pinged into her mind: Alan Paton's immortal line that South Africa was 'lovely beyond any singing of it'. She didn't really understand why it had suddenly and so quixotically occurred to her, except that she was inspired by it.

The satellite images were a mixed blessing.

They showed the Sniper exiting the fort, but he was wearing a hat and was unrecognisable. He joined the crowded pavement, ducking in and out of nearby roads in the course of a brisk forty-minute walk to Newtown Junction Shopping Mall, where he simply disappeared. Later, Lynn Green ordered, they would search the mall CCTV for any clues, because identification or whereabouts otherwise seemed impossible.

But at least they had their main prize: the Veteran's location. That had been straightforward. The images weren't bad at all. Two people running into the Old Fort and lifting the clearly injured Veteran and placing him in a van, which it was easy to follow straight to a small private hospital.

The two figures were unknown, probably a bloke and a girl. They were secondary – could be followed up later. The priority – the prize in their hands – was the Veteran. *But don't involve the Russians in that*, Lynn Green decided. Too dangerous, too conspicuous. Instead she contacted iPhone Man.

Later, after exhaustively consulting colleagues, she decided to fast-track a search for the three cars identified outside the presidential compound. Now they all knew that her boss Moses Khoza had been photographed repeatedly as he was followed, they had better be found, and soon.

Major Yasmin got the alert. They were after the Veteran.

Apparently, he was in a private hospital and in a bad way. She was already aware from the state-security grapevine that Khoza was dead and there were rumours circulating via the *Daily Maverick* on Twitter, questioning his whereabouts and whether he had had a fatal accident.

She quickly put the two together, called Thandi while she was being driven by Mkhize after they had left the hospital, and got the full story.

Major Yasmin paused, thinking. Rapidly.

'You said one of the doctors was a friend? Do you have a name and phone?'

Thandi scrabbled in her own phone and found the details.

'Critical you lie low for a bit. They've got access to a Russian satellite and they may try to track you, so go into a multi-storey car park and abandon the car. Then leave yourself, after a long interval, in the middle of a group of strangers. Remember also that your DNA will be in the van, with Isaac's.'

'Abandon my car!?' Mkhize interjected.

'Yah,' she said firmly. 'Because they will find you. Best to say it must have been stolen, that you know nothing about any plot. Get back to the reserve immediately and swear your colleagues to stick to the story you have been there working, not involved in something in Pretoria or Joburg. Try not to implicate Thandi. If she comes up, you have no idea who she might be. Hide your phones too, Isaac and claim your own personal one must have been in the car when it was stolen, or otherwise they will immediately track your calls, which will be lethal for you. They may go to your phone provider, but that will take time, or they may not bother.'

She paused again and changed the subject. 'By the way, the President is getting very worried about the coming ANC conference and the way it will go. Our intelligence is that his favoured successor is losing support to his main challenger. He is getting more desperate. So keep going – what you're doing is very, very important.'

Major Yasmin then acted decisively inside her own military security.

Her edict was followed immediately: a critically ill suspect to Khoza's murder was in danger of being abducted; her unit must get there fast and guard the suspect. She provided the address to the Corporal; who rounded up others: this would be logged as an official operation.

Then she called the doctor to explain what she was doing; initially the doctor was flatly uncooperative, her resistance only disappearing when she was reassured that Major Yasmin knew the name under which the Veteran had been booked in and the aliases of both Thandi and Mkhize.

Major Yasmin was taking a bit of a risk but could claim that she was acting in support of the President – even if his security apparatchiks were furious, there would be nothing they could do if she protested her innocence in justifying her stated purpose.

*

However, iPhone Man got there first. He inveigled his way into the hospital by charming the reception staff and flashing his security-services pass. There was a patient in intensive care whose security was paramount, and he needed to check it out. Could he be directed to the unit, please?

He was careful not to give a name, pretending to be interested in security in general for all patients. Directions were readily offered, and he set off down a corridor, pausing when he was out of sight to pull out a white coat from his bag and put it on.

Both because they were ravenous and needed to kill time so that they exited the complex after an hour or two to avoid being tracked on satellite, Thandi and Mkhize grabbed a snack and coffee in one of the eateries in the mall.

They endlessly talked through their situation. Then, fed up with going round in circles, Mkhize changed the subject. 'I'm going to have to get a Gautrain to the airport.'

'But your things are at the B&B,' Thandi retorted.

'Yah, but I cannot take a chance and delay my return by going to Pretoria in case they come soon for me. I will keep my secure phone hidden away in case the security police come hunting for me. Here – you take my old one; please take out the SIM card and throw the phone and the SIM away in different places.' He handed it over with his room key, asking her to collect his gear and keep it for him.

Then he called Elise and explained he was returning urgently, that she must corroborate that he hadn't been away at all, merely assigned on other duties, if any security police came asking. He would need collecting at the airport, please, could she come personally to pick him up?

They settled their bill and stood hugging and kissing before Thandi reluctantly tore herself away. Mkhize noticed her eyes were moist and wished to hell he wasn't being forced by Major Yasmin to abandon her – even though he knew that was simply the way it had to be.

Thandi also felt terrible at having left the Veteran.

Wearing a hoodie, with her face down, she slipped unnoticed out of the mall in a throng of black shoppers. Ten minutes later she was crammed into one of the many minibuses serving as taxis in the city, bound for Pretoria. While the other passengers chatted among themselves, she was silent, her mind transfixed by the trauma of the day.

333

While at the Veteran's bedside, she had recalled the day before and the painstaking, methodical way he had given her an induction to his world of leadership, with a clear intention of passing the baton to her. Then it had seemed surreal: although faithfully absorbing all his instructions and exhortations, she had done so rather going through the motions. Now it was all chillingly real. She grimaced, daunted by the sense of heaviness that had descended upon her young shoulders.

Mkhize returned to find Elise and his ranger colleagues had performed an extraordinary rescue of a newborn, badly damaged elephant. The baby had been unable to stand properly so couldn't suckle at her mother's milk. She was tiny and close to lifeless when they had rescued her, left behind by the herd. But they couldn't feed her with cow's milk, for it would have near poisoned her. Instead they had been recommended coconut oil with special nutrients in a bottle with a teat. Slowly Elise and her team had nursed the baby back to health and over the ensuing days gradually taught her first to toddle unsteadily, then gradually to walk. Weeks later she was released back into the herd, her mother scooping her along as she scampered off.

That night Mkhize anxiously studied a report on lion poaching, worried that Zama Zama might have to prepare for an attack different from that on their rhinos. A pride living in Mozambique's Limpopo National Park had been deliberately poisoned three times over the last few years. Nine lions had died, their faces and paws and tails gruesomely hacked off by the poachers, decimating the pride.

Apparently, lion teeth and claws had been found alongside elephant tusks and rhino horn in shipments bound for East Asia, as well as more locally in traditional magic in southern Africa. And with tigers reduced to just a few thousand globally, lion bones removed by poachers had become substitutes in Asian tiger cake and wine.

Next Mkhize read a report on why – like the American dentist who killed a local favourite, Cecil the lion, in Zimbabwe in 2015 – there were now a collection of hunters who spent small fortunes killing wildlife. One hunter, decades previously, had killed thirty-two elephants all by himself, in one go, over about fifteen minutes, explaining: 'It was a great thrill to me, to be very honest.'

A contemporary guide with a Danish hunting travel company described the motivation as a mixture of thrill, risk and challenge in faraway countries, chasing after all manner of wildlife. Giraffe were easy

334

to hunt legally and therefore cost relatively little – about R60,000 for a shoot. 'A giraffe is basically a very docile pile of meat. I could go shoot a cow in a field,' he said.

Lion or elephant, much harder to catch, were typically upwards of £400,000 for a shoot. 'It's amazing to see the number of young people in Manhattan who all of a sudden realise there's a world out there, that it's not just shares and stocks, and realise: 'We could actually go hunt animals, it sounds amazing."

Thandi would have harsh words to describe that – and Mkhize wouldn't fancy the chances of any hunting apologist up against her in full flow.

There was a tap on his shoulder. 'Time for the evening *braai*, Isaac,' Steve Brown said.

They both wandered towards the brightness of the fire shimmering in the dark and began chatting to guests. But Brown could tell there was a sense of distance about his friend tonight and didn't push the bonhomie.

Mkhize was consumed with worry about the Veteran, wondering also how Thandi might be. It was one thing to be in the middle of a poacher firefight – that was his territory. It was quite another to be caught up in firefight with the security services.

As they dreaded, the Veteran wasn't at all in good shape.

He drifted in and out of consciousness, his inner fight struggling against an overpowering weariness. It tried to consume him, to smother him back into lifelessness, but still he fought, his spirit resisting the weakness of the flesh, then subsiding, only to begin resisting again.

Guarding his room and keeping her abreast of the latest medical assessment – not good – Major Yasmin's team stayed alert, for she was sure there would be an attempt to kill the Veteran, if indeed he survived his injuries.

Her men were pros, and iPhone Man cursed as he surveyed them while pretending to go about his non-existent duties in the white tunic with a stethoscope around his neck he had purloined.

A man struggling to hang on to his life, an agent lurking to end it.

Oblivious, the Veteran slept on as the battle inside him between physical frailty and mental fortitude raged.

Major Yasmin plotted.

One way or another the President's men would find a way to kill the

Veteran. That was a dead cert. So she had to get him out of there. Yet her position was vulnerable. Not trusted to be part of the President's inner security circle, yet so meticulously wily that she hadn't given them any excuse to dispose of her, Major Yasmin now needed to throw caution to the wind and act decisively.

In breaking a bit – just a bit – of cover, she was comforted by even more crucial intelligence that the President wasn't getting it all his way, as he had been accustomed to in the run-up to elective party conferences.

There seemed to be a shift away from his favoured successor – despite everything he had contrived. Despite the 'ghost' ANC members who had died but were being kept on branch membership lists to inflate the numbers of conference delegates pledged to vote for him in Mpumalanga province. Despite the going rate of R10,000 for local branch secretaries and R3,000 for delegates to swell his camp's votes – money from the Russians routed through the Business Brothers. Despite the large number of party apparatchiks on his payroll. Despite all that, he was losing ground to the Challenger.

The President was demented with frustration. And that meant his heavies would be severely distracted.

Major Yasmin called the Veteran's doctor, explaining they were living on borrowed time and gave clipped instructions.

Thandi eventually staggered, exhausted, through her parents' front door.

She didn't tell them about the obnoxious, testosterone-filled taxi, nor the drama of her mission, nor about the reason for collecting Isaac's gear and checking him out of the B&B, nor her wrenching worry about the Veteran.

Thandi didn't tell them anything at all. She just went to bed and fell into a deep sleep.

Which was why she didn't know anything about the drama her parents had watched on the late eNCA news, announcing the mysterious death of Moses Khoza and the even more mysterious death nearby of a Russian citizen. Nor did she see the *Daily Maverick* tweet with an online link to its breaking news.

Thandi slept like a baby.

With Mkhize absent, Elise had yet another problem, so had called for help from her other rangers. A young bull elephant, which had been expelled

336

from the main herd in accordance with custom once it began chasing females, had charged a Land Cruiser with safari guests, the party only narrowly escaping as their driver reversed frantically.

It was the third such incident with the same bull – behaving rather like an adolescent youth who needed a strong father to assert control – or in this case, a patriarch. They had to find one from another reserve and had immediately started the process of trying to do so, beginning with seeking permission from SANParks.

Shooting a dominant bull elephant could often trigger rogue behaviour by younger bulls. Equally, when a senior bull entered the territory, a ferocious fight often ensued, which is exactly what Mkhize had predicted when he returned and a patriarch arrived.

It was a brutal collision of giants, powering into each other like immovable forces, each crunching clash taking minutes, the earth juddering, the whole affair going on for a couple of days with breaks to eat and drink. After what seemed like an age, it finally ended with the older bull placing his trunk on the younger one's penis and giving it an almost belittling flip, as if to say: 'I've won and the females are mine now.'

Relations between the two later settled down into wary mutual respect and the young bull gave no more trouble to the guests.

The fire alarm in the hospital rasped shrilly.

An order for immediate evacuation followed. Staff with patients on trolleys rushed helter-skelter for the entrance. iPhone Man – desperately trying to look over his shoulder for a glimpse of the Veteran – was forced to join the throng, regular staff noticing him for the first time with some suspicion or curiosity: a stranger in their midst attired as a medic. It was a modestly sized clinic in which he suddenly stood out.

Slowly and carefully the doctor and his paramedic colleagues began moving the Veteran, thin medical tubes sprouting from his body and still attached to drips. They levered him out into one of three ambulances parked under a hard cover at the back of the clinic. Major Yasmin had been very specific: there must be no possibility of scrutiny by satellite.

At the front entrance other patients were also being bundled into ambulances out in the open. It was chaotic and iPhone Man couldn't get near enough to see what the hell was going on, who was being taken where, and to which nearby hospital or clinic for temporary shelter.

To the rear, three ambulances pulled away from out under the hard cover, one of them containing the still unconscious Veteran, the doctor and his team.

The other two were empty.

Major Yasmin's phone call jolted Thandi wide awake.

Her instructions were clipped and clear. She mustn't use a cab; she had to drive herself immediately to a military intelligence safe house in Midrand, just outside Johannesburg, north towards Pretoria where the Corporal would await her. The Veteran was being moved there.

'But he's in a critical condition!' Thandi exclaimed.

'Yah,' Major Yasmin replied coldly, 'it's a big risk, but they would have killed him back in the clinic because I got a whisper they had located him. Grab some clothes and toiletries and take them with you. I don't know how long you will be needed there, but I cannot spare my people or suspicions will be roused. You will be my agent at the venue, doing whatever you have to: nursing, shopping, security – whatever. There are medical facilities installed in one room, with a nurse in attendance, and the doctor will do her best to set everything up for you.'

'Okay,' Thandi mumbled, 'but I cannot leave my dad's car there.'

Major Yasmin thought for a moment. 'I'll get the Corporal to drive it back to your parents' house.'

The Sniper hadn't slept at all that night after arriving to stay at Elise's house.

He had been thrilled to see her and enjoyed her affectionate peck. No more, no less. He was pleased but disappointed all at the same time, because he realised he craved her. But even if she had wanted to recip-rocate his feelings, she wasn't ready to show or do that yet. The Owner's death was too painfully recent. She was still emotionally battered – which he both understood and respected.

Elise had poured them both a glass of wine, and they'd walked out onto the verandah to survey her kingdom. It was nightfall, but the moon was high, and the squeaking, burping, rasping, chirping, grunting sound of the bush was simply magical.

She started talking fast, as if to substitute for a more personally engaging conversation.

'Look at all this,' – she swept her elegant arm expansively around – 'all under threat – less from poachers than from all of humankind, with sixty per cent of mammals, birds, fish and reptiles wiped out in the last five decades. It's now such an emergency, civilisation itself is threatened. A sixty-per-cent cull of humans would be wiping out North America, South America, Africa, Europe, China and Oceania.'

The Sniper, entranced, could listen to her all night as she continued to talk.

They stood silently enjoying the sound, enjoying the view, taking it all in, and turned to each other, clinking glasses as they went back inside to get refills – then sat down to eat before heading for their separate bedrooms.

As he closed his eyes, the Sniper found his mind surging and whirling. It would be like that all through the night as the events at the fort consumed him and collided within him.

And he couldn't even tell her anything about it.

Just over an hour after being woken up and having an argument – yet another argument – with her dad about taking his car, Thandi arrived at the safe house.

It was a standard large, newish six-bedroom family home spread out over one floor in an upper-income suburb, with standard surrounding walls painted mid-grey. Only the curious or the discerning would have noticed the especially forbidding steel spikes overhanging the walls, the ubiquitous CCTV cameras and the intimidating steel doors at the gates, with armour-protected glass inspection panels and intercom.

As instructed by Major Yasmin, she had called a number to give her car registration when approaching the gates, and they began to open just as she pulled up, allowing her to enter seamlessly and without attracting the slightest attention in what was a heavily gated neighbourhood. She drove forward towards a second barrier guarded by machine-gun-carrying men in khaki gear who checked her out and searched the car, a sniffer dog on a leash prowling aggressively around it. Then she was waved forward, and the Corporal stepped out of the house towards her. She pulled up, handed him the keys and gave him her parents' address, which he entered on his Google Maps app.

As she walked through the front door, the Corporal drove off.

The inside of the house was functional, with a bare minimum of decorative accoutrements. A housekeeper was waiting, introducing herself, polite if rather aloof – as if to say: 'And what are you doing here?'

Ansie Pottgieter, a white woman in her early sixties, clipped grey hair, wearing a prim grey dress, had probably been in charge of the house under apartheid too, Thandi presumed.

'Please come with me.' She turned and Thandi followed, the woman indicating where her bedroom was, and waiting fussily outside as Thandi dumped her scruffy grip bag and had a quick pee in the cramped en suite bathroom.

Then she was pointed to the back of the house. 'Your friend is in there; please let me know if I can help at any time. There's a button in his room and a similar one in your bedroom. I am here all the time. Security is all around us. There's a nurse and doctor on hand too, plenty of food for you as well – just help yourself in the kitchen.'

Thandi gingerly pushed the door open. To her relief, the inside resembled a medical clinic. The Veteran, dozing, she thought, was hooked up to various tubes, at the end of which were drip bags or electric monitors.

A young Indian doctor welcomed her with a smile, and an older Coloured nurse as well.

Thandi introduced herself: 'I'm a close comrade.' She chose the label 'comrade' deliberately, almost to test them out.

It appeared to work. She was important.

'How's he doing?'

'I am really not sure,' the doctor replied, looking worried, though he seemed to have a permanent frown anyway. 'He's only been with us a short while, but the doctor from the clinic briefed me fully that it was seventy to thirty against surviving.'

'He's very important to the future of the country. He's got to survive,' Thandi said grimly. She didn't say it accusingly, just extremely firmly. She wasn't used to giving instructions, but that's what the Veteran had entrusted her with.

The doctor looked even more worried. 'I know. The major made that perfectly clear. Perfectly clear. We will do all we possibly can, and we have a new ID for him if he needs intensive care in a proper hospital. At least he's stable – for now. But we're worried about brain damage.'

'Is there anything I can do?' Thandi asked.

The doctor shook his head. 'Suggest you sit on the chair over there in case he stirs.'

Thandi sat down and started checking her safe phone for news and messages.

Over the next hour she waited, looking up periodically as the doctor hovered and the nurse came in and out. The Veteran slumbered quietly, seemingly endlessly, as if there was no fight left in him any more.

Anger consumed iPhone Man.

He had a reputation for delivering. As he'd done repeatedly for Moses Khoza in the past – from surveillance to assassination – and as he was determined to do for his successor. But the target had simply disappeared. It was baffling and frustrating in equal measure.

What the hell was going on? iPhone Man wondered. Who was the enemy? What resources did they have? He was part of a huge security-service operation – the deniable part of it. Yet he was getting no answers, and certainly no traction.

His mentor, Khoza, was dead. That was unimaginable. He'd been told it was a clean kill by a professional. Who was the guy? Presumably the same guy who had also shot the Russian, supposedly an invincible pro himself. And now there were rumours that the President's dummy successor was losing ground. Surely that couldn't be true? The President had never, ever lost an internal party battle. Never.

If the Challenger won, it could be curtains for him. For the first time in a very long period, iPhone Man was worried. And to cap all that, there was the testimony of that bastard, the former finance minister, who claimed that he had been misled and targeted with a torrent of lies and abuse as he sought to curb looting by the President and his cronies.

He was speaking at a Parliamentary inquiry, revealing that honest public servants were dismissed or shuffled sideways as the President took control of state-owned enterprises and interfered in the management of government institutions by placing his people in them. There his cronies ruthlessly plundered with impunity. Anybody seeking to expose this, including the former finance minister himself, was sacked.

He also stated that investigative journalists were placed under surveillance by the State Security Agency, especially if they had uncovered corruption, state capture or abuse of power ... And to deflect attention away from the cause, state capture became a sophisticated racket that advanced false narratives, including re-racialising politics with racist sentiments.

Or so the former finance minister alleged: he should have been taken out a long time ago, iPhone Man thought. In fact, they had discussed doing that very thing. But Khoza had vetoed it. The man had too much

341

media support, too much respect within the ANC as well: though not among the President's apparatchiks, for they all hated him.

iPhone Man had never really given much thought to his own future, for under Khoza it seemed to take care of itself. He had a decent home – not plush like Khoza's – but more than decent enough for him. His wife and boys were content enough with their standard of living. He'd even been able to save a bit for a rainy day.

But now he was starting to feel insecure: his world wasn't behaving as it had for the last ten years – certainly not as it should.

Mkhize was subdued and silent.

Steve Brown had forwarded two online reports and the two of them crouched over his laptop.

United Nations experts were insisting children born today might well be the very last to experience the wonder of tropical coral reefs in all their glory – reefs that had thrived and survived for tens of millions of years.

'And then some influential politicians have the gall to deny climate change is happening!' Mkhize snorted.

'Yah,' replied Brown morbidly, now looking at a second report. It will cheer you right up – I don't think.'

Scientists researching climate change reported that melting ice, warming seas, shifting currents and dying forests could cascade, domino-like, and tip the Earth into a 'hothouse' state, making policies to curb emissions and reverse climate change pointless.

'It's real end-of the world stuff,' Mkhize said morosely. 'And it might already be too late for humankind to do anything about this.'

Brown shook his head. 'Makes you wonder whether our little contributions here in Zama Zama will make any bloody difference at all.'

'We have to do our bit,' Mkhize insisted, reflecting that he sounded rather like Thandi on politics.

Then his phone rang. It was the Zama Zama office. The police had called wanting to speak to him about his car.

In a moment his world had changed. 'No idea what they want,' Mkhize said, knowing full well that he did.

The hours dragged by in the safe house.

Thandi's mood swung between intense anxiety about the Veteran and anticlimax as time remorselessly drifted on.

Nothing seemed to be happening.

Night came, still the Veteran hadn't stirred, and suddenly she felt totally drained – the drama of the last couple of days catching up with her. She told the night nurse at the Veteran's bedside that she was going to bed, but to wake her immediately if he stirred out of what seemed like a coma.

The President was feeling the heat.

For years he had seemed impervious to all the evidence and allegations of corruption, fiddling and looting. But the rhino-horn furore had rattled him. The main wildlife NGO, Save Our Rhinos, had applied to take the case to the Constitutional Court, where Justice Samuel Makojaene would look into the legal background.

In all the cases against the President brought to the Constitutional Court, including the reinstatement of criminal charges against him for receiving bribes before he became President, the issue of whether he could be compelled to appear in court to face a criminal charge while serving as a President had not been raised. In the USA, when President Bill Clinton had been threatened with criminal prosecution for lying under oath, the Supreme Court had ruled that any criminal or civil charges against him would have to be postponed until he ceased to be president. But South Africa's top court would not be bound to follow that decision.

Especially in this case where its Parliament had ratified the Convention on International Trade in Endangered Species of Wild Fauna and Flora (CITES) in 1975.

Then there was the question of domestic South African law. The National Biodiversity Act of 2004 provided the statutory basis for the protection of vulnerable species and ecosystems. Also, rhino poaching and trafficking was a crime in the country.

Therefore, it seemed to Makojaene that an action could be brought against the President for violating the duties of his office to uphold the Constitution and the law. however, he could not preside over the case, because he had given rulings on illegal wildlife issues before. The Chief Justice would preside because of the President's involvement. Nevertheless, Makojaene would have ample opportunity to make his views known in the vigorous conclaves the court had on every matter before it.

Van der Merwe was usually phlegmatic about shocks and invariably found a way to ride them, but Khoza's death had seriously flustered him.

343

The security chief had been his pipeline to information, tasks and, above all, cash income. They had trusted each other completely and now he was on his own again. Also held at arm's length because of the rhino-horn smuggling scandal and the very unfortunate way in which he had been fingered. Not so much fingered as exposed, bang to rights under a glare of media attention.

The media had camped outside his house for a day and he had been forced to lock himself inside – until eventually other stories beckoned and they went away, leaving notes through his letter box to call. Some chance.

Peering from behind the curtains, he had felt imprisoned. Now he felt like a leper. Once-friendly neighbours, chatting or in the past enquiring solicitously after his sick wife, didn't want to know him any more. He dared not pursue his research on likely poaching ventures in Limpopo province because his name was too well known – for now at least, though he worried that even when media attention moved on, those in the wildlife world would have had reason to clock him and, the danger was, recognise him if he booked into a reserve or was seen poking about.

In any case his conduit, Khoza, was no more. Wiped out – how on earth was that possible? He hadn't a clue, had tried to make enquiries, but Khoza's team was cool and keen to keep a distance from a now con-taminated operative.

Van der Merwe sipped at another very large brandy. Then he had an idea.

One of Khoza's several most-trusted protégés in the National Intelligence Agency had become an acquaintance. To call him a friend was pushing it. But the man had always been cooperative and affable. Van der Merwe called him, and they fixed to meet – very discreetly, it went without saying.

He poured himself another glass and began reminiscing.

South Africa – his very own South Africa – was a total bloody mess. All the chat among his circle was of sons and daughters, or grandsons and granddaughters, being overlooked because of so-called affirmative action for jobs, even university places, by people often less qualified, sometimes downright incompetent.

The white man had made South Africa their country. What the hell – they had made South Africa. Where would the place have been without them, for goodness' sake? Whites had brought skills, investment, entre-preneurialism and sheer fucking hard grind to make the country the most modern by far on the continent, in some respects equal or even better than modern industrialised nations in the northern hemisphere.

Then they had handed over power to Mandela without a war. And what thanks did they get? 'Sweet Fanny Adams', as his best friend from army service used to say.

To be fair, it had been pretty good under Mandela. And then later had come the President, looting and pillaging, bringing the country down.

Yes, it had to be said, he personally had done okay under the President. In fact, he had thrived these past few years.

'But that's not the fucking point, man!' van der Merwe raged out loud in the empty house. 'I've lost my country.'

His world had disappeared. His wife had disappeared. His provider had disappeared. What on earth next? Maybe he should disappear into one of those Afrikaner white enclaves in South Africa's far rural north?

Then his mind switched to the emptiness of the house, his black maid having retired to her quarters a couple of hours ago. She was decent and competent, but vastly overweight. He thought back to the slim, curvy carer wistfully. Maybe he should recruit a new replacement maid like her?

Oblivious to the contradictions between his anger and his yearning, he staggered to bed, a lonely, getting-to-be very grumpy old man.

For another oldish but diametrically different white man, memories. Lots of memories. Whirling around, colliding, and evaporating into an amorphous blancmange of semi-consciousness.

His armed and dangerous days vivid – then slipping away, unreachable. The comradeship, the danger, the courage. Above all the conviction of justice and the high ground enjoyed by the freedom struggle under the outstanding yet undersung Oliver Tambo, as well as the iconic Mandela. And to crown it all, the astonishment and joy of victory, so long and so determinedly fought for against such fierce odds, and the bubbling, pulsating joy of the new rainbow country.

But then the betrayal. The trashing of their values and their ideals. The venal corruption. The gangsterism infecting his old party, the ANC. The grotesque inequality chasm between those at the top and the masses below.

And the pain which that brought, together with the awful, searing loss of his brave wife, who wrapped around him a cocoon of comfort and love and passion, partners both in bed and in the struggle.

345

The Veteran opened his eyes. Where was he? What was going on? What had happened?

Then he closed them again – easier that way, because he had no strength or even purpose any more. So tired. So very tired. Easier just to slip away completely. To wander along the coast of his cherished Cape Peninsula with his wife – she was beckoning him now: 'Come and join me.' The sun was bright, the breeze cool, the sea shimmered turquoise and deep blue, the colours of the flora stunningly sharp, the vista summoning him like an aura gradually enveloping his whole persona. It was so enticing. That was now his chosen path. That was where he would just slip away, to relax, to stop the endless struggling and stress.

But suddenly from somewhere far away an unwelcome distraction, tugging him back.

'It's me, Thandi, I'm here. I'm looking after you. Everything will be all right.' Her voice pleading, gentle, warm, vibrant, like a homecoming summons.

No! He didn't want that. It was too hard, and he had no will any more. He wanted to go with his wife into the alluring glow.

'Please speak to me! Please!' She sounded desperate – but also warm, comforting, reassuring. He felt the glow receding, his wife now disappearing. He couldn't see her any more. He was being drawn back.

It was such an effort and he wasn't sure he really wanted to, but the Veteran somehow summoned up the energy to open his eyes again.

Thandi had noticed him stirring and had moved quickly to his bedside.

She deliberately hadn't asked permission from the nurse or doctor, because they would probably have refused. In any case, Major Yasmin's instructions had been clear: she was in charge.

She smiled and spoke gently, putting her hand in his, squeezing lightly. Another glow, another aura. The Veteran felt warmer. 'What is going on?' he stammered, wheezing with effort, his diction blurred, his voice faint.

Thandi gently reminded him about the meeting and the shootings, explaining how they had collected him from the Old Fort, bleeding badly, and rushed him to a discreet hospital. From where he had been evacuated to the safe house he was in now.

The Veteran closed his eyes again. It was all so exhausting, so utterly exhausting.

Then Thandi's caressing, tender urgency summoned him half awake.

346

He hadn't the energy to ask more questions but, as if she intuitively understood that, she was talking slowly and calmly. He mostly listened, mostly understood, her hand somehow transmitting energy into him.

They'd never held hands before, never had any need to. But Thandi knew from a friend who was a reflexology and reiki therapist the importance of human energy in healing – if and only if, of course, you had the sort of personality and empathy that gave you the ability to transmit yours to a patient. She stroked the top of his palm and lightly stroked his shoulder and brow, hoping she could do something similar, however amateurishly or imperfectly.

The Veteran relaxed, more attentive now and a little more engaged, as Thandi went over the drama slowly and simply – until she realised she was still speaking and he was back sleeping.

Van der Merwe awoke and prowled about the house, getting himself breakfast.

'Always eat a good breakfast,' his mother used to say, 'for it may be your last food for the day. You never know what any day might bring.' Then she would plonk down steaming ladles of sausages and bacon with scrambled egg on toast piled high, and he would tuck in, leaving a clean plate.

But these days he couldn't be bothered to have a cooked breakfast – in fact, hadn't had one since his wife became incapacitated. It was too much sweat – even prepared by the maid. Instead he'd become used to cereal and toast with strong coffee and three spoons of sugar.

After gulping it down, he had a shave and a shower before heading off to visit Mrs Moses Khoza. Funny that he had never used her first name – always 'Mrs Khoza'. When he had called to fix a convenient time, she was hysterical. She simply couldn't survive. What should she do? And so on, and on and on.

But by the time he called by to commiserate, he found her in good spirits. What a wonderful, caring President the country had. She had this very day been appointed chair of South African Airways on a stipend that substituted almost entirely her husband's salary. That she knew nothing about running an airline, had never been on a board and didn't have any commercial expertise whatsoever was no problem. She was ideal for the job, the President had called to say.

Oh, and another small compensation: the Business Brothers had so thoughtfully paid off the outstanding loans on their – now her – prestigious house and state-of-the-art Jaguar XF saloon.

Life wasn't too bad for her after all.

Unexpectedly there was an odd sound – one of reverberating rustling, like a low, piercing, strong wind utterly focused in its intensity. They had no idea what it was.

'Red driver ants!' said Mkhize, chuckling. 'Look down for them now and be careful! Don't step on them! They'll eat you alive!'

He looked around. 'There they are!' he pointed.

Through the scrub came an army on the march, millions of them, it seemed, single-mindedly hunting, devouring anything in their way, small reptiles, beetles, the lot. Capable of attacking animals, they would pour through buildings stationed in the bush, gobbling up insects, rats, mice, cockroaches, as well as bugs, dirt and grime, leaving everything pristine in their wake.

'You cannot resist, just get the hell out of their path!' Mkhize urged, enjoying the guests' gawps of spellbound horror as the deadly convoy moved determinedly onward. Their morning bushwalk was proving to be full of the sort of alarming novelty that captivates the luckiest safari lovers.

Traversing a gulley, Steve Brown hissed urgently 'Stop!'

He pointed ahead and to their right at the extraordinary sight. An adult rock python, five metres long, its skin glistening brown-gold, was wrapped around a young springbok, the powerful snake's mouth hinged so wide open that it was swallowing the animal whole, horns and all.

'Be quiet!' Brown whispered. 'Or it will get frightened, regurgitate the buck and then slither off, possibly not to eat again for weeks until it finds another prey to ambush.'

They were transfixed, backing off slowly from the cruel splendour of the ferocious wild.

After an enjoyable lunch, the wine flowing and the conversation lively as Mkhize explained how rising ranger deaths from poachers had turned them into paramilitaries rather than conservationists, the guests sloped off for a kip or a read before the afternoon game drive.

Mkhize sat contemplatively, thinking not any more about poaching but about the coming police visit. Normally he worked closely with the local police investigating poaching. Now they were investigating him, and he didn't like it. In fact, he was worried stiff. He had rehearsed his lines with Major Yasmin, and just hoped the police found them believable.

Thandi waited, watching tenderly as the Veteran slumbered gently.

Her eyes were moist as she willed him on. She wasn't at all religious and she would under no circumstances pray for him. But she did the next best thing. She closed her eyes and concentrated all her energy fiercely and determinedly upon him. *Survive. Fight. Don't abandon us now. Never ever give up. Isn't that what you taught me?*

It was as if everything she had to offer him had been sucked right out of her, and she felt utterly exhausted. But she redoubled herself, reaching into her reserves. She couldn't allow herself to be distracted, couldn't even allow herself to think of Isaac, of anyone or anything else.

She focused so hard on the Veteran that, when the nurse came in to check on him Thandi was fast asleep herself, chin on her chest, but still holding his hand.

Van der Merwe sat in front of Khoza's protégé in the National Intelligence Agency, transfixed at the account he was hearing. Some of it wasn't clear because the protégé wasn't clear. But both the presence and the death of the Russian hitman was startling.

Startling, because to import a hitman from Moscow was a huge thing – and then that he was killed, with all the explaining and excusing required. Well, humiliation didn't even begin to explain the extent of the grovelling the President's men would have been required to undertake, and maybe the President himself as well in a call to the Russian president, the nuclear deal personal to them both.

But who the hell had killed him? van der Merwe wondered. Must be some helluva guy. And how had the Veteran got hold of him?

An old MK shooter? No – they weren't good enough for that sort of thing, van der Merwe concluded. Somebody else. Somebody else entirely. Somebody top class in the art of assassination.

And none of them had a clue who he was.

Van der Merwe returned home to his empty home and his emptying brandy bottle. And he pondered long and hard into the night.

When he eventually woke in the early hours, slumped on his sofa, just a smear left in the bottom of the bottle in front of him, feeling cold with a gnawing headache, a sudden blinding thought struck him.

Everything to do with his clandestine activity these past months had a common denominator: executions of those within his close circle. Executions of not just the African poachers, but those ultimate pros he'd recruited, Momberg and Botha. And now executions of his ringmaster, Moses Khoza, and the Russian hitman.

Was there a link? van der Merwe wondered. No, surely not. How could there be?

On the other hand, he was not a man for coincidences. Surely there must be a link.

It was just a whisper, but iPhone Man heard it first.

The Veteran's evacuation was so professional, it must have been an inside job of some sort, his source maintained. But if so, who?

He began asking around. Very discreetly.

The police officers from Richards Bay – two of them, in full uniform, brandishing guns and batons, one a man, the other a woman – looked bored.

They'd been sent by senior bods in Pretoria to find out why a car had been seen parked up the road from the President's official compound, when they had far better things to attend to – like an internal ANC faction trying to maintain its privileged access to gravy trains by killing fellow ANC activists who persisted in raising difficult questions in KwaZulu-Natal, for instance, as the numbers of deaths kept rising. Or theft, violence and drugs barons.

As far as they had been briefed, no offence had been committed involving the parked car. The driver hadn't breached any traffic regulation, and there had been no collision. Pretoria wasn't very forthcoming. It was all rather odd.

Mkhize knew both the officers, as they had visited Zama Zama after the attack on the orphan rhino cubs, and they greeted him warmly in their native tongue, Zulu. Their questions were officious but perfunctory, and they wrote down his answers very fully and very carefully.

No, he had no idea what the officers were on about. He had never been anywhere near the presidential compound. So, why then had his car been spotted up the road on CCTV? Mkhize shrugged his shoulders, looking puzzled.

'What was my car supposed to be doing there? How far up the road was it parked? Could the number plate have been mistaken for someone else? Was there an accident?' Mkhize asked, taking control of the interview as Major Yasmin had advised.

The officers, looking embarrassed, couldn't say, then asked: 'Can we see the car, please?'

'Sorry, I have left it with a friend, as I had to fly back the other day,' Mkhize explained, adding, 'I leave the car in Joburg or Pretoria sometimes. I don't get much time off as a ranger, so it's sometimes easier to fly and get the Gautrain from Joburg airport. By the way, what day was the car supposed to be left there?'

The officers consulted their notebooks and gave a date.

Mkhize looked at his Samsung smartphone. 'Sorry, I was on duty here in Zama Zama that day. You can check in the office register next door. But I know I left the car with my friends. Do you need a name? I'd have to find out who had it. Are you really sure it was my car number? Could there be some mistake?'

The officers looked at each other in exasperation. They shrugged. 'We'll get instructions and call you back.' They shook his hand and went off.

Mkhize breathed a sigh of relief. So far, so good.

He immediately called Major Yasmin, who listened intently to the sequence of the interview.

'Good,' she said, 'it seems, as I suspected, that they were simply checking out your response, and they don't have much more detail. If they were certain, they would have sent their security goons down to interview you. That they didn't confirms security have much more urgent and important duties than chasing down a mystery photographer – like fixing the forthcoming ANC conference to choose the President's successor. I hear that's all they're really concerned about at the moment.'

'So am I likely to hear from them again?' Mkhize asked.

'Although I can't be certain, I rather doubt it.' She paused. 'But if they do get back in touch, I'm afraid the next interview could be far tougher, and we will have to discuss it again beforehand. The important thing is to stick to your story and try not to give details on your "friends", certainly not Thandi's name. Anyway, we will talk further at the time if it materialises.'

Mkhize, only partially reassured, asked if he could call Thandi, as she had been worried too.

'Yah, do. But if you get no answer, text her, because she's looking after the Veteran in a safe house.'

So that was it – Mkhize had wondered why she had apparently gone to ground after leaving a garbled message on his voicemail.

'One other thing to remember in all this,' Major Yasmin said, 'you are now on their list as a marked man. Make just one mistake and they will have you.'

This time when the Veteran opened his eyes it was different. Instead of feeling like closing them the whole time, he was alert, wondering.

Somebody was holding his hand. Odd? That hadn't happened in the same way since his wife had passed. She used to hold it really tightly sometimes.

He tried to turn his neck, but it hurt too much, so he swivelled his eyes, and they came to rest on a familiar figure. Who? Who was it? He knew her, but he didn't? No – that was wrong, surely? He did.

It was Thandi. He tried squeezing her hand back, but he couldn't. He was too weak, and sank back with all the effort.

But Thandi stirred.

The story was too big to be kept secret for long.

It began to leak out in an untidy way: two murders and the disappearance of the Veteran. Police leaks – instantly denied by the security service – suggested a foreign national might be implicated, and that an unknown pedestrian had told police she had walked into the Old Fort while sightseeing, stumbled upon the dead Khoza, and seen two men taking another body away in a black bag.

Having reported this, an opinion piece by a leading journalist from the *Daily Maverick* suggested the public wasn't getting the full story and demanded a statement from the President himself. An opposition MP soon pressed for a public inquiry.

In the safe house, Thandi conferred with a now lucid Veteran propped up in bed, though still frustratingly weak, permanently exhausted, and prone to fall asleep in the middle of talking to her. He was clear: he had to issue a public statement, and she would have to read it out for him.

Major Yasmin, who had called by, was in on the conversation and strongly recommended against this. Thandi was a clean skin. Nobody knew her. If she went public speaking for the Veteran, everyone would want to know who she was. The media would dig – understandably

352

so – that was their job. Other questions might be asked. She would come under security service and police scrutiny. It was far too risky.

But, the Veteran countered, at some time Thandi would have to come out. She had agreed to carry on his work – hadn't she? He looked at her.

Thandi nodded – rather hesitantly.

'What is more, from what you have both told me, the President is more vulnerable now than at any time since he was elected. This story of a plot to kill me could be a clincher on top of everything else.'

Thandi was unusually quiet, saying nothing: Was it a moment of truth for her? she wondered.

Sensing her dilemma and knowing of her reluctance to be in the spotlight, the Veteran continued. 'Thandi, remember how I explained that in politics timing can be everything? Sometimes there's a moment for change which, if you don't seize it, can pass – maybe not to return, either ever or for a long time. I cannot be sure, and I'm not able to consult trusted struggle comrades. If I surface in any way publicly at this critical stage, the enemy might kill me. They nearly did. But I think we are in one of those must-be-seized moments.'

The Veteran sank back, propped up on his pillow.

Major Yasmin had gone quiet.

Thandi didn't know what to think, because she was at once convinced by the Veteran and worried about her own ability to face the inevitable media storm if she did as he recommended. Yet somebody had to do it, didn't they? And there was nobody else he could ask except her.

He was getting nowhere, and that frustrated iPhone Man beyond belief.

It had to be an inside job, but only he seemed to believe it. Certainly, nobody was owning up to how the Veteran had been moved from right under their noses to just disappear into thin air.

As for the new (and maybe temporary) security chief to the President, Lynn Green, she had come straight to him at the outset, but hadn't really confided when he reported back that he'd drawn a blank. In fact, she'd seemed almost dismissive, preoccupied as she was with other pressures. The coming ANC conference vote on the President's successor was at the all-consuming top of her list, he was certain.

On that, her future – indeed his own future – and the same for many others, depended. And from what he'd picked up, the race was looking uncomfortably close.

Maybe he ought to hedge his bets and make himself available to those close to the Challenger to the President's favoured successor?

Van der Merwe, who always kept his ear close to the ground, had the same impression. Yet the President had such a grip on the party machine, he could swing any vote, any time. Always had done.

He climbed out of the cab, to a regular gathering of members of the South African Institute for Maritime Research, in its heyday a formidable gang of mercenaries linked into the heart of the militarised apartheid state. Known for their toughness and effectiveness, they were recruited for operations throughout Africa.

Always working clandestinely, they had supported coups and served different elites engaged in nefarious sorties. Declared 'anti-communists', they could not conceal their racist mission to retain white supremacy in Africa. They even claimed to have organised the notorious 1961 plane crash that killed United Nations Secretary-General Dag Hammarskjöld, seen as a champion of decolonisation in his support for newly independent states, and therefore a threat to the white elites that had ruled Africa in the colonial era.

Some of them, van der Merwe knew only too well, had also discussed an armed uprising to thwart Mandela's impending rise to power in the 1990s, offering expertise and weapons to other white conspirators. Having flirted with the notion himself, he'd concluded it was too reckless and, anyway, Mandela soon outsmarted and snuffed out threats of white resistance on the eve of the 1994 majority rule elections.

Van der Merwe circulated easily among the attendees, bumping into old friends and contacts, at home among them, the glasses continuously refilled by courteous black waitresses circulating amidst the boisterous gathering and pretending not to hear the racist banter.

They were relics from the past – each and every one of them. Proud to be 'White Africans', passionate about the continent, yet united in their militant zeal that everything was going to pot and resentful that black Africans now ruled the roost.

After a sumptuous lunch concluded with a speech from the top guy, cheered to the rafters, he retreated by Uber, considerably the worse for wear but happier nevertheless.

CHAPTER 24

For years the President had seemed cloaked in his very own form of impunity.

The economy was weakening relentlessly. Foreign investors had a self-imposed boycott – ironic, Thandi thought, since they never did that until the dog days of apartheid. Local protests multiplied daily over deteriorating community services. Erstwhile allies in the ANC had begun deserting him as they realised defeat beckoned at the looming general election. The Russians, preoccupied with the nuclear deal that was their bridge into the subcontinent were getting fidgety. Very fidgety.

But the President remained oblivious and smiling through it all. Whatever was thrown at him, it had seemed that he was impregnable. He didn't realise that he wasn't any longer: the noose had started to tighten.

The Constitutional Court announced it had accepted as within its jurisdiction the case brought by Save Our Rhinos and set down a hearing date.

There was also NGO pressure on the International Criminal Court. Although its priorities were genocide by governmental or military leaders, the international outcry was such that its prosecutors and judges in The Hague had signalled they were looking into it.

Therefore, if he travelled to any European Union country he would almost certainly be arrested by Interpol, which had issued a Red Notice on him. That might be triggered in other countries too, so he was virtually confined to his home, South Africa.

Scorpio seemed to have a new revelation about presidential wrongdoing almost every other week, as leaks began pouring from whistle-blowers sensing the tide was turning.

Bob Richards MP, taking advantage of the scope at Thursday's regular House of Commons Business Questions, threatened to expose more corruption if further whistle-blowers contacted him. In an interview and podcast for the influential South African online BizNews, he explained more fully that he expected many more such exposés, so long as the President remained in office.

Through his weakness and suffocating tiredness, the Veteran was crystal clear.

This was Thandi's time. An ideal opportunity to catapult her from the shadows and onto the stage to carry his mission – their mission – forward.

He would never be back to his old self, the doctor had sympathetically but firmly warned. In fact, his very survival even to this point was against all the odds. His disability was permanent. This time he really would have to 'retire from retirement', as Madiba had so memorably described it in 2004, aged eighty-six after five busy years of post-presidential activity and global campaigning, with a typically witty and self-deprecating turn of phrase.

Major Yasmin had reluctantly agreed, though she worried about the risks of exposing Thandi, for these were potentially huge. There was no question Thandi would turn herself into a target for the people around the President, and some of his gangster cronies too. The danger then was the trail might lead all the way to the rest of the tight circle. Maybe even to her and the Sniper, and that had to be avoided at all costs.

The Veteran began dictating a statement, which would be issued in his name. Thandi typed it into her laptop and corrected the draft, with Major Yasmin's beady eye helping to avoid any bear traps.

After several redrafts, it was finally ready, the Veteran exhausted at the effort. It described Khoza's invitation to meet and his pretext for doing so, but omitted key details, such as the last-minute switch of venue and any mention of the Sniper whatsoever. There could be a common interest with Khoza's security people to eliminate the Sniper from the story, Major Yasmin surmised.

The Veteran quickly agreed – the last thing the security people would want was to create an even bigger story about a mystery sniper, though they would certainly try to hunt him down. Better to focus even more media attention on the identity of the Russian hitman, whose existence was out there anyway.

'But will that really stand scrutiny in the long term?' Thandi asked.

'Remember,' the Veteran said, his energy at near zero level and his voice now almost a whisper, 'remember what the economist John Maynard Keynes said about the long term: "In the long term we are all dead."'

Under Major Yasmin's worried guidance, Thandi made elaborate arrangements for delivering the statement.

A senior reporter on the *Daily Maverick*, together with the eNCA's top political correspondent (both personally known to the Veteran) would be the only ones invited under terms of strict secrecy. The eNCA would have to 'pool' the recorded interview with other broadcasters once the two outlets had broken the story. Similarly, only once their exclusive had gone online, the *Daily Maverick* had to offer their own photos and story to other print and online media.

Other conditions applied. The two journalists must tell nobody else about the arrangements for the interview. Nobody else. Not even their editors. They would be picked up at the second-floor exit of the Rosebank Mall parking block, from where they would be guided to a nearby van, invited to climb into the windowless back and driven to a secret venue.

Their mobile phones must be switched off and handed over, and they could only bring video equipment and a digital camera without any Wi-Fi connection. They would be searched for any other device that could enable the interview location to be identified, either then or subsequently.

Afterwards, they would be returned in the same way.

Meanwhile, Thandi used WhatsApp to call Bob Richards.

And later that same afternoon, having tipped off select South African and British journalists still following the story, the MP questioned the British Foreign Secretary at his regular monthly appearance in the House of Commons: 'Has he had any information or intelligence about the presence of a Russian assassin involved in the attempt last week to kill a former anti-apartheid struggle hero and South African government minister in Johannesburg?'

He named the Veteran, and a startled Foreign Secretary gave the usual anodyne reply about 'never commenting upon intelligence information'. And then (to cover his back) promised to write to Richards if he had anything more to report in future, adding that the government deplored any attempt on the Veteran's life.

Within a few minutes the story started trending on Twitter.

After a phone call from Thandi, the Sniper was distinctly uncomfortable. Although he understood why she was going public to tell the truth after all the media rumours, he was paranoid that in the subsequent furore his role might be revealed, even if inadvertently.

'Don't worry,' Major Yasmin, standing by Thandi's side, had quickly called to reassure him. 'The President and his security henchmen will never admit to the presence of the hitman. Although the coroner will inevitably find the mystery bullets in Khoza's body, there's no way of tracing these to you – unless someone makes the connection to the bullets in your poacher victims at Zama Zama. But as I understand it, the rifle you used on the poachers is stowed away at the reserve, and is not your other one, used at the Old Fort. In any case, there will be that risk regardless of Thandi's statement.'

Meanwhile the Sniper's personal life had taken a distinct turn for the better. He was enjoying his regular commutes between his Joburg base and Zama Zama to discharge oversight of the IT upgrade needed at the reserve. And to his pleasure, Elise always insisted that he stay at her home and eat with her whenever she was around.

His daughter noticed that he had a new spring in his step and was much more considerate towards her. She seemed to have got her dad back, and he was even talking of taking her away for a long weekend in a game reserve. His son also seemed warmer somehow – or was he just imagining it?

A friend who worked there had tipped off Mkhize about a radio-producer vacancy in a local studio at Richards Bay.

He was excited yet nervous, and resolved to discuss it with Thandi. Then they could live together, he continuing with his work, she with a new job nearby. There was the complication of her political dedication, but surely that could continue wherever she was based, he planned to suggest.

But now the public spotlight was on her, and that made sustaining a relationship, which would inevitably become more widely known, much more difficult. It could even risk the police connecting him and his car to

358

her – with potentially ominous consequences. He checked himself – not 'potentially', but 'likely'.

Mkhize's elation turned to despondency, until he consoled himself: she might even say 'YES!'

Nothing surprised her any more about the lengths to which the President would go in order to install his favoured successor at the coming ANC elective conference.

What Major Yasmin had discovered – or rather stumbled upon – was pure dynamite. Public funds were being syphoned off to bribe conference delegates. The Independent Police Investigative Directorate (IPID) was being blocked by police chiefs from accessing data on a R45-million slush fund of public money laundered through the Crime Intelligence (CI) unit to buy votes at ANC elective conferences, not just the impending one, but earlier ones too, where the President had won the day.

The slush fund was controlled by the CI acting head, previously Head of VIP Protection Services and one of the President's most trusted bodyguards, acting with an adviser to the Minister of Police. The two of them were present at a secret meeting at the Courtyard Hotel in Arcadia, Pretoria, Major Yasmin was briefed.

If the President got away with this on top of everything else, not only could his favoured successor snatch victory from what looked increasingly like the jaws of defeat, but he would be omnipotent.

What to do, she pondered? It was dangerous for her to be in the know. It would be even more dangerous to act herself. She couldn't brief the Veteran, because he was on life support. She'd better call in Thandi: maybe the girl could get the information out via their MP contact in London?

It was mid-morning, the guests had come back from their early bushwalk, and the Sniper was briefing Elise and Mkhize, sitting together on the verandah looking out from her home and sipping rooibos tea.

The subject was drones.

They'd made successful use of them to rebuff the high-powered poacher attack on their rhinos, but the Sniper was anxious to explain how drones could be used to attack Zama Zama, not only to defend it as they had so far done.

'In Syria and Iraq, Islamic State frequently used drones, as did the

Russians, Americans and British. Drones were also used by terrorists in Iraq to guide armoured suicide trucks full of explosives towards targets.'

'So how would we prevent drones being used against us?' Mkhize asked.

'There's a shoulder-mounted, air-powered cannon called SkyWall that launches small nets, entangling its rotors and making it plummet to the ground. There's also an "octocopter", which has a gun that fires a net to trap and carry off rogue drones.

'In Iraq the British electronically jam the drone-control signal, blocking the commands from the operator. The Israeli-developed military Drone Dome system can also do that and also destroy drones with a laser beam. But there are also new generations of autonomous drones preprogrammed and very difficult – maybe impossible – to stop, even programmed to fly in large, coordinated swarms.'

'Good God!' said a horrified Elise, not at all reassured.

Thandi's briefing to the two outlets went rather untidily.

The journalists and crew were picked up by the Corporal, bundled into the back of a black van with its number plates temporarily covered and driven around for an hour so that when they arrived in the garage of the safe house, they hadn't the faintest idea where they were. Nor were they allowed to look around the house or out into the garden. There was a nondescript storeroom adjacent to the garage with some chairs, and they were shown in.

A few minutes later Thandi walked in, introduced herself as 'Thandi Matjeke of Pretoria and an activist for justice'. She may have seemed calm, but was churning inside.

She was guided by the eNCA journalist and a camera operator to sit on one of the chairs in front of the whitewashed wall and given a microphone. The *Daily Maverick* reporter took a photo of her; smile, the Veteran had instructed, so she did, albeit cheesily and nervously.

When the two reporters were ready, notebooks on their laps and ready to record, she began, looking up as much as she could – again as the Veteran had advised during their rehearsal.

'I have a statement to read out, but I apologise in advance that I cannot take certain questions. You were brought here secretly because we are being hunted by the President's security gang, who will capture and kill us if we are found.

'The Veteran was badly wounded four days ago after the President's security chief, Moses Khoza, had invited him to a meeting, then tried to have him killed. Fortunately he had taken the precaution of wearing a bulletproof vest, and the bullets simply knocked him to the ground. Khoza must have had some sort of assassin secretly nearby. But when he realised the Veteran was dazed but not dead, Khoza, who had come armed with a Makarov, tried to kill him as well, but the bullet instead wounded his neck and damaged his spine. I am sorry I cannot be more precise, because I wasn't present and the Veteran, who is critically ill and still cannot speak for himself at this time, has tried to explain to me what happened.

'The meeting was requested by Moses Khoza, who claimed he wanted to defect from the presidency and reunite with the Veteran – they had worked together in exile during the liberation struggle. Although the Veteran was extremely suspicious, he decided it was worth the risk to meet, but took some precautions, including the armoured vest. Soon after they met, there were long-distance shots fired, which hit the Veteran on the armoured vest. It was very confusing. He thinks there might have been a shooter somewhere. But then Khoza pulled a gun and fired a bullet or bullets, before Khoza himself was killed. The Veteran is not sure exactly how, I am afraid, because he fell to the ground with a life-threatening injury.

'We believe this was a state-sponsored trap to kill the Veteran by the President's security chief, which is why we have had to go into hiding.'

Her description over, she moved to her own role, as both the Veteran and Major Yasmin had advised.

'I am here because I enormously admire the Veteran's values and integrity. These are the values of Nelson Mandela, and I am fighting to restore them and save South Africa from the evil of corruption and growing inequality. I am a Born Free because of Mandela, Sisulu, Tambo and all the other freedom fighters, including the Veteran. I urge my generation to rise up and fight to defend their legacy, as, in a small way, I am trying to do.'

Thandi paused and looked up as per the Veteran's script: 'Thank you. I will now go and collect my comrade in his wheelchair so you can photograph and film us. But, as you will see, he is incapable of answering questions.'

She turned and exited the room, the two journalists at once exhilarated by their scoop and frustrated at the inability to ask follow-up questions.

361

Was there another assassin? If so, what had happened to him? Who killed Khoza if the Veteran hadn't? Was it Khoza's own shooter?

Five minutes later, she signalled by first knocking then opening the door and wheeled in the Veteran, bandaged around his neck and with portable drips attached to his upper body, the video rolling and camera snapping.

Although recognisable to the journalists, the Veteran looked a mere shadow of his former self, unable to respond to their questions. The journalists were shocked. But they had the photographs and the video footage and the huge scoop they came for.

Within a few hours, via a reverse journey in the back of a van, their story was headlining and the speculation on social media went viral.

Major Yasmin was at once alarming and reassuring.

If the President's crony won the election to succeed him, then the dogs would be let loose to track down Thandi, Mkhize and possibly even the Sniper. On the other hand, if the Challenger won, the dogs would be reined in, to find they were now targets for investigation and likely prosecution.

The Highveld wind was up, blowing through the city streets, howling round the buildings, shrieking through window openings.

It was quite a distance, by far the longest since his army days, decades before. And the Sniper was on his own.

Because he had no spotter with a range finder and instruments to feed him the necessary data, he had to estimate for himself wind and distance. Otherwise, if he had only placed his cross hairs on the target's head, by the time the bullet arrived seconds later it would have missed, maybe hitting the chest or veering off entirely.

He settled, his scope steady, his only sight now through his optics. Those were his eyes. He forced himself to relax. His blood pressure dropped. His heartbeat slowed. His breathing deepened. His concentration was total.

There was nothing else in his life. No son or daughter. No girlfriend – except maybe, or maybe not – Elise. No rhinos. No shooter to kill. No distractions. No other thoughts. Just cold, clinical focus. On his target.

The man never moved in public without a minimum of twenty-two armed bodyguards drawn from the hundred-strong presidential protection unit. Grim-faced, with ubiquitous dark sunglasses, their pockets bulged and their earpieces crackled. They were intended to intimidate and certainly did just that.

All vetted by the intelligence services, whose chiefs the President meticulously appointed for loyalty – to him, not to the country – the bodyguards could be a law unto themselves. How much they resembled the old apartheid security operatives, former freedom fighters observed. Similar intimidation. The same aggressive attitudes. Identical arrogance. That they were black, not all white as before, made no difference. They were of the same breed. Not so much protectors as oppressors, by instinct and mandate.

The Sniper had seen them begin to emerge from the building, which some had never even entered, instead remaining outside near the armoured limousine, eyes constantly swivelling. But they had not spotted the Sniper, holed up in a tall, empty commercial building, once part of the business hub of Johannesburg's centre, long abandoned to squatters and since cleared. It would doubtless soon be requisitioned for yuppie apartments. But now there was only him in it.

The barrel of his rifle rested on the glassless window ledge. Funny how empty buildings always seemed to have no glass in their windows, he had thought when he first scouted it.

The bustle on the pavement confirmed the moment was imminent.

Where once he had been assigned to protect a president-to-be, now he intended to kill a president-in-service. It seemed to be the only way to get rid of him. Because whatever happened, the hated President seemed to survive.

The Sniper was ready, trigger guard released, when the man suddenly appeared, surrounded by burly men in sunglasses.

Never pull the trigger, just squeeze.

He squeezed.

The face imploded. There was a pandemonium of sunglasses and wild gesticulation and pointed fingers.

Pointing right at him.

The Sniper knew exactly what to do next. Methodically dismantle the rifle and store it carefully in the tailored bag. Then move down the stairwell and out to his car, ready to escape. The getaway had been just as meticulously planned as the assassination.

But he couldn't move.

He was frozen rigid. Stuck there in the open window, with the sunglasses coming to get him. He tried to jerk up, but some higher force pinioned him down. Terror engulfed him. The Sniper strained against the huge force cementing him to the dirty, dusty floor as the sun glasses came swarming all over him . . .

Then, just as suddenly, it was all over.

He jerked out of his trance. Sweating, his heart pounding, disordered.

He wasn't at the window ledge after all – he was sitting bolt upright in his Zama Zama bed, the nightmare over, but his brain still pounding at just how near he had come to assassinating his country's President – whose very office it was once his duty to protect.

It couldn't be true – surely not?

The announcement of the vote had been delayed by two hours, and rumours were spreading like wildfire among the five thousand delegates to the ANC's conference.

The President's Challenger had won!

Never! thought Thandi.

Possibly! thought the Veteran, who had close contacts within the Challenger's inner circle. One had told him: 'We get delegates coming to us for advice and saying they've been offered thousands of rand to vote for the President's successor. We tell them "take the money and still vote for us!"'

Apparently many had done exactly that.

As he sat in his wheelchair, the Veteran let his mind wander freely. He imagined once again, looking out from his home over the dazzling, enchanting False Bay as the whales circled and breached in season.

His False Bay, known to some as the 'Serengeti of the seas', with its amazing diversity of marine life found among the very rocky, sometimes mountainous, eastern and western shores of the bay, with large cliffs plunging into deep water.

The Veteran chortled to himself. Maybe, just maybe, his strategy had succeeded. Only time would tell. He would be disabled for the rest of his life. No more criss-crossing the country and even continents to speak and continue the struggle. He would have to find other ways to ensure his influence, and one was sitting right next to him.

The Veteran turned to Thandi, who was excited by the rumours.

'If we have won – if we have, because this President has never, ever lost an internal party fight – then this will be only the first of many, many battles to come.'

'*A luta continua.* The struggle continues – as it always does, Thandi. If you ever relax because you think you've won, that is when you start to lose.'

EPILOGUE

Sometime later . . .

With an international outcry over the stolen smuggled rhino horn and a warrant out for his arrest, the President was eventually forced to resign.

After a ruling drafted by Justice Samuel Makojaene, the Constitutional Court upheld the demand by the International Criminal Court for the President's extradition, and he was seen in handcuffs boarding a South African Airways flight, flying first class to London, then to be transferred via a connecting Schiphol flight to The Hague.

The Business Brothers had meanwhile fled to Dubai, where they continued to thwart efforts to track down the billions they had laundered and went on lavish spending sprees . . .

Having narrowly won the ANC's presidential election, the Challenger succeeded to the South African presidency after Parliament had endorsed his assent without opposition. He immediately set about the task of restoring probity to the government.

But, with the ANC leadership still split between him and the former President, and corruption together with cronyism remaining deeply embedded, it was an uphill task, to say the very least.

One of his first Cabinet appointments was Major Yasmin Essop, with a mandate to clean up the security services, including military intelligence.

And that was also an uphill task . . .

Both their mothers were deeply shocked.

First by their simple marriage ceremony in a register office, which abandoned the traditions of their separate communities. Second,

366

when, by mutual pre-agreement, Thandi never uttered the standard words 'I promise to obey', as she pledged her future together with Isaac Mkhize.

However, so delighted and surprised was her father at his daughter's unexpected betrothal that he never noticed the omission; her mother told him in a stunned whisper during the couple's riotous but low-cost reception afterwards, where the Veteran delivered a moving and witty speech of congratulation as he stood with difficulty, leaning on the lectern, having been helped up from his wheelchair by the bridegroom.

He was followed by best man, Steve Brown, who entertained the guests with stories of Mkhize's wildlife escapades and the unexpected appearance of the bride in his life. Although there were allusions in Brown's speech to rhino wars in Zama Zama, guests noticed a tantalising absence of detail.

Except for the tiny band of conspirators, none of the guests had a clue that among their number was the Sniper sitting close to Elise, both enjoying their own company and the occasion.

Just as over his Madiba guardian role, nobody else knew what he had done — and for that he remained mighty relieved, hoping nobody ever would.

Sometime later still . . .

The seals bobbed lazily and provocatively around the bubbling waves bursting against the foundations of Kalk Bay's Harbour House Restaurant. The sun was high, the atmosphere of the lunch party exuberant as the Veteran reached up from his wheelchair to welcome and hug his guests.

Glasses of his favourite Sauvignon Blanc and Pinotage, both from different wineries in the Franschhoek Valley, were raised repeatedly. More bottles arrived and still more as the sumptuous angelfish was eaten, the hours drifting by in warm chatter and laughter.

Bob Richards and his wife, out on holiday and staying in nearby Noordhoek over the British Christmas parliamentary recess, had organised the lunch in tribute to the Veteran and his band of conspirators, who were all present, as well as Elise and the VETPAW guys Clint and Ken.

The only ones not sharing the wine, because that would have contravened their Muslim faith, were Yasmin Essop and Solly Naidoo, but that did not stop them enjoying the festivities to the full.

*

367

And even later . . .

An agitated Thandi was on the phone to the Veteran.

'What should I do?' she asked.

To her utter astonishment the now established new President had, right out of the blue, called her asking that she agree to stand for Parliament.

The sequence remained crystal clear in her mind. First an unknown caller; she answered cautiously.

'Please stand by to take a call from the President.'

A dumbfounded Thandi waited during a delay and then a series of clicks, as the warm, familiar voice greeted her and explained what he wanted.

'But I have never been active in the party before!' Thandi protested politely, still flabbergasted.

'That is exactly why I want you. We need fresh blood with the values of Madiba in our Parliament,' the President explained. 'You have performed a brave service to your country already. Now you have an opportunity to do so in a different way by standing at the next election.'

Sensing her confused surprise, he asked Thandi to think it over, promising: 'Please take my call tomorrow morning.'

Expressed as a request, it was actually a summons, she ruefully reflected as he ended the call.

She spoke to a shocked Mkhize as soon as he was free from his duties in the reserve.

Understanding both her excitement and her worry, he responded carefully yet plaintively. 'It is a great honour. But what will it mean for us?'

'That I really don't know,' she replied wistfully.

They had recently set up home together in a modest apartment in Richards Bay, where she had been appointed a senior producer to the local radio station, their lives bumping along happily, even if, as before, in parallel universes, her frequent flights to Johannesburg, Cape Town or other cities on political missions consuming much of their spare income and his ranger duties confining him to the reserve for long periods.

'Ask the Veteran,' Mkhize suggested, 'he's been an MP, and he knows what it's like. And he's probably the only other person you can trust for confidential advice.'

And so Thandi had done so.

'It is a fantastic opportunity for you,' the Veteran had begun, disclosing that he had supplied Thandi's phone number on request to the President's chief of staff.

'You what?' she exclaimed indignantly. 'And you didn't even tell me?'

The Veteran brushed her protest aside and continued: 'As I say, it's a chance to make a real difference. But you must go into it with your eyes very wide open. The ANC is divided right down the middle between the corrupt gravy-trainers and those trying to reclaim its heritage. Also, party politics can be a greasy pole. Lots of factionalism, infighting, careerism and jealousy. Compromises too. I compromised, we all have to in life – in our families, our personal relationships, our work, our leisure. We very rarely get our own way on everything – or anything. So it's hardly surprising that happens in politics too. The key is to stick to your values, your principles, and above all your integrity. But that is very hard. Most people get sucked into the culture and lose their roots. Others stay well away, pure in their armchair disdain but without any influence.'

Thandi listened, wrestling with the enormity of her choice.

'On the other hand, as we ourselves have demonstrated together, change never comes from within the system alone. The political establishment – any political establishment – is so hemmed in by pressures from different interest groups that decisions get gridlocked.

'Pressure from the outside can then be decisive. Apartheid was only defeated because of the liberation struggle, the international campaign and the country becoming near ungovernable with the economy in crisis. Although it needed a President de Klerk from the inside to recognise that change was essential, he would never have made the changes he did had it not been for the external pressures on the state.'

The Veteran paused, allowing his point to settle in Thandi's mind.

'The reason I resigned my ANC membership was because I believed I couldn't change it from within any more. And in my own case I think I was correct. But within the ANC progressive forces were needed to defeat the old, corrupt President and install a new and better one in the Mandela tradition of public service, not self-service. And the President needs more allies because there are still too many enemies, too many corrupt cronies of the old President in the ANC and in the system.'

'So what should I do, then?' Thandi asked.

The Veteran was silent, her question hanging between them.

'Talk again to Isaac. Sleep on it. Wake up in the morning and be ready to answer the President when he calls.'

Pausing again, and understanding she was about to object, he added quickly: 'I have given you my views, Thandi. But only you can make this choice. I will support you whatever you decide, and I will be there for you so long as my health lasts. Call me anytime.'

Then before she could say anything, the Veteran quickly bid her good-bye with a, 'Solidarity, Thandi.'

Sitting in his wheelchair and looking out over False Bay twinkling in the sunshine, he had a smile of both nostalgia and pride as he wondered what she would do.

GLOSSARY

Action for Southern Africa:	successor to the British Anti-Apartheid Movement
amaBhungane:	an independent non-profit investigative news group based in South Africa that promotes an open and accountable democracy
ANC:	African National Congress
AWB:	Afrikaner Weerstandsbeweging, an extremist racist white South African group
baas:	Afrikaans for boss, and usually used to refer to a white employer or other white male deemed superior under apartheid.
bakkie:	pick-up truck
Bantustan:	one of the territories set aside under apartheid for black inhabitants designated by their ancestral origins
Black Consciousness Movement:	an anti-apartheid movement promoting black self-empowerment and pride
Black Economic Empowerment (BEE):	a policy to give black South Africans access to business ownership and opportunity the preserve of whites from the apartheid legacy

371

Boere mafia. Boers (Boere):	a term for white Afrikaners, often used pejoratively by English-speaking South Africans. Boere mafia: a clandestine, para-military and corrupt group of powerful Afrikaner whites
boetie:	brother, mate
braaivleis/braai:	barbecue
Coloured:	short for Cape Coloured, a mixed-race ethnic group in South Africa
CBCU:	Customs Border Control Unit
CITES:	Convention on International Trade in Endangered Species of Fauna and Flora
die hele boksendais:	the whole lot
DA:	Democratic Alliance, the present-day opposition to the ANC
dassie:	a hyrax, a type of rodent
duiker:	a small antelope
EFF:	Economic Freedom Fighters
ESPU:	Endangered Species Protection Unit in South Africa
fynbos (Afrikaans):	'fine bush'; refers to plants associated with the mountains of South Africa's Cape region
FRELIMO:	Mozambique Liberation Front
impimpi:	informer
kaffir:	derogatory term used by white people to refer to black people during the apartheid era
kopje:	small hill

KZN:	KwaZulu-Natal, a province in South Africa
lekker:	cool (originally 'delicious' in Dutch)
MK:	Sizwe (Spear of the Nation), the ANC's underground wing
necklacing:	a form of execution that involves forcing a fuel-filled tyre around a person's chest and arms and setting light to it
ORT Airport:	O. R. Tambo International Airport, Johannesburg
PAC:	Pan-Africanist Congress, a rival to the ANC
panga:	machete
parastatal:	a publicly owned enterprise
Poqo:	armed wing of the PAC
rooibos:	redbush (tea)
SADF:	South African Defence Force
sanctions-busting:	disregarding restrictions and trade imposed upon a country like South Africa under apartheid
SANDF:	South African National Defence Force
SANParks:	South African National Parks
SARS:	South African Revenue Service
Scorpio:	the *Daily Maverick*'s investigative unit
sjambok:	a heavy leather whip
SSA:	State Security Agency (in South Africa)

state capture:	political corruption driven from the top of government to benefit an elite of ruling politicians and their business associates
SWAPO:	South West Africa People's Organisation, the Namibia liberation movement; in government there since 1990
three-line whip:	a written notice instructing MPs to attend a parliamentary vote. It is underlined three times to show its importance
toi toi:	a combination of singing, dancing and chanting
UDF:	United Democratic Front, a South African anti-apartheid movement in existence 1983–91
UNITA:	National Union for the Total Independence of Angola
veld:	open grassland
volk:	people
Voortrekkers:	nineteenth-century Afrikaans-speaking colonists who travelled from the coast of South Africa to establish settlements in the interior and escape British rule imposed upon them
ZANU:	Zimbabwe African National Union, which fought against white rule in Rhodesia

ACKNOWLEDGEMENTS

My wife Elizabeth Haywood has been an enormous support and made detailed points and corrections. Ronnie Kasrils also gave important comments and suggested alterations.

I am grateful for their help to Zohra Ebrahim; my best school friend in Pretoria, the late Dave Geffen; my daughter-in-law, Dr Kirsten Hain; Fiona Lloyd and Albie Sachs; and drones expert Arthur Michel. Also to Kate Quarry and Laura McFarlane, whose insightful copy-editing improved my text.

Jean Marais, an amazing South African game-reserve ranger, made invaluable wildlife corrections to my first draft, though neither he nor others should be blamed for anything I still might have got wrong.

I was privileged to visit the wonderful Thula Thula Game Reserve near Richards Bay; as may be apparent from the text, I thoroughly recommend it.

For his encouragement, thanks to Eugene Ashton, CEO of Jonathan Ball Publishers and also the nephew of my favourite teacher, the late Terry Ashton of Pretoria Boys' High School.

I am also grateful to Sarah and Kate Beal of Muswell Press for their publishing expertise and enthusiasm.

Among the books and publications I relied upon during my research are:

Lawrence Anthony, *The Elephant Whisperer* (London, Sidgwick & Jackson, 2009)
Lawrence Anthony, *The Last Rhinos* (London, Sidgwick & Jackson, 2012)

John Hanks, *Operation Lock and the War on Poaching* (Cape Town, Penguin Books, 2015)

Peter Hounman and Steven McQuillan, *The Mini-Nuke Conspiracy: Mandela's Nuclear Nightmare* (London, Faber & Faber, 1995)

Ronnie Kasrils, *Armed and Dangerous: My Undercover Struggle Against Apartheid* (London, Heinemann, 1993)

Ronnie Kasrils, *A Simple Man* (Johannesburg, Jacana, 2017)

Françoise Malby-Anthony, *An Elephant in My Kitchen* (London, Sidgwick & Jackson, 2018)

Kobie Kruger, *Mahlangeni: Stories of a Game Ranger's Family* (Johannesburg, Penguin Books, 2015)

Rachel Love Nuwer, *Poached: Inside the Dark World of Wildlife Trafficking* (London, Scribe, 2018)

Ronald Orenstein, *Ivory, Horn and Blood* (Buffalo New York State, Firefly, 2013)

Jacques Pauw, *The President's Keepers: Those Keeping Zuma in Power and Out of Prison* (Cape Town, Tafelberg, 2018)

Sharon Pincott, *Elephant Dawn: The Inspirational Story of Thirteen Years Living with Elephants in the African Wilderness* (Johannesburg, Jacana 2016)

Julian Rademeyer, *Killing for Profit: Exposing the Illegal Rhino Horn Trade* (Cape Town, Zebra Press, 2012)

Daphne Sheldrick, *An African Love Story: Love, Life and Elephants* (London, Viking, 2012)

Christopher Vandome and Alex Vines, *Tackling Illegal Wildlife Trade in Africa: Economic Incentives and Approaches* (London, Chatham House, 2018)

Hennie van Vuuren, *Apartheid Guns and Money: A Tale of Profit* (London, Hurst Publishers, 2018)

Investigative articles in the *Daily Maverick* and online articles in the *Guardian* were also very useful.